I0677314

AN
IMMORTAL
SPY
NOVEL

THE
CAPTURED SPY

K. A. KRANTZ

For Krathpy
Forever my partner in mayhem

CHAPTER 1

The prickling of the skin. The brittle air raking across the nape. The weight of regard pressing against the body. Old spies knew to pay attention to these sensations. Old spies knew how to leverage those sensory details to track the hunter to a general location. Old spies survived by knowing when to take cover, when to bait, and when to confront.

Every day for the past week, Bix had visited this pyramidal library that existed in a pocket of displaced time and space. Every day, she played the part of oblivious prey. Every day, she ambled the rows and stacks of untold treasures while she waited for her observer to make a move. A thick, sparkling carpet of blues and greens muffled her footsteps and those of her watcher. Backlit frescoes of fantastical races offered soft lighting from the panels of the peaked ceiling in such a way as to deny every chance of shadows even in the deepest recesses of the seven stories wrapping around an empty atrium. No chairs. No tables. No plants. No clocks.

What the library had in abundance was books, artifacts, and magic. Lots of magic from all Worlds—Upper, Under, Mids, and Other. Dustless spines of tooled-leather tomes leaned against stacks of frayed and stained pages bound by fairy wings, bestial claws, or gut strings. Every book, pamphlet, scroll, and origami napkin had been marked in languages Bix couldn't begin to translate.

However, a librarian could.

No way had her future-self gone through the trouble of shipping this treasure trove back in time without giving her a resource to understand everything in here. In the future, a brutal war was destroying the Mid Worlds, reducing the number of Worlds from hundreds to a mere three. The native armies had been decimated. The civilian death toll was beyond the trillions. The odds that the last three Mid Worlds would survive were nil. Her future-self had created this library as a Hail Mary to try to change the past and stop the Other World invaders before they took root.

The Bix of the present, the today, the now, had only recently identified those foreign invaders and learned of their plans. Devourers, they were called. They were old foes of the gods, created during the same unknown era. Unlike gods who nurtured the Mids as farmland for the souls on which they fed, Devourers wanted only to consume. No investment, no maintenance. Just total obliteration.

No way, no how would Bix let that bleak future come to pass. She'd sworn to protect and defend the Mids from all threats foreign and domestic. Not because she was particularly patriotic or enamored with an ideal. Hell, she wasn't even from the Mids. No, she'd taken that vow because of the relationships she had with specific residents of the Mids. Interpersonal connections, the kinds that went deep? Those were the things that mattered when you couldn't die. Stuff, power, and wealth? Hollow comforts and superficial in the greater scheme. What mattered were friends. True friends. Some of her truest friends had died in the line of duty defending the Mids, and she honored them by continuing their mission. She was blessed to also have true friends who were alive and well and fighting shoulder to shoulder with her; their solidarity held value beyond measure. No matter how the political landscape delighted in screwing her, she was committed to her friends and to the fight for the Mids, now and in the future.

Too many lives had been sacrificed to catch this magical football flung through time. Bix's present-self was keen to put this mass of intel to good use…once she figured out how.

The friends in her present day who could help her decipher all these books and resources couldn't get in because of the security spells. She couldn't take objects out because of the same security spells. Future-self had instituted a strict nobody-in, nobody-out policy to which she was the only exception.

That meant the librarian was her stalker.

Since said librarian had refused every opportunity to introduce themselves, despite her repeated congenial solicitations, she was going to have to be a little less nice. Not exactly the way she preferred to start a relationship, but not one to which she strenuously objected either.

She inhaled the library's heady aroma of myrrh, cardamom, and antiquities as she continued to browse the shelves, trailing her fingers over tung-oiled wood. Tentacles of darkness pushed through her skin from nape to small of back, silently coursing along the carpet and over the top of shelving units until they made contact.

A masculine curse. Heavy footfalls. Running. With a limp.

Her darkness seized its prey and suspended it over the atrium.

"Damn it, Bix, wait," shouted a voice she couldn't quite place.

Mid World magic, potent yet tainted, surged against the corporeal shadows subservient to her will. The taint wasn't surprising considering the prevalence of Devourers in the future, nor was it a surprise that Mids' magic shoved at her in its futile attempt at eviction. Mids' magic didn't like her because she wasn't from the Mids nor did she contribute to its power. Existing on the Worlds it imbued was a bit like enduring the jostling of a train. The effects of being near a life-form it had created varied depending on the amount of magic bestowed upon the individual.

Whoever she'd caught was at the top of the heap, either a

royal dragon or an archangel. Curiously, he hadn't counterattacked. He wasn't really struggling to get free for that matter. Perhaps the librarian knew exactly who she was. Maybe he was a friend from the future? Odd. She didn't have many allies among the leadership of the Angelic Host or the Dragon Horde. She could count the dudes on one thumb, and the timbre of the voice in the atrium did not match that lone ally.

Intrigued, she went to see whom she'd snagged.

Six stories of gilded balconies encircled the atrium, affording unobstructed views of the painting on the ceiling. Bookshelves diverged from the wide walkways ringing each layer like rays of sunshine. There was a baroque beauty to it all.

Including the man wriggling in the thick coils of her darkness.

Apple-red hair feathered down to broad shoulders covered in a fine-gauge green sweater. A sharp chin sported a Sir Francis Drake–styled short beard with streaks of blond adding a bit of character. A peeved aquamarine gaze lifted and held hers.

Her stomach soured.

Of all the people her future-self could've stuffed in a time capsule, why had she chosen the Phoenix? He was the lone dragon-angel hybrid, the living power gauge of Mid World magic, doomed to die every five hundred years at her hands so Mids' magic could reset itself. He was a dude with a shitty destiny, who'd thus far lived a shitty life. He did not like her at all. Not even remotely.

The first time she'd met him, that she could remember, he'd kicked her ass and dragged her before the powers that be to stand trial for attempting to rob the Angelic Host's armory. The last time she'd seen him, he'd been a maimed, emaciated, shell of a man who'd still fought her. That time, she'd won, but it hadn't been a fair fight. He hadn't been able to lift his head, much less stand.

Admittedly, had their positions been reversed and the powers that be had tasked *him* to be *her* executioner, she wouldn't care much for him either. She didn't know how she'd drawn the short straw, but it was a date she'd reportedly kept for millennia. Went with the title of High Executioner for All Worlds. She couldn't remember how she'd earned that either, but then again, she couldn't remember much of anything beyond the last thirty years. Memory issues. She had them. One of her many failings.

"Feng? What…how…who…?" If she kept spitting random words, the right ones were bound to surface. "Future or present?"

"Future, I'm from your future," he said, his accent a European polyglot that exposed his upbringing among the angels. "I'll explain everything after you let me go."

"Nah, you don't have a great track record of playing nicely with me. Consider this a restraining order, of a sort." Bix rested her forearms on the polished railing. They were five stories up, and Feng was a superpower. A fall wouldn't kill him, just sting his pride.

"Resist your instinctive urge to evict me," he cautioned. "The library and I are a package deal. Removing me from here breaks the spell and catapults all this and me back to my original timeline."

"That seems mighty convenient for you and a bit stupid on the part of future-me," she scoffed.

"Due to your ignorance of Mids' magic, I'm sure it does." He dropped his head back, staring at the frescoes. It took a few heartbeats before he inhaled loudly and slowly, then deigned to explain. "The time-traveling spell is a spell of opposites. You and I are opposites in all ways—woman to man, destroyer to creator, untethered to moored, eternal to mortal. You are the fixed element, you exist always. I am the variable with a beginning and an end. I reincarnate, cleansed of past ills, and begin anew."

"Not convincing me that you were our last hope, Obi-Wan," she countered.

He closed his eyes. "Think of the spell as the necklace you are wearing."

She glanced down at the two pendants she wore.

"You are the clasps. Time is the cord. I am the pendant, able to slide back and forth." He tipped his head from side to side. "I knew when to stop the slide through time when I lost one of my dewclaws and you took to wearing it. The binding of our magics caused a pucker in the flow of time, a buckle in the cord."

She closed her hand over the seemingly silver pendant of a dragon's wing seared to an angel's wing. In their hollow was indeed his golden dewclaw. All parts shrunken and bound by a Berserker commander who'd made Mids' magic his bitch. As long as she wore the pendant, the potent magic of displaced body parts was contained, minimized by her Other World magic.

"If you could choose any point in time to return, why not pick the exact day I took to wearing your claw?" she challenged. "Why let me fumble around?"

"Until you faced the Devourers in person, nothing I could have said would've convinced you of the veracity of my message and my mission. You would have been suspicious of the recording you left yourself in this library. You would have assumed it was a trick and that I was the perpetrator. Our history is rooted in the presumption of guilt." He opened his eyes and pinned her with a gimlet stare. "Even now you don't trust me. Even now, when time is of the essence, you insist on playing this game of pointless suspicion."

"You've shadowed me for a week instead of immediately introducing yourself. I'm feeling pretty justified in my trust issues." She wagged the pendant at him. "The Feng I know is a dick, but he's also insufferably formal. Lurking is rude."

"The journey *through time* took more out of me than I'd anticipated. I apologize for the delay my recuperation demanded." He rolled a shoulder and winced. The image of him flickered, then steadied. "Do you mind? This is very uncomfortable."

"I could be more accommodating if you dropped the glamour and let me see the real you." She poked a shadow at his deceptively robust physique. "I know what you went through, Feng. I know the scars you should have and the deformities from your time as a captive of lunatics."

He huffed and shook his hair from his eyes. "I am the personification of native magic's health. Having a flawed body—a body made by Mids' magic—would be a sign of magic's weakness."

"Mids' magic, in your timeline, is anemic due to the invasion by the Devourers. Devourers are toxic, leaving behind vapors so poisonous in the aftermath of their destruction that creationist gods will not spawn new Worlds where the old have been for fear of contamination." She propped her chin on her palm. "Go ahead, lie to me again. This trust game is a lot of fun."

Sadly, as tempting as it was to simply end Feng now and take her chances with the library surviving without him, she couldn't. To kill the Phoenix before his scheduled death date would screw up Mids' magic, and the internecine warfare would leave the Mids utterly exposed to the Devourers. He was *that* important.

He was also that irksome.

"Maybe we should focus on the missions you sent me here to impart to you, if you and your motley crew of misfits are going to alter the chain of events and save the Mids from the Devourers," Feng groused while holding fast to his glamour. "Within this library is the evidence collected on those who are enabling the Devourers to attack the Mids."

That piqued her interest.

"The faction within the Consortium?" She straightened. "You know who they are?"

The greater Consortium oversaw the defense and welfare of the hundreds of Mid Worlds. Comprised of the four races of superpowers—dragons, angels, gods, and Fates—the Consortium not only created the thousands of magical races and humans who populated the Mids, they also maintained the linear flow of time for those Worlds. Most of the Consortium's members despised Bix for being their bogeyman. She had a few allies among the superpowers, though "ally" was probably too strong a word. Feng, on the other hand, had been the Consortium's darling, their lead investigator, a man beyond reproach…until he'd been too good at his job and run afoul of the wrong people.

Politics. Nasty stuff.

"Some. I know who some of them are. Damn it, put me down and allow me to be the guide you sent me back in time to be," he demanded in frustration.

"Oh, now you want to get to work." She snorted and reluctantly recalled her darkness, dropping him unceremoniously. Massive wings snapped from Feng's back. The thickly scarred and discolored membrane expanses were visible for a heartbeat before the glamour of lush red and yellow feathers took hold. He alighted at the bottom of the atrium and glowered at her.

She smirked and opened gates, one at her side and one at his. Her aspect of a gatekeeper allowed her to create doorways from anywhere to anywhere as long as she held a clear mental image of the origin and the destination. Size was irrelevant. Heel cap. Hippodrome. Heart wall. Whatever. The effort came from maintaining the boundaries, so she didn't displace more than she'd intended. One step delivered her from the balcony to the main floor.

"You need to take a new tack against the faction within the Consortium. Proof of malfeasance is no longer an effective tool. They are too well entrenched. Regardless of who presents the evidence, the faction will twist facts to place the blame on *you*." Feng rolled his shoulders and tucked his wings under his skin. The rips in his sweater repaired themselves as he strode past her with an obvious limp. He waved at the empty center of the atrium floor. A bar table and two stools appeared. "Once the faction successfully tricked their peers into convicting you of a crime for which you could not logically have been at fault, you became their ideal scapegoat. That was their purpose in having me intercept and arrest you. That was their goal in having you stand trial. It was a test of their peers, and the faction got exactly what they wanted."

"Except, hello, I'm the Chimera." She grimaced, taking a seat the table. "I've done the Consortium's dirty work for eons, and they had the balls to turn on me? Idiots."

"It's a pity you didn't realize your power over them at the time it mattered. When you lost your memories, you lost the leverage, control, and outright fear you wielded over the Consortium. You made yourself an easy target when you returned to the Mids in your lesser capacity." Feng retrieved an orange drink coaster from a shelf, then spun the disk atop the table. "Your sentence was intended to keep you out of the Mids while the faction opened the doors to the Devourers. Your early parole presents a problem for them and an opportunity for us."

"Whoa," she breathed and sat back as the coaster whirled faster and faster, levitating as lights burst from it. "Keep in mind 'us' is a very small group. Like, handful kind of small."

"In this case, a tight-knit group of spies working in the shadows is more effective than an army. Large public actions will only incite panic among the masses. Panic works in the faction's favor. Because of the faction's reach, we cannot rely on the Consortium to save the Mids. That burden falls to you and your team. Fortunately, the evidence in this library and my experience from the future give you the tools you need." He sat across from Bix and danced his fingers above the coaster. Light bent and twisted, folding over on itself as two images built.

Words failed her as a face came into focus.

Heterochromatic eyes—one pale blue, one dark pink—too wide set in a vulpine face, looked askance through the hologram. Bix's heart skipped three beats, then resumed at a frenetic rate. Staring at her was the high-value package she and her last Dark Ops team had been trying to retrieve the night a traitor had redirected them to the Angelic Host's armory. That same mission had had Bix and Feng duking it out while her team had been slaughtered by angels. It had culminated with the Consortium sentencing her to exile for a hundred and eighty years.

She would never, ever forget the fellow operatives she'd failed to bring home. The guilt for the blown op and for whatever had happened to that lost agent weighed heavily upon her.

"Fymmi," she whispered. "Why are you showing me this?"

"You have to complete the mission, Bix." Feng pulled the second image into focus and enlarged it. It looked a lot like a brass collar and articulating spine from a sci-fi movie. "This brilliant piece of engineering masks the presence of its wearer from all types of magic. It is fused to her body, invisible to the naked eye."

The cyborg addition was some sort of cloaking device that existed as a part of Fymmi? That explained why the CWIG, the Cross-World Intelligence Guild, had been desperate to get their agent back.

"It's been ten years." Bix toyed with her pendants and leaned back, shaking her head. "Fymmi's probably dead by now, thanks to you and the Consortium."

"Once you were sidelined, the faction had Fymmi exactly where they needed her until she escaped. Now the Devourers have taken up the hunt." Feng tapped his middle finger to an erratic beat. No, not tapped; it was a tremor, proof of the weakness in Mids' magic caused by the Devourers in his timeline of the future. "Once the Devourers get their hands on Fymmi, they will replicate the cloaking tech of her implant and infiltrate every branch of government and defense organization. Their commanders will sit among the members of the Consortium with no one the wiser."

Of the many abilities the godlike Devourers possessed, shapeshifting down to the DNA of any life-form worried Bix the most. Only the superpowers and the uppermost caste of the Mids' magical races could detect the tainted displacement of native magic a Devourer's presence caused. Even then, they had to be looking for the anomaly. Bix could sense them with a bit more ease, and she was training herself to develop the unconscious habit of doing so. Unfortunately, Devourers could also detect her presence because one of her suppressed aspects forcibly repelled them, thus the element of surprise was null and void once she hit the stage. She was still plotting workarounds for that.

"The existence of the tech didn't hit our radar until a quarter of our ranks were gutted from the inside by our own leadership," Feng continued, his mien darkening. "Leaders you and I recruited were replaced by Devourers who had replicated this tech. The tech gave the Devourers a stealth ability we could never counter. We were doomed before you and I rallied the troops."

Damn it all, if Fymmi was still alive somewhere out there, it'd be a miracle. It'd be an unbelievable second chance, the kind only the Fates could offer. The same Fates who'd put Bix on a collision path with Feng and the angels years ago. Mind, there were as many Houses of Fate as there were pantheons, and they notoriously worked at cross-purposes to be catalysts of chaos, but... Could it be? Could the fractious Fates really be giving her a second chance at the same mission?

Or was Feng setting her up to be served to the faction within the Consortium again? That future-her had stuffed him in this library spoke to some sort of eventual alliance, but when her darkness had held him, it had also held the proof of the taint of Devourers poisoning his person. She'd be a fool to ignore that.

"You still don't trust me." He sighed wearily and shoved his quivering hand through his hair. "You want proof of my message. Proof of my intention."

"Trust but verify, as the saying goes," Bix admitted. "I'm not asking for your firstborn son, but I need something that'll give me a reason to trust a man who despised me on sight, then was horrifically tortured for years, and has supposedly been fighting a noxious enemy since."

"A madman," he huffed. "You think I've gone mad."

"If you were still the lead investigator for the Consortium, and I'd drawn you into my secret lair to tell you this story, what would you think?"

"Fine." He pursed his lips as his eyes darted left and down, the body's language for searching recollections. "Let us talk about your memories, and the lack thereof. Your future-self left your present-self a message within this library urging you to continue the acquisition of your divided memories."

Over three hundred years ago, Bix had split her memories among seven gods to prevent her enemies from stealing her secrets. She'd known she'd be too weak to protect herself after giving her last bit of magic and wherewithal to repel the Devourers' first attempt to invade the Mids. So far, she'd reclaimed two out of the seven sets. They were meaningless blips of moments unrelated to each other. Sounds, scents, images, tastes, and textures poured across her brain like an upended can of cake sprinkles. Lots of potential but utterly useless. They gave her wicked weird dreams and random ghosting sensations during her lucid moments. Until she had more pieces of the puzzle that was her past, she was still vulnerable to nameless foes and clueless to the breadth of her supposedly awesome power.

"Future-me mentioned not having the courage to weather the insanity that comes with the memory merges." Bix shrugged. "Now that I know to expect a bad case of the crazies, I can forewarn my friends and put a plan in place to deal with the mind mush."

"In my timeline, you destroy Worlds while in the throes of your madness. After your third memory merge, I rise early from my rehabilitation to try to minimize the damage, but I have no recourse against the gates you open in the protective layers that allow the Devourers through."

A chill snaked down Bix's spine. "I what?"

"It takes you months before you are lucid, and by then, you've done more to aid the Devourers than the faction of the Consortium did in all the years of their existence." He looked at her with pity.

Bix held a hand over her mouth as a wave of nausea crashed over her. She knew the Chimera of old was a monster of unmatched ruthlessness. Her greatest fear was devolving back to that heartless entity once she regained all her memories. She'd lived eons as the old Chimera and a mere three decades of being the new. The odds of which of the two Chimeras would win were in the monster's favor. She had no idea how to stop that from happening. Conversely, the old Chimera had way too many enemies who had already started coming for her and her friends. Protect and defend, that was her vow and she'd do it for as long as she was able…which might not be as long as she'd hoped.

"Proof," she whispered, swallowing the burn of bile as her training took over and squelched her emotions. "You paint an effective and gruesome picture, Feng, but you've left out the proof of why I should give your spiel any credence."

He raised his hands in small surrender and inclined his head. "How long do you think you and I have been allies?"

"Pfft," she sputtered, eyeing his hands as his tremor reappeared. "Only when we had no other options."

"When you leave here, go see the dragon twins." He tucked his hands in his lap. "Ask them about the pendant you wear, the one with my dewclaw. Let their answer be your deciding factor in the pursuit of Fymmi."

"If I don't like their answer, I'll leave you in here to languish." She studied the hologram of Fymmi's artificial spine, committing the engravings on each plate to memory. "How long have you and I been battling the Devourers?"

"In my timeline? One hundred and seventy years," he murmured.

Bix snapped her gaze to his. The Phoenix burned every five hundred years. The last time he'd burned was just before she'd given up her memories. She could manage basic math. "That's the end of your lifecycle. You're slated to die—"

"In two months," he cut her off. "I have no idea if or how existing out of my timeline changes the date. This may be the only mission I'm able to impart to you before you…"

Before she had to execute him, either in her timeline or his.

It wasn't that she hadn't killed before; it came with the job. However, bumping off someone with whom she had a relationship was not something to which she looked forward. It was inevitably worse when the target knew it was coming. Feng had had centuries to stew in anticipation.

Miserable.

"The incursion by the full Devourer army is inevitable, whether it's by your unintentional actions or the faction's deliberate exploits." Feng cleared his throat and shook his hair from his face. "Therefore, I have chosen the operation most likely to have the greatest positive impact on our future to be the first I share with you. In your timeline, the Devourers have been in the Mids five years. They are already among us, establishing camps and building their infrastructures. Once they get their hands on Fymmi, they will go dark and we will *never* find them until they're slavering over our dying Worlds."

The Devourers were big bads that needed to be rebuffed once and for all from the Mids. No question. They were the enemy. However, the faction within the Consortium, they were the real villains. To swear to protect the Mids, then lay them bare to an invading force? Unforgivable. It was the ultimate sin of all sins. The most heinous transgression.

Bix *would* get all her memories back and with them access to all her magics. Regardless of which Chimera survived the merger, she would take down every member of the faction in a manner more horrific than their imaginations could conceive.

First, however, she had to ask the dragon twins about the pendant she wore. A huge part of her wanted future-Feng to be right about Fymmi, that the operative was still alive and still in play; yet a notable part of her dreaded him being right about everything else.

"I know you think I haven't earned the faith I am asking of you." Feng waved both his hands at the projection, and the images vanished. The coaster slowed its spin until it teetered and toppled, flat once again as if waiting for a big mojito to dribble on it. "I hope your visit with the dragons proves otherwise."

"Leave issues of faith to the gods." She stood and smoothed her skirt. "To ensure the survival of the Mids, I'm willing to operate on mission-level trust with you. Just don't expect me to believe we become bosom beaus."

He gave a sharp nod.

"Then your mission, Bix, is to locate Fymmi before the Devourers do, and to destroy the cloaking tech so it cannot be used against us."

Chapter 2

It wasn't that Bix couldn't trust a madman trapped in a library and tossed through time. She'd danced with the devil under the pale moonlight. Often. However, intel had to be verified before action could be taken if an operative wanted to stay out of enemy hands. So, before she took on the Fymmi mission and asked her team to risk their lives in support of it, she had to do her due diligence.

Future-Feng had given her the means to establish mission-level trust with him. That kind of trust ensured both operatives got out alive but didn't last beyond a single assignment. Thus, she stood ankle-deep in fragrant tilled soil that served as the floor of a massive silo. The lack of windows and doors meant the only illumination came from the ring of singing stones softly humming gentle songs of nature. Undisturbed dirt lay within the ring. Beneath that dirt lay present-day Feng, currently in a state more Sméagol than Smaug.

The dragons had taken him in after the Consortium had turned their backs on their precious lead investigator. This quiet place of healing was a rookery, the dragons' equivalent of a NICU. That Feng was over three hundred years old made his sitch kind of funny. However, it was present-day Feng's guardians she was after, not the Phoenix himself.

"Chimera," whispered the shadows along the perimeter of the rookery. The light Danish accent was barely perceptible in the single word.

"Raspoine?" Bix kept her voice low as she studied the shades of dark beyond the circle of light, searching for the dragon queen ascendant.

The Dragon Horde was ruled by seven queens, each queen to her own cycle, each queen faithfully supported by her enforcer. In Raspoine's case, her enforcer was her twin brother, Rummir, who should also be here. Whether they were in human form, dragon form, or something else entirely, well, that was what Bix was trying to discern. The last thing she wanted to do was chat up the south end of a north-facing dragon.

"You usually join him while you are fast asleep," a deeper and definitely masculine voice answered from the other side of the rookery. The thick Danish accent confirmed the speaker was Rummir. "That you are awake is…interesting."

"Some people snore. I travel. My subconscious dictates the destination. Sorry if I've been triggering alarms and whatnot." Bix's gatekeeper magic took her body wherever the images in her mind told it too. Her subconscious was trained to relocate her often while she slept as a defense mechanism against the entities that hunted her. Her brain feeling the need to check on Feng while her body rested was odd, but whatever. Another thing to add to her list of personal issues.

"Your visits are the only time his mind truly quiets." Raspoine's voice accompanied the sound of a long slither scraping lightly against the walls. Large violet serpentine eyes glowed amid the black. "But you did not come here tonight in your passive capacity. Is something amiss?"

"I wanted to talk to you two about him." Bix silently prayed that future-Feng hadn't set her up to piss off the token allies she had among the Dragon Horde. Like the other superpowers, the dragons didn't number among her fan base. Raspoine and Rummir had proven to be the exceptions. They'd sidestepped politics and the edicts of their reigning queen to come to Bix's aid when she'd needed help. In the aftermath, the twins had ended up as present-day Feng's new guardians. As far as she knew, they couldn't see into the future, but there was no one else who came close to an objective and informed third party when dealing with the Phoenix and the Chimera.

"Does this have something to do with the bubble of displaced time and native magic in which you've been loitering?" Rummir asked through a yawn.

Bix's lips formed words that did not accompany sounds until one word escaped. "How…?"

Raspoine twitched the tip of her tail, causing a gust that blew Bix's hair back. "The anomaly clings to you like sawdust from a construction site."

"Ew," Bix groaned and held her arms out from her sides, searching for the evidence.

"It is faint, perceptible only to royals or archangels," Rummir grumbled. "It will fade the longer you are away from its source."

"That you are able to maintain a presence in the bubble is intriguing," Raspoine added. "May we be bold and ask how you have achieved this?"

Bix stared at her feet. At the ground, actually. At the Phoenix quietly resting under it.

"Curious," Raspoine murmured. "Perplexing is perhaps more accurate. This means the two of you have collaborated in the present and the future, which will have ramifications all along the timeline. A dangerous choice of actions that accompany an unheard-of partnership."

"Dangerous? In what way?" Bix asked. She had a lot of questions about the residual and concentric effects of the time travel. She and her Dark Ops team had debated those topics ad nauseam during mission downtime. Months' worth of yeah-buts and what-ifs, and they still hadn't covered all the bases. It was the opening to a rabbit hole she'd explore later. Much later. When the Mids weren't in jeopardy. "Did we spawn a black hole or something?"

"*You* can do that without the Phoenix's aid," Rummir harrumphed.

"The danger is in second-guessing our actions, reactions, plans already in motion, and strategies in their nascent stages," Raspoine clarified. "The temptation is to avail ourselves of all information from the future, no matter the cost. However, the Fates are the first to advise caution about deciding our present based on a singular view of what is yet to come."

"You offer us a perilous enticement, Chimera, and there will be a time when we are hard-pressed to resist," Rummir warned.

"For the spell to work, the Phoenix is the one who moved through time. Whatever his reasons, our traditions demand we respect his actions." Raspoine exhaled loudly, and a curl of lavender smoke drifted across the illuminated stones. "At least we now know your absence from the timeline is why he has been so restless recently."

"Wait, if it's a pocket of displaced time, how does present-day Feng know when I'm not in the 'now'?" Bix pinched the bridge of her nose as her brain throbbed behind one eye from trying to keep Feng-one and Feng-two straight; as if she didn't have enough crazy to juggle.

"It's the pendant you wear," Rummir explained. "It allows him to track you and help you as much as you permit him to. Surely you have felt his interventions?"

She had indeed felt Feng's assistance. There had been times when she'd been severely weakened that she'd felt Mids' magic aiding her, diverging from its natural propensities. The first time she'd noticed it, she'd been starving after relocating a crime scene. He'd helped her stay tethered to the World as the delirium of hunger had taken hold.

More to the point, Rummir had provided the unsolicited proof of future-Feng's veracity. Spies preferred organic answers to questions the interrogatee didn't realize were being asked. Those responses minimized prevarications, omissions, and half-truths.

"Never occurred to me that it was a conscious effort on Feng's part. It seems contrary to our relationship and his current condition." Bix stood straighter as the weight of a new mission, the Fymmi mission, settled on her shoulders. Along with it came the mind-numbing panic that she would bring ruin to the Mids by opening gates for the Devourers when she gained her next segment of memories. There had to be a way to prevent that. The point of knowing the future was to stop bad things from happening. Right? Right.

"Agreed," Rummir groused. "Yet he still helps you in his way; hence, why my sister considers your collaborations perplexing."

"Well, that makes two of us," Bix admitted. Knowing that Feng had helped her from the moment she'd taken to wearing his dewclaw—from the moment their magics had been bound together—that was straight-up unnerving and confusing. That meant he'd chosen to be her ally while at the lowest point in his life. His decision hadn't changed despite a war, his impending execution, and her future utter betrayal of the Mids in the throes of her memory assimilation.

Feng was either a stalwart friend in the making or a new strain of nutbucket. Didn't matter either way. She'd said she'd take the mission if he could prove she could trust his story. He had, so she would.

"You said you needed to speak with us about Feng," Raspoine gently prompted.

"Right." Bix mustered up her courage and prayed her confession wouldn't blow up in her face. "Feng is going to rise soon. I don't know the exact day and time, just that he's going to wake up convinced that he needs to save the Mids from *me*."

The sound of two massive heads lifting accompanied twined curls of lavender smoke drifting across the singing stones.

"This is how it starts, with a seemingly benign statement of what is to come." Rummir slashed his tail through the air. "We modify our plans. Reassess his treatment and progress. Make changes that even now are altering the future. It's a snowball effect."

In a future where the Devourers reigned over the Mids, yep, changing even the most minor things could help. In this case, if Feng could complete his rehabilitation, then he could be a greater asset in the war.

"Will he be correct?" Raspoine pressed. "Will you become a threat to the Mids?"

"Maybe," Bix hedged, closing her hand over the pendant holding Feng's dewclaw as it warmed against her skin. "But I'll take steps to minimize it. The point is *he* will be in no condition to make things better. In fact, he'll make the situation and himself worse. It will not do the Mids any good to have us going at each other way ahead of our scheduled date. So, please, will you make every effort to keep him on the peaceful path to recovery and out of my way?"

Their silence was long, giving Bix plenty of opportunity to regret telling them she'd be a threat. They were royal dragons. They couldn't kill her, but they could wreck her up in all kinds of unexpected ways. Yeah, telling them the truth was probably not her best move.

"Will you turn to the Berserker commander for assistance in containing the threat you pose?" Rummir not so much asked as he demanded, making it clear the Berserker's involvement was a condition of the dragons' potential agreement.

Unfortunately, Feng wasn't the only one with whom she had trust issues. Tobek, the Berserker commander, knew her from the days before she'd lost her memories, but he wouldn't talk about it. He was a good guy by all other standards. She totally classified him as a friend… a friend with secretive and therefore suspicious motivations. Hell, she lived with him, so their problems weren't insurmountable. They assisted each other whenever the need arose and did so without quibble. Plus, Tobek had a unique capacity for bending Mids' magic to his will. If there was a way to prevent her from going nuclear, he'd be the one to figure it out. The last thing she wanted to do was hurt anyone while in the throes of a memory merge.

"Tobek is my next stop," Bix confirmed.

"Then, in exchange for your honesty, we will do as you ask," Raspoine conceded. "However, we will be watching, Chimera. We will act accordingly if the Berserker fails you."

Bix wasn't sure if that was a threat to her or to her friend, but she wasn't dumb enough to inquire.

Chapter 3

Bix moved through gates to the parking lot of a renovated coal plant in Old Town Alexandria, Virginia, Primary Mid World; her cartoonish "elves being gored by reindeer" platform pumps arguably not the best footwear given all the black ice. A bitter evening wind rolled up from the Potomac River, causing the gentle tumble of snowflakes to dance across the beautifully landscaped, twenty-five-acre compound that was home to a battalion of Berserkers.

White holiday lights decorated barren trees, while festive city banners hung from replicas of historic gas-lantern streetlights. At the main building, more white lights limned the black awning of the body-modification shop Dysmorphic. To one side of the shop, a charming mural of a fantastical community feast had been painted in the long windows of the beer-hall-slash-classroom. To the other side of Dysmorphic, the high-security mirrored front of the clinic and morgue remained caustically unadorned and utterly uninviting. The apartments above the shops, however, sparkled and glowed in merry array from myriad decorations.

For long-lived soldiers in the Mid World Army who knew the ugly truths behind all kinds of religions, the Berserkers still embraced the joy of community at the heart of the winter holidays.

The big lugs.

Grinning, Bix scampered into Dysmorphic. The bell above the door chimed as a blast of warm air melted the tiny snowflakes sticking to her dress. She stamped her feet on the acid-stained concrete floor etched with countless wards. The shop was busy tonight with Chwedlonol—the catchall name for the many magical races who occupied the Mids—in search of early solstice tattoos, scarifications, piercings, subdermal implants, and whatever else magic or technology could provide. The Berserkers who manned the shop were artists with remarkable talent, most of whom gave Bix the chin-high salute as she made her way to the last ironclad stall.

A hulking, heavily tatted blond bent over a magnifying lamp. One gloved prosthetic hand held taut the red skin of a fire-eating kobold. The natural hand held a fine-tipped nozzle connected to a tank of liquid nitrogen, steadily carving minute details into an elaborate backpiece.

"Sweetheart," the blond drawled, not looking up from his task. He didn't need to. If her pumps didn't identify her, the way her Other World presence caused his blend of Mids and undefined magic to dichotomously push and pull at her was enough to do it.

"One day, Tobek, you will call me by my name," she lightly chided. For whatever reason, he refused, flat-out, not even in conversations with other people, to use her name. Everybody had their own special weird. That happened to be one of his.

His deep chuckle made his chest vibrate and the beads in his long, braided beard clatter. "You're back earlier than I expected."

According to her internal clock, she'd spent the better part of the day inside the library. Apparently, when one existed outside of time, time in the present still moved, but at a different rate. That was somewhat similar to the time variances between Mid Worlds and the other types of Worlds. She would have to train her mind to track and adjust accordingly.

"Don't mean to interrupt your workday." She rocked up on her toes and clacked down on her heels. "I'm checking in, so you don't send out search parties for me. I'm going to head home to do some research."

Tobek graciously shared his sprawling basement home with her and the goblin superintendent of the compound. As the commander of this Berserker battalion, Tobek gave Bix great leeway in availing herself of his resources. All he asked in return was that she not make him hunt her down, oh, and that she not bring friends home to the supersecret lair that most people didn't know she shared with him.

Rent-free luxury in the highly secure heart of a Berserker command post? She could totally abide by his rules.

"Your girlfriend can hang," the kobold said, his face planted in the padded headrest that kept him looking at the ground. "I don't mind. She's got a nice voice."

"Thanks, man, but the piece is done." Tobek reached behind him and turned off the tank, not bothering to correct his customer's erroneous assumption. He blotted the kobold's back, then moved the lamp out of the way. Next, he applied some sort of orange menthol-smelling unguent to the entire scarification, then wrapped the kobold's torso in clingwrap.

"Damn, that's cold." The kobold sat up and flexed his shoulders, shivering. His red-orange eyes flicked to Bix. His flirtatious smile slid into a slack-jawed gape. He jumped up from his seat and bowed to her, wincing. "Mighty Chimera, forgive my familiarity."

Bix leaned back and looked at Tobek. The Berserker failed miserably to hide his grin as he snapped off his gloves and tossed them in a biohazard bin.

"We're good," Bix said, giving the kobold two thumbs-up. "Compliments don't make me angry. Please don't do anything to muck up your scarification. It looked beautiful. An avian celebration scene under the full moon?"

The kobold hung his head.

"Sun," Tobek corrected. "The Phoenix bringing forth the heat of the weak sun to beat back the long winter's night."

"The Phoe—oh," she drew out the last, finally grokking the kobold's reaction. Stories of the epic cyclical battles between the Phoenix and the Chimera were making a resurgence in Chwed pop culture now that she—the bogeyman wrapped in darkness—had been unmasked and spotted in public. It was kind of a cool way for her to relearn her own past, barrels of salt for the exaggerations included. "It's all good. The Phoenix deserves a fan club. You fire guys have to stick together. No hard feelings."

The kobold cocked his head and blinked rapidly.

"Here's your aftercare packet. Make sure your uncle wears clean gloves when he changes your wrappings this time, eh?" Tobek handed the kobold a bag and motioned him out of the stall. The kobold bowed twice again to Bix before heading for the front door.

Bix smiled and waved goodbye to the guy, then turned to Tobek with a brittle smile. "Still creepy being recognized as the Chimera."

"Probably doesn't comfort you that we get a lot of requests for your portrait these days." Tobek loaded up a tray of used tools and set about sanitizing his station.

"Dude, it hasn't been that long since I was outed," she muttered under her breath, then paused. "Where are people putting my picture, exactly?"

His laugh was a little too wicked, which told her more than she wanted to know.

She grimaced. "You better have a no-groin policy."

"They ask for the image, but we don't agree to do it. You're on the list of superpowers whose likenesses we don't replicate lest we mark our customers for certain death."

"Really? Except gods live to be worshipped. Dragons and angels are already everywhere and on everything, so I'm thinking it's the Fates who are a little particular about their image. Your big-big bosses not big-big fans of the one-eyed hag look?"

Berserkers were the Fates' contributions to the protection of the Mids. Fates plucked great big men—specifically men, specifically combat-proven soldiers, and typically human—from highly mortal lives, made arrangements for some level of physical restoration and longevity, then tossed their new-and-improved dudes into the Mid World Army. Berserkers were easily identifiable by the vibrant blue eyes they all got alongside their lifetime military commissions. They were a glorious blend of ethnic diversity… not gender or Chwed diversity. There were women in the other branches of the MWA just as there were Chweds in the other branches. Those other branches hadn't extended any offers of assistance to Bix, so she stuck with the Berserkers who had. Plus, she liked their company.

"The kobold was my last customer for the night." Tobek handed her the tray of used implements and toed the cart on which the nitrogen tank sat, rocking it back to its wheels. "Head for the clinic. I need to sterilize those and put this away. Whatever it is you're up to, you can tell me when we get there."

"What makes you think I'm up to anything?"

"Because day follows night?"

"Fine. I'm up to something." She carried the tray to the iron corridor running in front of the utility rooms at the back of the plant. The stainless-steel door to the clinic slid aside as she neared. "Memories. Mine, specifically."

"We've discussed this. I cannot reveal our history." He parked the nitrogen tank beside two others, then tapped his pec, the pec into which a curse had been etched, a curse that prevented him from discussing the past that he and the Chimera version 1.0 had shared.

"Not asking you to." She handed him his tray of dirty implements, then perched on one of the half-dozen rolling stools in front of the wall of morgue refrigerators. "It's come to my attention that the next infusion of memories I get will break my mind."

"This caution is from a source you trust?" He took the tray to the trough sink and set about cleaning.

"I don't trust the source, but I'm choosing to heed the

warning." She poked at the scars on her arm. "At some point, I'll reclaim enough fragments that they'll start making connections with each other, which will enable me to intentionally recall the memories, peppered with holes and partial truths though they will be. So, yeah, I can imagine the short trip to Crazy Town becoming a very real thing."

He glanced over his shoulder at her and nodded. "Okay, then we'll deal with that when it happens. There are mental spells, artifacts, totems, etcetera, created for the sole purpose of managing memories. The challenge will be finding one that works for you."

"Then there is the small matter of the gods themselves," she mumbled. "The seven gods I burdened with my memories? Turns out what I did drove them mad. Of the five remaining, those whose pantheons haven't locked them up are coming for me. I can't control when, how, or where they'll appear. Asking a god to 'hold that thought' until reclamation is convenient for me will end badly for everyone."

He grunted. "I see what you did there, punny girl."

"Seriously, Tobek. The gods are a big enough threat, and if I lose my mind, I'll be ten times worse. 'Destroyer of Worlds' kind of worse. I don't want to hurt you or your guys. I'm aware my presence here is enough of a risk to them."

"A risk they welcome," he countered.

"I am also aware that I travel in my sleep, and that I often travel to you." She bit her lip. "So even if I try to keep my distance, I can't guarantee I'll succeed."

He stopped what he was doing and came to her in two strides. He lifted her chin with the edge of his soap-bubble-covered finger. His eyes glowed faintly with the dawning rage of a Berserker. "I always welcome you. Wrath, pain, joy, madness, all of it, all of you. Always."

Heat flared along her cheeks. It took a few deep breaths before she could speak coherently. It was moments like this with Tobek that confused her. With Feng, their history made it easy to cut him off at the knees. But Tobek would say these things, and better still, prove these sentiments through actions. Eighty percent of the time, she felt all safe and snuggly in his presence. But that missing twenty percent was instinct, and she'd be a fool to ignore it.

"What if I kill you?" she whispered.

"Sweetheart." He stroked her cheek with his wet thumb. "You don't know how."

A surge of Other World magic chased by Mids' native magic shoved against her. He staggered back into a mortician's table. The pattern of an Eternal Knot burned through his Henley shirt.

"Tobek?" She leapt up from her stool.

He warned her off with a look, clutching his chest. Green magic encircled the fingers of his natural hand, sending tiny silver spears to pierce his skin until his blood flowed into the pattern of the knot.

The curse of silence took its due.

"I'm sorry, I didn't mean to provoke it." She looked away, tremendously curious even as she inwardly cringed. Did Tobek's comment mean that she had *tried* to kill him in the past? And he still wanted her at his side? Was that a "keep your enemies close" thing, or had they had one of those highly violent sort of frenemy relationships? Yes, there was a definite connection between them, but with each of their unique issues, she didn't see how they could've been compatible as lovers. Not that she hadn't thought about them in that way, because, hello, look at him, but…mmm, no. Whatever was between them, at its core, wasn't wild lust, not exactly. She didn't have that same visceral feeling with anyone else, so she couldn't identify it, couldn't put a name on the "it."

Clearly, he couldn't either.

He puffed a few loud breaths, grunted, audibly shook off the pain the curse inflicted, and grinned. *Grinned*. Silly man.

"You and your pain fetish," she drawled.

"It's invigorating." He winked, then hobbled to the sink, returning to the tools of his trade. "Now, then, about those memories."

"*Miiidniiight,*" warbled a young woman's voice from the

morgue cooler. "*Not a hound in Hel's baaaasement.*"

Bix and Tobek looked at each other, then at the wall of square steel doors. Bix motioned for Tobek to stay as she silently approached the door from which the singing came. In this bastion of security, there was only one interloper who'd have the ability and the balls to hide inside corpse cold storage. Bix unlatched the door and pulled out the long tray, revealing a rather lively dead girl with rainbow-dyed pigtails and a gel manicure of Munch's *The Scream* drumming against her freckled cheeks.

"Hiya, Bixie." The girl giggled.

"Misheard show tunes, Drew?" Bix grinned at her best friend, a draugr, a body thief of sorts. Drew preferred corpses since the souls had already vacated, but she was capable of occupying the living too when necessary. "And why are you hiding in here, of all places?"

"I was going to come see you in the morning, but I had a minor misunderstanding with this suit's landlord." Drew hopped off the tray and gestured to the logo of her T-shirt promoting a hot-dog eating championship. "Turns out the landlord watched me choke to death on a wiener. Needless to say, he wasn't keen to let me stay until the lease expired. However, he was quick to call the cops, a medium, and some poor immigrant he swore was a voodoo priest."

"Are you in need of protection?" Tobek asked, rinsing his tools.

"Aw, ever the gentleman." Drew blew Tobek a kiss. "I've been doing a lot of body-hopping, chasing leads on the Devourer infiltrators. I just needed a place to rest without fear of violation or cremation. I knew you'd relaxed the wards to allow me to meet with Bixie in the beer hall, so I took a chance the free pass extended to the morgue too. Mad props to the goblin. He keeps this place spotless."

"I take it you heard our discussion." Tobek shook the water from the tools and put them in an autoclave, setting the timer for sterilization.

"Well, yeah, it sort of echoes in there." Drew tipped her head at the coolers and frowned down at her chest, picking at a grease stain. "Bixie, did your source give you the names of the gods who have the rest of your memories?"

"No." Bix rebraided one of Drew's pigtails that had started to unravel. "My source would rather I not pursue my lost memories."

"You need those memories," Tobek snapped, far too emphatically. "The Devourers would likely love nothing more than for you to opt out of remembering how to kill them. The sooner you get those memories back, the better for all of us. I got you on this one."

"Thank you," Bix said in earnest, making a mental note of his reaction. While Tobek allowed folks to believe he was human, she had proof to the contrary. Her working theory was that he was an old demigod, screwed over by his pantheon, and somehow caged by the Fates with the contract that had made him a Berserker. He, naturally, couldn't talk about it, which made her think the pre-memory-wipe Chimera had had something to do with his constrained state. If she—with her full knowledge restored—held the key to his freedom, then that could explain his dogged loyalty. That was her positive take on it. She chose not to dwell on the negative possibilities. It was another layer of complexity in their unusual relationship.

"Anudrengr, you are welcome to rest here for the night," Tobek said far more evenly, calling Drew by the ancient name she despised. "I'll let my men know you are on the premises."

"That's not going to be necessary, I think. I know a place in need of a long-term tenant." Bix plopped down on a stool and rolled to the clinic's computers. She tapped a key, and the screens lit up with the MWA logo. "Cian? Cian, are you there? Cian, Cian, Cian?"

"Sweetheart, the young Sage moved out, remember? The Houses of Fate and the MWA denied his continued sanctuary here. He's no longer networked into our system." Tobek spoke with all the bitterness he still held for being overruled by his big bosses.

"Hold up, you think I should move in with the kid?" Drew squawked. "Are you insane? Mmm, let me rephrase that…"

"Drew, you read his mom's soul." Bix took Drew's cold hand and patted it. "It makes you the most qualified for the gig. Emotionally, he needs someone to be a touchstone. Strategically, we need him alive and monitored by someone capable of recognizing a Devourer or one of the superpowers should they come looking for him. I'm not asking you to be in his back pocket, just to keep an eye on him."

"Asset management, eh?" Drew rolled her eyes. "It would be a place to sleep, and I wouldn't have to move every few days. But living with the living? Y'all are icky."

"A teenage boy is much worse," Tobek noted, not at all helpfully.

"Give it a try? Please?" Bix gave Drew her best sad-puppy imitation.

"You know I can't refuse you." Drew sighed. "But this is temporary, right? I might kill the kid on principle if he pushes me too far."

"Agreed." Bix spun back to the computer. "Cian, Cian, Cian?"

"Sweetheart, you can't reach him through this system," Tobek reiterated. "That's not how current technology works."

"Oh, you old fogey," Bix tutted. "Once he hacked your system, you were never going to be free of him. Right, Cian? Cian? Cian, Cian, Cian?"

"Our security is exceptional," Tobek protested. "We cleaned, patched, and closed all the holes he exploited."

"This is probably the one arena in which age works against you." Drew pressed her cheek against Tobek's arm. "Welcome to the party."

"Cian, you let them think they'd kicked you out of the system, didn't you, Cian? Cian, Cian, Cian. I know your mother raised you with a healthy sense of paranoia, Cian, Cian, Cian." Bix chittered irksomely. "I know that means you coded some sort of alert to register every mention of your name, Cian, Cian, Cian, Cian. I can keep this up all night, Cian, Cian, Cian. You have no idea how annoying I can be, Cian, Cian, Cian. Answer me, Cian, Cian, Cian, you little herb nerd."

"Herb nerd," Drew gasped. "Did you just call him an herb nerd? I'm stealing that. Totally stealing that. Herb nerd. I'm dying."

"You know, most people would use a phone." Tobek snickered into his fist.

"Ciiian," Bix sang. "Ciiian, Cian, Cian, Ci—"

"Oh my god, Bix," blasted through the speakers as the monitors flicked to the image of a bleary-eyed teenage boy. His shaggy ginger hair pointed eighteen different directions. The purple ring around one of his green eyes was not from sleep deprivation; neither was the scab on his puffy lip nor the slight purpling on his bony bare chest. Of greater interest was the way a neon-orange light from a sign outside the windows fell around him and a very familiar couch.

"Yay, there you are," Bix cheered with way too much enthusiasm, just to further irritate the kid as she smirked at Tobek. "Aw, who's the lump at the end of the sectional?"

"Bix, don't—" Cian blurted.

"Incoming," she warned, throwing open gates and taking Drew with her.

Chapter 4

Bix and Drew stepped into a two-bedroom second-floor apartment in a four-unit town house that'd last been renovated in the 1970s. The worn parquet floors started in the teeny entryway and went everywhere orange-and-yellow floral linoleum didn't. The padded flooring in the kitchen matched the harvest-gold range and the microwave-hood combo nestled between knotty pine cabinets whose doors didn't align properly. The edges of the faded orange Formica countertops had been chipped and torn over the years. A dented almond-colored fridge from this decade was hooked up in the living room. Three feet separated the fridge doors from a beat-up overstuffed brown leather sectional and an exasperated seventeen-year-old Sage hastily untangling himself from a headset and laptop.

"Bix," Cian whispered, doing a double take at Drew, "you can't be here."

"Dude, I helped your mom move into this armpit before you were born." Bix deliberately waited to introduce Drew; besides, the stench of boy funk and stale Thai takeout was overwhelming. "That damn couch is how she discovered I'm a gatekeeper. Didn't you ever ask her how she got it up the rinky-dink stairway? 'Cause it didn't come through those narrow windows, which, by the way, open them, it reeks in here."

"It's snowing outside. The heat only works sporadically." He lurched up to bodily block her from getting near the windows and the end of the couch on which the blanket-covered lump softly snored.

Bix artfully avoided tromping on Cian's bare toes but had to clutch his shoulders to keep from tripping over a heap of messenger bags and textbooks. "Clearly none of the Berserkers taught you the art of the hookup while you were with them. Look, the stinky food is the excuse you use to open the windows. The cold air then requires the heavy blankets under which you and your girl must cuddle to stay warm. Cuddle. Together. Not at separate ends of the couch."

The thing about pasty white boys was when they blushed, it went from scalp to toes. "It's not like that."

"They say scents trigger memories," Drew whispered loudly. "This is not a scent any of us will remember fondly. Please, for the love of anyone who had a nose hair in the history of ever, open the windows. It's super bad when I can taste the ick in the air."

Cian rolled his eyes but did as they asked. As he struggled with the heavy warped wood frames, Bix moved to the lump on the couch.

"You can come out anytime now, honest," she murmured. "I'm not judgy. Poke one finger out if you need pants. Two fingers for a shirt and pants."

"Bix," Cian cried.

A melodious laugh answered from the lump as the blanket fell away, revealing a diamond-shaped face with vitiligo framing the brightest smile. Long hot-pink bangs and side fade dared anyone to overlook the girl. She was fifteen, maybe? Definitely within a year or two of Cian.

"Oh, aren't you darling?" Bix gasped. "And you're wearing a classic arcade T-shirt. Are those...are those fuzzy *dragon* slippers? Where did you get them?"

"Cian gave them to me for my birthday," the girl said, sitting upright and tugging up the legs of her plaid fleece pants to show off the hairy green slippers with felt horns and fangs.

"Bix, Onyeka. Onyeka, Bix," Cian muttered. "She's not my girlfriend. She lives upstairs. We've known each other since Mom adopted me. Our parents would step in for each other when the other one had to work late."

"Cian was helping me study for exams," Onyeka explained, drawing the blanket over her shoulders. "I fell asleep. Honest. Nothing happened."

"Her dad would kill them both if it did," Drew said as she picked up a box of takeout and sneered. "Ew. Cold curry. How many times did your mom tell you this needs to be eaten hot?"

Onyeka and Cian stared at Drew, heads angled at the same degree.

"You know my dad?" Onyeka asked.

"Hmm?" Drew picked up three more containers and sniffed them. "What? Your dad? Oh, no, no, honey. His mom. She was so grateful that you and your dad have been there for Cian."

"If you two change your minds," Bix jumped in to say before Drew further rattled the human girl, "there's a spring under the third cushion that should really be avoided at all costs, and you will not know it until it's too late."

"Oh my God," Cian groaned, slapping his hands over his face. "I can't believe…Mom's been dead a week. Can't you show a little respect?"

"What? She would've agreed. She was the one who found it." Bix winked at Onyeka. "And I'm sorry if I offended your delicate sensibilities."

"This pigsty would've offended hers." Drew plucked a filthy T-shirt from the floor and gave Cian a reproachful stare. "She was way too uptight to tolerate a mess like this. Do you need a house brownie?"

"A what?" Onyeka slid to the edge of the cushion.

"Nothing, just a joke between me and Mom," Cian rushed to explain, shooting Drew a "shut it" look as he snatched the shirt from her and put it on.

Bix hid a smile. So, the kid was adhering to the "keep humans in the ignorance bubble" rule by which all Chweds had to abide. Ninety-nine percent of humans didn't possess any kind of magic; they grounded it, which kept native and disparate magics from tearing apart Worlds. Cian belonged to that one percent of human exceptions. He was a Sage, a Fate-in-training, just beginning the gauntlet of tests and trials that would end in his death, his transformation into a long-lived supercomputer in the Grove of Sages, or his rebirth as an immortal Fate with destinies to weave.

His adoptive mother had been an Oracle, the feminine half of the Fates-in-training. She hadn't passed the bulk of her tests, so the Fates had pulled her from the game. They hadn't bothered to wait until her kid had reached the humans' age of majority. It was a pointed reminder of how cruel Fates really were.

"Speaking of housekeeping and your mother's passing…" Bix moved a textbook off the arm of the couch so she could perch. "Are you set up okay? Lease? Income? Tuition? I assume you're going to finish grad school, not punk out?"

"Mom and I had a deal. She didn't care what kind of school I was in, it just had to be accredited and I had to attend until I was eighteen. I'm almost done with my thesis and have put in for the doctoral program already, so yeah, I'm staying. I've got one more year to keep my promise to Mom. As for the rest…" He shoved his hand in his hair. "A benefits counselor from her old employer is securing the lease and handling all the legal and probate stuff. My scholarship will take care of the tuition. My job should cover books and food. I should be good."

"All you need, then, is a roommate." Bix gauged his reaction from under the fall of her bangs.

"No, no, I do not," he blustered as any teenager would.

"Yeah, yeah, you do." Bix pointed at the two tattoos of leaves on his arm that marked the grades he'd received on his first Fate-based trials. A disk of crystals covered one of the leaves, the side effect of a disease for which there was no cure. He was the first to live this long with it. "You're an actual genius with an addiction to drugs and information. You jumped into the deep end of the criminal pool with your online shenanigans, alerting the wrong kind of people to your existence. Then there's whatever ass whooping you recently endured. Do I need to get into the details of the other dumb-dumb things you've done since we met?"

"Bix," he hissed, cutting a look at his friend.

"I told you one day you'd hack the wrong people," Onyeka tutted, seemingly unsurprised and unfazed by the litany Bix had laid down. "The fight, though, he was defending me."

"Some guys need to be taught that not every girl is interested in them." Cian scowled, then winced as the cut on his lip bled again.

"Okay, Prince Charming, that bakes the cake. You're definitely getting an adult roommate, one who can teach you how to block more of those punches." Bix glanced at Drew, who nodded. "No, you don't get a say in who it is. It'll be someone familiar enough with your special snowflakery."

"Are...are *you* going to be my roommate?" he stammered, recoiling.

"Cian," Onyeka whispered with reproach as she folded the blanket she'd used.

"Me? Oh gods, no." Bix mimicked his disgust. "I kept my distance for a week to let you grieve, brood, brawl, and embroil yourself in deeper trouble. Now you have to put on man pants."

"Don't worry, kiddo, your new roommate will help you box up your mom's stuff while being fully considerate of her memory," Drew added with a touch of compassion.

Cian stared cow eyed at the dark bedroom off the kitchen. "I...I don't know...I..."

"No matter what you've been told, it does *not* get easier." Bix shook her head. "You simply get stronger. That's the part that takes time."

He looked at her with eyes reddening and jaw quivering. "Did they know her? Whoever you're bringing in, did they know my

---

mom?"

"Better than she would have liked." Bix grinned. "Make no mistake, though, your roommate will not be her surrogate, will not be your nanny, and will definitely not be your doormat."

"Damn skippy," Drew muttered.

Onyeka chuckled. "I cannot wait to meet this new roommate."

"I suspect the anticipation will be mutual." Bix deliberately did not look at Drew this time. The frequency with which the draugr changed bodies meant Onyeka could be meeting someone new every week, if not more often. "Now that I've crushed your dreams of premature independence, Cian, when you're done with your winter finals, I have a project with which I need your help."

Cian perked up. "I took them early, while Mom was in a coma. Professors are super understanding about provable family emergencies, especially in single-parent situations."

"He could use the distraction. Spring semester doesn't start for two months." Onyeka gathered up her books. "It was very nice to meet you, Bix, and your friend here. If you will please excuse me, I need to get home before my dad thinks we're up to no good."

"I'll walk you up." Cian scrambled to help Onyeka gather all her papers, books, and laptop, then pack her messenger bag.

Bix and Drew gave the pair their space, ambling to the kitchen.

"You think it's still here?" Drew murmured.

"Teenage boy? Hell yeah." Bix peered under the microwave hood and grimaced at the wealth of tomato spatter staining the ancient surface. She also noted the fingerprints in four distinct places. Ah, some things never changed. The range hood had never worked. Cian's mom used to hide Bix's shoes in the gutted appliance in an effort to prolong Bix's visits.

Bygone days for sure.

Bix waited until the front door closed before pressing her fingers into the tomato prints. Latches released, shifting a notable weight onto the tray. Bix slowly lowered the base. Shiny, well-oiled brackets extended, exposing the hidden compartment. A taser, refill cartridge, two pistols, four preloaded clips, and a black-magic bag.

"It's all here," Drew sighed. "Small favors."

"Hey, what are you doing?" Cian slammed the front door and rushed to the kitchen. "I need those."

"When you demonstrate proficiency with each of these to Tobek's standards and prove to me you fully comprehend the personal trauma and responsibility of taking a life, then maybe you'll get some of them back." Bix used gates to relocate all but the taser and cartridge. Nope. Second thought. She moved the taser too. He'd probably try to light up Drew, and Drew did not respond well to electrical jolts. "Where's the rest of it?"

He thrust his jaw forward and looked away. "I don't know what you're talking about."

"Your mother stole weapons and munitions from the CWIG armory capable of blowing up people, trains, city blocks, power grids, and much more." Drew crossed her arms and leaned against the counter. "You availed yourself of a few of them."

"You're one of *them*, aren't you?" Cian flicked a disgusted look at Drew. "Another one of those agents the CWIG uses to babysit me, eh? Are you part of the group they moved in downstairs or the ones they put in my university? Oh no, let me guess, my work? The CWIG thought a hot chick would be able to lead me around by my dick while I blabbed every dark secret my mom ever had? Suck it."

Bix pushed the emptied tray back into place, dying laughing inside. "Cian, meet Drew, your new roommate and the draugr who kept your mother alive long enough for you to say goodbye to her."

Cian leapt back like his nuts had been scorched. "A d-dr-draugr?"

"Listen up, herb nerd," Drew said, mirroring the kid move for move as he backed toward the windows. "I'm also the only other survivor of the burn job your mother set in motion for a CWIG Dark Ops team."

"H-how?" Cian blanched to a paler shade of ghostly, his eyes as wide as swelling allowed. "Mom told me everyone but Bix died, that angels burned the whole team to ashes."

"Flesh suits are flammable. I'm not." Drew smiled with menace. "Now, I don't work for the CWIG anymore. They think I'm dead, much like they think your mom told the truth when she laid the blame for that mess at Bix's feet."

"She didn't have a choice," he muttered.

"Bullshit," Drew cooed. "I read your mom's soul. I know everything about her, even the things she forgot. So, let's put our cards on the table, shall we? I didn't like her. I'm glad the Fates snipped her threads. I haven't decided how I feel about you yet."

Fear morphed into mulish anger in Cian's posture and expression. Good. If the kid was ever going to trust Drew, Drew had to put the truth out there so it couldn't be used against either of them. Better to deal with the emotions now while their relationship was new, so they didn't fester and explode into betrayals later.

"If you know everything about her, you know where the weapons are stashed," Cian sniped.

Drew laid her hand on Cian's rapidly rising and falling chest. "I do. Bix knows I do, but I'm not the one she asked, am I?"

"You, Cian, can tell me, or I will gut this apartment down to the studs and send everything out to the ether where it will be destroyed in seconds." Bix leaned on the counter, flicking cereal crumbs across the kitchen. "Everything. Every piece of furniture. Every scrap of clothing. Every photograph. Every everything. You will have nothing but the clothes on your back. Do you understand how little patience I have for deceit within our core team?"

Cian knocked away Drew's hand as he stood straighter. His chin rose. His pursed lips wriggled as though struggling to keep invectives from getting him in more trouble. She let him wage the personal war. The kid's longevity depended on his ability to know how to make good decisions, not necessarily the consistently benevolent ones, rather the ones that took into account the And Then Whats. That was the attribute at which Fates excelled far beyond their superpower peers. It was how they'd outsmarted the pantheons and won their independence. Sure, normal humans didn't develop that part of their brain until their midtwenties, but Cian wasn't normal and his brain had long ago outpaced typical human growth.

"I sold most of it," Cian mumbled at last. "Traded, really, for information about the faction that set up Mom, me, you two, and a lot of other people."

That right there was the reason he needed managing. All the book smarts, none of the street. In the recording future-Bix had left for present-day Bix, she'd spoken of the demise of the Mids and that Cian had died when his mom had. That he still lived in this timeline made the kid a variable, a valuable one, if, and only if, he stayed alive. It'd be a challenge. The boy was going to find trouble no matter what. He couldn't help it. Being a Sage made him an addict, and knowledge was his drug. His quest to sate that constantly evolving need would lead him into ever-changing crosshairs. By directing his attention to certain information troves, Bix's team could anticipate the threats to him and try to thwart them. Somewhat. Sort of. He'd come close to dying a couple of times already.

"Oh, herb nerd, you have got to *stop* painting a bull's-eye on your forehead." Drew laughed sadly and smoothed Cian's hair. "Maybe we start with that as your first lesson in keeping you alive, yeah?"

Cian hung his head but nodded.

"Put together a list of what you sold, your buyers, their pics, and images of their favorite haunts," Bix said. "Send the completed files to me. I'll review them for anything that needs to be reclaimed. The other goodies you haven't yet sold, gather them up, then ping me when they're ready for transport. When you're done with that, I need you to find a connection among a list of dead CWIG agents and MWA soldiers, a connection that got all of them killed but only some replaced by Devourers. Then I need you to take it one step further and identify who is missing from that list and whether they're still alive. There was a pattern to the assassinations, but the person who'd cracked it is dead. I need you to pick up that ball."

His eyes lit. "Is this the Consortium's hit list? You think they're after more agents and soldiers?"

"We have the right hand of the MWA versus the left hand of the CWIG. The two will cock-block each other in the name of cross-World security integrity." Drew hacked and slashed at the air like a bad kung-fu movie actor.

"They don't trust each other enough to get the real answer." Cian dodged Drew's blows. "Mom used to complain how much of a problem it was with departments inside the CWIG. I can only imagine it's ten times worse with the MWA."

"Ding, ding." Drew landed two light hits to Cian's throat. "Since you're part of our rogues' gallery, you're going to bypass their pissing contests and maybe save some lives."

Cian rubbed his neck and nodded. "Yeah. I'm in. I've seen what happens when the Consortium turns against the people it's supposed to protect."

"Good." Bix smiled. "I'll send the names of the confirmed dead once I get your weapons report. Do you have sufficient access to the MWA's network or do you need me to facilitate that?"

"I'm buried deep in their stuff, so we're good there." He eyed Drew. "But, it's going to take some serious effort to get into the CWIG's network. Whoever secures their data is damn good. I've never been able to hold a hack with them. I'm usually forced out at fifty seconds, all my worms defeated at ninety."

Bix knew quite well who in the CWIG kept kicking Cian out of their network. They were next on her visitation list.

"You and I can work up a plan, kiddo." Drew playfully punched Cian's shoulder. "It will not be the first time I've helped hack the CWIG."

"The plan is pretty straightforward." Bix pushed away from the counter. "Cian is going to get a winter internship with the CWIG."

"At HQ?" Drew gasped and giggled. "Brill."

"No, no." Cian waved his hands in negation. "I have a job at the bar. I like that job."

"But you don't have school for a few months," Bix reminded. "The best way to hack the CWIG is to be on the inside. Plus, résumé building, and blah, blah, planning for your future, blah, blah, adulting."

"Herb nerd, think about it." Drew grabbed Cian by the shoulders and shook him. "Access to *all* the CWIG data. Tell me your skin isn't prickling at just the thought of that much information at your fingertips. Centuries of secrets. Worlds you don't even know exist, their national security in the palm of your hand."

"Yeah, like they aren't going to try to trip me up with misinformation to see how fast my brain bleeds." He scratched his cheek. "This is just a temporary gig, right?"

"You'll be there for the proper length of an internship. It's what we call seeding a legend. You lay the foundations so in a year or five or whenever, you can leverage that position into a rock-solid backstory when you go deep under in a high-risk assignment." Bix drummed her nails on her hips. "Charm the folks at the CWIG, and you'll get a recommendation that can land you in countless intelligence hubs on this World and many others. You're going to need that to keep feeding your information addiction."

"They might even hire you full-time." Drew hugged Cian's arm and turned to Bix. "Look, honey, our very own mole."

"One problem." Cian tried to shrug out of Drew's grip, but the draugr was worse than a curious gecko. "Internship slots filled up weeks and weeks ago. My university department has to approve all nonstandard positions, and then the potential employer has to—"

"It's like he doesn't really understand what the CWIG is," Drew whispered loudly.

"Be ready for one of your babysitters to announce that you have a meeting." Bix wagged a finger at the kid. "And remember, you're still on probation when it comes to state secrets. This may not be a Fate-based trial, but make no mistake, I am testing you and so will the CWIG. You're not the first Sage to cross their radar. They will attempt to abuse your abilities and confuse your loyalties, so be on alert."

"I know, I know," he huffed. "The CWIG is Lawful Evil."

"Gamer geek," Drew teased.

"Speaking of Lawful Evil." Cian snapped his fingers, then grabbed his bag from the couch. "I almost forgot. Bix, you lost your smartwatch and earwig on your last mission."

Bix pouted. "And my bug. They didn't survive my travels."

Items created by Mid World magic couldn't exist beyond Mids, and Bix spent a lot of time in places other than the Mids. She didn't always remember to take off the Mid World tech before she bounced. Sometimes urgency didn't allow for a quick change. It was why she had to rely on gods to make most of her wardrobe since they could manifest durable materials.

"How do you feel about glasses?"

Bix curled a lip. "My gatekeeper aspect is completely dependent on imagery. I despise anything that mucks with my sight."

"Okay. We'll put these aside, then." He pulled a hard-sided glasses case from his bag and tossed it on the couch, continuing to rifle through his bag.

"Here. Use this the next time you want to get ahold of me, instead of blowing my spyware hack at the coal plant." Cian hooked a smartwatch with a band of different delicate metals around her naked wrist. "Features are the same as your last one. Projection, nanocomputer, voice commands, preloaded numbers and data from the last backup. I tripled the storage for the next time you steal intel from top-secret data servers."

"Thanks. What do I owe you?" She stroked the shiny metals with delight and fired up the phone feature. The keyboard projected on her long sleeve, allowing her to send a text to someone whose help she needed with the Fymmi mission.

"You don't owe *me* anything. The MWA footed the bill. Couple of the Berserkers brought over the parts. I think it was their excuse to check on me." Cian turned her palm over and dropped a half-dozen earwigs in it. They resembled simple silver or gold cartilage cuffs rather than the gaudy full-ear sleeves he'd made in the past. With all the odd encounters she had, she needed an earpiece that clamped on rather than one that rested in the ear canal.

"Oo, what do I have to do to get a set of these?" Drew picked up one of the earwigs and held it up to the neon-orange light.

"Not suck as a roommate?" Cian stuffed his hands in his pockets.

"Oh, it'll be like living with a different person every day." Drew batted her lashes.

"Luckily for you, Drew is coming with me to secure a recommendation for your internship. She'll move in tomorrow." Bix affixed a cuff to her ear and used a pair of gates to deposit the others on her bedside table back at the coal plant.

"That I will," Drew confirmed without hesitation. They'd worked together for so long that following each other's lead was second nature.

Bix glanced at her watch as it vibrated from a responding text that displayed an attached image along her sleeve. Meet confirmed. No questions about the who, why, or where. Good. Better still, her contact was immediately available.

Future-Feng had said the Devourers were already hunting Fymmi. That meant Bix didn't have time to waste. Since the faction never stopped searching for Fymmi—and they had eyes and spies everywhere—briefing her contact and Drew about the mission had to happen at a clean site, a place no one would think to look and a place Bix had already scrubbed for surveillance bugs. An apartment building crawling with active CWIG agents didn't fit the bill.

"While we're gone, Cian, pack up your mom's arsenal and try not to detonate anything." Bix shook her watch, shutting off the image projection. "I expect those traded-items files in the morning."

"Yes, ma'am," Cian mumbled.

"Ma'am," Drew chortled, then yelped as Bix shoved her through a gate.

Chapter 5

The clean site, clean World to be specific, had been abandoned by the Consortium eons ago. The thin air didn't move through its atmosphere. No currents stirred the evaporating oceans. Bottomless pits littered the terrain; their perpetually crumbling expansions offered the only sound. The place was completely uninhabited.

The Mid World of Vuornis had once been a jewel teeming with life. It'd taken one god spreading an antagonistic religion to convince the inhabitants they were mightier than the dragons and angels. The foolish people had hunted the creationist superpowers for sport, so the dragons had stopped feeding the seas and enriching the loam. The angels had stopped planting crops and purifying the air. Neither race would create new fleshy bodies to house the souls provided by a god whose prank had gone too far. Without bodies, the souls could not live, they could not grow fat with experiences that would feed the god. The Fates had refused to intervene no matter how pitifully the god had pleaded. So the god, much like the World he'd ruined, had withered, his name forgotten.

Deep inside canyon walls long abandoned by rivers lay the ruins of advanced cities that'd relied on geothermal heating and cooling while crystalline vents invited sunlight to illuminate what had been city centers. If one didn't mind the skeletons and the risk of everything caving in, it made for a lovely bolt-hole. It was one of many secret sanctuaries across the Mids that Bix had claimed during her tenure as a spy.

While she wasn't keen to expose all her hideaways, even to her best friend, this location had the records and the privacy they needed to conduct an effective briefing on the Fymmi mission.

"Bixie, when you take me out at night, I look forward to glittering dance clubs, pulsating beats, and young people too stupid to value their lives." Drew planted her hands on her hips and toed a divot in a cobblestone path. A crack deepened and spidered beyond sight. Ominous crumbling echoed in the distance. "What are we doing on a dystopian futuristic film set?"

"The draugr asks a pertinent question, shockingly," drawled a masculine voice, a smooth tenor with a hint of a carefully cultivated accent that played to the illusion of a modern, well-educated globe-trotter. While Ashtad Ba'al was undoubtedly brilliant and capable of existing on any World, he wasn't exactly modern. The demigod was pushing four hundred.

"Ashtad." Bix turned with a smile to greet her former boss, the man who'd trained her to be a covert agent, the only one inside the CWIG—other than Drew—who'd believed she wasn't the felon her enemies had painted her.

She stopped in her tracks.

Ashtad typically favored the finest in casual elegance. Today, however, he'd apparently run afoul of an angry tween who'd forced him into printed leggings, a sparkling half shirt, quilted moto jacket, and shaggy white boots. The normally gold streaks in his curly dark hair were now teal, two shades brighter than Bix's natural color.

Drew audibly gasped, her hands slapping over her mouth a heartbeat before she doubled over laughing. Bix had to look away before she too succumbed. When Ashtad had answered her text with a photo so she could create his origin gate, he hadn't made it a selfie. Now she knew why.

"Go on, get it all out, you two," Ashtad drawled, tugging a jewel-tipped false eyelash from his neon eye shadow.

"Good to see you're back to fighting form," Bix struggled to say with a straight face. The last time she'd seen him, he'd been reliant on a cane while recovering from a gruesome battle in which he'd engaged on her behalf.

"Take a picture," Drew wheezed. "Quick, Bixie, take a picture. I want to have it painted on the side of a skyscraper."

Bix's two closest friends didn't care for each other. To say it was a personality conflict would ignore the interpantheon rivalries and bigotries. Purely for her sake did they make the attempt to play well together, which she appreciated immensely.

"Don't make me fry your smartwatch," Ashtad cautioned, sparks dancing along his fingertips. The son of a storm god, Ashtad manipulated electricity with ease. It would hardly be the first time he'd lit Bix up like the Vegas Strip, though, this time, the picture might be worth the joules. "Your message said it was urgent?"

"I'm sorry to pull you from whatever undercover op this getup required." Bix paused an extra beat to give him the chance to dish, but he didn't take the bait. "We have a CWIG agent in distress. One in need of recovery."

Her friends swapped wary glances.

"And *we* care about this because...?" Drew prompted.

"It's Fymmi," Bix blurted. "She's alive, in danger, and a critical player in the war against the Devourers. We need to find her. Fast."

Ashtad's hot-pink lips formed a perfect ring as he stared at Bix.

Drew groaned. "There's a name that haunts my conscience."

"Mine too," Bix admitted, leading her little troop under the arched doorway of a building that resembled three large eggs toppled against each other with bits of their shells missing. Crystalline shelves and lockers lined the walls. Curved tables made concentric circles that led to a dais and podium at the heart.

Some of the tables were still intact, and half the podium remained upright. Heaps of debris dared an imagination to run amok envisioning everything in its original state and splendor.

Ashtad called a ball of electricity to hand, then tossed it in the air, where it stayed, illuminating the massive chamber. All the crystalline furniture sparkled, giving off a faint glow.

He whistled as he took in the space. "How'd you stumble upon this place?"

"I like looking through illustrations to see if I can open a gate to the depicted places. Sometimes an artist's vision is an old memory their soul carried into this life." Bix pulled a very ordinary file box from a wall locker and set it on the nearest table. "It makes for interesting dinner conversations."

"Pfft. The way you eat dinner? I don't think your dining companions are worried about conversation." Drew opened the box and tugged up a file. "You scamp. These are hard copies of our final op for the CWIG. All the prep work, all the records. Photos? Of course, you kept the photos."

"I was running another mission when all this went down. Give me the highlights." Ashtad joined them at the table, examining the picture of a brown-skinned woman with heterochromatic eyes who looked like she'd just finished filming a Bond movie from the '80s. Lots of satin, lots of shoulder pads, lots of leg, and lots of big hair.

"The famous Fymmi," Drew explained. "The CWIG's perfect operative. She could go anywhere undetected, even looking like that. No security system could catch her. No one with a libido could refuse her. Oh, and she knew a thousand ways to kill you with a bra wire."

"Management thought it'd be a good idea to introduce her to Bix? Someone up the food chain had a bigger op in mind to take that kind of risk." Ashtad skimmed through the paperwork. "How'd Fymmi end up needing a rescue?"

"Fymmi was chasing a big-time buyer of chemical weapons." Bix brought a second box to the table. "The CWIG had busted the manufacturing ring but lost the cache to an unknown buyer during the op. Fymmi tracked the bombs and the buyer to the Crimson Market, then things got sketchy. She missed meets with her handler. Wouldn't name the buyer. Wouldn't say where the bombs were headed. Last time anyone had eyes on her, she wasn't looking too healthy."

"Management suspected she was compromised." Drew rolled her eyes. "They believed she'd started working *for* the buyer. Love, leverage, money, who knows what turned her. Whatever Fymmi was up to caused the syndicates who run the illegal market to arrange for a direct transport to an Undine prison, bypassing any official law enforcement involvement or a pesky trial. An informant inside one of the syndicate's transfer teams alerted the CWIG to a big fish about to leave the market. That's when we got the call."

Ashtad glanced up from a pile of reports. "Why your team?"

"We'd wrapped a year-long op at the Crimson Market not too long before." Bix sifted through the second box, searching for the packet of photos of the Undine Royal Navy's fleet, and the floating prison ship in particular. "We probably missed Fymmi's arrival by a week or two. Alas, even if we had overlapped, she wouldn't have known us or we her."

"Dark Ops teams are highly compartmentalized for their safety." Ashtad nodded as he reviewed the files. "We know why *you* weren't able to rescue her, but why plan on taking her during the transport to the Undine instead of from the market you guys knew best?"

"Dude, a *year* undercover. Those were legends we didn't want to burn if we didn't absolutely have to. Hindsight, though, I'd roll into the market wearing a sandwich board with CWIG painted on it if I could have our old gang back." Drew stared at a sketch of their team that one of the members had drawn during some downtime. Pictures of the team together were against regulations. It was a safety measure to prevent the bad guys from stumbling across covert agents' real identities. Bix had usually opened a gate for her teammates to take turns chucking the drawings in the highly destructive ether, but every once in a while, she'd diverted a sketch here. With the state of her memories, she hadn't wanted to risk forgetting the men and women with whom she'd shared a unique and unbreakable trust.

"I'm sorry." Bix squeezed Drew's hand and held it an extra beat. "I'd change the outcome of that op if I could."

"It was never on you, Bixie." Drew double-squeezed and offered an evil smile. "We're going to find those rat bastards who set us up to die, and we're going to make them suffer. I had a long time to come up with my list of methods, and I know you did too."

Bix drew a deep breath and shook off the wave of melancholy. "Ashtad, while you were looking through the gaps in the case against me, was there ever any mention of the CWIG sending other teams for Fymmi after we'd failed?"

Ashtad hadn't been a member of Bix's doomed Dark Ops team; management had separated the two of them years before. However, he'd recognized the frame job surrounding her conviction, so he'd jumped divisions from clandestine services to counterintelligence, specifically, to the branch of the Internal Affairs equivalent in the spy game. Although deep undercover, he was still an active CWIG agent reporting to the director of the CWIG with a mission to identify and dismantle the network of leaks inside the guild. That network was linked to the faction inside the Consortium collaborating with the Devourers. As ugly as the circumstances were, they were nonetheless a justifiable reason for him to collaborate and share intel with someone the CWIG had privately disavowed and publicly branded a terrorist.

That and he was an unwavering friend.

"Twice." He dragged the second box of files in front of him. "We tried to retrieve Fymmi from the Undine twice, failed both times. Lost team members. Those who escaped tell some pretty nasty tales."

"We were trying to get her *before* she was handed off to the sea serpent shifters because we knew once she was with them, getting her back would be next to impossible," Drew muttered, thumbing through a file. "Undine are one evolution away from dragons. I'm surprised the CWIG still went for her, especially if they thought she'd turned."

"We got close enough the second time to rattle the Undine. They misread our efforts as an enemy attack against their sovereign territory. To ensure their high-value prisoners didn't escape during naval warfare, they requested a transfer for every prisoner aboard ship." He pulled a folder and scanned the contents. "Do you know most of this intel isn't in the official file on your final op?"

"Not surprised. Scrubbing the file would've been part of the cover-up." Bix scratched the scars on her arm. "You said the Undine requested a transfer of the entire ship's prison population? To where?"

"To the Consortium supermax detention facility," Ashtad said, rifling through a folder. His scowl etched deeper and deeper lines in his makeup. "The Undine sailed the ship through a special gateway and no one—prisoner or crew—was seen or heard from again."

"A *Consortium* supermax?" Drew sneered. "Why the hell does the Consortium need a prison of any kind? Run afoul of those guys, and you're executed or husked. That's part of their charter. It's the oogie-boogie of being on their bad side. Unless you're Bixie, then you get exiled, and that's only because you're truly immortal."

Drew gave Bix a toothy apologetic grin. Bix smirked. Truth was truth. No point in being offended.

"Getting that sort of sentence from the Consortium presumes the prisoners stood trial," Ashtad corrected. "The Consortium maintains a menagerie of their most despicable creations. Those creations are kept in supermax storage until the cyclical Great War when they are used as weapons, then purged. Though, there are rumors of the occasional work-release pass during the intervening years."

"I don't know why I'm surprised." Drew shook her head.

"The angels are evil shits, the gods are utterly deplorable, and Fates are…well, Fates. Maybe I'd held out hope that the dragons would've insisted on some sort of compassion for their creations."

"That's what's called wishful thinking," Ashtad drawled. "Even the dragons are flawed. Comes with the longevity and the excessive power."

Drew wiped her undereye with her middle finger. Ashtad winked.

"Did the CWIG know which supermax facility received the Undine deposit?" Bix asked, finally locating the file of fleet photos.

It was Ashtad's turn to look bemused. "I was unaware of there being more than one."

"Six." Bix spread the photos out on the table. "There are six supermax prisons. I don't know how many gateways or where they all are, but I do know there is a heavily warded one in the middle of a Berserker battalion."

Both Ashtad and Drew looked at her with brows raised.

"Guess we're not asking Chief for his help on this op, then," Ashtad grunted.

He meant Tobek. Everyone but Bix referred to Tobek as Chief. She called Tobek by the name he'd asked her to since he had that weird thing about names.

"Damn it, I'm going to miss my infusion of beefcake support." Drew slapped the back of her hand to her brow. "How shall I ever survive?"

"Same way you did before Bix came back from exile?" Ashtad rolled his eyes. "Are we assuming all gateways are guarded by the MWA?"

"Strangely enough, Tobek isn't keen to discuss the prisons or the portals with me." Bix studied the photos of the prison ship, refreshing her memory of the ship's details. If the ship still existed, it could be a clue to finding Fymmi's new jail cell. "The one time he did let deets slip, I learned the gateways are configured to redirect any unauthorized persons to welcome centers on random Mid Worlds."

"Which means all attempts are logged and reviewed either by the MWA or the Consortium's security forces." Ashtad exhaled loudly. "We need to get you an image of the facility. Bypass their efforts."

"It's got to be the right facility on the first try. Once we trigger their security protocols, pretty sure the MWA will be the least of our concerns. We're not the only ones looking for Fymmi. Devourers are after her too." Bix stared at the picture of the engine room of the prison ship and attempted to open a small gate. Denied. She pulled the photo of the galley and tried opening another gate. Denied again. Either the ship had gone through significant changes so that these critical areas no longer resembled the photos, or the ship had been destroyed.

"Oh, this just gets better and better." Drew stuck out her tongue and gagged. "Devourers have the hookup with the faction inside the Consortium. They might already know which facility. Good thing they're hampered by the protective barriers surrounding Mid Worlds. They're stuck using regular transportation."

"But they can use gateways as whatever form they're impersonating." Bix collected the fleet photos and slid the file back in the box. "That includes guards and security personnel. In that, they have an advantage."

"That begs the question, if the faction inside the Consortium wants Fymmi, why don't they just take her out of their own lockbox?" Ashtad took the files from Bix.

"Pfft," Drew snorted. "I bet they've looked for her, but they can't find her due to her handy ability to exist undetected. Apparently, even by superpowers."

Ashtad grunted his concession. "If we can't track the ship and we can't track the woman, what, exactly, is your plan here, Bix?"

"By tracking the one thing every prison has in common, regardless of who runs it, which World it's on, how it's built, or what sort of prisoners they're keeping. Care to guess?" Bix looked to her partners in crime; both of whom shook their heads. "Oh, come on. We've all been in the clink before for various missions.

It's the ubiquitous thing for Under Worlds, Upper Worlds, Mid Worlds… No? No guesses?"

Ashtad and Drew shook their heads, synchronized negation.

"Contraband," Bix enunciated slowly. "Cup of real water in the Under Worlds, a nice fat soul in the Upper Worlds, a crate of drugs in the Mids. The wardens allow it because contraband symbolizes hope, and hope is what makes incarceration miserable."

"I think you've spent too much time with the gods, there, sweetie." Drew patted Bix's shoulder.

"No, she's right." Ashtad nodded slowly. "One prison absorbed a ship's worth of felons who, presumably, had a standing order with smugglers. We need to figure out what the order was and where it's being delivered now. The catch is which ring of smugglers had the contract back then and which ring has it now."

"All smugglers of note are based in the Crimson Market." Bix eyed Drew. "It's been a while since I was there. I might still have an in, even though the CWIG outed my real identity."

Drew eyed her back, scowling. The scowl softened as they stared at each other for a few heartbeats before Drew's eyes widened and she slapped a hand over a giggle. "Yukiko? Oh, she… are you sure you want to go back there? To her? She is *not* going to thank you for the way you ended things."

"But it would be great to see the people of the subterranean city again." Bix grinned wistfully. "Remember those chaneque plumbers? We always knew when they were working the pipes by the rhythm of the water coming out of the faucets."

"Who can forget every time they made the toilets in the neighborhood flush to the bass beats of live entertainment up in the main market?" Drew snorted. "Or the fireworks during the salamander parades when it was time to change the color of the streetlights to denote when night had fallen aboveground? Man, the subcity had more action at any given moment than Manhattan on New Year's Eve. I hated to leave that place. Crazy fun that was."

"It's been over ten years since you were last there. Things might not be as you remember them," Ashtad cautioned. "That said, whatever your cover was, everyone knows you're the Chimera now. You can work that in your favor. We're talking about hardened criminals wanted on every World but their own. In their eyes, you *are* one of them."

"Are you ready to own it, Bixie?" Drew grabbed her hand. "Being the Chimera? If we go back to the heart of the Chwed illegal market, you will *have* to be the bogeyman of legend, not the charming fixer of your old undercover persona. The original Chimera chapped a lot of asses and won you the wrong kind of fans. That Chimera protected herself from the masses by never revealing her identity to the Chwed community. That's all out the window now. You're reentering the game as the notorious executioner unmasked. Are you sure you want to go that dark and stay there for the length of the op?"

"In the war against the faction and the Devourers, we all have to step up, right?" Bix offered a smile she didn't feel. Playing at being the thing of which nightmares were made for effect was one thing. It was a character, a part in a short-lived production. No different from any of the many legends she'd adopted in twenty years of being a spy. She knew some of the stories about the original Chimera. She could pretend to be a monster, as long as she didn't lose her way back to the true-her of now. She liked the person she was today, all her broken bits, missing parts, excess baggage, annoying habits, the whole shebang.

"The Chimera of old worked alone." Ashtad massaged his jaw. "You've been spotted with me more than once in the time since you've been outed. Chief too, along with a few of his men. That's something that might make the syndicate leaders nervous."

"I suspect my legacy is well enough established that no one of importance would begrudge me a date with some sexy men." Bix leered at Ashtad.

Ashtad crossed his arms in front of his face, warding her away and laughing.

"Hey, I'm right here," Drew said indignantly. "I can get a manly meat suit."

"It's not the gender at issue." Ashtad lowered his arms and sobered. "Chief and I are our own brands of infamous in the market and beyond. We're viewed as power players. Chief for obvious reasons. Me, because outside of a handful of people within the CWIG, I'm known as the challenge broker for the demigods. If it's suicide missions for obscenely illegal gains, I'm the guy who vets the jobs, then retains the players, for a hefty fee, of course."

"Hanging with the Chimera didn't hurt your rep, did it?" Drew snapped her fingers and her chin from side to side. "Does this mean I'm the faithful lackey, or are you sidelining me to babysit the Sage?"

"Babysitting is a part-time gig," Bix assured her. "I'd never pull you from a second run at Fymmi. No, while Ashtad and I work our angle via the criminal establishment, you're going shopping at the Crimson Market for someone who can break in anywhere. Your story is that there's a Mid World guardian with something you want. You need someone with the chops to steal from a god."

"And by a 'god,' you mean the Consortium." Drew nodded. "We're looking for a rogue, unaffiliated with a syndicate, who keeps trade secrets close because anything less would get them added to the menagerie."

"Exactly. The Consortium's greatest weakness is their egos. They will assume the security they've put in place at the prisons is sufficient. A rogue at the top of their game will know if that's true." Bix glanced at Ashtad. "Make sure you frame the job as something a demi wouldn't touch, though. We don't want them tattling to curry favor with the Consortium."

"I'll help you with that," Ashtad offered. "Give me twenty-four hours to wrap up the op I'm working now, then I'm all in with this one."

"Thank you," Bix said.

"Maybe you can dress with a bit of dignity for the market, yeah?" Drew cracked. "Not that you don't have the ass for leggings, Sparky."

"I think I can swing it. It'll be fun to play arm candy for a change." Ashtad winked and pointed at Bix's smartwatch. "Meantime, if you give me that, I'll make sure neither the young Sage nor the MWA are overreaching in our investigation. I'll give it back when this op is done."

"Speaking of the Sage and investigations…" Bix thrust out her arm and let Ashtad take her new toy. When it came to tech, Ashtad made Cian look like a Luddite. Ashtad was the one who kept Cian from burrowing into the CWIG's network.

"Why don't I like the sound of that?" Ashtad tossed the watch from hand to hand.

"I need you to write a recommendation for him to intern with the CWIG this winter."

He tilted his head. "A little late in the season for internships. Our first class is heading for orientation next week and their security clearances have already been processed."

"Cian's already under CWIG observation," she countered. "His background is up to date. Security doesn't need to run any additional checks. His file with you guys is current and complete. Plus, he's a bit aimless right now what with his mom dying while on duty."

"Going for the guilt, are we?" Ashtad rubbed his neck. "I don't like him near HQ. Addicts can't be trusted."

"Look at it this way, Sparky," Drew piped up, "He's a genius who's at the crossroads of choosing to be Lawful Good or Chaotic Evil. Surrounding him with agents and analysts who are passionate about the CWIG's mission will hopefully divert him from his path of revenge against the Fates. You do remember what it's like to be young, powerful, and stupid, right?"

"I'll talk to the director about him. That's as far as I'm willing to go." Ashtad grimaced. "The kid's already logged as a valuable asset to be managed. They know he's a Sage, they know he has ties to the MWA, and more importantly, they know he is part of your inner circle, Bix. He's going to be used, and not in a 'go get me coffee and six copies of this document' way. They will make every attempt to turn him against you."

"I expect no less. I am the CWIG's public enemy, after all." Bix shrugged. If Cian was going to turn on her, better now than later. "It'd be great if you could recommend him for the taskforce researching what the Devourers are after. Because he's linked to me, the director might be a bit more amenable to that particular placement."

Ashtad huffed and wagged her watch at her. "You have him looking into the list of dead agents and soldiers. The former ward of the MWA. I got you now. He's the cross-link."

"We're not going get the answers without a bridge," Bix admitted.

"Can't argue that. Since your mole has a focus, I can build a proper cage and make sure he doesn't roam too far. I'm slightly more comfortable with that. Now hand me your earwig." He pointed at the silver cuff on her ear. "You don't want to take tech into the market. You'll come back with more bugs than an entomology museum."

"Oh, right." Bix quickly handed him the earpiece.

"Drop me at home, please." He pocketed her watch and earwig. "I'll be ready for off-book mayhem by midnight tomorrow."

"Thank you, again, Ashtad." Bix opened gates and sent him to his penthouse in the Primary Mid World. Drew crossed her arms on a file box and stared at the team sketch, sighing loudly.

"I miss them too, you know," Bix murmured.

"Honestly, Bixie, I'm more afraid I'm going to lose *you* on this op."

"Drew, I'm immortal. You can't lose me." Bix tipped her head, confused.

"Tell that to the original Chimera, yeah? The next time you look in a mirror, ask yourself whether the old you is gone, lost, or lying in wait." Drew sniffed and slid the picture across the table to Bix. "If you'll send me back to the kid, I'll help him pack before I shop for a new suit. You know where to find me when it's time to go to market."

Chapter 6

Bix stayed on Vuornis. Guilt scrabbled at her conscience as she ambled from the city center to a small rotunda wedged between headless colossal statues fallen neck to breast. She grabbed a glow stick from the box by the door and cracked it. Limeade light bounced off moon-pale skeletons seated in a ring against the outer wall. Priests, probably, dying in prayer to the god who'd screwed them over. Above them, taped to inlaid crystal mosaics, hung charcoal portraits, pencil drawings, and napkin doodles done by one ageless Berserker commander. The subject common to all of them? Bix. A few of the drawings were of her since she'd moved into the coal plant. The rest? The Chimera pre-memory-wipe.

Tobek had the unconscious habit of sketching when he was deep in thought. With the help of their third housemate, she'd collected his mental wanderings, hoping they'd match a memory mote floating through her brain without context or connection. So far, no luck. But the drawings still told a story, one of how he viewed her then and now. His playful affection was apparent in the recent ones. His pain clear in the others.

She didn't like going behind Tobek's back on this mission. He was giving to a fault. Trusting her maybe too much. But she respected him enough to not put him in the untenable position of having to choose his duty or hers. Sure, they shared the same greater goal of protecting the Mids, but he had superiors who firmly believed she was the greatest threat. Breaking a prisoner out of supermax would go toward proving their point. Alas, he got twitchy when she didn't hatch schemes with him, and tasking him with the memory devices would only distract him for so long before he flipped to trying to guess what else she was up to. She didn't want to outright lie to him, but hey, price of befriending a burned spy. Right? Besides, he was a master of creative and evasive answers himself.

In the center of the rotunda lay a crystal-lined circular depression, possibly the dried basin of a viewing pool. These days, it hosted a hot-pink-and-white rocking chair with assorted shoes painted on the slats. A gift from a very special goblin. She chucked the glow stick in the lap of a skeleton and took a seat in her rocker. Setting her arms on the wide armrests, she rolled her shoulders and bid her darkness to come out and play. Tentacles set the chair to rocking as others reached for the shadows.

Darkness was the blank slate of all creation. Light was selective and small by comparison, sporadic and unreliable. The art of tapping the universal pool of darkness to communicate beyond boundaries was the purview of Shadow Casters. They were rare, but not unique. Bix was still learning the finer points of this aspect of her magics. It was a spy tool beyond wild imagination. Unfortunately, it was also an army of fire hoses blasting her brain with information. The risky part of tapping the pool lay in the other Shadow Casters. Some would try to steal information from her if she failed to keep up her guard. Others would attempt a full-on attack. So far, she'd yet to encounter overtly hostile presences in the pool, but she'd only been skirting the edges of the pool's potential. She had it on good authority that the Devourers had a few Shadow Casters among their ranks. She'd have to tread carefully, frame her questions responsibly, and hope to avoid drawing unwanted attention.

No direct inquiries about Fymmi. That might alert the Devourers' Shadow Casters and draw their attention to the answers. No, this time, she'd focus on the prisons' gateways. As a gatekeeper, she was attuned to the disruptions in the atmosphere and native magic a gateway caused. A preprogrammed gateway that only went from Point A to Point B interacted with its surroundings in a different manner from a gateway programmed to go from Point A to Points B, F, N, and X. Living directly below a gateway to the prisons, she was well familiar with its unique signature.

It was a long shot. A shot in the dark. A bad pun waiting to happen.

Slightly amused with herself, Bix closed her eyes and willed her darkness to tap into the universal pool of night and nothingness. The initial deluge of images and sounds assailed her brain, a disorienting cacophony. It took precious minutes for her to calm and throw out dampeners. Sounds lessened to whispers; images to static. She pushed out sensations, the ones she derived from the gate at the coal plant, and requested images of locations from those who felt some, most, or all of what she transmitted. She didn't know of any other gatekeepers, so she didn't expect anyone to respond with an exact match. But she did expect *some* response.

For a rather disconcerting time, there came not so much as a peep from the darkness. There was a general sense of unease; tension, perhaps. Anticipation, definitely.

Annoyed, she pushed the sensations again. This time she didn't ask nicely.

Answers rushed forth. Desperate. Eager. Pops of sensations flooded her first, most with only a passing similarity to her request. Images bubbled up, some obviously not from the Mids. Those she quickly discarded. Each image she let pierce her awareness triggered her gatekeeper magic, relocating her to the destination. On and on she went, from place to place, her darkness disengaging and reengaging with the pool to a tempo that played in the back of her mind. Bounce. Bounce, bounce. Bounce. Slow, quick-quick, slow. Nowhere she went resembled an obvious prison. Nowhere she went exuded a punishing excess of Mids' magic that would be indicative of a hidden menagerie.

Frustration built alongside exhaustion as she pursued hundreds of false leads. The vine of malice rooted deep inside her sprouted a new leaf along the way. She was being played. Idiots and fools thought it funny to prank her. She had no choice but to go along on the off chance that one, just one, lead was the right one. The more places she went, however, the more her anger roiled.

Enough.

She was done being led around by the nose. Seething, Bix returned to Vuornis and tapped the damn pool one last time. She didn't ask a question. She didn't demand attention. She just sat there amid the deluge, blocking out the images and listening to the sounds. To the song. The volume built. Slow, quick-quick, slow. Rumba. Basic steps. The song that had kept her company hadn't originated in her head. It'd originated in the pool. Over the beat there came words. Screams. Scream, shout-shout, scream. Words she didn't understand. Languages lost with her memories. The sound grew and grew, pushing away every other noise until she had no choice but to focus on it.

Pain tore through her darkness, sharp like claws' long drag through prey. She yelped, one part agony, one part indignation. Her retaliation involved no conscious thought. Soft, shapeless tentacles morphed, jagged and honed, thorns and blades, talons and fangs. A few became thousands, limitless in reach, lashing out, swift, fierce, and overflowing with wrath.

With them, they carried her full sonic fury.

Everything stilled. Quieted.

Her breath came in short bursts amid complete silence while she waited for the next attack. The pool held its collective awareness in check. No images. No sensations. No emotions.

A gentle swish and flutter of a lone sheet of white paper tumbled toward her as if skipping on a breeze. Faintly, ever so faintly, a high-pitched bark and howl echoed across the pool. Her darkness reached for the page. Paper burst into tiny fibers and dissipated.

She lingered a bit longer in the eerie lull permeating the pool before the throbbing in her shoulder demanded her attention. Perturbed, she withdrew from the disembodied community and bid her darkness to return. The movement sent white-hot twinges across her back, and she shouted through clenched teeth, banging her head against the back of her chair repeatedly until the hurt ebbed. Mist and midnight trickled down her spine. Whatever had happened in the pool, she'd sustained real, actual physical damage.

Shit.

"You divorce yourself from all awareness of your surroundings while you're playing with the pool," derided a familiar yet unexpected masculine voice. "A fool's mistake."

Bix opened her eyes. Dim burgundy light filled the chamber of the rotunda on Vuornis. A very tall man in a well-tailored suit perused the collection of pictures on the wall. Thick, dark hair tumbled freely over harsh features and dared to dust his collar. Twin scabbards crossed his back. Seemingly bronze hilts shimmered in the light.

"Phobos," she greeted the Greek god of fear as she dabbed at her back, trying to get a sense of the damage to her body. Her skin was hard to pierce, so while she was intimately familiar with pain, she'd forgotten the burn and sting of this particular kind. "What are you doing here and why are you armed? I haven't seen you with your xiphoi since the days I used to watch you sparring with Hades in the Under Worlds."

She'd had the mental maturity of a toddler back then. She'd been so fascinated by their strangely beautiful dance and the music it made that after one particularly violent session, she'd picked up one of Hades's blades and tried to engage him. Hades had laughed so hard, he'd caused the Under Worlds to quake. The blade, the spear, the bullet, they were not her weapons to wield, he'd told her. Instead, he'd encouraged her to master gates as tools of offense and defense. But man, oh man, watching half-naked gods supremely skilled in the art of combat had made her a voyeur of warriors of all genders and all races using their bodies as the primary weapon in the fight for dominance. Everybody had a kink; she had a few dozen.

"Your distress summoned me, as it inevitably does," Phobos explained as if talking to a child. "It does not seem to have summoned the Devourer on whom you last fed. Fortunately."

Embarrassment burned her cheeks. She hadn't meant to feed off the anti-gods the first time one had attacked her. It'd been self-defense gone awry. Apparently, a side effect of her feeding off the primordial essence of the divine and not draining said dinner into a cataleptic husk was that the feeding created some sort of bond that neither she nor Phobos understood. Novelty was priceless to an immortal, so Phobos endured the inconveniences of being her portable meal without getting overly pissy with her. For a god, he was damn near a good sport. Sort of. Tiny bit.

However, his annoyance was no excuse for him to lie to her right now.

"It wasn't distress, it was anger. You've never come running just because I was pissed. Why are you really here?" She massaged her temples, seeking relief from the throbbing borne of the information onslaught of the pool. "Is the real reason for your visit, oh, spymaster of the Greek pantheon, because you have a mission for me?"

He had the grace to feign indignation. "What do you mean?"

"Don't try the innocent routine. I've been wondering how it was that you just so *happened* to be in the right place at the right time on the one night I was desperate to find a dinner source." She groaned. The sound of her own voice was too loud for her headache. "Gods aren't omnipotent, despite you guys pretending like you are. I think you were tracking me, looking for a way to bait the ol' compromise-the-asset hook. Did you know about the binding thing when you decided to reel me in? Got to admit, it's one heck of a handler-asset relationship we've got going here."

"You are not amusing. You are not even mildly entertaining." He strode to her and took a sheet of paper out of her lap.

Wait. Paper in her lap?

"Let me see that." She held out her hand.

"It's blank." He flipped the page and skimmed his hands over both sides. "Why did you bring blank paper out of the darkness?"

"I didn't. The only piece of paper I saw in the pool was destroyed." She snatched the paper from him and inspected it. It really was just a blank piece of copy paper available in any home or corporate office in the Primary Mid World.

"You did," he insisted. "It was not in your lap when I arrived. It manifested before you withdrew from the pool. Surely your doing?"

"Surely I don't possess the Mids' magic necessary to create copy paper," she sniped. "It's not made of souls, so it's not god created. How did it survive the pool if it's made of Mids' magic? Things made of Mids' magic can't survive beyond the Mids. Pretty sure the pool is classified as 'beyond.'"

"I didn't say you created it. I said you withdrew it. Whoever you took this from is also in the Mids. *There is another Shadow Caster in the Mids.* That is my point." He arched a winged brow. "Temper, Chimera. I am not your enemy."

Another Shadow Caster? A Devourer? Or someone else? Regardless, it couldn't be good.

"I'm still waiting for you to tell me why you've hunted me to my sanctuary." Bix unfolded from the chair and taped the blank sheet to the wall alongside Tobek's gallery. She'd really liked this place, but now that Phobos knew where it was, she was going to have to find a new bolt-hole. The entire point of this sanctuary was to store her secrets and lie low without being found. Bringing Drew and Ashtad here to the old city hall had been an acceptable risk since neither of them could transport without a gateway. Gods, on the other hand, could go anywhere they wanted. Like here. Damn it.

"Hold," Phobos commanded.

She froze. His usual stoicism made it easy to forget he was a battle-proven leader of gods in the Greek pantheon's army. He was maybe the spymaster for this era, but that only added to the danger he personified.

He placed both hands on her shoulders and angled her away from him, her back under his close scrutiny. The light inside the rotunda brightened and shed its red cast.

"Claw marks," he murmured. "Wild animal, not a mythical beast."

"Rabies, not archaic plague?" She allowed him his inspection. Without a mirror, she certainly couldn't see what had been done to her.

"No mere animal did this. They could not have ripped your skin."

"It happened in the pool. It was another Shadow Caster."

Cursing under his breath, he released her. "You are too depleted to heal yourself. Feed."

She turned and ogled him, entranced by the sensuality of a man in a suit unbuttoning his jacket, his vest, then his dress shirt. Suit porn. Definitely a reason that existed. Not that she would bang Phobos. She'd learned in the most unpleasant way never to screw her food source. Fortunately, Phobos also wanted to keep that line in the sand. Deep line. More like a trench. Like the Mariana Trench. Better for both of them.

"Before I take you up on your offer and possibly render you unconscious along the way," she paused and held her hands in front her, keeping him at bay, "perhaps you want to tell me *why you're here*. I know you didn't stop by to have a chat purely for the giggles of it. Of Ares's many spawn, you're the least loquacious, except for maybe your twin, Deimos."

"You cannot throw a tantrum in the pool of omnipresent night and not expect repercussions." He glowered, sliding his hand in his slacks pocket. "All of us who are even tangentially connected to it felt your displeasure. It reverberated throughout every pantheon, every World, and every race."

"I was attacked," she objected. "By something with claws. What did you expect me to do? Roll over?"

"You awakened sleeping giants," he snapped.

"Good," she shot back. "If they're powerful enough to be connected to the pool, then they're powerful enough to pay attention to the Devourers threatening the Mids. Maybe there are allies out there for whom nap time ought to be over. Maybe they needed to know the Chimera is back and that she is not amused. Whatever the case, the era of complacency is over."

"You assume what's out there is not worse than the Devourers. You assume that your fit of pique didn't reveal the mighty Chimera is not all she once was." He pursed his lips, then curled one finger over them. Three long beats passed before he spoke again, this time his voice softer and controlled. "This ignorant state of yours is increasingly problematic. Your conscious mind fails to conceive of the immense power you wield, while your subconscious flings it about like an irritable child. Instinct is overtaking rational thought. What you just did is a short tumble to feral. Hades trained you better than that, so do better."

She recoiled, and her barely simmering temper spiked. Darkness answered, slithering from her spine. The pain of her injury intensified her anger.

"Don't you dare chastise me for protecting myself," she snarled. "I've done my time scrabbling in the dirt, a victim of those who delighted in my vulnerability. I don't put up with that shit anymore."

Unfazed by the darkness encroaching on him, Phobos stepped to her. His chest unyielding against hers. His red pupils, common to all gods, glowed, bleeding into the amber of his irises.

"What were you demanding from the pool?" he murmured. "What are you so desperate to find that you let your wrath threaten eons of peace accords? Were you looking for the Mid World guardians who hold your memories?"

Her heart sped, and her skin turned clammy at the mention. She backed away from him. Of the hundredish gods tasked by their pantheons to protect the Mids as a payment to the Consortium for reaping the benefits of playing in the Mids, only five of those guardians held the fragments of her memories. Five divine guardians who were hunting her, desperate for her to take back her memories. The next one she obliged would result in her opening the floodgates for the Devourers into the Mids.

"What's this?" Phobos caught her head between his hands, forcing her gaze to stay locked with his. He snorted. The snort protracted into a malevolent guffaw. "Fear, I sense your fear. You're *afraid* of getting your memories back. This is new. What happened to tracking down those keepers and wresting back that which is yours?"

She tried to pull her head from his grasp, but he wouldn't allow it. His grip wasn't cruel, but it wasn't gentle either. She rolled her shoulder, antagonizing her injury, hoping the pain would stave off the sticky creep of pressure amassing from external sources. Future-Feng, the dragons, Tobek, every god who knew she needed those memories to awaken her repressed magics and defend the Mids against the Devourers. Every innocent life who didn't know their own peril. Every agent, soldier, and investigator trained to expect and counter domestic threats, yet who trusted their superiors to shield them from Other World enemies. Superiors who couldn't rise to the occasion; superiors who wouldn't. She was quite clear on who was depending on her regaining her marbles and on the urgency that she do it now.

Yet doing so would come at the cost of the lives she sought to protect as the Devourers invaded unchecked and unimpeded.

Her throat constricted, making breathing harder.

"The last time we were together, you'd consumed the essence of a Devourer and it somehow muted your fears." Phobos stroked her cheekbones with his thumbs. "Now you have new fears. Strong ones. This is deliciously disturbing. What changed?"

"Breaking. I fear breaking." She whispered the half-truth, focusing on the errant lock of hair resting between his brows that had escaped the perfect side sweep of his dark layers. She couldn't tell him about the gates she'd inadvertently open. He'd have to report that threat to his pantheon, and then she'd have far more than the guardians coming for her. No, she had to rely on Tobek finding something that would help her keep a modicum of control during the next assimilation of memories.

"Gods go through this adjustment after being husked. It is their reawakening. Their reintegration to the pantheon, the reintroduction to their powers, and most of them come back stronger for the respite." Phobos cocked his head and released her. "You knew this as the original Chimera. You often said the reset was the purest form of justice, the best chance at rehabilitation, the best odds of reducing recidivism. Your fear is unfounded."

"Gods don't get their memories back," she argued, demanding her darkness return to her, embracing the pain as it dulled to discomfort. "They hear stories about themselves while maintaining emotional distance. They are like children, listening to the tales of the infant years they can't recall. It is pabulum fed to them in palatable bites. They accept what part of the stories they wish, and ignore the rest. That's not what happens to me. It is a self-conducted surgical transplant. It is agony, physical and mental. It is drowning while burning. It is imploding while exploding. It is days of recovery before I can draw a breath without choking on my own blood. And that's just from tidbits floating disconnected in my mind, unable to push their way into my consciousness. Imagine what's coming. Imagine what will happen when my memories start making connections, when they start demanding conscious review and introspection. Can you fathom the hallucinations that will come from those fragments? It only gets worse from here."

"Why have I not been summoned to tend to you in these moments?" He scowled, reaching into his vest pocket for the fob containing a still-beating heart. He rolled it across his long fingers like a magician with a coin. "Your suffering is not something I am capable of ignoring. What is between us does not allow it."

She wiped away a tear threatening to fall. "I don't know, Phobos. I don't know. It's happened twice. The anticipation of the next time scares the hell out of me."

"It's not the pain that frightens you, though. It is your mind turning against you." He slid the fob back in his vest pocket. "Yours is not an uncommon fear, but it is one that often bears out."

"Thanks for the pep talk." She huffed.

"Come to me." He waved her closer. "Come, feed. Regain your equilibrium. You will need to be on your guard more than usual until we know the fallout from your actions in the pool. It is, perhaps, time you expanded your network of allies beyond your handful of misfits."

She fisted his lapels and his opened shirt, moving close enough to feel his divinity prickle her exposed skin. "I still don't fully understand the pool or who has access to it. I'm learning as fast as I can. Is what I did really that bad?"

"Far worse, which is why you need more supporters." He scooped her up in his arms and spun around, landing in her rocking chair with all the grace of a dancer. He draped her legs over one of the armrests. His hand settled lightly on her knee. His other hand gripped the other armrest until his knuckles whitened.

"If I amass an army, the Consortium will come down on me hard and fast. They'll execute any and everyone associated with me. That will become the distraction that plays into the hands of those conspiring with the Devourers." She adjusted her seat in his lap, pushing his clothes off one heavily scarred shoulder. Her fingers trembled as they traced the damage earned during his demigod trials. Those trials were the only times in a god's interminable life when their bodies could be permanently flawed. Once they ascended to full godhood, any damage to their bodies was temporary. The damage to their minds, however, was inevitable. The curse of immortality.

"Who said anything about an army?" he rasped. "That's not your stock and trade, is it? Nor is it what you are currently best known for."

"I'm infamous for being a…" She frowned against the round of his shoulder. "A criminal mastermind? You think it's time for me to live down to my modern reputation?"

"Own the underbelly, Chimera." He tucked her hair behind her ear. "That is always a monster's weakest spot."

She met his searing gaze. Own the underbelly, eh? She didn't want the administrative burden of being a crime boss, but she wasn't above manipulating the leaders already in place. Good thing her next stop was the Crimson Market. Guess she'd double down on her bad reputation and roll in like the ruthless bitch everyone believed her to be.

The Chimera was about to get her evil on.

Right after she fed.

Chapter 7

Bix delivered Drew in his handsome new meat suit to the Crimson Market by himself two hours early to divorce him from association. The draugr would return to the Primary Mid World by public gateway to complete the illusion of an independent broker. More times than not, brokers new to the scene were tailed as a means of vetting their business. Drew relished the chance to lead a tracker through a gauntlet of absurdities, changing bodies just to mess with whoever had drawn the short straw. Bix would sync up with her BFF at Dysmorphic once she and Ashtad finished their meeting. The public shop in the Berserker stronghold should cap off confounding whoever was following the draugr.

Bix and Ashtad arrived during the middle of the day within the vermillion shadows of red prismatic monoliths of a Mid World hollowed out during the Great Wars of eons past. The remains of the World reached up like clutching hands joined at the wrists, its blood-coated fingers home to the permanent residents of the illegal market. Warrens of stalls, storefronts, and stockpiles belonged to highly territorial gangs and syndicates. Chweds from all races dealt in the illicit and the proscribed. Social constructs and mores had been sanded away by the brutal economics of supply and demand. Reviled goblins sold the services of lofty light elves.

Banished fae hawked infants of various races stolen from their cribs. Mercs mauled and maimed, barely able to hold a weapon, prowled the streets as disposable muscle for hire. Dwarves sold custom-built war machines, while sprites wove tailored glamours. Gamblers and gladiators, hackers and cleaners, everything for everyone. Even members of the superpowers desperate enough to trade their dignity for whatever fed their addictions could be found within the red glow bathing the entire World.

Nothing was taboo in the Crimson Market, except a conscience.

"Does it look the same as last you were here?" Ashtad walked a half step behind Bix, his hand resting possessively on the small of her exposed back. The damage wrought by her turn through the pool had been erased after a nice rich meal of divinity.

"Not quite, and for that, I'm rather proud." She started to grin but stopped herself, recalling the character she had to play. "Our assignment had been to effect regime changes among the syndicates trading in cross-World classified intel. If I did my job right, there should be significant differences."

There *were* notable changes at first glance. While the structures built into the landforms hadn't been modified one whit, who occupied what stalls certainly had. Awnings, signs, and markers were all as new as the faces in the liveries of the syndicates' security teams. The layout of the market's main square had been revised to encourage lingering, with garden and bistro vignettes surrounding fountains and small stages where sellers paraded fashions and demonstrated curiosities. The square and the storefronts immediately surrounding it had become less of a writhing sea of opportunity and more of a destination point for a higher caliber of clientele. Bix was willing to bet that behind the façade of relative refinement, the seediness still reigned.

"*That* was your team?" Ashtad cried softly. "Congratulations. You sufficiently complicated my side business for a while. I recovered fairly quickly in comparison to other vested parties, but some of the big players never did."

Bix paused at a stall of moon-faced changelings, shackled

and on their knees. Their attire, slightly dirty, boasted haute brand names in children's wear from the Primary Mid World. These were not children, however, but members of a race of Chwedlonol who aged…differently. Changelings were frequently placed in human homes as agents of corporate espionage. Humans never suspected the children they brought into their lives and workplaces of stealing secrets. Humans merely mourned them once they disappeared. Some humans, that is, those who had a shred of decency. Those humans who had a penchant for abusing children, well, they soon found themselves quite dead once the intel was gathered. Usually victims of some horrible "accident." Dick in a blender happened to be her personal favorite tale of revenge. As sweet as they seemed on the surface, changelings were quite vicious.

She cupped the chin of a tow-headed changeling and tipped his head back. He had sixteen flecks in his brown eyes. That made him one hundred and sixty years old, middle-aged for a changeling.

"Which addiction got you shackled, changeling, eh?" she asked, her voice crackling with the icy disdain being the infamous Chimera demanded.

He puffed and whimpered, trembling in her gentle grip. A dark stain spread across his lap and puddled on the polished stone floor. She released him with a disgusted sigh and scanned the stall for the vendor. The gaudily-dressed hobgoblin hid behind a rack of children's clothes, doing her best to appear unaware that she had customers, but the furtive glances ruined the pretense. Bix laughed on the inside, yet held to the part of the heartless executioner on the outside as she reached for a strawberry-haired changeling farther down the line.

A white arachnid the size of a baseball crawled across the back of her hand, heading for her sleeve. Bix caught the spider in a small cube of gates and brought the syndicate's foot soldier up to eye level.

"Tell your mistress to meet me in twenty minutes where we shared our first meal. Tardiness is a personal offense." She blew on her hand for the show of it, but gates dropped the spider shapeshifter on the barely perceptible network of webs running along every ceiling, cornice, and balustrade in this sector of the market.

To the community of spider shapeshifters, those webs were akin to fiber optic cables. One bite hooked them into the information superhighway. Within heartbeats, their leadership would have the message. As an agent embedded with the spiders' syndicate, she'd often marveled at the complexity and efficiency of that network. It spanned across Worlds. Anywhere a web could exist, the spiders did their damnedest to put one. The more intimate, the better. Cuff of a pant leg, sole of a shoe between the heel and the arch, collar of a suit, elaborate hairdos, dangling earrings, headphones, laces of a corset. No place was off-limits.

"Hobgob," Bix snapped, startling the shopkeeper so badly, the woman knocked over a rack of small overalls. "Clean your wares. You lessen your profit when they are covered in bodily fluids."

The clatter of the hobgoblin's wooden shoes mixed with the whispers of onlookers. Bix wrapped her fingers around Ashtad's bicep as she tucked herself to his side, making eye contact with each person who dared look her way. No one was brave enough to hold her attention. Wise. She didn't like being gawped at, even when she was playing good Bix.

"You're enjoying this," Ashtad murmured.

"Not as much as you're enjoying shocking me with your built-in bug zapper." Electricity prickled her skin every place her body touched the demigod's as they strolled through the spider-run section of the market.

"I like to keep you on your toes." He dialed up the wattage to make his point, then throttled it back. "To which of the many exotic dining establishments are we heading?"

"Aww, you're cute." She cooed and patted his arm. "Have you ever worked with a jorōgumo?"

"A spider queen? No, can't say I've had the honor. Have had many a demi request an assignment with them, but the spiders have never been in need of our services."

"The one we're about to meet is young by their standards, yet she is twice as old as you. She has been trained by and has trained some of the most notorious warriors, emperors, and priests in Chwedlonol lore."

"You saying she could give me a run for my money?" he teased.

"Better for you if you two run different races." She paused at a large fountain where a Lorelei played her alluring harp atop the uppermost basin while piranhas nipped at the fingers of those who tossed coins into the bottom basin. "The most important thing for you to know, my dear arm candy, is that she is carnivorous. Her favorite dish is a man: handsome, virile, and still breathing."

"Still…oh." He cleared his throat. "So not a restaurant, then?"

The Lorelei glanced down at Ashtad and smiled broadly until her attention slid to Bix. Horror overtook the girl's sweet expression, and her fingers mangled the song.

"No." Bix looked upon the Lorelei with thin-lipped reproach. Normally, she would've reassured the girl in some way, but she had to be the evil Chimera. "And if the jorōgumo offers you a seat, don't take it. The chairs are designed to ensure you'll never stand again. I wouldn't trust the tea either."

"This ought to be educational," Ashtad drawled.

"If we're lucky." Bix rolled her eyes as the Lorelei flubbed another song. The girl would get herself killed by a syndicate goon if she kept screwing up like that. Quality was the hallmark of the market, and that included whoever they retained for entertainment. Bix flicked her wrist and opened gates, removing the terrified Lorelei from the square. No one needed to know she'd put the girl in a public restroom to compose herself. All that mattered were the optics of an annoyed Chimera.

"Well, that move made sure folks took notice of us." Ashtad lifted Bix's hand and kissed the air above her knuckles.

"Needs must," she muttered. "Keep in mind, you are playing the very important role of barometer. How the jorōgumo treats you correlates to the type of business relationship she wishes to have with me. If she threatens you and I intervene, then she will not trust me in a commercial partnership because I have already demonstrated I do not trust her. If she threatens you and I do *not* intervene, then I have insulted her by bringing a disposable asset to our meeting."

"Smacks of a trap with no positive outcome." He resumed their stroll around the square.

"That's the way of the jorōgumo. If she threatens you, we walk. No further discussion needed. No chance of partnership, ever. However, if she doesn't threaten you, then we'd better be ready to pay through the nose. This game of overtures and introductions is a test I have witnessed many, many fail." She repressed the pangs of disappointment as shoppers fled from her path. She'd spent so many years alone without any kind of contact that physical rejection still bothered her. It probably hadn't bothered the original Chimera, though, so she raised her chin and accepted their avoidance as her due.

Ashtad pulled her closer to his side, as if sensing her blues. "Minding my Ps and Qs, got it."

"Let the adventure begin." Bix opened gates to a place with a frenetic pace and frantic people whom she missed rather badly.

Chapter 8

An excess of native magic shoved against Bix's Other World presence as she arrived in the surprising pitch-black and silence of the rendezvous location. The salamanders' streetlights should have thrown a warm orange glow through cracked circular windows and gaping floorboards. Sylphs should've churned lily-scented breezes. Instead, the air was stagnant and stale. A peculiar quiet gripped the space where once the clamor of too many people engaged in the constant percussion of life had been overwhelming.

The entire subterranean city of poverty-stricken merchants, maintenance workers, and lowest-level syndicate employees had become a ghost town. No matter the state of prosperity, there was always someone on the bottom rung. Where had they gone? Where were her old friends, acquaintances, contacts, and assets?

"This is not at all how it should be," Bix whispered as unease scraped across her senses.

"It's been years since last you were here. Things change," Ashtad gently reminded. Blue sparks built into a glowing orb in his hand as he gathered enough electricity to subtly light the studio apartment that Bix had once shared with her target for the duration of the op.

Spatter-stained rice-paper paintings bubbled and peeled

from bone-and-daub walls. The tatami mats had a marbled look to them. A thin, lumpy mattress stuffed with hair peeked from beneath a feather comforter. The dark brown duvet's wear spots were more Rorschach than Roebuck. Then there were the man-eating chairs. Four seemingly innocuous club chairs upholstered in tightly woven spider webs.

On many Worlds, insects would have gobbled up the decades of blood and gore embedded in the room, but this was a spider's lair. Nature's cleaners had gone extinct long ago on the World of the Crimson Market. They were pricey imported delicacies these days.

"This place hasn't changed one iota since last I was here. Depressing then, depressing now." A sharp feminine voice emerged from the shadows on glossy red lips belonging to a jorōgumo in the heart-stopping beauty of her fully humanoid form. Long black hair, plank straight, and fine yet thick, dusted pale, petal-soft shoulders deliberately bared by a highly structured white floral wrap jacket secured by a wide black silk sash. The sash was tied in such a way as to augment the extreme tapering of her waist. Black silk cigarette pants whispered the brushing of thighs strong enough to crush a man's ribs, yet shapely enough he'd thank her for it.

Bix stowed her confusion and slid back into the role of the ruthless Chimera, allowing a slow leer to sneak across her face as she recalled exactly what it had been like to be between the jorōgumo's thighs. She untangled herself from Ashtad, putting a bit of distance between them to allow the leader of the spider syndicate to play the game of overtures.

"Depressing, Yukiko? Didn't think you'd miss me that much," Bix purred.

The sound of the slap stinging Bix's cheek echoed through the apartment.

"How dare you?" the jorōgumo hissed, her bright eyes flashing as more bodies emerged from the shadows. A baker's dozen of guards armed with black-magic bags, swords, and guns modified to shoot more than copper-cased gunpowder stood at the edge of the light.

"Pretty sure the notches commemorating just how much I dared are still above the bed, right where you made them." Bix curled a lock of Yukiko's hair around her finger.

Yukiko's ageless symmetrical features distorted, revealing the three smaller eyes above each dominant eye and the mandibular fangs. The guards crept closer, hands on their chosen weapons. Ashtad remained perfectly still; the weaponized light in his hand grew no stronger nor did it weaken.

Bix didn't shy away from the sight of the spider ever present within the woman. Instead, she skimmed her finger along Yukiko's jaw, collecting the deadly venom beading at the tip of the spider's fang. "I remember the first time you bit me. That you couldn't pierce my skin terrified you. That I was immune to your venom perplexed you."

"I thought you a god come to torment me." Yukiko gestured to her men to stand down. "Instead, you became my enforcer, and for one glorious year, we rose in the ranks, changing the balance of power. Until the day I killed my aunt and seized her place at the top of the heap, the day you abandoned me."

"You didn't need me anymore. The entire syndicate was yours to command. Had I been there when you faced your aunt, your authority would've been questioned. My presence was a contentious point among your faithful, ever the outsider in your family business."

Spiders gave birth to a hundred babies at a time, providing plenty of family members to run their vast empire. That empire extended to every habitable Mid World. Yukiko had more power, practical power, than half the Consortium.

Yukiko nodded, retiring the features of the spider in favor of the woman once more. "True. After you left, I *was* challenged. Repeatedly."

"Is that what happened down here? This city was the heart of the everyman for multiple syndicates."

"Fools battle for short-term gain without an eye on the future should they win." Yukiko ambled to a cracked window and stared out its murky pane. "Rivals, keen to oust the new leadership of the market and too confident in the value of a swift slaughter, planted chemical bombs throughout this underground city. We lost far too many in the initial wave. Even those we evacuated to the surface eventually succumbed to the side effects."

Chemical bombs. Detonated inside a closed space. Mass slaughter. The news hit Bix harder than a wrecking ball. She swayed, and Ashtad reached out to steady her.

She'd known these victims, their stories, their quirks, and their penchants. Down here, everyone had been some kind of miscreant or reprobate. They'd welcomed her as they'd welcomed all newcomers—with keen eyes, open arms, and healthy caution. For a solid year, she'd been part of this once thriving community. Their acceptance of her had been a memory she'd held close during her years of exile.

Gone. All of them.

If Bix hadn't had a part to play, she would have sunk to her knees and wept. Instead, she closed her eyes and sighed, letting the facts penetrate while she tucked away the emotions in a little internal box to be opened when she wasn't actively on mission.

"There were a quarter of a million people down here," Bix said with a deliberately disaffected tone. "No words can sufficiently express my condolences for your loss."

"This place is still riddled with the bombs." Yukiko tapped a nail against the window frame. "They're networked. Pull one and you'll set off a chain reaction that will contaminate the whole market, from tower to square."

Fymmi. She'd chased the buyer of chemical bombs right to the market, but at what point had the buyer moved from imports to installations? Had Fymmi known? Had she tried to stop it?

"The market has been sitting on live bombs all this time?" Bix fought down a wave of ugly wrath enticing her darkness. It pushed against her spine, eager to escape. With great effort, she held it in check.

"Adds to the thrill of the most dangerous place in the Mids." Yukiko walked around the room, seemingly reacquainting herself with the squalor. "In the wake of that tragedy, the syndicate heads consolidated down to five families to rule the market. We cemented our leadership and our alliances. While underlings and lieutenants inevitably jockey for better roles, the top is solid and solidly against external interference in our livelihood, which brings us around to you, here, today. What does the Consortium's number one enemy want that the Crimson Market could possibly offer?"

Bix resisted the silky invitation in the jorōgumo's voice. The lure was part of Yukiko's magic, part of the bait to lead prey into her web. Bix completely understood why mortal men succumbed. But, like any ex-lover, one eventually became inured to the tricks.

"I need information," Bix said.

"And you thought to make an appeal to me based on our past?" Yukiko paused at the bed and laughed. "No syndicate leader in their right mind would refuse *the* Chimera. Aligning with you publicly is good for business. Next time you want to meet, we needn't do it in a death trap. You are welcome to stroll through the front doors of my home. I'm sure you remember the place."

Bix lifted a brow. "Hard to forget the night your aunt served me up as the main course."

Bix had allowed herself to be captured so she could learn the layout of the family's estate and plant listening devices for the CWIG. Her escape from the bamboo serving platter had humiliated the former jorōgumo leader. In a fit of rage, the crazy old spider had eaten her entire household, including her faithful lieutenants. By morning, the bulk of the spider syndicate had shifted their loyalty to Yukiko. Sanity in the face of madness.

"The seneschal of the demigods, however, should remain in the market square." Yukiko pivoted sharply and stepped to Ashtad. "It is unwise for him to appear to be aligned with one syndicate over the others. Wouldn't you agree?"

Not a threat. Sound advice. Interesting gambit.

Ashtad inclined his head but said nothing. Good little barometer.

"So, what is it you need, specifically?" Yukiko walked a tight circle around Ashtad, assessing him covetously.

"Insider's information on the Undine navy regarding a prison ship that disappeared about ten years ago." Bix refrained from mentioning Fymmi or the special arrangement the syndicates had had with the Undine navy. There was a fine line between a question and an accusation, and Yukiko was the sort to enjoy taking offense.

"The prison ship?" Yukiko nodded, continuing her inspection of Ashtad. "Yes, I remember it. Good customers. One of five ships that sailed through a gateway, reportedly for off-World maneuvers. Rumor is all five vessels were sunk by enemy forces."

The Consortium likely had sunk the ships after prisoner intake. They'd probably killed all the Undine aboard too. Supermax was for unique individuals, not noble races.

"Safe to assume your customers extended beyond the crew to the prisoners on that ship?" Bix asked baldly. Smuggling was highly profitable, and no one could beat the spiders' syndicate in the smuggling game. Supplying goods and services to criminals was their bread and butter. The Undine navy happened to be a necessary secondary customer.

"Don't tell me the Chimera wants to get a foot in the provider racket?" Yukiko teased, sort of. The jorōgumo was far from stupid and naturally suspicious.

"Couldn't be further from my interest. You know me. I much prefer to take. Things. Hearts. Lives. Revenge." Bix studied her manicure but didn't miss the swift inhalations of Yukiko's guards or the jorōgumo's amused grunt.

"Ah yes, your methods of revenge were quite…satisfying." Yukiko bobbed her head. "And that is the reason you've come today. Something about that old ship is going to help you get revenge in the here and now, eh? Color me intrigued. How can I help?"

"Prisoner and crew rosters of the ship. Particularly the

unofficial prisoners."

"Complete prisoner lists? Of course, I'll give you those. They've been dead for years. No one cares about them now." Yukiko waved that off. "You can have the crew listing too, but it will be of little good. They all used pseudonyms to prevent any association with their family members. The contacts we had aboard vanished with the ship."

"Also the records of goods provided to the ship, what they were, when they were ordered, how frequently they were delivered, who paid for them. Say for the last three years before it vanished?" Yes, Bix was after a subset of that data, but if she was too specific and Yukiko had something to hide, then she'd hit a wall.

"That's a lot of proprietary information, some of which is still relevant today. It exposes my suppliers, my subcontractors, my network." Yukiko gave Bix the side-eye.

"Many of whom I already know now, don't I?" Bix didn't flinch from the jorōgumo's cold assessment. Risks. Gains. Trust. It wasn't hard to imagine the calculations running through Yukiko's mind.

"I don't do favors for free, not even for old friends." Yukiko sidled up behind Bix and whispered in her ear, "I am a businesswoman, after all."

And there it was. The product of the wheels of scheming turning behind Yukiko's casual façade, evaluating the price of the information. Deliberating the value of revenge for Bix abandoning her years ago. Deciding on how to trumpet her ties to the Chimera in front of her peers. Weighing how much she could demand of the Chimera before it backfired. There'd been a time when Bix had been the sounding board off whom Yukiko had bounced her cost analyses.

"Then let the negotiations begin," Bix drawled, grinning as Yukiko completed a half circle around her.

"I propose a bit of barter." Yukiko ran a sharp nail along the sweetheart neckline of Bix's dress. "I will give you every scrap of information about the prison ship and provide unlimited assistance in your revenge scheme. In exchange, you will safely remove the damn bombs from my market. Deal?"

Bix *could* gut the subterranean city in an instant, but doing so without weakening the foundation of the market above would be a challenge. She needed the guidance of a structural engineer to do it properly. But that wasn't what made her hesitate.

"What's the catch?" Bix held Yukiko's hand to her bosom. "Why are the bombs still here? No one has more resources than the syndicates, particularly the united syndicates."

"None of our resources can get within ten feet of the grid to which they're networked. Wards. More powerful than anything our experts could counter." Yukiko leaned into Bix and pushed up on her tiptoes, her glossy red lips a breath from Bix's. "The Chimera, on the other hand, has a reputation for removing all kinds of problems."

Wards? Wards that were too much to tackle for any of the superpowers begging for a fix in the market proper? What kind of nightmare had Fymmi discovered before pissing off the syndicate leaders? These little pieces of intel did not fit the CWIG narrative, probably because the CWIG didn't know the whole story. Their agent had held out on them. A too-familiar tale.

Bix had no issue removing the bombs; it was more about who she had to call in to help her. Yet, her mission was to find Fymmi, and she couldn't do that without Yukiko.

Bringing in a third party to help with bomb cleanup it had to be.

"I expect complete compliance," Bix murmured against the jorōgumo's lips, "no records withheld, no hesitations to fulfill my requests no matter how irrelevant they seem, and no subcontracting without my prior approval."

Yukiko claimed more of the kiss, then pulled back, her smile slow and supremely sultry. "It will be a pleasure, I'm sure."

Bix purred in the back of her throat and stepped away from the jorōgumo, wrapping her hand around Ashtad's bicep. "I'll be in touch."

Chapter 9

Bix returned with Ashtad to his penthouse in Rosslyn, Virginia, Primary Mid World. The setting sun blasted roses and lavenders across the white marble and mosaic tiles of his pristine bachelor pad. The perpetual rush-hour traffic played the distant tunes of honking horns and idling engines as harried commuters fled across the bridge from Washington, DC.

"Before you even ask, no, I didn't know about the bombs at the market." Ashtad tugged a tissue from a box on the coffee table and handed it to her, gesturing to her lips. "I did know the warrens had been cleared and condemned."

"Yeah, you could've been a bit more specific than 'things change,'" Bix chided. "Warning me that everything I'd known was gone would have been useful."

"Yukiko needed to see your surprise, or she might have believed you were behind it," he countered, tapping the end of her nose with his finger. "Not even you can fake the heartbreak you showed when she told you what had happened."

"I thought I'd hidden that." Bix puffed her hair from her eyes.

"Not to anyone who knows you, and she clearly did." He toed off his shoes and placed them in the boot box by the front door. "Market security forcefully removes anyone who loiters too long around the old openings to the subcity. Those openings have been sealed, unless you can shrink down to spider size, apparently."

"I suppose their method of sealing the city explains the excess native magic. Those and whatever wards are protecting the bomb grid." She wiped Yukiko's lipstick from her mouth and perched on the arm of his aqua couch. "I take it you weren't there when the bombing happened?"

"No, I was six Worlds away and eighteen sheets to the wind, trying to wrap my mind around what had happened to you when I heard there'd been an incident at the market." He headed for his kitchen and his beloved teakettle. "But back then, incidents were still common, what with the trickle-down leadership changes. The market went from nine major families down to five in the wake of the explosion."

"We propped up spiders, the drow, and the trolls. Are they still in control?"

"They are." He lit the burner and set to preparing his tea. "The brownies sold their stake in the physical market for an increased presence on the virtual market, which allowed the Penates to move in. The serpents were victims of a hostile takeover by the imps."

"The CWIG has to have details about the bombs. They *must* have sent somebody to look at the grid before deciding to leave those things in place. The Crimson Market is too important to the spy game to let it fall." She stared at the smear of two different shades of lipstick on the tissue. "Did the CWIG task a team to work Fymmi's final op? To pick up where she'd left off?"

"One would hope. Give me a second and I'll log in to the CWIG network."

"She was after a chemical bomb buyer, who clearly sold them to someone in the market who then had them installed. There's a whole ring of sickos involved in something like that, which would've necessitated a new CWIG operation, a bigger one." Bix clacked her heels on the tiled floor. "She probably didn't want the help, didn't want the risk of new faces making the bombers nervous. That's probably why she stopped reporting in."

89

"If the wards are stronger than any resource of the syndicate, then Fymmi could well have gotten in over her head. Swimming after bigger and bigger fish is the danger of being in this job too long. Eventually, you'll run into an aircraft carrier." Ashtad ambled to the simple white stone desk abutting the back of the couch. The clicks of latches unlocking hidden compartments echoed. A moment later, his rubber-encased laptop appeared, and he settled in for work. "Are you going to ask Chief for help with deactivating the bombs? He and his pet goblin are experts in chemical warfare and magical wards."

"That's a curious thing, though, isn't it?" She tipped back to sprawl on the couch, her heels dangling over the armrest. "Tobek's battalion is a collections unit. Their job is to gather all the intel from the MWA's vast network, farm it out to their analysts, collect it again, then distribute actionable intel to boots on the ground. There's no way they didn't know about the bombing of the subcity, which makes me wonder why the MWA left live ordinance in place."

"Law enforcement of any stripe isn't exactly welcomed in the market, and Berserkers aren't built to blend in." Ashtad made music with the speed at which he typed. Clickety-clack and tap, tap, tap.

"Maybe. Or, maybe the greater MWA likes knowing they can erase the whole market with the flip of a switch." She folded her arms behind her head. "Yukiko said the bombs were networked. That's your wheelhouse."

"I'm the wrong guy to take a closer look." He huffed. "We're fortunate I didn't blow the space just by calling a light ball. Any spark from me could detonate those bombs. Based on where we stood, I didn't sense an electrical grid, and ley lines don't cut through the city. Whatever was used to create and power the network isn't obvi…"

She waited for him to finish his statement. Waited. The kettle whistled, and still he didn't react. She sat up and glowered at him. Something on his computer owned his complete attention.

"What'd you find?" she called over the kettle's piercing wail as she went to the kitchen and took the noisy thing off the burner. There was a line of pinch pots on the counter leading to a cup of fine china. Three pots had dried weeds. One contained small snail shells. A few others she wasn't brave enough to guess. "Hey, which one of these is edible?"

He didn't answer. His mouth didn't open. He didn't blink. His chest inflated and deflated with regular breaths, so she didn't freak. Plus, his finger twitched on the trackpad, so reading was still on the table.

She eyed the line of possible tea mixings and the teacup. The cup was too small to hold all the fixings, so she dumped them into the kettle. There were rules for steeping. Three minutes seemed like a good compromise for that many kinds of whatevers. She counted down the minutes, cutting her attention between the kitchen clock and Ashtad. Three minutes came and went without him coming to his tea's rescue, so she poured a cup. Clumps landed with a splash. She scowled at the clumps and poured them back into the pot, looking around for a filter. Failing that, she used gates to keep the gunk out of the cup. The stuff smelled like a men's locker room, but the foulest-smelling stuff was usually the healthiest...or something like that.

She set the cup in its usual place on his desk and waited. More minutes passed. He reached for the cup and took a sip.

Choked.

He shoved away from his desk and staggered back, his eyes watering and nose running. With the preternatural speed of a demigod, he fled to the kitchen and shoved his head in the sink and the sprayer in his mouth.

Bix cringed. "Did I steep it too long?"

It was a while before his sounds of gagging ebbed and he stopped hosing down his entire head. He grabbed a towel from the handle of the wall oven and blotted his face. Golden eyes, reddened and puffy, peered at her over the edge of the towel.

"Um, sorry?" She offered with chagrin.

He set the towel on the counter and held up a gold tin with the letters *t-e-a* emblazoned on the front. "This is where I keep my tea. You made me a cup of crusting spices for an atomic pork recipe I was going to make for dinner."

"So, I nailed the 'hot' part?"

He laughed through a wheeze and picked up the towel again, dabbing at his eyes and the corners of his mouth. "On my computer is the CWIG file about the bombs below the market."

She looked at the tiny font and large page-count number. "The short version is…?"

"The subcity bombing happened shortly after Fymmi was delivered to the prison ship." He got a glass from a cabinet and a box of buttermilk from the fridge. "CWIG records back Yukiko's accounting of the bomb grid. The CWIG sent experts undercover with the drow contingent to evaluate the situation. The network is mostly visible to the naked eye, but protected by tamper-proof spells that enforce a ten-foot distance."

"And they're sure the bombs are from the chemical manufacturer they busted? They confirmed they're part of the lot from Fymmi's nameless buyer?"

"Fit the description, but no one could get close enough to confirm." He gargled with the buttermilk, then spat it into the sink, exhaling loudly with relief. "There are sketches of the clustering and of the bombs, but they're nothing remarkable. Smooth-surface cylinders, presumably some sort of silver alloy. Constructed to appear as an ordinary gas canister available on any street, any shop, any lab."

She paced the shadows cast through the balcony doors as the winter sun ducked behind the humans' war memorials. "Did the CWIG task a new team to locate the bombers? Fymmi's missing buyer, the installers, the mastermind, any of them?"

"They did, but the new team got nowhere. Kept hitting dead ends. Literal dead bodies." He took another swig of the milk, this time swallowing it with a cringe. "Management believed the syndicates were trying to squelch any further investigation."

"Or the syndicates were doing a better job at investigating than the CWIG's B team." Bix kept pacing.

"Bix, I know we're focused on Fymmi, but I need to redirect my attention to where she left off." He repeated the buttermilk mouthwash cycle. "If there's even the slightest chance that the subcity wasn't the only place these bombers pulled this stunt, I have to find the other locations. We're talking hundreds of thousands of lives, and who knows what governments and guilds being held over the barrel. I mean, gods, just the idea of these bomb grids propagating over the last ten years…"

Bix planted her hands on her hips. "The last agent who tried to run this mission alone failed badly. The CWIG's already proven it can't handle it either. So, you're nuts if you think I don't have your back on this. The best thing we can do is continue our search for Fymmi. She has the intel on that group."

"And if the CWIG is correct and she joined the other side? Are you sure you want to spring her?" He poured himself another half glass of buttermilk and swallowed it with a wince and a shudder.

"The other side is the faction within the Consortium who want to trade her to the Devourers. Even if her loyalty to the CWIG faltered during her last op, pretty sure she's kept herself hidden for the last ten years because she knows far bigger powers are after her." Bix scratched the scars on her arm. "However, I'm not going to assume the worst until I have her accounting of events. An agent with a long history of protecting the Mids? She deserves the benefit of the doubt."

"She's not you." He rinsed his glass and set it on the counter. "Don't fall into the trap of thinking of her that way. The conditions of your exile were one kind of physical and mental torture. Her time in supermax is guaranteed to be another. The fact is, she will not be the same agent she was when she went in, regardless of where her loyalties lie."

"Understood," she sighed.

"I hope so." He came around the counter and stood in front of her. "We'll have to decide what to do with her once we've sprung her. If she refuses to cooperate with us, how are you going to handle that?"

"We will not play games with what is and isn't the truth. Our favorite draugr will read Fymmi's soul and rip the intel on the bombers from her." Bix stared at the wadded-up tissue in her hand. "If she cooperates, then her odds of surviving Drew's unique method of interrogation are good. If she resists, Drew will kill her and still take the intel. Ultimately, the choice will be hers."

Fymmi would likely wish to be dead before anyone successfully removed the cloaking tech fused to her spine. Hell, Fymmi might beg to be killed due to her stay in supermax. The worst-case scenario, however, would be if Fymmi was still a sharp-witted defender of the Mids. Then the matter of destroying her spine would get awfully complicated.

"If it's all the same to you, I'd like to try to debrief her before the draugr has a go." He took the tissue. "Think of it as a first-run psych eval."

"As long as you're not planning on putting her back inside the CWIG. She'd be a sitting duck for the faction and the Devourers."

He gave her a flat stare. "You don't say."

"Yeah, yeah." She shooed him aside. "I'm off to solicit help to make the Crimson Market safe again. I'll be in touch when I'm done."

"The moment Chief gets his hands on those bombs, he's obligated to report it to the MWA, and they'll launch a manhunt for all involved." Ashtad chucked the tissue in the trash and settled in front of his computer. "Make sure you have a plan to divert him from Fymmi's trail unless you want the army participating in our prison break."

Chapter 10

Bix followed the scent of grilled beef and caramelized onions wafting across the basement of the coal plant. The aroma of Tobek's dinner guided her through the hallways of books and ancient artifacts, past the tapestries from empires long forgotten, around the TV room and its extra-extra-long leather couch, to the stainless-steel armory and the adjacent modern kitchen where her housemates dug into their respective meals.

The goblin, hunkered over the mortician's table in the armory, looked up. His big bulging eyes lit. His mottled brownish-green fist paused halfway to his mouth, clutching the gnawed butt of an automatic machine gun. "Pretty lady home!"

"Hiya, Gurp." Bix smiled and motioned to the melted, twisted, rusted, and otherwise useless weapons spread out before him. "Saving the grenade for dessert, are we?"

The goblin grunted happily and chomped on the gun butt.

"Sweetheart." Tobek wiped his mouth and stood from his place at the quartz island, gesturing for her to join him at the row of barstools positioned so he and Gurp could still talk to each other without Tobek's food getting contaminated by whatever the goblin was dining on. "Can I get you anything?"

"Keeping gods in the pantry now?" she teased as she took the offered seat beside him.

He grinned. "That'd be something, wouldn't it? Going shopping for the week based on your pantheonic preference. Excuse me, I'd like two Mayans, a Roman, and a, um, German to go."

"No, no, we had hunters last week, dear, let's try a fertility goddess tonight." She patted his hand and feigned seriousness.

He laughed into his stein. Judging by the wealth of foam clinging to his mustache, he'd opted for a stout ale.

"Speaking of gods, Gurp pulled together the first round of memory artifacts. If you're lingering long enough, we could give them a go, see if they'll work on you." Tobek speared chunks of steak with his fork, leaving the foam on his upper lip.

"Thank you, Gurp, I will definitely want to try those, but I was hoping we could do a little something different after dinner. Assuming you two are available, of course," she hastened to add.

"For you, I am always available." Tobek winked, and Gurp belched his agreement. "What do you have in mind?"

"A little complex bomb removal, perhaps?"

Gurp squealed with delight. Tobek paused midbite.

"I think Gurp's in," Bix whispered loudly. "You?"

Tobek set his still-laden fork on his plate. "And the location of these bombs is what you went looking for in the pool of omnipresent night?"

"What? No. Why…" She sighed and stared at the exposed ventilation and piping running across the industrial ceiling. "You know about the kerfuffle in the pool?"

"Did you really think I wouldn't? I'm a very old warlock, remember?"

"Is that what we're calling you today? 'Warlock'? That term's sort of reserved for Chweds, and we know you're not one of them." She met his stare, daring him to keep going down that path. Phobos riding her ass about what had happened in the pool was bad enough. Two dudes doing it would send her around the bend. Male patronization. A big button of hers that read Do Not Push.

Instead, Tobek scratched at the spell in his pec. "Are you injured? Do you need assistance?"

"I'm fine," she said a little too crisply. "And yes, I do need assistance. With disarming live ordinance in the Crimson Market."

He licked a tooth and placed both forearms on the counter. "The subterranean city. You found the chemical bombs."

"Damn it. The MWA *did* know." She slapped the counter with her open palm as the box of emotions she'd carefully packed away during the meet with Yukiko tumbled from its mental cubby, losing its lid. "And you let those bombs stay there? Two hundred and fifty thousand lives ended. The entire population of the market remains at risk. And the MWA did *nothing*? What about your mission to protect the Mids? The market is one of the Mids."

"We learned of the chemical attack *after* the fact." He looked at her quizzically. "We heard no chatter beforehand, had no inkling it was coming. The market doesn't welcome our presence, officially or unofficially. We could either go to war with the survivors or let them deal with the tragedy themselves. We chose the lesser evil."

"Two hundred and fifty thousand lives lost," she repeated quietly, fighting back tears. "Your precious army couldn't work out how to get *into* a war zone? Do you really expect me to believe that?"

"We chose to minimize total casualties. We chose not to make it a million lives lost. We chose to extend an olive branch, and when it was refused, we chose to stand down." He shifted in his seat to face her fully. "The MWA isn't the CWIG. We don't have the authority to invade without an invitation from the local government or without a directive from our superiors. We had neither."

"For all that you revile the CWIG, they at least tried to help." She dropped her head in her hands and dug her nails into her scalp as the first tear fell. "You know what, forget I mentioned the bombs. I'll get someone else to help me."

"Hey, I'm not saying no." Tobek nudged her knee with his. "I'm trying to understand why an old tragedy matters to you.

Clearly, it matters a lot. All I'm asking is why."

"I used to live there, just like I used to live here before you and your battalion took it over," she snapped, lifting her head and meeting his gaze as tears streamed down her face. "I knew those people. I played with their kids. I danced at their celebrations. I helped newlyweds move and families dispose of their dead. And I guarantee you, when those first bombs went off, more than one of those trapped people prayed that *I* would show up to save them."

As she spoke the words, her heart shattered with enough force to cause physical pain. She did *not* let innocent people suffer. Hell, she didn't even let bad people suffer. Someone had to be a special sort of evil for her to extend someone's process of dying. She knew how it felt to be on the cusp of death, so certain that her next breath would be her last, yet so desperate to keep living. She'd experienced that at least a dozen times before she'd discovered she was immortal.

For the people of the subcity who'd never questioned their mortality, that prolonged dying must have been beyond horrific.

"You just learned what happened to your friends. Ah, sweetheart," Tobek groaned and stood, gently tugging her into the safety of his embrace.

She finally let the reality of what had happened to the subcity escape the careful compartmentalization in which she'd separated the data of her jobs from the emotions of them. Yes, the people were long dead. That didn't stop her mind from imagining their terror at being stuck, or the stampede of residents trying to escape through the few exits to the surface. It was too easy to think of those who'd died from being trampled by their neighbors, and of those who'd lived long enough to watch their children succumb to chemical warfare. To attack the subterranean city like that required a hateful, twisted soul.

A soft square of fabric was pressed into her hand. She looked down to see Gurp rubbing one foot atop the other as a fat tear trickled down his cheek. The purity of the goblin's concern tempered her wild emotions.

"Thank you," she whispered, blotting her face. "I'm sorry, guys. I shouldn't have lashed out at you. You couldn't have known."

"But we do now, and because it matters to you, it matters to us." Tobek smoothed his hands down her arms. "Give me a moment to gather some gear."

"You were in the middle of dinner when I interrupted. You should finish," she demurred.

"Bombs." Gurp patted his belly and waggled his brows. "Yum."

"Containing chemical agents, not just explosives," she warned, not knowing the limits of his palate. Little dude ate radioactive material like humans ate breath mints, so his digestive system was its own wonderland. "Also, the place is wired with something that doesn't use electricity or ley lines. The entire configuration— such as has been identified—is warded to keep prying eyes at a minimum of ten feet. The city itself is a sealed tomb. Being down there is like wading into a bog of native magic."

"Gurp, we're going to need some special items from the vault." Tobek grinned, his blue eyes dancing. "And a pair of oxygen tanks."

Chapter 11

B ix delivered Gurp and Tobek to a flattish rooftop at the center of the subterranean city of the Crimson Market. Ten square miles had been carved into the belly of the World, the residents stuffed like alfalfa sprouts in multistory homes constructed with no regard for safety or aesthetics. Building codes hadn't existed, but it'd been a matter of syndicate pride to ensure the basics of plumbing, lighting, and clean air had been functional and abundant. Since the market above never slept, the city below hadn't either. There'd always been something to do, somewhere to go, a spot of small-scale, free fun to be had. Sleep cycles had been regulated not by circadian rhythms, but by pills.

"I see it's maintained its mausoleum status," Tobek drawled as he fitted his night-vision goggles over his respirator mask. The oxygen tank was strapped to his back like a diver's. Gurp wore a similar setup, though smaller to accommodate his size. Bix's eyesight in the dark was enough to keep her from tripping over large furniture but nowhere near good enough to read a book. As for the oxygen, she wasn't worried about breathing contaminated air. If it was going to affect her, it would've happened during her meeting with Yukiko.

"When this place was occupied, the din was such that noise-canceling headphones came with your first paycheck. The style you wore denoted your status and your syndicate. Losing those headphones was worse than a death sentence, and getting caught with stolen ones was an instant execution." She pointed to a crooked house that looked like a stack of paperbacks ready to tumble. "There was a cobbler in the middle apartment whose addiction was dryad diet pills. A side effect of those pills was a craving for manure. His favorite kind was from a wagyu beef farm in Nebraska. I challenged him to make me the most comfortable stilettoes in exchange for steaming fresh pucky. His neighbors were not amused, but, man, I wore the hell out of those pumps."

"Shit for shoes?" Tobek guffawed, pulling a deflated balloon from his duffel bag and handing the flaccid rubber to the goblin. "I've made worse trades. Gurp, if you would do the honors?"

Gurp grunted happily, took the balloon, removed his oxygen mask, held the balloon to his lips, and let loose a belch that would win awards at any frat house. The balloon swelled and strained until it turned clear. Inside, rainbow glitter swirled. A quick knot, then Gurp released the balloon. It drifted up, up, and up.

"You know from living with him that Gurp's digestive system releases all kinds of curious gasses," Tobek explained. "When mixed with the contents of the balloon, we get a chemical reaction that is one part magic and two parts science."

The balloon popped. A great sea of glitter blew across the ceiling like millions of fireflies twinkling in the night. Bix gasped and clapped.

"Wait for it," Tobek urged.

The tiny lights swirled and danced, seemingly searching before settling as a map of neon lines and pastel clusters across the entire ceiling.

"It's beautiful," she breathed. "They look like little dirigibles journeying around the world in eighty days."

"Those are bomb canisters. The lines in between are the wires. The big circles are the power cells." Tobek pushed his goggles up to his forehead. "The brightness of those lights corresponds to the strength of native magic inherent to each component. That, sweetheart, is the source of the excess native magic you feel."

"So the wiring has more juice than the bombs." She walked the perimeter of the roof, scanning for patterns and anomalies. "There are thousands of bombs up there. The dark blotches must be where the canisters that exploded in the initial attack were staged. How did they not blow the others?"

"Did the subcity have its own closed circulation?" Tobek asked.

She nodded.

"Then 'explosion' wasn't really the issue. The canisters didn't need to detonate to disperse the chemicals. All they needed to do was open and let the forced air do its work. That's why the structures are unaffected and there are no blast scars on the ceiling." He paced the roof in the opposite direction of her wanderings. "We need to get our hands on the emptied canisters and a random sampling of those unexploded ones to see if they all contain the same thing or if we have actual explosives mixed with chemicals, different chemicals, bioagents… The possibilities with this many are damn near limitless."

Maybe that was why Fymmi had delayed turning in the buyer she'd followed here. There'd been more bombs on the way, more bombs in the stockpile. Maybe even more buyers, more middlemen, and more than one installer.

No doubt, Fymmi had been in way over her head. This was too much for one agent, no matter how skilled, to tackle alone. Teamwork, it was how spies stayed alive. No operative was an island. Etcetera, etcetera. Something must have compelled Fymmi to continue the mission alone. Who, what, and why were good questions, but not ones for which Bix had answers.

"Now that I have a map of what I need to cut away, I can get you the samples, that's no problem." Bix laughed to herself; really, it wasn't a problem. All these bombs would keep the MWA busy, far too busy to figure out Fymmi's involvement. "I just need to know if I can do it without weakening the market above."

"All I've done is illuminate the obvious. We can't know how much you need to cut until we break the protective wards around the power sources." He pointed to a dozen huge circles glowing brightly across the map, the closest a few houses over. He hefted his duffel bag of magic goodies and leapt rooftops until he was under the nearest bright spot. "Sweetheart, how sure are you that you want these canisters gone?"

Bix used gates to join him, bringing Gurp along with her. "As sure as any compassionate entity can be. Why?"

"Then you and I are going to have to make a bit of magic together."

"Tobek," she gasped with mock affront. "There is an impressionable young goblin here."

Gurp snickered and waggled his brows.

"Gurp hasn't been young in ages." Tobek retrieved five bronze-looking urns from his duffel bag. "You said the CWIG was down here at some point and couldn't defuse this. The power cells are why. I need you to place these urns at five points of a pentagram along the perimeter, using this spot as center. Commit the details of the locations to memory."

Fortunately, she and Yukiko had spent many a date on the rooftops of the subcity. Sure, it'd been to spy on the residents and permanently remove select individuals, but the point was Bix already had the visual map ready for recall in her mind. A gatekeeper couldn't open gates without the destination image, and she didn't have the time to create that map right now, not if she wanted to get to Fymmi before the faction caught wind.

She took one urn at a time to make the pentagram while Tobek and Gurp assembled something between a monstrous harpoon and a lightning rod set upon a stand with a treadle.

"What can I do next?" She rocked up on her toes, eyeing the ten-men-tall rod.

Tobek removed his shirt and his prosthetic arm, handing both to Gurp. Sometimes magic caused the tech to go haywire, so for spells that involved a lot of wherewithal, removing the prosthetic was a precaution. The shirt? That didn't happen in public too often, but she'd never complain about eye candy. Tobek had an apocalyptic stripper look going, what with the respirator and low-rider jeans.

"First, send Gurp home," he said, snapping her out of her ogling.

The goblin chittered something that sounded a lot like angry dissent in a language she didn't know.

"Of course we still need you," Tobek assured Gurp, "but once we tap into the cell, there will be no neutral surface anywhere in this cavern. She'll bring you back when it's safe."

"I absolutely will," she concurred, even while a frisson skittered across her skin. Tobek clearing the decks meant this wasn't a simple or even moderate bit of spell casting about to happen. "Once it's safe."

Gurp glowered at both of them but nodded. "Okay."

Gates delivered the goblin back to the basement armory and his interrupted dinner.

"How bad is this going to be?" she asked.

"When it comes to power grids, you have two choices: overfeed it so it shorts out, or starve it." Tobek adjusted his position under the moon-bright power cell. "Causing the magic to surge down here will detonate what's left, so you and I are going to drain the magic. Specifically, you are going to drain me."

Her heart stopped. "Dr-drain you?"

"As you would a god," he said softly.

Her heart kick-started, and a coy smile dawned. "You want me to snuggle up to you, lave your naked torso, and drink the magic as it spills out of your every pore?"

His wicked chuckle made goose bumps pepper her arms. "I'll never object to those first two, rest assured. But I mean 'drain,' not 'feed.'"

"No, no." She shook her head as goose bumps gave way to clammy chills. "You're not a god. You're not an anti-god. You will not survive what I do to them."

He pressed his forehead against the lightning rod. "So you have fed from a Devourer. That explains some of the changes in you."

She stepped back, a kid with her hand in the cookie jar. He didn't know her well enough to judge. Then again, he'd known the original Chimera well enough to have been cursed by her. Okay, fine, maybe there were some minor changes she couldn't see. Changes both he and Phobos had detected. Whatever. Navel gazing could wait for another day. This was about the Crimson Market, Fymmi, and defeating the faction.

Priorities.

"So what? I don't retreat to the coal plant when I'm injured or in distress." She dismissed with a wave. "You don't have to worry about a Devourer showing up there."

"Doesn't stop me from worrying about *you*." He stared at her with a glimmer of something she couldn't name, some kind of sadness laced with hostility.

"I know you're not mortal by Consortium standards, but that doesn't mean you'll walk away from what you're asking me to do," she groused, irritated by what felt like his disappointment. "At best, you'll bleed out. At worst, I'll take a whole lot more than I mean to. I'm not an expert at wielding my darkness yet."

He shrugged. "The Fates will restore me."

"In three to five days, also known as the 'humbled and hampered' clause in your contract with them." She crossed her arms. "You're putting a lot of faith in the idea that I am incapable of killing you outright. I am the High Executioner for All Worlds, so whether I mean to do it or not, I'm pretty sure ending anything not a fully evolved god is in my wheelhouse somewhere."

"Sweetheart." He pointed at the light. "This was done by a superpower, upper caste or one of the ruling. The magic in each of these cells is too advanced for a plebian. Who else managed to install miles of complex bomb tracks in the ceiling of an overpopulated city without anyone noticing?"

Meaning that the installer didn't simply work for the faction, they were a member? Anger spiked and tentacles of night emerged from her spine, but logic quickly charged to the forefront. Why would an upper-caste superpower, one whose magic could create the very walls around them, use bombs? Why stoop so low to use basic Chwed, no, worse, *human* technology? Why, when they could sneeze and decimate everything, would they resort to primitive methods?

Facts. They did not fit. The players, the motives, the CWIG's case against Fymmi…

Unless.

Unless Fymmi had been turned by one particular type of superpower. The ones who thrived on fear.

Not Phobos. He was staunchly anti-faction and knew the danger of the Devourers. These idjits, not so much. Not yet.

"A superpower. An excess of native magic. And miles of terror hardwired throughout a population who is very much aware of the threat beneath their feet." She tapped her bottom lip. "Golly gee, I wonder which of the big four it could possibly be."

"You don't know for sure it's the angels," Tobek chided.

"Really? Dragons feed off the fun times. Angels eat misery. I'm not a mathematician, but even I can manage remedial probability." She was biased, true, but for lots of good reasons. Mostly involving every interaction she'd had with any of their miserable lot.

"How about you take that anger and focus it right here." He pointed to the spot where the curse of silence had been branded into his skin. "If you hit me from the front, it will hurt me less."

"Since you get off on pain, are you asking me to attack you from the back? It's hard to know with you." She lifted her chin.

"Once I connect to the cell, I'll become a conduit." He tightened his lone hand on the lightning rod until his knuckles whitened. "Those urns will draw upon my energy, enacting a counterspell that will break the warding around the bombs. I need you to wait fifteen seconds, then hit me. When all the power is completely drained from the cells overhead, count to fifteen again, then dump the urns in the ether. Don't wait too long or move the urns anywhere else. Their integrity will be too unstable, and they will blow."

"Uh-huh." She crossed her arms. "And afterward, do I dump your crispy carcass on Gurp's mortician table or in the Berserker clinic?"

Crinkles formed at the corners of his eyes. "The clinic will do."

"I hate you for not telling me your suffering is the price of neutralizing these bombs." She scowled.

"What good is being really smart, really strong, and really powerful if I can't use any of it to impress a girl?" He winked.

"Jackass," she groaned. "You're actually looking forward to this."

"Old soldier versus an indomitable foe. How can I resist?"

"What about Gurp? Is he going to be surprised by the condition in which I'll return you to his care?"

"No." He adjusted his respirator. "That was part of the tirade he leveled at me earlier, but you will still need him to do the structural assessment before you remove the bombs. When you bring him back, he'll be carrying pictures of disposal sites for all this. Resist the urge to chuck the bombs and the wiring in the ether too. We can learn quite a bit about the who, what, and why from them."

Setting the MWA up against the Angelic Host? That'd be a fine political pissing match that'd give her plenty of cover while she located Fymmi. This was getting better and better. First, however, she had to try not to kill Tobek.

"Okay. Whenever you're ready." She gave him two thumbs-up and rolled her shoulders.

"My oxygen tank to the clinic, please. Don't want it to explode."

"Right. What's the point of purified air when you're going to be toast in a few moments?" She cut the man off from his air supply and returned the tank to the Berserkers' clinic.

"When I say 'go,' start counting." He wrapped himself around the harpoon lightning rod, leaving his curse mark exposed. He braced one boot on the treadle and took a deep breath of stale air. His foot tromped the pedal, launching the harpoon at the power cell.

She expected fireworks. She got the opposite. Like a jellyfish going for a swim, the bulbous head of the power cell fluttered open. Bright ephemeral tentacles unfurled along the wiring, connecting to the other power cells. Three tentacles braided down the harpoon and reached for Tobek.

"Go," he wheezed.

Bix started counting down. Within five seconds, the tentacles engulfed Tobek. Ribbons of his green and silver magic shot through the braid, straight for the urns. They struck with a low hum. A brilliant green pentagram lit the city. Green parted from silver, racing like cars around a track, humming a higher octave as it formed a circle around the pentagram. The glow of the green counterspell stretched for the ceiling and pushed down through the buildings.

It was breathtaking, beautiful, and slowly altering Tobek's body from a state of mass into energy. Five seconds. Four more. Three.

Bix closed her eyes and willed her darkness to strike true.

Tobek's agonized scream was nowhere near human. Tears cooled her cheeks as she siphoned Mids' native magic and more from him. Primordial seeds that had yet to germinate, a miasma of Other World distillate, and the barest hint of humanity. He contained an element of everything, of each superpower and then some.

What kind of entity was he?

Whatever he was, she never wanted to repeat this invasion of his person. The direct line of his potent native magic cocktail into her Other World body was far from pleasant. Mids' magic didn't like her, and it was doing its damnedest to escape her, causing her to jerk and flail. The pendant containing Feng's dewclaw burned her chest as his uninvited assistance kept her moored to the World, allowing her to stay connected to Tobek.

The onslaught of native magic wasn't the worst of it either. Draining an entity of any sort connected her to their emotions, and Tobek's were gut-wrenching. His dominant emotion, not the one he showed but what he consistently felt, was a vast, bottomless loneliness that surpassed any she'd encountered. For a man surrounded by people and activity, he was hollow, a master of putting on the good show. He knew others required him to exist in a certain state of equanimity and to augment it with tempered joy and zest. His men were long-lived just as he was, and they needed that reassurance, that confidence that their lives were more than an endless grind. But Tobek didn't feel what he showed. He was gutted. Mourning. Sad. Alone. Gods, so alone. She wanted to pull out, to run, to get away from that nothingness, but half the power cells were still bright.

The only thing she could do was exist there in the hollowness of self with him and weep.

He wanted me to see it.

The thought pierced through her as two more power cells went dark. Anger answered the revelation. Anger on his behalf, that he'd been alive so long and forced to remember all of it; all the people, the innocence, and the wonder he'd lost. But there was also anger *at* him, for showing this to her. Yes, it was something that he trusted her enough to expose his raw truth, but what'd he expect her to do with it? Was he trying to make her a hostage of his emotions? Was that the way he thought he could tether her? Did he intend for her to fix it, fix him? Sharing his black hole of loneliness, was it meant to guilt her into staying with him? They already had a dynamic that swayed dangerously close to stalker and victim with either of them being able to play both roles. What motivated him to give endlessly of himself to her? Was it a self-destructive need? Did he pray she could, in fact, end him? Was she his last hope of eternal rest? Choosing to be fried alive certainly lent itself to that interpretation.

The last power cell flickered, snapping her temper out of its spiral. The braids of native magic encasing Tobek weakened, then faded away as the overhead grid went completely dark. Tobek slumped to the ground. His shoes had melted, and his pants were incinerated. His flesh had burned beyond blistering. Her darkness gently wrapped him in a cocoon of dignity. She didn't dare touch the respirator that had fused to what remained of his face. His wealth of blond hair was gone. No beard, no eyelashes, no man bun.

Around them, the urns erupted with sonic energy, causing the air to ripple. Then, like popcorn, wards in the ceiling burst, releasing a shower of ashes.

Fifteen seconds. Bix counted down the last as the green and silver of the pentagram of Tobek's magic sputtered, then died. Gates dropped the urns into the destructive ether. Total quiet and opaque black returned to the subcity.

For a moment, native magic ceased to be the enemy.

Bix recalled her spearing darkness from Tobek's curse mark. Her breath caught. The eternal knot that held his curse glowed in soft shades of teal and midnight, the flesh into which it had been carved unharmed by the burns of native magic.

A strangled laugh escaped her. How weird their weird. How extreme their "it." How confusing and fearsome. One day she'd remember who he was to her, and she to him. One day she would understand why he did so much for her at such personal expense merely because she asked.

Regaining her composure, Bix opened gates to the Berserkers' clinic at the coal plant. Her darkness carefully placed Tobek on a cold metal slab. She caught a glimpse of Berserkers scrubbed in and standing by. Then there was Gurp, wearing his oxygen tank and a mining helmet. Photos clutched in his trembling hands. Her tentacles of night cradled the goblin and brought him through the gates. With one last glimpse at the damage she'd wrought in pursuit of her mission, she closed the passage behind him.

Chapter 12

Bix and Gurp stood in the quiet dark of the subcity, neither of them speaking as her heartbeat thundered in her ears. Twice she tried to form the words to the apology running through her mind. Twice all that came out was a gasp. Stubby, calloused fingers closed around her hand, squeezing gently.

"He choose," Gurp said, his voice distorted by his respirator mask. "Help make him happy. Happy important. Happy last. Burn not last."

"Tobek is a grown-ass man, more than capable of making his own decisions. I understand, logically." She returned the squeeze of their hands. "However, I see how much his choices in the wake of my requests worry you, and for that, for causing you distress, I am sorry."

"'S okay. You, I not angry." The goblin chuckled, surprising her. "Now we work?"

"Yes, yes, of course," she hurried to say. "Where would you like to begin? There are no air ducts or venting systems in the ceiling. It was all done by Chwed magic. The closest I can get you, where you can move on your own accord, are the tunnels leading up to the market proper. Those tunnels are sealed on the market end. Alternatively, I can use gates to create a sort of flying carpet to get you right up against the grid. The downside of that, I'm told, is feeling nauseous and trapped somewhere between floating and being disembodied. I don't want you to be uncomfortable, so you tell me in what way I can best help."

"Hmmm."

She couldn't see his expression in the dark, even if he hadn't been wearing a respirator mask.

"Carpet to tunnel?" he asked like a child requesting a chocolate cake for breakfast.

"Absolutely," she laughed. "Carpet to tunnel it is. There are eight tunnels aligned to the cardinal and ordinal compass points. We'll start in the northwest and work our way around."

She layered gates on progressive angles, slowly tipping them to their backs, mindful of his oxygen tank. Small grunts of wonder escaped him as he tested the stability of the gates lifting him off the ground. Grunts built into guffaws as she brought their flying noncarpet within a foot of the ceiling grid. He clicked on the light clipped to his helmet, then handed her the pictures he'd brought of the MWA's bomb depots. She committed the images to memory.

Gurp reached for the wires and snatched his hand back with a yelp. "No touch."

"We drained the power. How are they still live?" She too reached for the wires. Native magic speared the palm of her hand, knife sharp. Yes, she could have pressed through it to grab the wires, but she wasn't sure if contact of any sort would trigger a reaction.

"We move? With line?" Gurp held his hand at a constant distance from the wires as she floated their carpet parallel to the grid until they reached the first bomb canister. Again, he made a cautious approach, hand first. An annoyed grumble, a bit of wriggling, and a grunt of success repeated on a curious loop. Her companion developed a strong resemblance to a calliope. "Again? Move?"

She did as he bade, gliding them along the grid in a northwestern trajectory, pausing at each canister for Gurp to make his assessments.

By the time they reached the first tunnel, the scowl escaping his respirator had etched deep furrows in his wide brow. The grid ended at the lower mouth of the tunnel, yet Gurp had her move him all the way up to the sealed end, then back, twice. From there, he had no interest in inspecting the rest of the grid, just the tunnels.

The calliope of discovery ended on a distinctly sour note.

"So how bad is it?" she ventured.

"No cut," Gurp groused. "Wire come out of rock. Rock go up market tower. No cut. Tower cave."

A chill ran down her spine and prickled her toes. "The towers of the Crimson Market are wired into the bomb grid? If I remove anything from here, I'll blow the towers?"

"Yes. Market too. Grid follow street and hallway." He walked his fingers as though they were tourists on the streets above. "Four line, three power, and one bomb."

"Det cord? They've run det cord alongside the power wires?"

Whoever had run that was either an idiot hoping for an "accidental" explosion or a misanthropic genius with supreme confidence in their booby trap. Considering it'd been installed by a superpower, the latter was most likely.

"Yes." Gurp swiped his hand in front of him in sharp negation. "No cut. Leave canister and wire. Must. Or no market."

A slow clap broke the silence.

"Well done, goblin. Well done indeed."

Golden light blazed from the street below them. In the center of the light stood a tall, burly man. Black jeans, jump boots, and a tight manga T-shirt. The black buzz cut was new. His cold black eyes, highly familiar.

The Archangel Samael.

Chapter 13

Bix touched down on a subcity rooftop with Gurp, closing the gates of the flying noncarpet. In a single leap, Samael jumped from the street to a roof adjacent to her. Bix placed herself between the archangel and the goblin.

"Oh, I should have guessed this mess was your handiwork, Samael," she sniped.

"You know how much I like taking credit, but this…" The archangel held his hands up as if in holy surrender to the grid of bombs. "This is not my doing."

"Really," she drawled as her darkness slithered across the rooftops, lurking at the perimeter of the archangel's light. "The moment we drain the system, poof, here you are, as if summoned by your broken spells."

"Partially correct." He waved his hand, and light filled the subcity, brighter than it had ever been while occupied. Her darkness retreated from it, tucking into the safety of her flesh. Samael scratched his cleft chin as he eyed the ceiling. "Your shenanigans down here did alert me. After all, I reside in the tower above us. The breaking of the complex wards, some of which were against angels, finally allowed me access. They really did a doozy down here."

"Wait," she sniggered. "You *live* in the Crimson Market? You? An archangel. The highest echelon of the Angelic Host, the superpower of a superpower, lives among the myriad races who hate your ilk the most?"

"Don't do yourself a disservice," he mocked, his accent a mashup of European languages. "You're the one who hates angels the most. You can stop protecting the filthy goblin hiding behind your skirts. He's free to do whatever work you've assigned him. Harming him would cement our adversarial path, and I have a suspicion we need each other."

The audacity of angels, they really gave gods a run for biggest douchebag. Still, she didn't want Gurp anywhere near the archangel, so she returned the photos of the MWA's bomb depots to the goblin. Worry changed the angles of the wrinkles in Gurp's brow. She drew his gaze away from the archangel and clutched his hands twice, mouthing the words *thank you*. Gates returned Gurp to the heavily warded safety of the coal plant, far away from Samael.

Alone with the archangel, she let the vine of malice within her stretch and writhe.

"Cement our adversarial path?" Bix chortled with derision, returning her attention to the archangel. "As if my taking your wings didn't?"

"The pain was horrific, and learning how to balance myself without their weight has been a bit novel." Samael bent back and forth from the waist. Archangels could reconstruct every part of their bodies, except for their wings. Sure, they could replace feathers and heal torn membrane, but a wing amputated at the root wouldn't grow back. An archangel would have to surgically reattach the severed wing to their body and hope for the best. Native magic's special brand of punishment. "You like my wings too much to destroy them, though, which means you can give them back to me when it suits you. I can be patient until war comes calling, then I'll need them if I'm to defend the Mids."

"Patience isn't an angelic virtue." She toyed with her two

pendants. Samael was a hunter, an executioner of his own race when necessary, the doer of the dirty jobs his brethren needed done but didn't want to admit. He'd also been the first angel to offer her assistance, guiding her along the way, feeding her valid intel, then stabbing her in the back. The fact he'd been helpful at all was why she'd only taken his wings instead of killing him outright.

"Do you have any idea how old I am?" he asked out of the blue, his attention on the grid.

"Up there with dirt?" She crossed her arms under her bosom.

He snorted. "For most of the Mid Worlds, I'm far older than that. Any idea how I've stayed alive this long?"

"Probably has something to do with why you've been disavowed by the Angelic Host," she guessed. "Rogue archangel with his own army of fallen angels. Oh, wait. *Had* your own army until I gutted them, literally in some cases."

"Admittedly, I made a tactical error that night. We were both after the same greater end, though through different processes. I judged this broken version of you as I had the ageless version, anticipating your actions based on the many times we've gone round before. However, you don't address a problem as you once did. You are swifter to ruthlessness and violence now. It's fascinating, really. The executioner showed more mercy." He popped from rooftop to rooftop, his voice projecting in perfect clarity regardless of his distance. Angels of any rank could go anywhere in the Mids they wished unless the destination was warded against them. However, what they could take with them was a different story. They weren't gatekeepers, and even archangels had limits as to what native magic allowed them to do.

"So never making a mistake is how you've lived for so long?" she derided, not bothering to yell. If he wanted to hear her, he'd make the effort.

"Knowing when to be your ally even when the Angelic Host was set against you, that's what's kept me alive," he whispered in her ear, then popped away to another rooftop out of sight. His voice floated back to her. "I think that will prove true again. Your meeting with the jorōgumo is known to the five syndicate heads. We are all eager for you to get this crap out of here."

"'We all,'" she echoed as her brain put together the pieces. "You head one of the syndicates. One of the newer ones. Let me guess, the serpents? You're behind the hostile takeover of their business?"

"Guilty." He landed beside her on the roof, lingering this time. "Of course, I don't reveal myself to them as an archangel. You know how Chweds can be. My choir of the fallen and I go about our business here in a wholly different guise. I tell you this because if you're going to spend time in our lovely market, I'd rather you not rip more of my troops to shreds."

"As long as your minions play well with the legit Chweds running the market, I'll keep it in mind." She gave him the side-eye as the native magic he exuded simply by being an archangel pushed at her Other World presence, like an annoying sibling in the back of a car on a road trip. "Since you're one of the almighty, you must know everyone who worked on this horrible thing. Possibly even executed them already?"

"First, tell me why you're interested in the old Undine prison ship."

She closed her eyes and swallowed a curse.

"Spiders aren't the only ones with little spies." He smirked. "However, unlike your former lover, I know you've come back from exile with the Consortium in your sights. The ship brought you here, which means something about the Consortium led you to the ship. Dish."

"Cannot fathom why I would let you nose around in my business."

He leaned toward her. "Because you and I aren't that different. Because I'll share the historical knowledge that others cannot or will not. Because you know that despite our clashing the last time we worked together, I never lied to you. Because I know the Consortium is rotting from the inside. Because I know the cyclical war isn't the most immediate threat to the Mids. Most importantly, you'll tell me because you need me even while you're choking on the realization that I'm right."

He was right. She was choking on it. His position in the Angelic Host—blackballed or not—gave him access and insights not even Tobek had. Plus, Samael didn't have the conflict of interest regarding local military that Tobek and his men did. And with Tobek sidelined until the Fates reset him… Still, she didn't want Samael to find Fymmi. No, he'd use Fymmi as leverage to get his wings back, then kill Fymmi once he had them. However, Samael was a hunter and Bix *was* hunting, so all she had to give him was a target who wasn't Fymmi. Luckily for her, she had many.

"Remember when I came to you about rips in the protective layers of assorted Mid Worlds?"

"Yes. Ether is seeping in, slowly destroying the protection and adversely affecting native magic in the area." He crossed his arms and widened his stance. "There is a choir of angels dedicated to locating all rips and trying to patch them. It's slow going so far."

"At the time, you warned me about things from the ether sneaking through those holes into the Mids."

He grimaced. "And I was right."

"They're called Devourers and they've been coming through those holes for five years, setting up camps across the Mids."

He snapped to attention, cursing loudly and in many languages.

"They can't be killed by anything native to the Mids. In fact, they feed on native magics. They're here looking for things, but once they discover the Mids can supply them with sustenance for centuries—"

"They'll be like thieves in the palace," he interjected. "They come to steal the treasure, then get ideas about stealing the throne. Once they're in, the golden era is over and the empire falls to ruin. I've lived this story many, many times."

"Only when *this* empire falls, a new one cannot rise in its place. The Devourers are too toxic. The seed that resets with Feng's death and subsequent reincarnation will be poisoned, unable to grow."

"How did we not know they were here," he mused more than asked, his black eyes darting around the subcity. He slapped his thighs. "The rot inside the Consortium, yeah? They're affiliated with these Devourers. That's who you're really hunting. They're somehow connected to the Undine prison ship. Prisoners on that ship, probably. That's why you wanted delivery records. You don't care about the routes. You…you know where the ship ended up. You're looking for our menageries. The one that absorbed the prisoners the Consortium deemed interesting enough to keep alive."

For an angel, he was passably smart. Inconveniently so. What he called "the rot," she called "the faction," but semantics wasn't the issue. The location of Fymmi, on the other hand, was.

"Considering what you do for the Angelic Host, you must know where the facilities are."

He nodded. "Oh sure. I've made lots of deposits and the occasional withdrawal."

"Annnnd?" she prompted.

"And I'm waiting for you to tell me how a creation in the menagerie is relevant to the rot." He hooked his thumbs on his belt buckle and pointedly stared at her.

"The rot made a deposit. When they returned to make a withdrawal, the storage facility could not locate the item. The rot's buyers are now doing the legwork for them," she explained, mashing up metaphors.

"The Devourers want one of our creations, and you're trying to beat them to it." He grunted, nodding. "See? Told you you'd need me."

"You're gloating. That's not being useful," she argued. "Useful would be you giving me detailed pictures of the correct facility."

He laughed. "No, first you're going to help me. Then, we'll talk about the menagerie and whether I'll get the lost creation for you."

"And risk you stealing my prize from me? Again?" She gave him a flat stare. No way in hell would she tell him about Fymmi.

He mimicked her posture and expression. "Ever consider working together *all the way through* the mission so we both get to win?"

"That requires more trust than I'm willing to afford you," she countered. "Your turn. You said we're going to need each other. What is it you need from me?"

He gestured wildly at the ceiling. "I want the shit who hatched this plan. The one who put all the pieces together to grow a bomb garden. Once I get him, I get his minions, and I get the specifics on where else he's put down explosive roots."

The fact she'd already agreed to help Ashtad with the same issue made it a lot easier for her to acquiesce. Ashtad wouldn't care who got the credit for the takedown; he cared about the threat being eradicated. He would not, however, be happy about working with Samael. Neither would Drew or Tobek for that matter. Pretty much nobody on her team wanted to work with an angel. This one in particular. But he had insider's intel on the supermax facilities. Could she trust him? No. Did it stop her from working with him? No. Working with frenemies was a common hazard for spies. What mattered was if Samael was completely committed to *his* mission: to protect the Mids from all foes foreign and domestic. Those foes included the faction, aka the rot, and the Devourers. Would he help her bring them down and kick them out? Of that, she had no doubt. She just couldn't appear eager to work with him. That'd be one fake emotion too far for both of them.

"Why do you think I'll be able to help you find the mastermind?" she asked. "Surely you know more about this than I do."

"Within hours of you learning of this mess, you've done more than my choir and I have been able to since we caught wind of the bombing." He rubbed his stubbled jaw. "Whether you're aware of it or not, Chimera, you're doing exactly what you did before you lost your memories. You find bad guys, especially the ones who don't want to be found. You hunt them down. You judge them. You execute them. That's your life's purpose in a nutshell. Has been. Is. Will be."

"What about protecting the Mids? Did I always do that?" she dared to ask. It was odd to have someone who'd known the original Chimera who was willing to talk to her about her past.

"Always? Nah. You didn't care about a place that actively rejects you. No, you cared about a person who cared about the Mids. You protected this place for them."

That surprised her. "Who?"

"If I'd ever learned that, I'd have had so much leverage over you." He sighed wistfully. "You've made it easier this go-around, though. You have multiple people about whom you care and have made no secret of it. It'll bite you in the ass eventually."

"Spending time with you is a real joy killer," she noted drolly. "Now I remember why I don't do it."

"Oh, I'm growing on you. It's okay to admit," he taunted, then sobered, staring up at the bomb grid. "Angels aren't in on this. I know you like to think we are, but the wards you just broke? They were deterrents to all angels. Not merely a specific choir or specific angel, they blocked the entire Host. For the record, we can't make wards against ourselves. Ask your warlock. He'll tell you."

"So who can?" She didn't know enough about Mids' magic to guess, and Tobek certainly wasn't in any condition to talk. "This place was teeming with excess Mids' magic, the kind that comes from a superpower, but you're telling me the wards weren't done by one of your ilk."

"In this case, the superpower is a worker bee, not the brains of the whole thing. The wards prove that. Remember, we superpowers don't interact with Mids' magic the same way as Chwedlonol. How we do it is the backbone of our caste structure." He crossed his beefy arms. "No, the mastermind is definitely a Chwed. We get that Chwed, we get the whole cadre and the bigger picture. Each site would have a different team to minimize the risk of all sites being compromised should one of the flunkies get caught."

That could explain why Fymmi hadn't turned in the buyer. She'd probably hoped they'd lead her to the other buyers supplying the other sites. Surely the community of bomb makers and buyers was small enough to trace the leads. Yes, it would've been smarter to call for CWIG support; however, Bix could easily imagine five scenarios in which doing so could've compromised the op.

"Every year on the anniversary of the bombing, we—the heads of the syndicates—are sent a blank white piece of paper." Samael widened his stance. "It's a plain sheet of parchment common to the Primary Mid World, in every home, business, and copy shop. It's the only time we ever hear from whoever did all this. And the damn sheet just appears. No envelope. No deliveryman. One minute you're enjoying a beer, the next there's a piece of paper in your lap. Fuck all annoying."

She did a double take and rolled her shoulder, the memory of the attack from the pool still very vivid. "A blank piece of copy paper? In your lap?"

"Whoever ordered the threat under our feet is still out there, laughing at us, enjoying the terror they're stoking within the other syndicate leaders, terror that comes from *not* knowing who holds the trigger." He grunted and shook his head. "My choir and I arrived after the bombing to investigate it and keep the market safe in the meantime, yet I'm still included in the white paper tidings. So whoever it is still has eyes on the market."

She'd assumed Samael's interest in the bombing was because the attack had gone down on his doorstep, but learning that he'd come running afterward to seek out the perpetrator? That he'd stepped up when the other superpowers had turned their backs on this World? Gah. That was almost worthy of respect.

She slapped a hand over her bosom. "Don't tell me there's a kernel of compassion hiding inside you."

"Wouldn't that be horrid?" He made a face of disgust. "I've spent far too long looking into this mess, and the red herrings keep piling up year after year. It'll be good to have you with me on this."

She wasn't sure he meant for that last bit to be said aloud, so she stifled a smirk. "Well, now that the wards are down, we need to figure out who installed it so we can get them to undo it while we hunt the mastermind."

"Four rows left, eight north." He pointed to the spot.

"How did you…?"

"What did you think I was doing while we talked?" He held up his hand to stop her from answering. "Investigating. Following the pull of strong magic that isn't affiliated with the Host."

"Oh. Makes sense, I suppose." She hauled him with her through gates to the rooftop he'd indicated.

He grabbed his knees and dry-heaved. It took a few moments before he regained his composure. "Still not pleasant moving through gates with you."

"If you trusted me more, it wouldn't be so unpleasant for you," she jeered. "Plus, it's saved your ass more than once."

"I try not to dwell on that." He grunted and pointed to the ceiling, to a dead power cell. "Trapezoid in the center. Does it look familiar?"

Purple scrollwork formed the edges of the trapezoid framing a sigil of open maws and flared wings. Purple was the identifying color of one race, one superpower race. It wasn't the angels. They owned blue.

"Dragons," she whispered, grappling with disbelief. "They need joy to survive. Why would they do this? Why would they terrorize an entire World?"

"The problem is bigger than that. Way bigger." Samael ran his hand over his buzz cut. "That sigil belongs to a royal dragon. One of the seven queens to be precise."

Chapter 14

Bix had asked Samael to take his choir off World for a bit while she dealt with the exposed grid. He'd taken his angelic light with him, which left her staring through the pitch-dark at the damning sigil. She gripped the pendant of Feng's dewclaw until her nails threatened to break skin. She was probably going to get her ass fried for this, but she couldn't keep the secret of a dragon queen's involvement in large-scale slaughter. Not now that the wards were broken and anyone wanting a look could take a look. Not now that Samael knew. He wouldn't shout it from the rooftops, but archangels could co-occupy another angel's mind without permission. One snoopy snert and, bam, the Angelic Host would have plenty of political ammo against their natural nemeses the dragons. It'd feed the infighting among the greater Consortium that would distract them from the real problems: the faction in their midst, and the Devourers at their door.

She opened one gate directly beneath the trapezoid with a dragon queen's sigil and another inside the rookery where present-day Feng rested.

The air behind her rippled and native magic surged. Soft purple light bathed the rooftop, accompanied by a whisper of a song.

"Chimera," Raspoine greeted, stepping forward to stand beside Bix. The dragon queen ascendant held her humanoid form of ebony elegance. Long springy curls wreathed her sharp features. Pale scrollwork framed her hairline and disappeared beneath her flowing tunic. Violet eyes studied the ceiling bathed in darkness. The dragon's expression betrayed none of her thoughts.

"Thank you for coming," Bix murmured. "I, um, I found a can of worms."

"You *opened* a can of worms," Raspoine corrected, raising one hand toward the ceiling. Lavender light flowed from her fingertips, illuminating the grid, wires, det cord, bombs, the whole shebang. "A very curious can."

"Not one that I can close. I didn't want you caught unaware when word eventually gets out about this." Bix scratched her arm. "I'm fairly certain the reigning Dreigiau queen did not order the mass execution of two hundred and fifty thousand Chweds. I'm hoping that, had the Dragon Horde been made aware of what happened and what could still happen, they would've taken steps to neutralize the threat."

That snapped Raspoine's attention to her. "Neutralize?"

"Wrong word?" Bix asked.

"That depends on whether you are asking me to execute a fellow queen." Raspoine spoke not with hostility but with curiosity.

"No." Bix shook her head vigorously. There was bold and then there was stupid. "I know the reigning queen is a proponent of justice even at great personal cost. I also know there's notable unrest among the Horde about the continued rule of the seven queens. I'm thinking this doesn't help."

"True." Raspoine's attention drifted to the sigil. "Jekora. That is her royal seal. This is not her work though. It lacks her resonance."

"Resonance?" Bix echoed.

Raspoine nodded. "All powerful entities leave a signature in their great works. It is a harmony to the song of the magic to which the Dreigiau queens and their enforcers are attuned."

"That's really cool." Bix loved music but couldn't hear a lick of it from Mids' magic. Her relationship with it was all push-me-pull-you. "And that means you know precisely who framed one of your queens too, I'm thinking."

"What is proof without motive? It is a book with no words. When building a case, you must be mindful of who owns the pen." Raspoine tapped her fingertips together. "I need to take this, all of it. It needs to be evaluated."

That wasn't quite how Bix had pictured it happening. Did Raspoine know the complexity of what she was facing? Sure, dragons specialized in terra firma and all that, but gardening was more the purview of angels. She hated to suggest a joint effort almost as much as she hated to suggest the dragon queen ascendant was somehow not up to the task of undoing what another dragon had done.

Tact. She was really trying to be better at it.

"I'm told it's wired into the World, from the towers down," Bix opted to say. "I didn't remove it because I didn't want the World to explode."

"Whoever told you that is correct." Raspoine waved her hand in front of them and a hologram of the World appeared. "They began at the tips of the mountainous monoliths, driving the circuitry down as though it was the roots of a great tree, replete with offshoots. The canisters are akin to yams, onions, or carrots. There are four different root vegetables down here. I suspect those canisters that were emptied contained a fifth. It is quite insidious the way this was done. I will need my brother to help with the extraction."

They. *They* began. Multiple installers. Fymmi had been so screwed. There was no way a single agent could've countered this.

"Do you think the dragons who installed this also conceived it?" Bix gestured to the bomb garden.

Raspoine cocked her head, seeming to ponder the question. "No. I cannot see the benefit to a dragon to sustain fear. Those are ploys to which we revert during the cyclical wars, but only against our enemies. The population of the Crimson Market is not our enemy. They are criminals as defined by local governments, not by the queens or the Consortium. They are living robust lives full of experiences and emotions. That is the reason we created them. For all intents and purposes, the good people of the market are doing precisely what they were intended to do."

"There were wards protecting this bomb garden, wards put in place by a Chwed. Is there any chance you can detect his or her resonance?" Bix asked, daring to press Raspoine's patience. For whatever reason, Bix felt like an ungainly teenager rather than the über-powerful Chimera whenever she was around Raspoine. Maybe it was the size differential that made her confer greater respect to the dragon queen ascendant. Maybe it was the aura, the *je ne sais quoi* Raspoine exuded. Who knew.

Raspoine pursed her lips and arched one elegant brow.

"There could be other Worlds, other people, other communities who are being terrorized by the mastermind who conceived this scheme," Bix pressed. "While I fully respect the Horde's judicial process and your caution in framing the case properly, I've sworn to protect the Mids. Therefore, I need the Chwed who conceived this."

Raspoine stared at her, expressionless, for an uncomfortably long time. Yep, definitely testing the queen ascendant's patience. Still, Bix needed the answer to get Samael to help her retrieve Fymmi. Eyes on the mission.

At length, Raspoine inclined her head. "The Dreigiau are pleased to be of service to the Chimera Reawakened, as she will no doubt return the favor in our hour of need."

The formality of Raspoine's acquiescence raised the hairs on Bix's nape, but it was too late to backpedal. Raspoine held her arms out from her sides and whispered something Bix couldn't hear. Watercolor magic arced from the dragon's fingertips. Ashes levitated from rooftops and streets, drawing together in clumps and clusters, hydrating and plumping as Raspoine's magic reconstructed that which Tobek's magic had destroyed.

"Rummir?" Raspoine called.

Plum light dawned in front of Raspoine. From the glow stepped the queen ascendant's twin in his humanoid form. His serpentine gaze cut left and right as he mirrored his sister's posture, saying nothing. Dark jewel-toned magic leapt from his fingertips, running alongside Raspoine's paler magic.

Bix ground her teeth against the influx of Mids' magic attempting to boot her out of the subcity. It wasn't quite the potency of Tobek's undoing, but…damn.

Reconstituted fragments, bits, and chips pulled together, forming a series of humble clay disks with a large symbol etched in each. The disks danced in a ring around the twins' shoulders as the dragons lowered their arms and their magic subsided. The twins stared at each other, neither uttering a word. Raspoine's expression betrayed nothing, but the same could not be said for her brother. Rummir's nostrils flared, releasing coils of purple smoke. His lip curled. His hands twitched at his sides.

That couldn't be good.

"We recognize the spell work." Raspoine pinned Bix with an intensity that provoked goose bumps along Bix's arms. "Isoba. The Chwedlonol you seek is named Isoba."

"Ask the archangel whose funk still lingers in this tomb. Isoba is one of their creations." Rummir snapped his fingers, and the disks stacked at his feet. "You were to be working with your warlock on mitigating the threat you are soon to pose, yet his resonance is strong down here. *He* broke Isoba's spells."

"Yes?" Bix drew out the word, unsure of where Rummir's censure was heading.

"That means he is in no condition to fulfill his obligation to you." Rummir leveled a piercing glare at her.

"He has some gewgaws that might work," she hedged. "I have to test them, of course, but we've started."

"We are watching, Chimera," Rummir reminded and gestured to the ceiling. "This is a distraction you can ill afford."

"The lives on this World matter to me, Rummir, so I'll be the judge of what is and is not a waste of my time." Bix didn't cool the lash in her tone. While Rummir was a proven ally whom she liked, he did not elicit the same kind of respect as his sister.

"One World for the many. These lives for the others you hold dearer," he growled. "You would do well to reconsider your priorities."

The malice inside her wanted to rise to his baiting, but the spy she was trained to be kept an eye on the mission. Break Fymmi out of the supermax facility. Thanks to Raspoine, she now had the name of the person Samael wanted in exchange for the intel on the supermax facility. She'd gotten what she needed. Plus, the twins were going to remove the bombs, thus fulfilling her promise to Yukiko. Wins all around. Therefore, Bix took a big step back, physically and emotionally. She painted on a smile and laced her fingers in front of her.

"Since you two are going to make the market safe again, my concern here has been addressed. Good luck prosecuting the dragons who did this. I'm sure Jekora will be grateful that you're keeping it in-house. Should you need my help putting the right words in the book, you know how to find me."

She opened gates and got out of the twins' way.

Chapter 15

Getting out of the twins' way didn't mean Bix wasn't keeping an eye on them. She stepped out of the subcity of the Crimson Market and into an adjacent Mid World.

Structurally, Mid Worlds existed in a cluster. Those closest to the center, to the core of the Mids, were the oldest and most imbued with native magic. Those on the perimeters were newer and not as saturated with the native magic that bound them all together. Every Mid World had a protective layer containing its atmosphere and shielding the World from external influences. Destructive ether existed as a vast barrier around the cluster and in the crevices between Worlds. It bumped up against the protective layers, constantly searching for a way inside. If one had the misfortune of being within the ether, it was endless. However, if one happened to be a gatekeeper of uncommon skill, then one knew how to leverage ether as a sepia-toned filter through which one could view an adjacent World, devoid of sound, where only the strongest magics appeared in color. One could also be so brazen as to use gates to exist in one World while strolling through another undetected. Mostly undetected.

Remote observations. A habit Bix had developed before becoming a spy, and a skill that had come in very handy afterward.

Like now.

Bix's viewing spot in the adjacent World provided a satellite's perspective of the Crimson Market. Ether formed its filter between Worlds, showing her streaks of purple magic building in power, glowing brighter through the filter. Bix steepled her fingers and pressed them to her lips as she watched the future of the market rest solely on the ability of the twins to undo what their own race had done. If they screwed up, the World would be gone. Every life she'd intended to save, ended. If they pulled it off, however, they alone had the proof that could send the Consortium into a tailspin. It was a trade she'd had to make. She'd presented Raspoine with the evidence of a crime and had to leave it to the queen ascendant to do her duty to the greater Mids. If there was going to be justice within the Dragon Horde, the twins were uniquely positioned to exact it without involving the Consortium.

Besides, if they didn't execute the dragons who'd done it, Bix could always do their job for them after she got the full story from Fymmi.

A wave of native magic crashed against her.

"So this is how you track your prey." Samael looked through the viewing gates. "Now that's a nice trick. Frick and Frack undoing the damage?"

"How'd you find me?" she asked as the power of the twins surged, whiting out the filter of the ether. She closed the gates and braced for the concussive waves of a World exploding. None came. That was a good sign. She'd give it a few for the dragons' power to ebb before checking on the Crimson Market again.

"Me. Hunter." Samael pounded his pecs like an ape. "Truthfully, though, I pursued Feng for so many years I can follow his magic anywhere in the Mids. You are wearing an excess of it like a disco ball. Probably from when you broke the wards."

"I've got to learn how to scrub that off," she muttered.

"It fades as long as you stop letting him help you." Samael folded his arms across his chest. "You get a name from the twins?"

"It wasn't the queen whose sigil was up there."

"Yeah, I warned you about those red herrings. That wasn't my question, though. Did they tell you who really did it?"

"They'll handle the dragons who installed the bomb grid. They're kicking off their own investigation and keeping it in-house. They did confirm the mastermind isn't a dragon."

"Obviously," Samael grumbled. "A dragon could fart and gas the market out of existence. There's no win for them doing something as elaborate as that grid. My money is on a rotten Fate putting a very conniving Chwed in a position to finagle an IOU from a royal dragon."

Of course. The Crimson Market had addicts who were angels and dragons stumbling through its streets. Sure, those addicts were lower level, but that was only because royals and archangels did a better job of hiding their indiscretions.

"Well, you're probably right," she conceded. "The Chwed's name is Isoba. They said you'd know about him."

"Isoba?" Samael slapped his hand over his face. "Isoba. Yeah, sure. That makes total sense, except for the part where I put him in supermax some hundred-odd years ago. He's a special kind of fucked-up creation."

"Well, the bomb grid's been up for ten years, so somebody let the nutter out."

"Probably the rot," he drawled. "You still have that arrangement with the jorōgumo, right?"

"Once the twins are done, I'll have delivered my end of the deal, so yes." She held out her hand. "I've also delivered the name of the mastermind to you, so it's your turn to ante up. Images of the facility."

"Pics aren't going to do you any good. They're outdated the moment they're taken." He waved off her demand. "We'll need your whole band of misfits to break in and out. Before you assemble them, however, you and I need more information. Take that meet with Yukiko, but this time, pay attention to the prisoner list of that Undine ship, not the goodies or the smugglers. Check for Isoba. He's crafty enough he'd hide in plain sight right under my nose while using the Undine navy as his unwitting accomplices. That's probably how he arranged to have those blank sheets of paper delivered to the syndicate leaders on the anniversaries of the bombings. Once you've done that, check for his associates. She'll know who they are. The spiders have been Isoba's main supplier for generations. They're how I caught him in the first place."

So many responses to that rapid-fire series of commands, but only one made it out her mouth. "Wait, why aren't photos going to do me any good?"

He started to say something. Stopped. Huffed. "I'll explain everything once we're ready. Just…we trust each other all the way through the mission, right? That's our agreement. I'll deliver. I need you to do the same."

"Yeah, fine," Bix muttered. Samael was way too agitated, uncharacteristically so. If he flaked, she was going to need Yukiko's intel anyway. "Where do I find you once I'm done with Yukiko?"

"It's the market. Believe me, I'll know when you're done." He made to pat her shoulder, then snatched his hand back as if he'd been zapped. "We did good today. We've disarmed the immediate threat. I can't say I'd be surprised if we had an influx of active-duty dragons incognito at the market to protect it should the rotten ones attempt a direct hit."

Shit. Retaliation for an old case hadn't occurred to her. "Your choir going to behave?"

"We'll be all Montague and Capulet for sure, which means we'll blend in with the usual back-alley nefarious happenings." He jerked his thumb over his shoulder. "I'm going to check that menagerie where I stashed Isoba and make sure the rot hasn't started an early release program. Could take me two or three days. These places aren't small. Keep that in mind when it comes time to plan the break."

Before she could say anything else, he was gone. Running straight into a danger he didn't fully comprehend.

It was a Shadow Caster who'd delivered those sheets of paper to the syndicate leaders. They'd used the pool to do it, which was why Samael couldn't follow the trail. If the Shadow Caster was the same as the mastermind, then Isoba, a Chwed, was a Shadow Caster. It might not have been the rot that had sprung Isoba. It might have been a fellow Shadow Caster in the ranks of the Devourers.

Devourers could only be killed by god-forged weapons in the hands of deities, or by, well, Bix herself—assuming she had all her memories and full access to the magics she was subconsciously suppressing. Since she didn't, the best she could do was weaken them.

An angel had no recourse against a Devourer. Samael was about to pick a fight he couldn't win.

Chapter 16

Bix returned to the early winter winds of the Primary Mid World, smothering a yawn. She hadn't seen her pillow in far too long. Before she engaged in a battle of wits with Yukiko, she needed to get some sleep. Reset. Refresh. Reassemble the gray cells. The twins were still working on the Crimson Market, so she had a legit excuse for a break. But first, she had to circle back with Drew for an update on the draugr's search for a rogue.

The cheery holiday decorations of the coal plant welcomed her as she threw open the door to Dysmorphic. Ink guns paused their humming as Berserkers looked up from their work. Tension snaked through the shop. Apparently, it was no secret she was the reason their commander was out of commission. She forced a smile and headed for the back of the shop.

Small fingers wrapped around one of hers. A young boy, five, maybe six years old, blinked up at her with dead eyes.

"Drew," she whispered on a breath of relief.

"The big guy is in the clinic. The goblin is keeping vigil." Drew tugged her along the back hallway toward the clinic. "The goblin, however, is more worried about you than Colonel Crispy. Been muttering about a bad angel. I tried to explain they were all bad, but that didn't comfort the little guy. Go figure."

"Our good buddy Samael is back on the scene," Bix said as she used gates to enter the locked clinic with Drew at her side.

Gurp's shriek outdid Drew's. Gurp lurched off his stool and ran at her, hugging her tightly.

"It's okay, Gurp. It's okay. *I* am okay." She patted his back. "Because of your help, I was able to call on some higher powers. They're taking care of the bombs as we speak. The market will be safe very soon. Thank you so much for what you did."

Gurp released her and stared up at her with frightened eyes. "Angel?"

"He's an enemy of the battalion, but a frenemy of mine." She let genuine warmth infuse her smile. "Sometimes we work with people we don't like because they can do things we can't. In the end, we all want to protect the Mids. That's what matters. Right?"

Gurp rolled his eyes and muttered something. Drew snorted and gabbled right back at the goblin. The two kept up their banter before looking up at her with wide but far from innocent eyes.

"I feel like I'm in the middle of a half-pint anarchy," she drawled. "Gurp, I'll sit with Tobek for a while. Why don't you get some rest? You've been up for way more than twenty-four."

The goblin's worried gaze drifted back to the charred remnants of the seven-foot-tall Berserker resting beneath a plain white sheet.

"Is there a single soldier in this battalion who would let Tobek come to harm?" she asked, fairly confident in the answer. She hadn't met them all, which was sort of odd considering she lived among them. Her social gaffs aside, Tobek sure as hell knew all his men, which meant the goblin knew twice as much about them. Gurp was a master of anticipating needs, a feat he accomplished by knowing way, way more than he ever let on. One of the hundred and one reasons she had mad respect for her goblin housemate.

"No. No harm." Gurp shook his head.

"Hey." Bix crouched in front of Gurp. "I know you want to be here when he wakes up, but it'll be a few more days before the Fates reset him, so sneak in a nap while you can. Once he's up, he's going to hog the shower and make a mess of the kitchen. Then there will be a return of the random weirds escaping from the altar room while he does we-don't-want-to-know-what in there, am I right?"

Gurp chortled and mumbled something that sounded like a litany of other offenses.

"Go on, claim some me time. You've more than earned it." She stood and straightened his collar. "Want me to drop you at your dinner table or the shower?"

"Hmmm. Shower?"

"You got it. Thank you, again, for everything." She opened gates, depositing Gurp at his favorite hiding place in the basement.

Once there was nothing but the faint hum of the machines around her, she scanned the clinic and checked the morgue drawers, making sure she and Drew were well and truly alone. Drew watched her with a curious expression but said nothing. Bix grabbed a stool and rolled it to Tobek's table. Drew followed suit, adding a few thick medical books to the seat before clambering atop them. The moment the draugr settled, Bix opened layered gates of privacy, gates that swallowed sound and distorted images. Gates that thwarted surveillance systems.

"The clinic is wired out the wazoo, and we know your new roommate listens in too," Bix explained.

"It's slightly cozier than a desolate World, though the view could be better." Drew waved a hand at Tobek. "The sheet just makes it worse, and I have to say, less burned chicken more burned cobra for the olfactory offense."

Bix closed one eye. "I can't tell if that's a dig about Samael and his choir in the market or if you can really smell Tobek's char."

Drew gestured at himself. "Child's body. They don't exactly have fully developed senses as it is."

"So, angel dig." Bix nodded. "I know you're not a fan."

"Oh, Bixie, that's an understatement. Burned alive by angel fire. Going to take me a long while to get over that."

"Yeah, fair," she conceded. "So, the update on Yukiko is—"

"No need." Drew held up a tiny hand. "I got the lowdown

from Samael's little angel boys and girls. You see, when you put out an ask for someone who'll steal from a god, you know who answers?"

"Angels," Bix said, knowing the question was rhetorical.

"Angels," Drew repeated. "Cocky little shits, don't even bother to vet before showing interest. I don't care what sort of meat suit they're wearing—and the ones they've chosen are a hoot—I know an angel when I touch one. Do you know what angels can't do?"

"Lie," she said at the same time as Drew.

"Oh, they can twist some truths, but hello." Drew motioned to himself again. "Raised the daughter of a chaos god. Know how to elicit the answers I want."

That talent had made Drew an incredible interrogator and critical member of their Dark Ops team. Yes, the borrow-a-body ability also added to his team value. He had two weaknesses, though. One was the deep streak of spite that ran through him. The other was his impulsiveness. Put those two foibles together with a choir of unwitting angels, and Bix was afraid to ask the question, but she had to.

"Did you thank these angels very kindly for their interest, then send them on their way?"

"Pfft, pfft, pfft," Drew sputtered. "No. I made them useful."

Bix dropped her head in her hands, covering her eyes. "Drew, what did you do?"

"Don't worry, I didn't out Fymmi." He sniffed. "We have another problem, and I put them on that."

Bix splayed her fingers and peered through the gaps. "Which problem? Cian?"

"No, no, the kid is balls deep in Devourer research," he dismissed with a wave. "Frighteningly amazing with the raw data he can sift through, and that's before he gets his mitts on a computer. However, I think he's going to overreach inside the CWIG and get his peepee whacked by the director. He hasn't quite puzzled out that Chwed tech is more cyborg than not. For all his numbers smarts, he has no clue how to cope with the biological components."

"What'd you do to the angels, Drew?" she asked again.

Drew tied little knots in the edge of Tobek's sheet, deliberately not looking at her. "Like I said, I put them to work on another problem."

"Unless it's making you an endless supply of meat suits, I really do need to know what dangerous assignment you gave Samael's choir." She reached across the table and took his hands in hers. "Our mission could be in a lot of trouble if Samael thinks we're working against him. So how screwed are we?"

Drew puckered his lips and stared at the ceiling. "Probably a lot."

"Drew," she groaned, withdrawing her hands. "What did you do?"

"There are five nutter gods hunting you. I put the angels to hunting them." Drew shrugged. "I told them I didn't need them to steal *from* a god. I told them I needed them to *steal a god*."

Bix bounced her forehead against the cold lip of the table. "Tell me they turned you down."

"Of course not." Drew derided. "The whole choir is a bunch of restless bounty hunters. There's only so much fun to be had tracking errant Chweds. Hunting gods who lost their marbles at the end of the last Great War? I mean, I barely got the word 'crazy' out of my mouth before they were shaking my hand and closing the deal."

There was no way any part of Drew's improv plan was going to end well. "On the off chance they're successful and bring you a rando god, what did you promise to pay them?"

"Bixie, sweetie, you don't know your own value." This time Drew patted Bix's hands. "They want a private audience with you."

Bix barked a laugh.

"You weren't around for this part, but I killed a lot of them. Recently, even. Like since I've been back from exile." Bix turned her hands up and held on to Drew's. "Pretty sure they're asking for a private meeting so they can give me a beat down."

Drew grunted. "That'd be appropriately stupid of them. I never promised they'd survive the meeting."

Bix pinched the bridge of her nose. "Drew. We're in the throes of a truce with their archangel."

"If we can round up the remaining five gods and bring them together all at once, then you can take your memories back all at once." Drew's bottom lip quivered. "There will be no surviving dangerous half stories and faulty truths. There will be no prolonged suffering for you or us while you repeat this Sisyphean punishment. You take one horrible, awful hit just once. Then we, your friends, put your pieces—all your pieces—back together. And there you go. The Chimera reborn in her full glory, for better or worse."

Panic, wild and bountiful, froze Bix's lungs, squeezed her heart, and clouded her brain. Ringing sounded in her ears. All the memories. All at once. She couldn't handle one infusion without her brain bleeding and her body locked in a fetal position for days on end. All the memories? At once? Her brain would never be able to handle it. Her body might recover, but her mind? It'd be ruined forever. She would break. She would become far worse than the monster of lore.

Then there was the small matter of having to drain the gods who held her memories until they were hollow shells, the closest to death a god could get. She had yet to successfully husk one, and they did not go gently into that long good night. She'd have her memories, their emotions, and the total disastrophy that would be her undoing. It was a surefire path to the uncontrollable destruction of countless Worlds, that was all before she opened the numerous gates for the Devourers to invade the Mids.

The whole concept was more than she could manage.

The room spun around her, faster and faster. She was vaguely aware of tipping off her stool, of the cold floor pressing against her cheek, of a child screaming her name, and of a cloud of mulberry and navy enveloping her in soft scents of sandalwood, black pepper, and musk with a hint of gardenia.

Chapter 17

Screaming. Full-bodied, anguished screams. They weren't coming from her, and for that Bix was grateful. Cool silk cradled her cheek; firm cushions supported her hip and shoulder. Warm air brushed her exposed back. Her fingers crept forward, confirming the edge of a chaise. A silk chaise. She didn't know anybody with a silk chaise. She reached out with her senses, and Other World magic answered, welcoming her. Not in the Mids, then.

Something else lay beneath Other World magic's greeting. Taint.

Devourers.

Her eyes flew wide. Sun-bleached limestone floors stretched to carved columns admitting salty breezes from shimmering aqua seas that stretched out before the...patio? No. Temple. Circa the heydays of ancient Greece. When the gods did retro, they went all-in.

Another brutalized scream rolled forth, chased by a dry masculine laugh. The noise of torture in progress came from behind her in the cella.

Bix struggled to sit upright, pressing a hand over her heart. Her chest ached as if a titan in soccer cleats had danced a jig up and down her sternum. Wincing, she swung her feet off the chaise and grimaced.

Someone had taken her shoes. And changed her clothes. While she normally wore fitted dresses that fell to the knee, the extra-snug fit below the knees confirmed who had taken care of her.

"Phobos?" she croaked.

Amber irises and crimson pupils blinked in front of her. She jerked back with a curse. "Whoa, personal space invader."

Phobos crouched before her. Tar-black gunk and blisters streaked up one cheek, following the path of two deep scars that ran from lip to hairline. Black spatter stained the collar and shoulder of his…rust-colored duster, leaving small holes. His white T-shirt also showed signs of damage. His coat sleeves were rolled, revealing living tattoos that writhed around his forearms. Fresh wounds covered his hands.

Not Phobos. Deimos, his twin. Fear was Phobos's domain. Deimos leveled up to pure terror. The kind that turned hair white and induced strokes. He said nothing as he snatched her by the upper arm and dragged her into the walled center chamber of the temple, toward the sound of screaming.

Bix had to run to keep up, and she despised running, doubly so in a dress that didn't allow for it. The balls of her feet struck the compacted souls that were the basic building blocks of all Worlds. A god's will made those emptied souls look and feel like whatever the god desired. In this case, it was pocked limestone solid enough to bruise. Add to that being bullied by a dude and her temper sloughed off its slumber just in time for her to be flung unceremoniously into a puddle of black gunk.

Deimos jabbed his fingers in her hair and jerked her head up. "Look at what you've done."

Phobos, the actual Phobos, slumped in a chair. Half his dress shirt and vest had been eaten away, fringed in black. What remained was saturated with his essence. It bled through his fingers, fingers that were stained black and weeping. Blisters pushed against raw skin running from nail to temple. His once flawless face had been ravaged. He looked like the victim of an acid attack.

Unholy wrath slithered from Bix's spine as she swept her fingers through the black puddle in which she'd been tossed.

Devourer blood.

It didn't burn her skin because she wasn't a god. However, she'd seen its effects on a top-ranking goddess once. The goddess had looked a lot like Phobos did right now. The goddess had been able to shake off the damage, but Phobos, powerful though he was, was not in the same class as the head of a pantheon.

"Let her go, Deimos," Phobos rasped.

Deimos pulled up on her hair, forcing her to roll to her knees. His lips brushed her ear as he seethed. "You did this to him. You and the thrall in which you hold him."

"Brother, for your own sake, let her go," Phobos insisted, the breathy demand labored.

Unlike most divine siblings, particularly those in the Greek pantheon, these brothers truly loved each other. Recognizing that was the only reason Bix kept her darkness from impaling Deimos. Instead, it crept over him, shoes and shoulders, knees and elbows, throat and hair.

Deimos swore and slowly uncurled his fingers, releasing her. She didn't return the favor. Pouting, she massaged her scalp as she regained her feet. She scowled at her now gooey, disheveled state, then glared at Deimos.

"You didn't think this part through, did you?" She indicated the Devourer blood dribbling over her, at the tatters of the once beautiful dress. A dress created by a god's magic, therefore trashed by the anti-god's blood. "I could hug you and you'd be as wrecked up as your brother. Or I could dredge you through the puddle and you'd be worse off than he is."

Deimos struggled in the hold of her darkness, clawing at that which was both ethereal and solid, inclusive of all states by its very nature. Murderous intent laced with pain brightened his eyes.

"Because Phobos cares for you, I'll share with you a little

secret. When you fight my darkness, it turns your efforts against you. You are the cause of your own agony. You inflict your own damage." She stepped closer to Deimos, placing one blood-covered finger between his pecs. The black goo burned through his shirt and sizzled against his skin, raising a blister. He tensed but stilled. His nostrils flared and his jaw locked, but he didn't scream. "And if you lay a hand on me again, I will start by peeling your skin, thin layer by thin layer. I will stop only when I reach marrow."

"Enough, Chimera," Phobos whispered. "Your point is made."

"Is it, Deimos? If I release you, are you self-possessed enough to think beyond your emotions? Is the greater picture of what we're all fighting against within your grasp, or does your futile anger shape everything you see? Hmm?" She held the god of terror's searing regard but didn't push. She waited as his attention cut to his twin.

It was said twins could hold intense conversations with just a look. If these two hadn't been gods, she'd believe that was what she was witnessing. But gods had the whole telepathy thing, so they were more like kindergarteners whispering in the back of class.

Boys.

At length, Deimos relaxed. His jaw audibly unlocked. She waited until his breathing calmed and his heartbeat no longer hammered against her darkness before releasing him.

"We good?" she asked with far more patience than she felt.

Deimos inclined his head.

"Excellent. Now, who wants to tell me what's going on," Bix demanded, not asked.

"You had a panic attack," Phobos whispered. "I answered your distress. I expected one…"

"My brother was prepared for one Devourer to show up, not a squad," Deimos finished for him. "A second one got him in the back. Real coward shot, there. I felt his agony and responded. Here we are."

"Ah, shit." Bix sighed and crouched in front of Phobos, listening to his wet breathing. She used gates to ensure she didn't accidentally get toxic blood on him. "I'm so sorry. What can I do to help you? Get you an infusion of mortal fears? We're still a few days away from Krampus scaring the hell out of bratty kids, but I think the iron dwarves are slated to sacrifice some light elves to keep their forges burning for another year. That's a two-week fright fest. Give you a little energy boost, eh?"

"Chimera." Phobos winced and gripped his knee until his knuckles turned white.

"Is it souls?" She bit her lip and shoved down the guilt threatening to make her darkness turn feral. "Do you need a snack of terrified souls? I'm more than happy to redirect a bunch of psychopomps."

"You have to learn to kill them," Phobos gasped. He didn't need to clarify "them." She was still wearing notable quantities of "them."

She huffed. "I'm working on it, but I'm missing some important details…like *how* I'm supposed to kill them."

"We will teach you." His oozing eyes looked at the ceiling. She followed his attention.

Pinned to the gilded tiles with Phobos's xiphoi and Deimos's spears were two unconscious Devourers. The still-bleeding sources of the puddle. Long black hair fell in mats and tangles around crowns of silver horns. Gunmetal-gray skin, taut across battle-honed muscles, bore the significant damage inflicted by god-forged weapons. There the similarities stopped. One Devourer wore a dark bronze uniform. The nipple-baring Queen Anne collar and elaborate embroidery along the right panel were a sight spiffier than the stark nakedness of the second Devourer.

Bix glanced over her shoulder at Deimos. "Your doing, I assume?"

"Gravity is a selective feature in the Other Worlds." Deimos shrugged. "Before they blacked out, we were able to learn the naked one was a prisoner of the god Ogun. The uniformed one was in the ether with his new squad. Neither could explain how they knew where you were beyond instinct. Said the summons echoed in the fibers of their beings, painfully irresistible."

Summoning implied intent, and she in no way meant to drag Devourers into the Mids.

Crap. The clinic.

"Did they breach the coal plant?" she asked of Phobos.

Phobos slowly blinked. "Within the confines of your gates, which confused them long enough for us to drag them away. The child protected the body on the table. There were others. I believe you will have explaining to do when you return."

Blessings to the powers that be…and blessings to Phobos. This could've gone a lot worse in so many ways.

"That black scrollwork on their right sides is their name, rank, and tracking beacon." She stood and crossed her arms. "If their brothers-in-arms haven't shown up yet, then you should expect them."

Deimos twirled a finger. "Why do you think we're at Dad's house? He's using this as a teaching moment for our siblings and niblings who haven't had the pleasure of dealing with Devourers before."

She scratched her brow. "One way for Ares to vent his aggression, I suppose."

"Unless you want the entire war contingent of the Greek pantheon to answer your summons from this point forward, I suggest, strongly, that you kill these bottom feeders now." Deimos hooked his thumbs on his belt buckle and widened his stance. "We can count on one hand the allies you have within our pantheon, and that includes the bestiary."

Not including the bestiary, her Greek allies were a whole two. She suffered no illusion that Deimos wouldn't strangle her with his bare hands if not for Phobos. He was proving to be a little dense like that.

"What part of 'I don't know how to kill them' did you not grok?"

Deimos snorted. "If you can husk a god, you can consume an entire Devourer, especially a scout."

Revulsion and chagrin hit her at once. It must have shown on her face because Deimos cocked his head and Phobos groaned.

"You can't husk a god." Deimos laughed bitterly, merrily, but still bitterly. "A toothless Chimera."

"Not toothless," she mumbled. "I can still make you suffer."

"And there are days gods are grateful for such suffering, merely to change up the monotony of our lives," Deimos ridiculed. "If you can't husk a god, what good are you?"

"Brother," Phobos chided, struggling to sit straighter in his seat. "Help or get out."

Deimos glowered at his twin. "Fine. Do your worst to the naked one, Chimera, let's see what we're working with."

"I'm not a circus monkey." She eyed the Devourers. There were side effects to feeding from an anti-god that were not present when feeding from a god. It changed her, so sayeth Phobos and Tobek. She wasn't sure she wanted to be changed. She wasn't sure which effects were temporary and which lasted. She was in the throes of a mission, and she liked to be in control during a mission. More people made it out alive that way.

"We feel your fear," Deimos groused. "What? What is so scary about them?"

She spun around and glared at the bossy brother. "You're looking mighty tasty there, grumpy, so back off."

"Chimera, your fears are deeply buried once you feed from Devourers," Phobos reminded her, causing his brother to swear. "We need you to embrace that, to desire that. We are at war, and war is no place for panic attacks."

Panic attacks had forced Phobos into a trap. His healing was slow, too slow. This damage was what happened to all gods within the spatter radius of a Devourer. Deimos had also been injured by it. Most god-forged weapons were from the eras where sword and spear held dominance. The smithies of the assorted pantheons weren't building remote-controlled drones. The internecine warfare among pantheons was intended to give the gods the ability to spit in the eyes of their enemies. The intimate violence was pretty much the point of the conflict. See Deimos's claim about the monotony of immortality.

But when it came to Devourers, that up-close-and-personal approach was a vulnerability that gave the anti-gods the upper hand.

"Go ahead," Deimos whispered. "Show me what a fearless Chimera looks like. How far are you willing to go to protect the Mids? How far beyond that *can* you go?"

If she could kill Devourers, perhaps her subconscious would lash out at them instead of opening gates to Mids while in the fit of madness she was doomed to suffer after her next memory merge. Plus, taking out an anti-god ought to put her one big step closer to being able to husk a god. Useful for self-defense and for when the five guardian gods came bearing her memories, memories that had driven them crazy.

She couldn't let those gods continue to roam the Mids with minds so warped and twisted by what she'd done to them that the gods' own pantheons feared what they'd become. It was a consequence of a decision she'd made as Chimera version 1.0, but it was still her decision. She couldn't run from that. She couldn't be the cause of *more* danger to the Mids.

Time to put on the big-girl panties.

She took a deep breath and sent her darkness to spear the body of the naked Devourer. His bright silver eyes snapped open as he gasped and let loose an ecstatic cry. She glanced at Phobos. He gave her a perfunctory nod. From the sounds of it, the Devourer didn't exactly mind being invaded. Of course, their race got off on pain like a certain Berserker she knew, so that didn't say much.

It took less than a thought to withdraw the raw energy from the Devourer. It was silken cold, numbing every pain receptor as it coasted through her body. Haze slithered through her mind, disengaging her regulatory ego from her impulsive id. There was no place for fear or doubt, much less consideration for anyone else. Impulse and instinct reigned.

"It's not working," Deimos complained. "Why is she failing?"

"Think, Chimera, you know why feeding isn't good enough," Phobos called. "You're just exhausting him."

"You said I had to *consume* a Devourer," she argued, rolling her shoulders and lifting her chin. "Is it possible your twin has no idea what I used to do?"

"I tried not to stick around when you went on a tear," Deimos drawled. "Self-preservation and whatnot."

"Coward," she shot back.

"Careful, brother." Phobos flexed his hands, now bright pink with fresh scabs. "Fearless is not far from unfeeling, which includes her capacity for compassion. That is the emotion that regulates the Chimera of today."

"Lovely," Deimos sighed.

Drain, not feed. Tobek's words from the subcity came rushing back to her. It was a different target; less of what the Devourer naturally generated and more of what enabled him to generate it.

Three more spears of darkness penetrated the Devourer. This time, Bix reached beyond his primordial essence, searching out the very things that made him a deity. This time, his cry sounded more like a zealot running toward rapture. His emotions crashed over her like waves. There was the shame of being captured, the confusion of why the fear gods had spared him, the admiration for the war god who'd held him prisoner and tortured him. When it came to her, it was…respect? Yes. Respect and a bit of awe for the High Executioner for All Worlds. He was proud to be in and of service to her. He was happy to die for her.

A few minutes ago, the notion would've horrified her, but now, filled with his taint, she had zero fucks to give about his opinions.

"He's shriveling." Deimos paced behind her. "You're husking him, not killing him. Devourers aren't gods. He can die. Now, stop playing with your prey, and end him."

Bix turned to the god of terror and curled a lip.

Deimos jerked to a stop. "By all that's…Phobos, do you see

this? She is becoming the darkness. It's replacing her skin. Look at the hollows of her cheeks, the frame of her hairline, the sockets of her—"

"Your eyes, Chimera," Phobos finished for his brother, the touch of his gaze a physical thing. "They're glowing with starlight. We've not seen that happen before, not even in your former glory."

"Worried that I am what I eat, Deimos?" Bix purred. She reached for the god's chest...and stopped. The tendons in her hand were black, her knuckles black. She flipped her hand and, sure enough, the lines within her palms were black; the nails under her manicure also black. She glanced at her legs, fully exposed by the tatters of her dress. They were still the shapely stems of a lifetime in high heels, but they weren't of flesh and muscle. No, they were like her tentacles, solid yet ethereal, and ever so dark. The effect faded across her hips, leaving her torso streaked but still familiar. The blood from the puddle in which she'd been tossed was gone now, absorbed by her darkness. It'd taken every drop and dribble from her clothing. She yanked up her sleeves and stared in awe as the scars on her forearm left by a god's venomous bite turned black, then smoothed into flawless skin.

The scars left by a god, undone by a Devourer.

She looked to the Devourer, then to Deimos, her mind churning with possibilities.

"No," Deimos said, shaking his head. "I know that spider-to-a-fly look. I perfected that look. Whatever it is you're conceiving, I will not participate."

She chuckled. "Aren't you cute, thinking you have a choice?"

"Me, Chimera," Phobos rasped, finally managing to sit upright but not without flinching. "Use me, not my brother."

"No, he's too weak." Deimos stepped between her and his twin. "Leave him be."

"You and I have the agreement, Chimera." Phobos dropped his head back and stared at the ceiling. "I hold you to that agreement."

"Gods and their infernal contracts." She sneered.

Darkness flicked Deimos across the temple. The double-whump of his body hitting the limestone wall, then the floor made her smile. She sauntered between Phobos's thighs and brushed her lips against his reforming ear. The power he exuded was slowly rebuilding, tickling her skin. A taunt, a lure.

Not yet. Too soon.

"Gods and anti-gods," she whispered. "To kill a Devourer, I must do the opposite of what I can do to you."

She husked gods. She took everything from them, leaving nothing but the hollow shell…or she would once she figured out how not to burst apart from the onslaught. To kill a Devourer, she needed to flip the switch, reverse the flow. They needed to burst from the excess.

It'd be messy and completely disgusting. It'd also serve as a pointed lesson to any witnesses. The question now became whether she had enough source material to overfeed a Devourer. One way to find out.

She held Phobos's wary gaze as seven tentacles dug into the Devourer. Darkness gave instead of took. It didn't give him back his essentials; no, it gave him the opposite. It gave him what she took from a god.

"Stop," Phobos whispered. "You're draining yourself. Think. You should be able to end hundreds of them at once. It did not require hundreds of gods to fall at your feet to do it."

She braced her forearms on the back of his chair as hunger crept up to her. "But I need to overfeed them."

"It's not a god's raw essence on which they feed, though, is it? Neither are they weakened by contact with our essence, as we are with theirs. If that was the case, we wouldn't need our weapons to slay them. We could just rip their hearts out with our bare, bleeding hands. Whatever it is comes from you, not us."

He had a point.

"They feed on native magic, but I am no repository for it," she mused aloud, searching for the answers as if they would appear in big neon lights throughout the temple.

"What do you have in abundance but is still limited?" he

pressed. "What is it that allows you to kill a hundred of them but not a thousand?"

She perched on his leg and tucked herself closer to his body, to his raw energy.

Raw.

That was the pairing of opposites. Raw versus refined. It would allow her to feed from the Devourers or gods, process their nutrients, then expel whatever she didn't need into the Devourers.

She ripped her darkness from the naked Devourer and drove seven tentacles into the clothed one watching everything wide-eyed and silent. Formerly silent, that was. She fed first, replenishing her stock as he cried out his exultation.

With a deep breath and wriggle, she flipped the switch. It took a few tries of conscious choice to divest herself of the things to which she normally paid little heed. It was, for all intents and purposes, the residue of her magic. Not the magic itself, but the chaff that was shucked whenever she called it into play. Theoretically, she had vast stores of magic. She was a co-creator of the ether, for fuck's sake. Without her complete memories, she didn't know the breadth and depth of her magic, but not knowing and not having were two different things.

She could do this. She was the godsdamned Chimera. She could do anything.

So she did. The darkness itself was an aspect of her magic, and it had no problems pumping its residue into the Devourer. The anti-god's cry took on a panicked tone, heavily laced with confusion, but he had little time to ponder.

He exploded.

Black tarry gunk flew everywhere, bathing his peer in blood and entrails. Darkness shielded Phobos, protecting him from further harm.

"Again," Phobos instructed. "Take down the second one. Prove it's not a fluke."

The naked Devourer shouted a war cry as Bix's darkness returned to him, filling him with the trash from her magic, then ending him with a revolting wet pop.

"Seek out the ones beyond the temple," Phobos demanded. "Verify this World is secure. Verify you have left yourself no weaknesses, no surprises. Do it now."

She complied without hesitation. Her actions proceeded as if by rote, as if an old habit had been renewed. There was no emotional thrill of achievement, no joy from a task completed, a lesson learned, or a test passed. Her senses stretched, seeking the additional taint of more Devourers. The numbing of her nerves didn't seem to affect her ability to hunt. She could still feel the noxious presence of a Devourer. It remained a beacon to guide her darkness.

Phobos kept close watch on her. His brows furrowed, and his lips thinned as his gaze drifted from her hair to her knees. He made no effort to toss her from his lap or hold her any closer as her darkness enveloped them in a protective shell while it tracked prey. She was a specimen being studied, and it didn't faze her in the least. A small part of her brain knew she *should* feel some kind of reaction to his scrutiny. He was teaching her how to be an executioner of all things, how to defend herself against Devourers and his own kind. She ought to be happy. Grateful, even.

Why couldn't she shake the stupor caused by the sustenance she'd taken from the Devourers? Consuming their essence had trapped her somewhere between a double dose of aspirin and a hit of morphine.

Still, her darkness continued to hunt until it located the lingering Devourers and destroyed them swiftly. With each Devourer she overfilled, the pitch painting her skin lessened and the haze of apathy thinned until, at last, she could feel *something* again. A hint of satisfaction warmed the cockles of her pitiless black heart.

No, really, her heart was warm. Warmer than the rest of her body. And Phobos was glaring at her rack. She glanced down too. A variant of an Eternal Knot glowed in green and silver across the swells of her bosom.

The knot was in the same style as the one on Tobek's chest, the knot that contained his curse of silence. The knot that brought him extreme pain whenever he attempted to communicate something about their shared past. Yet the mark upon her chest, shimmering in stark contrast to her increasingly natural skin tone, caused her no pain. If anything, it felt like reassurance, a reminder that she wasn't alone, an attagirl, a sign that someone was thinking of her fondly.

Had consuming Devourer's essence invoked it? Had killing Devourers done it? Perhaps it had nothing to do with the anti-gods. It could've been some sort of distress call from Tobek. After all, the Devourers *had* responded to her summons at the coal plant.

Shit. She needed to get back there. Now.

"I'm not the one to ask about that," Phobos said preemptively.

"No. However, I believe I am done here. Lesson learned. Trial completed." She stood and recalled her darkness, shuddering as it retracted beneath her skin, as though it'd been purified. She took a last look at the Temple of Ares, defaced with filth and dreck. Deimos reclined in a corner, flicking the black blood from his blistering cheek. He inclined his head and gave her a two-finger salute.

A shapeless woolen shift dress in charcoal gray replaced the tattered silken one that had been destroyed by anti-god blood. A parting gift from the terror twin.

Bix used gates to fetch the brothers' weapons from the ceiling. Chunks of Devourers dissolved into liquid as the spears landed at Deimos's feet and the xiphoi at Phobos's.

"Will I need these when next you summon me?" Phobos asked, surveying his weaponry.

Devourer essence had prevented her from feeling fear, from panicking. It had muted all her emotions and quelled her internal arguments. It had cleared a path for her instincts to override her brain. Those instincts belonged to the original Chimera, the monster Chimera, the monster she didn't want to become.

Yet, to survive the next memory merge without jeopardizing

the Mids, she might have to let the monster out, let it and its instincts be the thing that prevented her fear and wrath from opening gates for the Devourers to storm the Mids. But once free, could she ever return to the woman she'd been yesterday? Today? The woman with friends? The woman who *could* care about others, about protecting and defending loved ones alongside total strangers?

The risk of feasting from Devourers was second only to letting a ruthless monster roam. Her only hope was Tobek and whatever gizmo he could find to help her through the next meeting with a god too eager to return her lost memories.

Hopefully, Tobek would be restored and awake by the time she got home. Hopefully, the Devourers who'd attacked Phobos hadn't breached the gates to attack the coal plant in the process of trying to reach her. Hopefully, her fears and her ignorance hadn't caused more friends to suffer.

She bit her lip and took in the slow, slow progress of Phobos's recovery.

"Let us hope not," she whispered, "for your sake and the sake of the Mids."

Chapter 18

Bix returned to the clinic in the coal plant, bracing for the worst. On the upside, the clinic was still intact. No evidence of combat—physical or magical—smeared the polished floor or spattered the stainless-steel walls. The surgery stations were undamaged and unoccupied, as was the second mortician's table. A cube of distortion privacy gates still surrounded the table where she'd last seen Tobek and Drew.

All good…save for the chaos.

Silent alarms flashed red lights. Berserkers, eyes bright with rage, darted in and out of the clinic while others manned the few computer stations. Multiple monitors showed MWA reps from other branches alongside scrolling documents with all kinds of squiggles, hatch marks, and hieroglyphs. Gurp directed a group in the casting of complex spells. All focus was on the box of gates she'd left in place when she'd blacked out during her panic attack.

Apparently, the Berserkers were trying to undo the mess she'd left.

"She's here." The shout came from high behind her.

Trepidation wriggled through the lingering dampener left by the Devourers' essence as she turned and espied a bleary-eyed ginger genius on a ceiling-mounted monitor. His scruff said he hadn't shaved in days. Over his shoulder, a monument of canned energy drinks reflected the neon lights outside his window.

"They must be desperate if they called you in, Cian."

"What?" he shouted and grimaced. A few obvious strokes of his keyboard and the other monitors in the clinic went dark.

Cries of objection and curses in plentitude echoed off the metallic surfaces. They should have made her ears ring. Should. Didn't. With a passing thought, Bix relocated everyone from the clinic except Gurp to the Torpedo Factory on the waterfront a few miles away. It wasn't as if torpedoes were still made down there. It was an art gallery anchoring the tourist section of Old Town. The Berserkers were hardy stock and smart to boot. They'd realize the why of their circumstances rather quickly.

With her self-control still not up to snuff, she didn't want to risk harming Tobek's men when they inevitably challenged her about the gates and the Devourer attack. She didn't respond well to dudes getting aggressive in her general direction, especially when they outnumbered her. The section of her brain that housed her logic and empathy knew the guys had every right to be pissed. Sadly, that part of her brain wasn't the one directing her reactions right now. The quantity of dark gray still streaking her body confirmed it.

Gurp scrambled around the corner of the distortion box and spotted her.

"Pretty la—" The goblin stopped and blanched. Pallor with his skin tone was not a good look.

"Gurp? What's wrong?" She cocked her head and rechecked the clinic for what could possibly be worrying the goblin. There was no trace of Devourer funk.

"Four days." Gurp scratched the back of his hand, his gaze darting often to the privacy gates surrounding the table where Tobek and Drew should still have been. "Four days. Chief? Chief rise?"

"Is that what all this is about? Were you and the guys trying to bring down my gates?" She pointed to the box of distortion and the debris of futile spells scattered around it. "No Mids' magic can. I thought you knew that?"

Gurp made a pitiful little sound and hung his head.

A pang of remorse scrabbled around the part of her brain that could feel. "I'm sure that whatever state Tobek's in, he's fine."

"No signs of life from the big guy, but Devourers attacked the coal plant four days ago," Cian piped in from his remote location. "It's been all hands on deck since. Why do you look like an escapee from a zombie colony? What happened to you?"

"Had to deal with some of those Devourers," she dismissed. She didn't want to get into the details with the kid. "Why did the guys call you in? You should be at your internship."

"I was trying to get ahold of you—you know, via the tech I gave you that mysteriously went offline about an hour after I handed it over—while lending a hand here with researching spells that could connect us with Chief despite your barricade." He put a palm under his chin and pushed it to the side until his neck popped. "None of the spells worked. If you ever decide to hold him as your love slave, no one will ever find out."

"I'll…keep that in mind." She paced the edges of her gates, looking for any evidence that a Devourer had managed to breach the multiple layers she used to create the distortion. "Where did the Devourers strike, and how long did it last?"

A monitor adjacent to the one showing Cian flicked to life, playing a rather disturbing scene. The parking lot around the plant lay in ruins. Macadam jutted up and pierced down, mounds and holes. Vehicles teetered, twisted and mangled in downed trees and streetlights. The dark stains could've been motor oil or blood.

The awning over Dysmorphic hadn't been touched. The tempered-glass windows of the clinic and classroom were intact. The wards protecting the structure had held. How had Tobek known which wards would work against a Devourer? Then again, the guy was a master of research. He'd probably cooked up a homegrown bit of wizardry in the short time since they'd learned of the existence of the anti-gods. At least now she knew what he'd been doing while she'd been loitering in the out-of-time library.

"The attack lasted less than two minutes, yet they managed that much damage." Cian panned the exterior security cameras. The area of destruction had been confined to the coal plant property as if encountering some sort of containment field. "I think these guys scared them off."

Another monitor awakened and displayed a looped feed of two very familiar bellicose gods, Ares and Deimos. The exterior attack must have happened while Phobos had been inside the gates fending off the other Devourers who had answered her summons. Ares laughed with the thrill of the kill. Deimos appeared his usual unchipper self.

"A little father-son bonding there. So touching and unusual for gods." She crossed her hands over her warm heart.

Warm heart.

Probably ought to do something about that, like maybe learn if that was Tobek's distress call.

"To confirm, no one and nothing made it inside the building? Nothing escaped this box of gates I built? No strangers in the clinic, no magic at play other than what was done under your guidance, Gurp?" She glanced at the goblin, whose shoulders slumped ever farther forward.

"Not that any of their systems picked up," Cian answered, wiping orange cheese dust on his grease-stained shirt. "I checked in once the alarms triggered. Just so you know, my roommate hasn't shown in four days either. Should I be worried?"

"Time to find out, I guess." Now that she'd confirmed no one and nothing had gotten past her passive defenses, she dropped the gates. The stench of decay blasted the room.

"Nice of you to come back for us, Bixie." Drew sighed, wriggling out from his hiding place under the table. Rot had taken hold of the young boy's corpse he was wearing, yet the body moved with the admirable dexterity of the draugr inside it.

The charbroiled Berserker? He was anything but. A massage-style folded sheet granted Tobek modesty. His full arm was folded behind his head. His long, inkless legs crossed at the ankles. And on his heavily tatted chest, the matching Eternal Knot glowed in shades of teal and midnight. His vibrant blue eyes snapped to her, then jerked away, fixating on the ceiling. He made no effort to get up.

Gurp rushed to the table with a delighted squeal, unfazed by Drew's smell. The goblin's rapid chittering elicited a small chuckle from Tobek. She left those two to their reunion and faced the monitors.

"Cian, your roommate will be home shortly after he gets a new body," she assured the kid. "Thank you for bringing me up to speed on all that transpired in my absence."

"Yeah, sure." Cian rubbed his eyes and blinked rapidly. "That other project you have me working on? I have an inkling and should know for sure within a day or two. If I'm right, we have a ginormous problem."

"How ginormous?" Bix struggled to quash her instinct's reaction, to calm her darkness before it lashed out at Cian's vague caution. "Are we talking the sort where you've been compromised, or the sort that makes what happened at this compound look like a minor incident?"

"Both," the kid huffed. "Pretty sure my new boss is on to me."

"We'll come up with a CYA plan in the morning." Drew plucked bits of charred Berserker from his shirt.

"Cool." Cian glanced over his shoulder and leaned forward. "FYI, there are some shady guys hanging at the Thai restaurant across the street. Like, shadier than the usual clientele. I think they killed one of my CWIG guards. The one who was posing as the building super."

"You don't say," Bix drawled, glaring at Drew. "Any of the randos have black eyes?"

"Um, maybe?" Cian stifled a huge yawn, the resiliency of youth waning after being on station for the four days since the attack. "It could as easily be the bad lighting at the restaurant. I didn't get close enough to verify. The whole 'don't stare' thing got drilled into me pretty early."

"That's my ball to chase. I'll be home soon, herb nerd." Drew sniffed and eyed Bix. "I'm happy to see you, Bixie, always. Do me a favor, though? When you go home, take a look in the mirror and don't forget what I said to you when we started this mission."

Bix searched her memory and came up with the caution, the fear her best friend had had about losing her to the reemergence of the original Chimera. She snorted, grateful for once that the stupor of Devourer essence hadn't completely faded lest she succumb to another panic attack.

"This, coming from someone who wants me to take 'one horrible, awful hit just once' so it's easier for *you* to deal?" Bix put her hands on her hips.

"That was never what I meant," Drew argued. "If you want to choose your dosage, that's fine. I'm still going to get the product in stock, in case you change your mind."

By "product," he meant insane gods. Drew was so wedded to his harebrained scheme that he didn't see the huge flaw. Fortunately, *feeding* from a Devourer had buried the fear crippling Bix's thoughts, so *she* could think clearly. The emotional resistance to reclaiming all her memories at once was gone. However, she still had plenty of logical reasons why a batch draw was not going to happen. Despite her BFF's insistence.

"Better check that impulsive streak of yours, Drew," she cautioned. "Storage is going to be a problem for you and your product. Plus, it seems you've painted your own bull's-eye on the kid you're supposed to be looking after."

Before Drew could argue, she dumped him in his preferred hospital morgue that had the freshest corpses with the widest selection.

"If all's good again, I'm going to finally get some sleep," Cian said through another yawn.

"There's an Afghani joint not far from you that delivers. I suggest you develop a new craving, yeah? And keep an extra eye on Onyeka and her dad. A friendly eye. They're the only other non-

Chweds in your building." Bix glanced at her discolored hands. "You might find their situation becoming increasingly common on your block."

Cian gave her two thumbs-up, then rotated them down as he ended the video chat. The other monitors in the clinic brightened, the spinning MWA logo on their screens.

"Gurp, why don't you head downstairs and get the altar ready? She and I will be there soon." Tobek's rough rumble cut through the quiet settling in the clinic.

Gurp nodded and patted Tobek's shoulder.

"Do you want the express trip?" Bix offered the goblin.

Gurp shook his head as he kept a wide berth of her, then scampered out the door.

"That's unexpected." She pouted as she closed the heavy door to the clinic. Locks slammed into place. She glowered at the red light still flashing its alarm. "Care to do the honors of muting your surveillance system? I don't think your men will react well if I do it again."

"Big black button by the door shuts down the mics. The lockbox surrounding it shouldn't be a problem for you."

It wasn't, but the fact that Tobek had yet to *move* could be perceived as a problem.

"Do you need a block and tackle to help you up?"

"Is that really the question you want to ask me?"

She ambled to his side. The glow of his knot was fading, as was hers. She traced his with her fingertips, waiting for him to look at her. He seemed determined not to, resolutely staring at the ceiling.

"Why do we have a matching set?"

"You know I can't answer that."

"Bullshit." She laid her palm flat against the skin her darkness had protected from burning in the subcity. "You *chose* to embrace the pain of being fried alive, yet you *refuse* to do the same to answer my questions."

He sighed, still not looking at her. "If the only thing your curse did to me was cause me pain, we could call it foreplay as we talked for hours, now couldn't we?"

"We can't discuss foreplay when you can't bear to look at me."

"Because when you look like that, sweetheart, it brings to mind some difficult memories that are more than my heart can bear at the moment." The admission caused his curse to flare in angry blisters. He grunted and winced, but didn't rush to heal himself as he usually did.

"You don't have to admit when you're disgusted. It shows on your face, just like it did in the subcity when you learned I'd fed from a Devourer." She studied the lines of gunmetal gray that still stained her nails, joints, and veins. "I'm not sure what causes it, though. My choice of fuel source, or the color of my skin?"

"Not disgust. Concern," he corrected with an uncharacteristic lash to his tone as he adjusted his arm beneath his head. "Do you know every single man in my battalion has been on the frontlines more than their fair share? Things they've seen, things they've done, things they've had to endure and survive…it all has an effect. Some of the men can push through and come out the other side stronger for their scars. Others suffer deeper wounds that don't heal. It's not a flaw of the individual. It is simply a reality, twice so when there is only one way we can leave the army."

"Helmet on rifle," Bix murmured, referencing the Battlefield Cross.

"Right." He thrust his jaw forward, then to the side. "Returning from a campaign isn't like coming back from holiday. There is shit you've *got* to deal with. There are men who do so by acting out via overt aggressions, brawls, and beatings. Then there are those who seek to smother through pills, alcohol, and magic. Regardless of the path, each step is a necessary part of the process of finding the way to a new normal. But those steps are fraught with danger, personal and private dangers, that can easily create more problems than they solve. Spiraling self-destructive behaviors start with a desperate search for control of self and their environs, then manifest in repetitive thoughts and actions, increasing isolation and greater of loss of control."

Bix stiffened, disbelieving what she was hearing. "If you think it's any different for a clandestine operative, you're abso-fucking-lutely right. Soldiers get to fall back on their army family, the family who has been through the same shit in the same foxhole. They're allowed to talk amongst themselves about the horrors. Whether or not they choose to is on them. Don't get me wrong, I know you guys are big fans of the machismo thing and bottling everything up. But you have the resources to get help. The army *wants* you to get better. Spooks are expected to bite the poison pill so our secrets die with us. Management would rather put us down than fix us up."

"Addiction is one of the worst destroyers of good men and women," he rasped, seemingly dismissing her argument. "The worst of the worst is the addiction to things that create a state of numbness."

"You sanctimonious son of a bitch," she seethed with an anger hot enough to blast through her stupor. "The knot on my chest, it allows you to know what I'm feeling, doesn't it? It's not me battling Devourers that invokes it. Something about my state of disaffectedness triggers it."

"I've lost a lot of friends to addiction, sweetheart. Not going to let you be among them."

She jabbed a finger where his knot lay inert. "What about your addiction to pain, eh? Your addiction to riding the edge of death? Just because you can't die doesn't mean that repetitive behavior and that relentless desire are not fucking you up, and your relationships with other people along with them."

With preternatural speed, he pinned her hand to his chest with his lone hand. The brightness of his eyes betrayed his anger as they held hers. "At least I know my demons."

"I'm not a demon, Tobek, I'm a monster," she purred, leaning over him ever so slowly and holding his glowing gaze while her lips grazed the outer hairs of his mustache. His breath was fresh like charcoal and wintergreen mint. His heart thundered under her hand. "I'm not an addict either, and you don't know me anymore."

A sound like a feral wounded beast escaped him as they fought a battle of glares and stares. She refused to yield and so did he. Unfortunately for him, the dimming of his eyes betrayed the ebbing of his Berserker's rage.

She snatched her hand out from under his and smirked as she straightened. "I win."

"Hope so." He ran his hand over his mouth and jaw, his easy grin resurfacing. "If you have no more challenges for me, I need to get to my altar and reestablish the spells that were erased when the Fates reset this body."

Her lips formed a small circle as realization slapped her upside the head. "That's why Gurp watches over you like a hawk. You're weakened in this state."

"Vulnerable. I am vulnerable in this state," he corrected as if weakness was more distasteful. "When I signed my contract with the Fates, I knew an infinitesimal amount of what I know now. There are things both of my person and of public welfare that rely on me at my peak. Though I enjoy spending all the time I can with you, even when we bicker, I do need to get to getting."

"Right." She stomped her feet and planted her hands on her hips, physically grounding herself as more emotions crept toward accessibility. "Express pass or would you rather take the stairs like your terrified goblin?"

"Allow Gurp his trepidations. His experience with your darkness hasn't always been positive." Tobek sat up and swung his legs over the side of the mortician's table, holding the sheet over his lap. "I, however, would thank you for the expedient route. I would also recommend you head for the shower. There is a pot of what looks like gold glitter in the bathroom cabinet. It'll slough off the abundant layers of conflicting magics' residues in which you are covered."

"Ew, not again." She wrinkled her nose. After the kill school with Phobos, getting clean sounded delightful. Then she had a spider to see about a ship's manifest. She didn't want to think about what she and her darkness had done to poor Gurp pre-memory-wipe. She couldn't imagine hurting him, not on purpose at least. Never that.

"For the record, sweetheart, you shouldn't put too much credence into how historians cast your role in the Mids." Tobek massaged the scars of his amputation. "Most were on the payroll of your enemies."

"Yeah, well, when you're done playing in the altar room, I'd like to give a few of those memory gewgaws a try. I'm not keen to tempt the Fates, not on this topic."

She wasn't worried about becoming addicted to the Devourer brand of painkiller; her concern was suppressing the original Chimera. Just saying no to Devourer essence allowed her to stay in control...at least until her next date with a god carrying her memories.

Chapter 19

None of the memory spells, artifacts, or charms had yielded anything more than a headache. While Tobek and Gurp renewed their search, Bix headed to a long overdue date with a spider.

In the hollowed summit of a colossal red monolith, six stories of sweeping tooth-tiled rooftops held aloft by thick columns and carved lintels made of bleached bones nestled in an idyll of white vegetation imported from myriad Mid Worlds. Flora of every imaginable texture and shape were represented in carefully planned garden installations. Sylphs played on swings of blooming garlands, churning a fragrant breeze while sprites and pixies tended to the grounds. Inky water threaded through the landscaping and the main structure. Pearl bridges offered the illusion of safe crossings. During the day, sunlight refracting off the monolith bathed the ⎯⎯⎯or of the jorōgumo in dappled shades of red. Once the sun set, the all-white estate lit up like a fairy tale in pastel shades of the rainbow.

Bix vastly preferred the view at night.

Optics held immense value in the Crimson Market. No expense had been spared in the familial seat of the spider-shifter syndicate. Cutting-edge technology blended seamlessly with millennia-old traditional décor. While the main house may have looked minimally occupied, guards were stationed every six feet in gossamer webs out of sight. White drapes of spider silk danced in the open spaces where modular bone walls had been slid aside to welcome the cool evening.

Bix's heels clacked on the lacquered white floors, announcing her arrival. Out of courtesy, she entered on the main level, the one intended to receive prominent business leaders and affluent debtors. The beauty was in the simplicity that so well disguised the danger. Knowing Yukiko's voracious appetite, Bix didn't envy the servants who had to keep all this white pristine.

"Bix, to what do I owe the pleasure?" Yukiko descended the atrium on a thread of silk, shifting from her colossal spider form into her far smaller humanoid shape.

"You said to use the front door." Bix gestured to wall-less open space. "Since the problem in our old neighborhood has been resolved, I'm hoping for a thorough look at those records you promised."

"Your swift response to our issue was noted by all the syndicates. I believe that earns you unlimited grace. In the Crimson Market, that could prove useful, even for the Chimera." Yukiko held out a delicate hand. "The records you requested are upstairs in my office."

Bix clasped Yukiko's forearm without hesitation. The jorōgumo partially shifted her form so that her torso remained that of a woman and everything below her waist was that of a very large spider. Yukiko's front legs bound their arms together in spider silk. The jorōgumo paused and tilted her head.

"What?" Bix chuckled.

"Anyone else would be screaming in terror." Yukiko smiled fleetingly, or perhaps it was a wince. Perhaps it was both.

Bix snorted. "Anyone else would be having their flesh eaten away because of the toxin you produce."

This time, Yukiko truly smirked. "True."

The jorōgumo raised her free hand to one of the interior

balconies on the top floor and shot a stream of silk that coalesced around the traditional web-styled carvings of the railings. They ascended with a speed that defied expectations. Bix giggled as she zipped through the air, the currents rippling through her hair and dress. Yukiko swung them over the railings of the fifth floor, laughing.

"It has been so long since I've made that trip without someone weeping." Yukiko sliced the webbing binding them together, freeing Bix from her hold.

"I have fond memories of flying with you." Bix took in the plush décor of the upstairs. The white shag carpeting. The white leather-wrapped interior columns. The fine paintings beneath thick, thick clear coat. "Some gals roll up in fancy cars to impress a date. You took me swinging above the rooftops of the subcity."

"And you used to sing that infernal cartoon theme song whenever I did it." Yukiko smiled and motioned for Bix to follow her.

"I'd change the lyrics each time to see if you were paying attention."

"I always paid attention to you." Yukiko glanced over her shoulder, raking Bix with a rueful gaze. "That's how you caught me."

Bix's heels made no sound, and it wasn't just because of the carpet. Noise-dampening spells were in play. One part privacy, one part trap, one part necessity. It was the last part that niggled at Bix's mind.

"Yukiko, you're a woman of great renown," Bix hedged.

"In certain circles." Yukiko entered a room occupying the entire northern side of the building. Floor-to-ceiling white cabinet doors with the painted histories of the jorōgumo lined the interior walls. A long glass table with thirteen lethal chairs occupied the center of the room. There were plants in the corners and a fountain on the exterior balcony. The drapes had been tied back to encourage the breeze to come indoors.

"You've trained emperors, warriors, scholars, and even me."

Bix moved a plant off its ceramic stand and pulled the stand up to the long table, kicking a death-trap chair out of the way. "You've outlived protégés, friends, allies, civilizations…"

"I have been blessed." Yukiko opened one of the lacquered doors, exposing tomes and scrolls alongside external hard drives. She retrieved one of those drives and plugged it into the table. The touchscreen glass displayed millions of tiny spiders crawling across its surface. Yukiko had a keyboard and a bioscanner at her end of the table. She paused and eyed Bix's perch. With a snort and a shake of her head, she resumed logging into her network. "Is there a reason you are dancing around your questions?"

Bix scratched where her scars used to be on her forearm. "What do you do when your friends, true friends who have proven themselves time and again, flinch when you reach for them?"

Yukiko kept typing, and the images on the table kept changing. "Is this about the change in your appearance?"

Bix huffed. "A few hours ago, more of me was much darker. I'm uncertain if their reactions are about what I am or about who I used to be."

"True friends don't fear you." Yukiko laced her hands on the table and held Bix's gaze. "External events don't change the friendship. True friends don't always have to like you, but they never act against you. True friends are confident in themselves, in their relationship with you, and in your mutual respect for one another. True friendship allows for the individuals to grow, accommodates the growth, and encourages the growth."

"Even when the growth is into something they don't want you to become?"

"True friends understand that your evolution is not theirs to decide. They will either support you or they will move on with no animosity. Most relationships, even in an average lifespan, will be temporary. The challenge is in learning to let go with grace and in a timely manner." Yukiko leaned forward. "In our line of work, if it's any consolation, true friends will never be the ones you have to kill."

Bix grunted and considered the advice. Gurp's avoidance of her still festered. She'd thought of him as a true friend, reveled in the way he showered her with his affection. Maybe that was where she'd gotten confused. Affection wasn't friendship, it wasn't respect; it wasn't rooted, anchored, or tethered to anything more than one person's desire to engage in a positive manner. Some people were just wired to be kind. Gurp was that sort of wonderful being. He more than deserved her respect for his boundaries. Even if it did sting.

"These are the records you wanted. You'll forgive me for not providing you with your own copy, but the family business is mine to protect." Yukiko tapped the table, and the screens in front of Bix illuminated with handwritten and typed texts. "Also, I'd offer you refreshments, but I recall your preferences are a bit obscure."

"Thank you. At this point, what I need most is your patience and your insight." Bix called up the files, watching as a virtual translator turned the pictorial language into one she could read. Cian would make sense of all this data in two breaths and an overcaffeinated burp, so would Ashtad for that matter, but Yukiko wouldn't let them near this place, much less this information.

"Take all the time you need," Yukiko urged. "It's been ten years. Those records aren't going to change. I'll leave you to it. If you need me, call out."

Bix smiled and waved as Yukiko left. Alone with the data, Bix set her hands on the table and smirked as teensy needles embedded at random spots in the glass attempted to pierce her skin. This may have been Yukiko's office, but between the man-eating chairs and the porcupine tabletop, the jorōgumo did not trust the people she allowed in here. Knowing Yukiko, venom coated the needles that were also used to draw blood for DNA verification. If the meeting went well, the final offer of tea would contain antivenin. If not...

There were times she missed life among the super-paranoid syndicate.

Reminiscing aside, Samael had asked her to check the records for Isoba the Shadow Caster and any of his associates. He'd also said the spiders had been Isoba's supplier for generations. She set to type the Shadow Caster's name into a search box but paused.

Keystroke recordings.

Yukiko might not have been in the room with her, but the jorōgumo was absolutely monitoring everything Bix did. If Yukiko believed Bix was going after one of the syndicate's best customers, there could be problems, starting with missing data. Yes, yes, the jorōgumo had promised complete access and full cooperation, but Bix wasn't born yesterday. Bix's bonus skill set was not in tech; it was in understanding the motivations underpinning contracts. Those motivations allowed for loopholes. Without knowing Yukiko's personal feelings toward Isoba, those loopholes could be quite bountiful. Yukiko had a weak spot for smart guys; they became protégés or dessert. No in-between.

Shifting her strategy to one that accommodated third-party observations, Bix started her query with a cursory sort-by date. Her interest spanned the weeks bracketing Fymmi's arrival on the ship. The supermax facility had taken the whole ship. Any Undine prisoner who'd met the Consortium's criteria as an exceptionally awful yet useful creation would be someone with whom Bix and her team might have to contend during the breakout. It'd be stupid and careless not to plan for the worst while the intel was right in front of her.

The records reached back to the eras before the last three cyclical Great Wars. Yukiko had been at the helm of the spider syndicate for ten years, but her family had established the contract with the Undine millennia before. Good to know that when the apocalypse came, roaches and spiders would survive.

Cutting away the excess months and years caused a suspension of delivery notice to pop up beside the records: *Select vessels in the Undine navy departing World for six months. Deliveries to resume upon fleet return.*

Poor Undine bastards probably had genuinely believed they'd come back from supermax, blend in with fleet maneuvers on another World, then return home with no one the wiser. The

Undine royal family had learned a painful lesson about asking the Consortium for help.

Within her selected timeframe were the records of four hundred persons. One hundred crew. Those she discarded. The Consortium had no use for standup seamen or even measurably corrupt ones. That left three hundred prisoners, fifty of whom were off book. A three-to-one ratio of prisoners to crew. Not every crewman was a guard. Some of them had to sail the ship. The ratio probably wasn't bad; however, Chwedlonol guilds often sent their worst to the Undine as did the syndicates. The Undine's royal coffers had been filled by being a private prison provider for all kinds of governments and organizations. That they'd never suffered a prison break spoke to the power of the Chwedlonol upper caste to which the Undine belonged.

It'd be far more convenient to discard the two-hundred-fifty prisoners who'd been legit inmates, but if Isoba was as tricky as Samael believed, he could be among the greater number. That meant Bix had to familiarize herself with all three hundred inmates. Oh boy. Good thing she'd eaten and slept before she'd arrived.

Hours passed unchecked as Bix learned the details of the three hundred inmates, from their time aboard ship, what they bought from the syndicate, how often they ordered what goods, how they'd paid for those goods. The catch, and of course there was one, was the absence of prisoner names and photographs. Every prisoner was a number. It was simultaneously a pain in Bix's ass yet useful. Bix couldn't judge a prisoner by his, her, or its looks. She had to rely on the information provided. It was kind of like being back at the CWIG academy.

Prisoner records illuminated the entire conference table, sorted sixteen ways from Sunday. Bix paced around the table, sliding displays here and there like a grand jigsaw puzzle. She'd pause, perch, then pace again. Moving, resorting, reexamining.

Now, Bix knew from her team's failed attempt to rescue Fymmi, the exact date Fymmi had been brought aboard. There had been five inmates processed that day. Two of whom were off book. Those two went in Bix's Keep pile. Based on her experience with the Consortium and cross-referenced with notes in each prisoner file, she'd narrowed down the number of prisoners who were either Isoba or his associates to twenty-seven possibilities.

At best, the Consortium had added all those prisoners to their menagerie. It'd only cost them three hundred and seventy-three lives. A bargain from their perspective for sure.

"If you ask, I might be able to help," Yukiko cajoled softly, snapping Bix from her studies.

Bix rubbed her eyes. Sunlight slunk around the edges of the bone exterior walls that had been closed at some point. Similarly, Yukiko had changed clothes, looking every bit the businesswoman from chignon to silk blouse and pencil skirt. The jorōgumo leaned against one of the lacquered cabinets, a steaming cup of tea in her hand.

"Have I been here all night?"

Yukiko inclined her head. "All morning too. It's getting on midday. I'm not here to rush you, merely to offer assistance."

"I need the photos and names for these twenty-seven customers." Bix slid the digital packets she'd created to the end of the table.

Yukiko passed a disinterested glance over the files. "Why do their names matter? They're all dead."

"No records withheld, no hesitations to fulfill my requests no matter how irrelevant they seem." Bix studied Yukiko a bit closer. Something was off about the jorōgumo. "Those were the terms of our deal."

Yukiko swept Bix with cool regard but laid one hand on the table. The keyboard appeared beneath the jorōgumo's fingers, and she began typing.

"While you're at it, you can explain your frosty demeanor," Bix drawled. "It's not like I disrupted your sleep with my snoring."

"We've had an influx of satyrs to the market, picking fights, nosing about, buying nothing but a few rooms for an indefinite stay. Musicians mostly, with a rock-star complex. Not our usual clientele."

Bix massaged her temple, trying to help her brain shift gears. "And you think my love of music has summoned them here?"

"I will ask you one more time," Yukiko said with a lash to her tone. "Is the Chimera planning on entering the provider business?"

Bix laughed. Real, unaffected laughter. Oh gods, of all the absurdities. "Yukiko, I am neck-deep trying to expel Other World invaders from the Mids. I have neither the time nor the patience to deal with the mewling demands of entitled addicts and despots."

The jorōgumo stood straighter and her chin rose, eyes flashing. "Invaders? That's what all this is about? With the prison ship?"

"They're taking the slow approach to acquiring territory. I believe you, more than most, are familiar with that process."

"And how long it takes to do without anyone noticing, yes, that particular skill is a requirement for rising in the ranks of the syndicate." Yukiko swiped her hand across the table, and hundreds and hundreds of images filled the long screen before sorting and shuffling themselves into the respective files. "Bix, next time, just be straight with me. I believe our timelines have crossed again for a reason, and that reason is simple. You helped me rise to my place of power. It is my turn to do the same for you."

Bix didn't know what to say. Her mouth moved a lot. No words came out.

"Yes, you're welcome." Yukiko chuckled. "Every image we have of the twenty-seven inmates you've flagged. Their personal backgrounds. Criminal records. Known associates. Particularly those persons who betrayed them. Family members. Real estate. Holdings. Assets. Wills and beneficiaries. Tell me what other information I can give you."

"Isoba," Bix said baldly.

Yukiko didn't hesitate; she slid Isoba's file down the table to Bix. "He's a real piece of work. His father was a grifter who amassed magic by stealing it from fetuses after he drugged the mother. Isoba took his father's proclivities to another level, thus inspiring H. G. Wells to create Dr. Moreau. My aunt delighted in providing him supplies. Due to his practices, he had to move often, which meant we were paid handsomely to reestablish his network each time. I had the relo job at least a dozen times. He and I had a set-to more than once whenever he decided to use my delivery people as science projects loosed in the field."

Bix opened the file, and the first photo to greet her was that of a hideous patchwork man of indeterminable race. Extra appendages appeared to have been grafted to his torso. The eyes weren't right for the skull, nor did they match. If she stared hard enough, she could sort of spot the vestiges of a once-handsome man beneath all the implants. "Definitely not a face a mother could love, much less recognize."

"Isoba was an egomaniac. He believed himself an equal of the creationist superpowers. Better in many cases, and he craved that recognition. He eventually got it, which is how he ended up getting caught by the Angelic Host." Yukiko shook her head. "We thought he was dead, but he reached out to my aunt not long before you left us. When I took control of the syndicate, I cut him off. He went to the other syndicates, his reputation preceding him. They too refused him. His muscle decided to wreck a significant portion of the market to demonstrate his displeasure. That earned both of them a direct trip to the Undine prison ship."

"Sounds like he couldn't keep his pet on a leash," Bix snorted. "Who was his muscle?"

"Tashka, a troubled girl known to many of us in the market from back when she was just learning to walk." Yukiko slid a second digital packet to Bix. "Her foster parents worked for Isoba's father. His father used to bring Tashka here to test her skills. The girl was amazingly powerful but couldn't control her magic or herself. Eventually, she killed her foster parents and an entire village during a tantrum."

"That's when Isoba got his hands on her?" Bix opened the second folder. Her breath seized. Heterochromatic eyes. Vulpine features. Flawless skin.

Fymmi.

Isoba's second was Fymmi? Shit. No wonder Fymmi hadn't told her CWIG handler the name of the buyer. The mission had turned personal. Based on Samael's description of Isoba, the patchwork man was not the sort to fuck around—bomb grid being a prime example. Fymmi had likely known the explicit danger Isoba represented and hadn't wanted a CWIG team to fall victim. Bix couldn't blame Fymmi for making that call. Not one bit. Too bad the CWIG had assumed the worst of its agent.

"Isoba and his father had done their damage to the poor girl long before then." Yukiko gestured with her teacup at the file Bix was perusing. "Check the pictures. They'd had that muting collar made for her, then had it fused to her body. Sadly, her mind was so broken by their cruelty that even with her magic restrained, she was still a terrible force."

Most of the pictures were of Fymmi when she was a girl, not yet a young woman. In those pictures, Fymmi wore an engraved brass collar that grew from her clavicle and cupped her jaw. Another picture showed the long tail of the collar, bolted into Fymmi's spine.

The cloaking tech.

It wasn't at all visible in the pictures of Fymmi as an adult. Somewhere between magic and mutation, her body had absorbed it. Getting that out of Fymmi was going to be a huge problem

"Her parents let Isoba and his father do this to their child?" Bix grimaced, trying to imagine the agony Fymmi had endured for the sake of that tech. "No wonder she lost her shit and killed them."

"When word of the family's death reached the market, the trolls went looking for Tashka." Yukiko looked away, her gaze distant. "Taking pity on her, they put her on an uninhabited World where she couldn't hurt anyone."

"Uninhabited Worlds are rarely uninhabited. They're usually testing grounds of the Consortium for all kinds of weird sciences and new races." Bix shook her head. "An abandoned feral child with uncontrollable lethal magic, that's the best kind of toy to a bored immortal."

Yukiko nodded. "She became a fearless gladiator, taught and tormented by whatever existed on that World. The trolls would visit every now and then, bringing peace offerings, only to be frightened away. Then there came the day they couldn't find her. Spent months combing that World for her, yet she'd somehow escaped. The leader of the troll syndicate collapsed in the market square upon seeing her in the company of Isoba after all those years."

Tashka had vanished, all right; she'd become Fymmi, one of the CWIG's best agents, fighting on the side of good. Well, relative good. Whichever god had found her on that uninhabited World must have taught her how to harness her pain and hate into a fierce drive to protect strangers from suffering what she had. Bix could relate.

"Any of these other candidates an associate of Isoba or his father?" Bix gestured to the remaining twenty-five folders.

Yukiko swiped through the digital records. "No. Isoba would have considered all of them far beneath him. Wait, these few, these he used as parts. They were well on their way to dying before the ship vanished. I doubt the Undine exerted any effort to save them."

"So, twenty," Bix murmured.

"Twenty what? Twenty dead criminals who at one point or another reigned at the top of their respective games only to be hustled off to a prison ship that sank in foreign seas?" Yukiko shook her head as her brows drew together. "How does this help your fight against inva—"

"Mistress, forgiveness." A breathless spider shifter slid to his knees and pressed his brow to the floor.

Yukiko grunted. "Speak."

"There is an issue in the square," he gasped. "Our guards are unable to quell it."

"The satyrs?" Yukiko sighed, giving Bix a long-suffering roll of her eyes.

"Yes, mistress." He nodded vigorously. "And the imps."

The imps and the satyrs. Bix should've caught it earlier. *A Midsummer's Night Dream*. Shakespeare.

"I believe I can be of assistance." Bix snickered and held out her hand to Yukiko. "Shall we go together?"

The jorōgumo wiped the data from the table display, then handed her teacup to her messenger. With a broad smile, Yukiko placed her hand in Bix's.

"It would be my honor, *Chimera*."

Chapter 20

Mids' native magic surged in bursts, batting at Bix as she and Yukiko cleared the second gate by the Lorelei's fountain in the public square of the Crimson Market. Yukiko's shifters rushed to flank her as she and Bix stepped over the fallen bodies of market security from four of the five syndicates. Shoppers, vendors, and workers had all retreated to the perimeters. Crowds pushed and shoved in clogged alleyways and entrances to the towers, some wanting a better view while others wanted protection.

In the middle of the square, a gangly imp faced off against a bulky satyr.

At least the brawlers *looked* like an imp and a satyr. Little wonder the syndicates' security had thought it would be easy to subdue them. However, the native magic the brawlers exuded belonged to an angel and a dragon. Lower ranks. Foot soldiers. As the Archangel Samael had predicted, the royal dragons had sent protection to the market incognito. He'd similarly predicted the street brawling between his choir and the dragons. Natural nemeses couldn't let the other coexist in peace for the greater good.

The destruction around them said they could not care less for the Chweds they were endangering. Chweds they were supposed to be protecting. The brawlers moved with such speed that their actions defied sight. The mess they left in their wake proved their presence. Every time they separated, each bore physical damage, but nothing as bad as their surroundings.

Typical superpowers. Blinded by ego.

Bix glanced at Yukiko, who studied the fracas with narrowed eyes. "May I?"

"I have a feeling none of this is as it seems, so please do as you will." The jorōgumo gestured for Bix to proceed.

Darkness surged from Bix's spine, blanketing the whole square in premature night. Yukiko inhaled sharply but wisely stood very still. Bix expected chaos in the face of her darkness, but the Chweds among the onlookers hit the decks and stayed down.

Still, the brawlers persisted.

Tentacles moved faster than the fighters, grabbing them and all their kith peppered among the gathering. In a blink, every faux imp and fake satyr was pinned to the walls of the towers by unyielding darkness.

"Satyrs and imps, you will cease this primitive display of your lack of self-control." Bix didn't raise her voice while she studied the underside of her manicure, her nails slowly regaining their normal hue as the fuel of the Devourers continued to wane. "You will recall your duties or you will be removed from existence permanently. This is your only warning."

Some of the superminions were dumb enough to try to resist her, and they were dispatched to the ether forthwith. The remainder wised up quickly, ceasing their writhing. One by one, they raised their hands above their heads in the universal sign of surrender. She held them in place until their heartbeats slowed their frenetic paces.

Native magic surged to her left. Bix readied for an attack, then laughed to herself when she spotted the source.

The public gateway crackled, then glowed. A long-eared imp stepped through the gate followed by…Ashtad? Next through was a middle-aged woman in running gear in the company of Cian, who apparently owned a dress shirt, tie, and slacks. A half-dozen imps trailed behind them. The party drew up sharply, gazes swiftly assessing the paralyzed state of the market. Cian was the only one who marveled and grinned. When he spotted Bix, his eyes widened to saucers. He made to step toward her, but the woman at his side held him back.

The genderless imp leading the pack tromped forward; its thick, hooked toenails scraped along the ground. The trident tip of its long lizard-like tail poked and jabbed at the air, keeping anyone from wanting to get close. It stopped at the first pile of street rubble and licked its pointy teeth. Bright yellow eyes cut to the captives still pinned to the towers.

"Shakespeare?" it asked in a voice of high pitch and phlegmy distortion.

Bix curled a finger over her lips, desperately trying to stifle the laughter exploding within her. Behold, the Archangel Samael in his guise as the syndicate leader. Angels as imps. Of all the races he could have chosen to impersonate. So. Many. Comments.

"The Chimera has granted those willing to learn from their mistakes a second chance," Yukiko answered in Bix's stead.

The imp swept a grand bow in Bix's direction. "We are ever grateful for the mercy of the Chimera. Perhaps she will permit us to atone through repairs of all we have ruined?"

"I leave the justice of the market to its leadership," Bix managed with a mostly even tone. "For now."

Darkness sorted the imps from the satyrs and set them down at opposite ends of the square. Both parties had the grace to hang their heads. Satisfied, Bix recalled her darkness, allowing the late-day sun to once again blast its tinted red rays through the market. Ashtad caught her eye and jerked his head as life reanimated in the streets, stalls, and towers.

Bix turned to Yukiko. "Thank you again for all your help."

The jorōgumo smiled. "I have never seen you do that before. Like all Chwedlonol, I had heard the stories of sudden night and shadows coming alive, vivisecting whole armies where they stood.

It is magnificent to see its might and restraint firsthand."

Bix's cheeks burned. "Glad I didn't frighten you."

"Hitting the deck was my first inclination, but I trust you." Yukiko's knowing gaze flicked to Ashtad, Cian, and the woman waiting patiently for Bix to join them. "Remember what I said about true friends, Bix. They never fear you. They are confident in their relationship to and with you. Only one of those three fits that category. Be careful."

With that, the jorōgumo turned her attention to her fallen guards and the damage to her property. Bix headed for Ashtad, who swept her with a questioning look.

"You okay?" he asked, assessing her from head to toe.

"This is the afterglow of leveling up my defender skills." She studied the woman standing with Cian, noting the hint of blue around the nail and the lack of moisture in the eyes. Drew. In a new suit. Well, that explained...nothing really. "Are *you* guys okay?"

"Let's go with 'we were invited,' eh?" Drew eyed the imps still guarding them.

"Someone's deviation from the plan seems to have followed her home. Now she wakes up to find them in her bedroom," Ashtad taunted in painfully polite tones.

"Bite me, Sparky," Drew countered, all saccharine sweetness.

"Hey." Cian shuffled into their little group, closing the gap, his grin firmly in place. "This is it? This is the actual market, right? So much cooler than the virtual one."

"You stay close," Drew chided, unrolling Cian's sleeves and rebuttoning the cuffs. "From the sprites to the trolls, everyone here would give their left nut to steal a Sage. The smarter ones will go the other route and try to curry favor with you in order to reach Bix. That's why I didn't want you here."

"They didn't give us a choice." He stuffed his hands in his pockets.

"Hands out of your pockets when you're wearing dress pants. Otherwise, you look like you're playing with yourself." Drew smacked the kid's arm.

Cian rolled his eyes but removed his hands from his pockets.

Ashtad hid his smile in his palm as he rubbed his cheek. "She's been clucking over him all the way to the gate."

"Chimera." Samael turned sharply from addressing his cowed choir. A few more choice words in a guttural language directed at his disguised fallen angels, then he lumbered to Bix's side. "You tell her?"

"Not here," Ashtad scoffed.

"We'll do this at my place." Samael pointed a sharp metallic nail at one of the towers. "Frick and Frack blew the doors off the subcity, so it's hardly private anymore. You'll have to hoof it up the tower, Chimera. Think your stilts can make it up the stairs?"

The glib comment died on her tongue. This was the Crimson Market, and she was the Chimera with thousands of eyes upon her. Much like Samael, there was a certain image she had to maintain. She curled a lip and raked the angel-turned-imp with all the disdain she felt for his native race, while she mentally tested five destination gates. Four vibrated with readiness.

Samael's eyes narrowed, and his tail whipped.

Gates moved Ashtad, Drew, Cian, and their imp guards. Tittering and whispers bubbled up from the onlookers. Bix and Samael engaged in a staring match. At length, he looked down and away. Satisfied with his performance, Bix moved with him through gates.

Bix waited while Samael calmed his queasiness as she closed the gates to what had once been the serpent syndicate's war room in the southwest tower of the Crimson Market. The angels hadn't changed it that much. It was still one big circular chamber with a central stairwell up to the master's suite. That had changed enough that she couldn't open a gate to it, but this chamber was still predominantly tech-glass wall-screens lining the hewn red walls of the monolith. The floor was one massive mosaic of the serpents overrunning a mythical garden. A dozen round tables and accompanying stools denoted workstations. The air smelled of frankincense and lime.

"You need your own warning tag," Samael groaned, bending in half and clutching his knees. "Side effects may include nausea, vomiting, and a deep dislike of your traveling companion."

"Are you done being a wuss?" She leaned away from Samael as he surrendered the form of the imp to reclaim his angelic body. "P.S.? Took you long enough to remember an imp would be scared of the Chimera. Now, explain what the hell you were thinking bringing my crew to the market, particularly as one unit."

"Trust all the way through, right?" He slapped his cheeks repeatedly as he bowed his back.

"Trust is why you and I are standing here instead of on the precipice between the Mids and the ether. You remember the ether? The thing that makes your kind go poof?" She planted her hands on her hips and tapped her foot.

"I'm not a gatekeeper. Moving your motley misfits requires the use of traditional means. The moment your energy displaced the magic of this World, my choir alerted me. Before I explain any more, you really should allow your friends to join us. A lot has happened since you went AWOL for a few days. The demi and Sage have been extremely helpful in your absence."

Cian didn't know any better, but Ashtad? *Ashtad?*

She snorted. "Ashtad? Was helpful to *you*? Does he know who you really are?"

"Give him some credit, yeah?" Samael rolled his great big shoulders and stretched his neck until it popped. "Your demi is smart enough to understand the long game that is played among superpowers. He knows damn well he can't make it to full godhood without having an alliance with the other three superpowers. It's a prerequisite that's tested during the cyclical wars. That's why demis can't ascend in the off-season."

That…she hadn't known about the alliances being tested during a demi's final trial for godhood. Still, Samael and Ashtad had gone hand-to-hand in combat recently, and Ashtad had not been the winner. Then again, Ashtad *was* crafty, which explained why he hadn't been bristling when he'd arrived with Samael in the market. She'd take a chill pill until Ashtad signaled otherwise.

Three sharp knocks came from the floor.

Samael arched his brow and looked at her.

"I delivered them two stories below. Figured I'd get an answer from you while they hiked the final stretch." She shooed him toward the hatch in the floor.

"How did you…?"

"There isn't a hidey-hole in this market that I don't know." She smirked. "I may have been gone a few years while the people changed, but the market itself hasn't."

"I should've known." Samael flicked his wrist, and the hatch flew wide. Cian's ginger hair appeared first.

"This place is better than any RPG." Cian scrambled up into the war room. He had enough wherewithal to help Drew and Ashtad come through. None of Samael's choir followed.

Drew and Ashtad perched on tabletops while Cian made a beeline for the sleeping tech. One touch of the glass walls and all the screens woke. Samael shook his hand over his shoulder as if he were about to throw dice; a tablet appeared instead. As in tech, not stone.

"Your Sage is a mathematical genius. We're going to need him to guide us through the prison." Samael extended the tablet to Cian. "First, what'd you learn about Isoba and his associates?"

"There's only one associate. It's the one the rot is after, and the same person I am after," Bix hedged. Drew and Ashtad sat a bit straighter. "I'm beginning to think the rot freed Isoba to lure the associate out of the shadows. He was the bait for their trap before she eluded them again."

"She?" Samael crossed his arms.

"You'd probably know her as Tashka. We know her as Fymmi," Bix admitted.

"*Tashka?*" Samael echoed somewhere between a shout and a

guffaw. "The lost dragon. No wonder the twins are hot to trot on this. Odds are high it was Tashka's resonance in the bomb grid. That's why they handed you Isoba so readily. They want you on him while they look for her."

"Tashka is a *dragon*?" Bix swore. So much for Drew reading Tashka's soul for the locations of the other bomb gardens and the names of the other conspirators. Dragons didn't have souls any more than angels did. If Tashka couldn't or wouldn't divulge her intel, it was on Samael to draw it out of Isoba. No way did Bix want Drew anywhere near Isoba's corrupted soul.

"That's…unexpected," Ashtad drawled.

"How did we not know she is a dragon?" Drew cried. "There was no mention or even an allusion to that in her files."

"Aggressive editing is a known affliction." Bix shrugged. Tashka's cloaking tech hadn't been mentioned in her CWIG file either, and a routine physical would've told the doctors about her artificial spine. Somebody inside the CWIG had known; maybe they'd omitted those details to protect her. Might have been the same folks who'd recruited Tashka into the CWIG. The CWIG was forever looking for individuals with unique and powerful magic. The more broken the recruit, the better. Broken could be rebuilt as a dedicated operative. Every spy had a grim origin story; coming out on the other side of awful was what made them good agents.

"Look, I don't know what the jorōgumo told you." Samael held his hands up in peace. "Tashka is a stolen dragon kit, the first ingredient in a breeding experiment conducted by Isoba's father who was determined to create a dragon-angel hybrid."

"A phoenix?" Drew snorted. "He wanted to create a phoenix? Like Feng?"

Samael nodded. "He wanted an army of them, an army he controlled, an army capable of enslaving dragons and angels. He refused to believe the Phoenix is a creation of pure native magic, not of ill-advised rutting between our races."

"Well, now that's stupid," Ashtad muttered. "Anyone can see

it's like breeding a hedgehog with a tuna."

Samael scratched his neck with his middle finger. "Now, when someone steals a dragon kit, you can bet their nemeses in the Angelic Host want the thief, the kit, and the details of exactly how the perpetrators did it. I was two miles away from Isoba's father and Tashka when the girl nuked her town. Nothing but a smoking crater by the time I got there."

"How did the trolls find her when you couldn't?" Bix asked. Pieces of Yukiko's story seemed sort of convenient in this light. As if the trolls had wanted to control the narrative, as if they'd known who and what Tashka was all along.

"They didn't. She found them." Samael sniffed. "Imagine you're a kid who's been through everything she has, and possess a magic you don't understand and are physically prevented from controlling."

"You become an unholy terror," Drew said, probably having lived a similar situation with his first ward. "Everyone is afraid of you. You're afraid of you and them. A vicious cycle that just gets worse."

"Until someone comes along, breaks you out of the spinning decline, and teaches you the basics of you." Bix crossed her arms and silently thanked the powers that be for Hades stepping up to be her teacher while she'd been frightened and feral.

"No one with a hint of ethics intervened with Tashka, not in time, at least. That's why the trolls dumped her on that remote World where she was never seen or heard from until too late." Samael's gaze turned distant. "If only I'd known to follow the trolls instead of the spiders, the Fates wouldn't be shitting themselves quite so badly now. Ah well. Eventually I found Isoba, beat the truth out of him, then threw him in supermax. Which brings us up to the here and now."

Bix dropped her head back and groaned. "If the dragon twins know about the Udine prison ship, they're probably on their way to the correct facility. I have no idea if they're going after Tashka as friend, foe, or what. If they aren't aware that the real reason she was with Isoba this last time was to actually stop him from his mad scheme…"

"We have way bigger problems than the dragon twins," Cian piped in.

Bix raised her brows. "What problems?"

"Your Sage is tainted," Samael said bluntly. "He emits a kind of poison in the null space his humanity creates around him. I picked up on that same kind of poison but a whole lot more of it coming from the facility where Isoba and Tashka are being kept."

The poison to which Samael referred was a side effect of the disease afflicting Cian, the same disease for which there was no cure. A disease which the anti-gods had played no small part in creating. Samael detecting potent quantities of that poison at the prison could mean only one thing.

"The Devourers," Bix breathed in horror. "They've found Fymmi."

Chapter 21

Bix rubbed her temples and paced the angels' war room. "Fymmi's, *Tashka's*, ability to hide in plain sight is due to a combo collar and artificial spine that Isoba and his dad implanted in her as a kid. The Devourers are after that cloaking technology, so they can replicate it and move among us undetected and unhampered by Mids' magic. Even I will not know them."

Everyone in the room swore, including Cian.

"That tech was intended to mute her abilities and force her to maintain human form for the breeding process." Samael grimaced. "Someone inside the rot told these Devourers about it and about her. It's got to be the royal dragon who helped make it. The dwarves who forged it aren't with us anymore."

"Couldn't get the name of the royal dragon from them before you killed them?" Ashtad asked.

"Dragons are shapeshifters too, you know," Samael drawled. "Looked like a human, smelled like a human, produced magic that was decidedly not human. That's all the dwarves cared to know."

"If Devourers are already at the prison, we're past critical timing." Bix held out her hand and waggled her fingers. "I need those pictures of the facility. Now, Samael."

He laughed. And laughed. And finally realized he was the only one. "Oh, right. I forgot you don't remember."

Bix closed her eyes and pinched the bridge of her nose. "What, Samael, what don't I remember?"

"There were three requirements—only three—specified for the construction of the supermax facilities. One, contain the creations. Two, keep the creations alive. Three, keep the Chimera out." He bumped her elbow with his.

"Keep me *out*?" She stared at him like he'd lost his mind. "Why? The Consortium expected me to clean up their messes. I should've had a frequent-user card. Make six deposits and the seventh gets a room upgrade."

"You weren't a cleaner, you were an *executioner*," Drew reminded her.

"Precisely. Supermax stores our most despicable creations whom we want to keep alive. You didn't agree that we were entitled to play with our naughty toys. The Consortium's fear was that you would locate a menagerie and empty it." Samael drew his finger across his throat and stuck his tongue out the side of his mouth.

"Chickens," she muttered. "So, how did they keep me at bay?"

"There's only one way to truly stump a gatekeeper—constantly change the configuration of the destination so that you never have an accurate image." He donned a straight face. "Each facility exists on its own World, and that World is never the same from minute to minute. The configurations don't repeat. They exist in a perpetual state of transformation."

"Are you kidding me?" she cried. "You're torturing your creations."

"Yes." He nodded rapidly. "They'll be batshit crazy by the time we free them to create pandemonium during the cyclical Great War. Otherwise, the war can be predictable. We are a reprehensible mix of immortals and the extremely long-lived. Boredom is our greatest enemy."

"Isoba had been in there for years, then was released to bait Tashka. We ended up with a bomb grid in the market. Now Tashka's been there for ten years, and we have to wonder at the state of her mind too." Bix tapped her temple with her fingers.

Poor Tashka. She might not have intentionally gone dark to hide from the faction within the Consortium. She might have lost her mind, and her body merely reacted to protect her. Kind of like a certain Chimera in the pool of darkness.

"Let me guess, angel boss, you were part of the construction committee for supermax." Drew sighed.

"No, I'd long been blackballed by then. Had no input. Just delivery instructions, which, no, before you ask, I can't give to you, because how an angel locates a destination is a function of native magic. You three are from Other Worlds, so you can't exploit it. The kid and I can. Or your warlock, but I'm thinking you've kept him out of this due to his day job."

"If you can show me what Worlds are adjacent, I can get us in." Bix gestured to Cian. "The Sage doesn't come along, though. Not a risk I'm willing to take. Nonnegotiable."

"Your hunting thing with the gate looking into another World? That *might* work with the kid's help." Samael pointed at the wall screens to whatever simulation Cian was building. "The Consortium knows you're a Shadow Caster too, so they've flooded the place with light. It's a total white-out in there. For anyone who can see, there is nothing to see. Sound, sensation, and maybe the occasional taste are the senses that give inmates an indication of their surroundings."

Drew muttered her inimical opinion on that bit of exceptional cruelty.

"While I was there looking for Isoba, I used a combo of sonar and radar to map my location. I've given that data to the kid to see if he can extrapolate and anticipate what the prison looks like without all the light when it physically transforms," Samael explained. "It's the best I could do to live up to my end of the deal. If we get split up, you guys are going to need the kid to keep you from walking off cliffs you can't see suddenly manifesting."

"The kid doesn't come with us. Period," Bix repeated firmly. "There has to be another way. What about tech? Can he walk us through over earpieces?"

"Blocked, all kinds." Samael shook his head. "Come on, kid. Don't you want to be a hero? Boots on the ground? Thrill of the hunt?"

"Nah. I'm good with not dying," Cian said, wisely not opposing Bix and not looking up from his tech. "Consider me part of the rear echelon."

"What about your connection with your choir, Samael?" Bix suggested. "Can they buddy-up with us to be our navigators?"

"And risk another archangel using their eyes to spy on our prison break?" Samael tapped the corner of an eye. "Besides, I'm not letting one of my choir near Isoba. Dredging the information on where else that freak's made bomb gardens is all me."

"Guys, I might have a solution." Cian's gaze cut to the screens. "I can build the algorithm into the tablet, but one of you will need to fill in the blanks once you get there. I'll make it as easy as I can, but easy takes time."

"Just write the code, Cian, doesn't need to be easy. I can do the rest." Ashtad studied the screens, rapt. "Archangel, how do the guards manage to exist in supermax?"

"There are no guards *in* supermax." Samael crossed his arms. "The World itself serves that function. The gateways to the prisons are guarded, and additional guards exist within the gateways themselves."

"If something happens with the guards, that summons the MWA." Bix rubbed her brow and wrinkled her nose. "All the Devourers had to do to gain access was take the form of a creation and let someone from the rot check them in."

"They hacked the gateways themselves," Cian said with distraction. "The list you gave me? Of Consortium assassination targets? The commonality is who and what they'd been assigned to infiltrate or protect. The people and the locations weren't the same, but they all were, in some way, working on gateways. Scientists trying to improve the stability, capability, and deployment ability. Engineers trying to stop the natural degradation while enabling per-use customization. Doctors tracking the test subjects who use experimental gateways. Facilities where new gateway tech is tested. The whole product lifecycle. The agents who we know for a fact were replaced by Devourers are assigned to teams doing key development or to security for facilities."

"Since Devourers can shapeshift down to the DNA of whoever they're impersonating, no one but the superpowers can detect them. That explains why the Devourers replace worker bees rather than guild masters who have cause to interact with the superpowers." Ashtad covered his eyes with one hand and winced. "Staying beneath the notice of the guys who can out you is something taught the first day of any undercover class."

"With the faction inside the Consortium telling the anti-gods who to avoid and where, it's little wonder the rest of the superpowers never noticed the infiltration," Drew scoffed, retying her shoelaces. "Now we learn Devourers want personal gateway tech that allows them to move freely within the Mids—"

"Well, that's what everyone everywhere wants," Cian muttered, interrupting. "To be their own gatekeeper."

"Devourers *need* the gateway tech to bypass the protective layers surrounding the Mids that are keeping their forces out. A rip in a random layer isn't enough to allow the full army inside," Bix explained, simultaneously relieved and horrified. Future-Feng had said *she* was the means by which the Devourers would access the Mids en masse. But if they had gateway tech, they were going to get inside regardless of how she managed her memory merge. The issue now came down to timing. No wonder future-Feng had insisted on sending her after Fymmi to stop the anti-gods from hiding themselves from whatever the superpowers might enact as a countermeasure.

"It's a drip, and these Devourers want a deluge." Samael sneered. "The gateways plus Tashka's tech renders the Mids completely exposed. Sons of bitches. The thieves aren't satisfied with the treasure anymore, they're coming for the palace."

"That was inevitable." Drew tugged the bra band of her

running top. "They have a voracious appetite. The rank and file can survive on common quantities of native magic. However, the more powerful the Devourer, the more potent the magic it must consume. The Mids is like a freakin' shopping mall of delicacies to them."

"Magic's classic exchange." Ashtad tapped a finger against his lips. "You let your boss know about your discovery, Cian?"

Cian nodded. "Sent a note to Chief too. It's too big for our crew, and it's their people at risk. I didn't think it was right to sit on it."

"It was a good call," Drew assured. "Do we have any idea how close the Devourers are to having fully functional personal gateways?"

"Our researchers are decades away from figuring it out, according to CWIG intel." Cian shrugged. "Don't know how that translates to the smarts of a god army."

"Anti-god," Ashtad corrected indignantly. "There is a huge difference. Don't confuse the two."

"That the Mids isn't under full-scale attack right now says they haven't figured it out yet." Samael cracked his knuckles. "The intricacies of Mids' magic is likely their stumbling point, but who knows how much longer that'll stump them."

"We don't have spies inside the Devourer army, so it's moot until we catch a Devourer gate in action. Besides, if the MWA and CWIG are working the gateway issue now, then we can focus on Tashka." Bix clacked a heel against the floor. "We know how to get into the prison World by leveraging the view from an adjacent World. We know how to get around by using Cian's formula running on a tablet that Ashtad can power. Now, how do we find Tashka before the Devourers do?"

"You sure we're not too late already?" Ashtad asked the question Bix didn't want to consider.

A sheet of white paper wafted across the room. Samael snatched it before it hit the ground. His expression darkened.

"Blank." He held the sheet out to Bix.

"It's Iso—" Her words died in her throat as a second sheet chased the first, followed by another, and another, and reams and reams of white funneled in from the shadows where walls met ceiling. Drew shot from her seat and dragged Cian under a table.

"What the hell, people," Drew shouted. "Death by a thousand paper cuts?"

"All blank. Every last one of them." Samael grabbed random sheets as they flew at him, unfazed by the assault. "What is this? A threat to the market? Now?"

"I don't think so." Ashtad deployed a shield of electricity, singeing the edges of papers as they bounced off his bubble. A ball of sparks built in his hand. He passed a sheet over the sparks. An image took shape.

"Invisible ink, the purview of children and spies." Samael snorted and called a ball of angel fire to hand, waving a seemingly blank sheet over the fire. "I assure you, it hasn't been used on the pages sent to the syndicate leaders."

"Because there was no specific message until now." Ashtad passed his paper to Bix.

I'm waiting, Chimera, blazed in scorched script. *A broken kit for a broken mind.*

"It's from Isoba," Bix moaned. "He's a Shadow Caster. That's how the sheets of paper were being delivered to the syndicate leaders. He was reaching through the shadows in your respective chambers to deliver his antagonism."

Samael shook his head. "I know Isoba, every last pilfered part of him. He's no Shadow Caster."

"A Devourer, then?" Drew suggested, peering out from under the table.

"Doubtful." Bix stared at the font. "They've only been in the Mids for five years. These sheets have come for the last ten."

"Lower left corner," Ashtad prompted, looking at his own sheet. "Archangel, if you would?"

Samael waved his ball of angel fire under the corner of the page Bix held. A paw print emerged from the heat. Like a wolf's.

She rolled her shoulder, the memory of the Shadow Caster's attack in the pool still fresh. What was it Phobos had said about the damage she'd incurred? Claw marks from a wild animal, not a mythical beast.

"This is a god's work, Bix," Ashtad sighed. "You're being summoned by a god into supermax. One who knows too much about what we're doing."

"The broken mind, Bixie," Drew whispered. "It's a Mid World guardian with your memories. It's a mad god."

Chapter 22

Gray dots indicating Devourers peppered the supermax World, visible through the filter from the adjacent World. Two dots of purple denoted the presence of dragons, most likely the twins. One deep-red dot confirmed the loitering god. Powerful magic from supermax burst like popcorn, whiting out the filter, then ebbing. The process repeated: power spikes, whiteout filter, restored view. In addition to the problem of a superpower party going on in the prison, there was the issue of the constantly changing shape of the supermax World. One moment it was shaped like a mace, the next moment a Venn diagram of interlocking rings, the next a sieve.

Bix had to look away to keep her mind clear and ready to receive a snapshot image to open the destination gate. It'd be tricky, for sure. Capturing enough detail from a fleeting image was hard enough, but she usually had the luxury of filling in the mental blanks because the structure wasn't going to change.

This was a new challenge. If she screwed up, the best case would be that she couldn't open a gate. The worst case would be that she'd open a fragment that would cleave one of her friends when they dropped from the origin gate.

She could not, *would* not, lose more teammates in an effort to save Tashka.

"The plan is simple." Bix forced a smile. "The Mid World guardian knows where Tashka is and wants to make an exchange. I'll demand Isoba along with her, thus delivering on my end of the deal with Samael. Once you guys have hands on the packages, I kick you out."

The archangel scratched his jaw. "You know it's not going to be that easy, right? If that god has been hanging out in supermax for shits and giggles, he or she is more nuts than the creations who have no choice in the matter."

"Plus, there are the Devourers on-site." Drew coiled her ponytail into a top bun. "Thirteen of them per squad, minimum, and we don't know the full extent of their powers. It's more than shapeshifting, and, I assure you, they will impersonate the things or people we least expect. We have to verify that what looks like Isoba and Tashka are in fact Isoba and Tashka."

"Don't forget the creations are also threats." Samael crossed his arms over his broad chest. "There is no reasoning with them. You'll have to kill them, and you'll have to put a little gusto into your effort. Every one of them can muck with your senses. Every one of them can fell you in a hundred ghastly ways and rejoice while doing it."

"Add the dragon twins." Ashtad peered through the viewing gate and tapped on the tablet's screen. "Just because they've been allies in the past, doesn't mean they'll let us get between them and their lost family member."

Samael wagged a finger at Ashtad, grunting his agreement. "Finally, we have the World itself. It was specifically designed to keep out the Chimera. Once she's inside, who knows how it will react. That's on top of it constantly pulling the floor out from under us."

Bix stared at them. The corner of her lips twitched. Ashtad chuckled. Drew giggled. Samael grinned.

"Somebody has to do the shit jobs." Samael winked.

"Joys of being the best in the biz." Drew batted her lashes.

"The moment we cross into the World, the power players will

know I'm there." Bix rolled her shoulders as her darkness writhed beneath her skin. "Each of us plays to our strength. I take defense against the Devourers and the god."

"I'll kill creations and deflect the dragons." Samael rubbed his hands together. "Also, I'll be the one to manhandle Isoba since parts of him are toxic to the touch. I need him alive to know where else he grew bomb gardens."

"I'll take point on Fymmi nee Tashka and play navigator." Ashtad held the tablet up to the viewing window. The animation timing matched that of the changes in the supermax World. The grayscale shapes, hit and miss. "We have maybe a sixty-five percent accuracy with Cian's calculations. Not bad considering what he had to work with, but not good enough to trust blindly. It's a crutch, not a map."

"I'll cover you, Sparky." Drew peered over Ashtad's shoulder and frowned at the screen. "You can't recognize a Devourer. I can. And if your focus is on the tech, I'll keep you from stepping off a vanishing staircase."

"We have roughly five and a half seconds between exterior changes of the World." Ashtad glanced at Bix. "If that same interval applies inside, then we're good to go. Otherwise, I'll have to recalibrate."

"If we get separated, beware of any spot where light doesn't shine. The god isn't the only Shadow Caster. Devourers have a few among their ranks. They can use any unlit sliver to get at you." Bix steepled her fingers and pressed them to her lips. "As for exfil, it might take me a few tries to open gates inside supermax. Don't assume instant is an option. You'll most likely relocate midmovement."

"This ought to be fun," Ashtad drawled. "Hope no one gets motion sickness."

"Ready when you are, Bixie." Drew put a hand on Ashtad's shoulder.

Samael cracked his knuckles and donned his game face. "On your go, Chimera."

Bix closed her eyes. "Countdown to the next change, Ashtad."

"Five. Four. Three. Two. Now."

Six. That was how many attempts it took before Bix tuned into the rhythm of the supermax World. Like a breath building in the lungs, then expanding outward, the change was a ripple effect. On the seventh breath, she moved the team. They dropped through gates to a slick precipice overlooking a colorful landscape of a choppy sea amid a hailstorm. No way off but down.

"Always a damn storm," Samael groused, catching balls of ice in his hand. "We shouldn't be able to see this. This should all be whited out."

"Reminds me of Niflheim, and why gods avoid going there." Drew snorted, releasing a frosty cloud.

"Technicolor is the god's doing. I can feel the divine magic at work. Probably a welcoming gift." Ashtad huddled over the screen, trying to get it to respond despite the wet. "I need a minute to run a test."

Bix ground her teeth. Mids' magic on this World was abundant. Infinitely more potent than that in the subcity prior to breaking the wards. It pummeled her, like fists of fury trying to knock her out of the World.

"You okay, there, Chimera?" Samael gave her side-eye while he puffed out his cheeks.

She couldn't speak through the assault; she was too busy calming her instinct to retaliate against the World by ripping away its protective layer and letting the ether consume it. A temper, she had one, and it did not tolerate being attacked. The pendant containing Feng's dewclaw warmed against her chest. The ferocity of native magic's attack lessened, allowing her to focus on their changing surroundings.

It started with the sea, with tidal waves rising as green sod and crashing down on flat plains with loud bangs and booms. Hail tapered to land in a precise pattern, chalking out the lines of a baseball field. The rock of the crag on which they stood softened.

"Ashtad," Bix prompted. "Which way?"

"Bend your knees," Ashtad barked. "Count of three, jump left and be ready to roll through the landing. One. Two."

Her team vanished.

Rock turned to mud, collapsing in a slurry as a manic cackle built in the skies. Bix squeezed her eyes shut and lips together against the muck shoving her down as she tucked into the fall.

Her body thudded against solid terrain; the impact echoed all the way into her bones. She inhaled mud and dirt carrying the scent of sunbaked clay. With a wince and a groan, she loosened her fingers from her head and peered through the muck dripping from her hair into glaring light. Red desert surrounded her. Curved shadows stopped short of her legs. Pushing up on one hand, she used the other to shield her eyes against the brilliance. A large, striped rock formation framed a smooth-edged swirl, like a gong waiting to summon the gods or a portal waiting for the right passkey. Neither option was plausible. A portal would have beckoned to her gatekeeper magic. A gong that rang in the Other Worlds would have whispered to her Other World essence. No, it was an illusion manifested by the prison.

"Welcome to my home, Chimera." The voice was androgynous yet quivering with madness. Shadows shifted, hinting at a swish of a fluffy tail. Faint clicks denoted nails, no, claws upon stone.

Bix rolled her shoulder as her mind dusted away the excess pieces in the puzzle of the Shadow Caster god. Coyote or fox. Both renowned tricksters among their pantheons. Both of fickle allegiance to multiple pantheons. Either of them perfect candidates for the original Chimera to have inflicted her memories upon. None of her enemies would have looked twice at the rantings of a trickster exacerbated by the fragments of her mind burrowing inside theirs. Genius, really, but a wee bit problematic on the reclamation front.

"You asked me to come, so here I am." Bix didn't bother

standing. Even now the sky was changing color and texture. If she was going to plummet somewhere again, she might as well stay low. Plus, she wasn't entirely sure she hadn't broken something on the landing. There were parts of her that hurt more than they should. "But I must say, I'm disappointed. For a Mid World guardian, you're doing a crap job of protecting this place."

"So many visitors to our humble abode all of a sudden. I hardly had time to get the place ready. Vacuum. Pick up the magazines. Dust off the dolls." Shadows moved. A huge fulvous paw stepped from the dark, followed by unusually long legs, a large white chest, and the dappled body of a coyote three times its natural size. A size often worn by animal gods to convey their superiority. It sat at the edge of light, half in, half out. The artificial sunlight cut across its golden eyes, exposing the gleam of red pupils. "I was excited when the archangel stopped through some time ago. I'd hoped that finally, he'd riddled out the clues I'd left the Crimson Market's leadership over the years, but no. His obsession blinds him. His lack of wings makes him weak. His feathers function as a filter against the chaos of creation. They are as much rudder as sails. They grant him clarity of thought, intention, and purpose. Without them, he is as easily distracted as a human."

The coyote looked to the distance. A bubble built in the sky, then burst, revealing Samael running full-out through a transforming crystalline cave in pursuit of a...of a shadow of a man with extra appendages. It was just a shadow. A trick of a Shadow Caster.

A second bubble burst near the first. This time it was the patchwork man Isoba. Cornered by two Devourers while a third attempted to mimic Isoba's shape.

Bix had to warn Samael. She tried to open a gate in his path, but the gate refused, his surroundings changing too significantly.

"We haven't had a hunt here since the Consortium came looking for the broken kit," the coyote complained. "Now it's a melee of hunters."

Three more bubbles opened their views. The dragon twins

in their natural forms, pulling the magic of the World between them like taffy on a belt, destabilizing the rhythm and flow of the prison as they searched. Another bubble showed a full squad of Devourers following the pull of native magic toward the dragons. In another bubble, Ashtad and Drew danced back to back against a foursome of freed creations. The floor dropped out from under all of them. They fell with such speed they were streaks of colors within the bubble.

Again, Bix tried to open gates to her allies and friends; again, the World's changes denied her.

"So many searching for the broken kit, even you." The coyote inched closer, moving with the shadows but never fully from them. "The once and future Chimera, barging in to save the day, yet never once asking who is hunting you."

"You, coyote, you are my hunter," Bix said grimly. "I know what you want me to take from you."

His laughter built in the distance then rolled in with crackles of lightning and rumbles of thunder. "Take? *Take?* I want you to *take* nothing from me. I *like* the motes of madness you gifted me. They expand my thinking and provoke possibilities. No, I'm going to keep them. Just as I am going to keep *him.*"

A singular bubble burst right in front of her nose. A big blond Berserker led a small, heavily armed party through changing terrain. Green and silver magic radiated from a trinket carried in Tobek's natural hand. The blue glow of the accompanying Berserkers' rage lit the passage through which they trekked. The walls froze midmorph, long enough for the party to clear the spot before rushing through the next change. Tobek's magic? The coyote's? Both entities were powerful enough to bend Mids' magic to their will, but the coyote didn't need a token to amplify his ability. Tobek apparently did.

The Berserkers being here wasn't a complete surprise. The battalion had a preprogrammed gateway to this World in the middle of the coal plant, so the speed at which they'd arrived was expected. Bix had known from the moment she'd started planning the mission that either the Mid World Army or the Consortium would respond to the alarms triggered inside the supermax prison. If the Devourers hadn't done the honors, her presence definitely had. She would have preferred any unit other than Tobek's to be the ones tapped to respond, but Fates were assholes. Now, she had another team to keep safe in addition to her own.

"The Berserker occurs more than once in the blips of moments you stashed in my head, so I *really* hope he reaches us before the Devourers reach him. I have so many questions to ask him." The coyote sniggered. A paw directed her attention to the Devourers blending into the walls, trailing Tobek and his men, close enough to rush them, but waiting. Waiting for what?

Bix's heart hammered in her chest. Tobek was locking down the passages as his party advanced. The Berserkers moved as one. Left. Right. Left. Pause. Right. Left. Right. Pause. A tempo. One. Two. Three. One. Two. She pushed a gate, but the gate refused to open. The bubble blackened, then disappeared.

"Tut, tut, tut." The coyote pawed at the ground. "You didn't think I'd make that easy, did you?"

Why hadn't Tobek reacted to the Devourers? He could detect them. Come to think of it, why hadn't the dragon twins reacted to the approaching Devourers either? Why hadn't Samael, a proven hunter, not known he was chasing a shadow? Why were Drew and Ashtad the only ones not in jeopardy of Devourers?

Because one of these things was not like the others. That thing was the trickster god.

Isoba was definitely out of the game. The Devourers successfully replicated his patchwork body and fell upon him, consuming the flesh and bone that contained the wealth of native magic that had made Isoba one of the upper-upper-caste Chweds. They wove Isoba's threads of Fate into a cage for his rotten soul. A trophy to be kept purely to deprive a god from feeding on it.

Bix shuddered as the Devourers' skin, horns, and clothing absorbed the blood and gore. It didn't take much of an imagination to know a similar fate was befalling the other creations trapped in this menagerie.

"You've shown me everyone but the dragon kit. Did you lose her? Hmm? Are you as incompetent as the rest of the Consortium?" Bix taunted, sliding a finger along the edge of her muddy bangs. The mud seemed real enough. The bruises forming along her hip and knee? Those were very real.

The rest? The rest was controlled by a trickster god. The best tricks, like the best lies, threaded close to facts. The trouble was sorting which was which.

"Ah, yes." The coyote cocked its head, ears twitching. "The broken kit everyone suddenly desires. Behold."

Shadows scattered from the rocks, allowing light to gleam upon the center of the swirl. There cowered a woman, filthy and bedraggled, bruised and bleeding. Scraps of cloth covered her eyes. She trembled. The magic she radiated pushed at Bix's Other World existence.

Even from Bix's distance and despite Feng's ongoing intervention, the bedraggled woman's magic still pushed. Even with a muting collar, the woman's magic still pushed.

Just how powerful was Fymmi nee Tashka?

"Go on, go take your prize, Chimera," the coyote goaded, retreating into the shadows. "Take what you came for."

"How do I know this isn't another of your games, Coyote?"

"If I tell you it's not, I could well be lying," it snickered. "If I tell you it is, I could still be lying. The only thing of which you can be certain is that you can't be certain."

Definitely a trap, then. What kind of trap she couldn't know until she sprang it. All gods loved to do shit like this as a way to alleviate their boredom. The tricksters were masters of complexity and showmanship. Good thing she couldn't die. Her goal was not to let any of the good guys perish in the process of being the coyote's entertainment.

Bix forced herself to stand, swallowing a scream. Oh yeah, she'd broken more than her stacked heel upon landing. She limped forward, the pain going into a mental box to be expressed later. A snack of Devourer essence would've been nice to dull the pain, if not for the monstrous side effects.

"That's it, Chimera, claim your dragon kit," Coyote urged.

A fat ring of shadows separated Bix from Tashka. Finally, after ten years of guilt, the agent she was supposed to have rescued was right in front of her. Ten years. Too many dead. Too much blame to go around.

"Fymmi?" Bix whispered, reaching out a hand as she neared the rocks. She deliberately spoke the name Tashka had used while at the CWIG. It was a subtle code that Bix was there as an agent. The odds were high that in this hellhole, Tashka had heard her given name far too often in whatever sick games Isoba and Coyote had played. Hopefully, Tashka was still sane enough to catch the clue.

Tashka turned her head, one ear toward the sky, and pressed closer to the stones.

"I'm not going to hurt you, Fymmi." Bix paused. The magic around her rippled, shifted. That magic wasn't coming *from* Tashka; it was a bubble *around* Tashka.

Bix stepped fully into the shadows and tripped the trap.

Chapter 23

Claws of night scored Bix's spine. Once. Twice. A triumphant howl pierced the desert and shattered the illusion. The bubble displaying Fymmi burst. The red clay melted, and the stones dripped. The sky cracked and peeled. The picture crumbled, leaving everything too bright, too white, too washed-out.

Bix winced and blinked rapidly, desperately trying to discern shapes. Partial weightlessness alluded to great height amid vast nothingness. Yet she stood on something solid, something slow and smooth in motion. A glide. The smells…faintly of bleach and electronically purified air. The sounds, distant yet confined with her in a grand space, as if someone had hollowed out Shanghai Tower and left her atop scaffolding on the hundred and twenty-first floor.

Droplets of mist and midnight stained the area around her feet as her back bled from the assault of the coyote. The weed of malice that existed within her sprouted thorns and bent toward her pain, growing, demanding.

Of the many things Bix tolerated, an attack from a god was not among them. Tentacles of darkness surged from her, amplifying the pain of her injuries. She clutched that pain, held it tightly, and let it fester.

"How do you imagine this will play, Trickster?" she called into the whitewash surrounding her. "You needed me to step into the desert shadows for your attack to work, but it cost you. It cost you the illusion. You lack the ability to maintain a mirage while tapping the pool."

A single dark paw print appeared in the distance. A print made of her blood. Her darkness slashed at it. Missed. Another trick. Her wrath leveled up.

"This blank slate, this is the actual prison." She sneered. She might have caught on to the coyote's ruse, but this was still its turf. As long as her friends and allies were here, as long as Tashka was here, the god had the upper hand. "The Consortium built this to be devoid of stimuli that could excite their creations. The Consortium intended for the absence of opportunity to foment their prisoners' insanity. The clean canvas is what makes this World the perfect playground for a god of deceptions. You painted the scenery on the changing landscapes. You controlled what the prisoners saw, smelled, tasted, and felt. You made this your paradise, complete with a captive audience to entertain you."

The coyote gave no answer. Its silence was part of its game.

"Funny how light is the great excluder, which made this a place where no one of consequence could challenge you." She chuckled with derision. "However, darkness welcomes everything. Shadow Casters, Devourers, even me."

Bix's tentacles branched and grew, more thorns and talons than suction and grip. They wove a thicket of night, mapping edges, planes, and shapes. Finally, she could see the prison cells amid the changing passages. Nodules on a system of roots. The inspiration for Isoba's bomb garden.

She stood upon a taproot. The movement she'd felt was its undulation as it bent and swayed to accommodate the morphing World.

"I control who has access to which parts of this prison. I decide the what, when, and how of every encounter," the coyote whispered, its voice near and far. "I am a *god*, and this is my World."

"You had complete control until the Devourers came and threatened your toys." She guessed at the truth, baiting the god. "Did they come through the front door, or did they make their own?"

A bestial growl, artificially large. She'd irked the coyote. Good. This wasn't a traditional battle of might or magic. It was a test of wits, twisted and defective wits. Trickster versus Chimera. The physical damage was a provocation, nothing more. Neither of them would die from a blow. Neither would waste away from exsanguination. No. The coyote wanted something from her. Something Bix had overlooked. Something she'd misread.

"I'm betting they made their own door. The anti-gods come and go as they please, bringing friends along with them without a pattern for you to predict. Must be so frustrating for a trickster, to be unable to stop your uninvited guests from eating your toys," she said, picking at the god's ego.

"The gates they're using aren't stable," the coyote derided. "Many of them die trying to step through. Pitiful, though amusing to watch."

An organic answer to a question the interrogatee didn't realize was being asked. An answer that was more likely to be true. It verified the Devourers definitely had stolen Mids' gateway tech, and that they were definitely trying to modify it for their purposes. They were closer to being successful than Bix liked. Way too close, but she couldn't do anything about that now. Now was all about getting her friends and Tashka away from the anti-gods and the coyote.

"The amusement will end when they run out of food and come for you," Bix mocked. "What will you do then, Coyote? Your pantheon didn't give you weapons at your ascension because you're too capricious, so you can't kill the old foes. That's why you reached through the pool for me, and why you did it now. You need me to do your dirty work. You're *scared*."

"You wish," the coyote howled. "I don't need *you*. I need more of your memories. Somewhere in those recesses is the secret to destroying Devourers with the shadows. I can do it. I just need to know how."

A broken kit for a broken mind.

Oh, what an idiot she was. The coyote was craving *her* broken mind, not lamenting its own. Of all the inanities…

She laced her hands together and pressed two fingers to her lips. At the moment, she was a novice Shadow Caster. The god wasn't. She, as her former and far more knowledgeable self, had used the magic of the Shadow Caster to implant her memories in the gods. Now she had to use the same magic to extract her memories. Maybe the coyote, despite its tenuous grip on reality, knew enough to take what she didn't want to give.

That made the coyote a way more dangerous foe than his memory-keeping peers.

This promised to be ugly. Very, very ugly. And perilous for all those around her. Phobos had accused her, and rightly so, of the infantile abuse of her magics because she lacked the knowledge to recognize them, much less control them. Bix's subconscious would defend her at all costs, even if the costs were the lives of her friends.

To save her friends from her, Bix had to clear the decks. To do that, she had to use her darkness to locate everyone. If she'd only needed to evac her core team from one site, then multitasking wouldn't be an issue, but the addition of the dragons and the Berserkers complicated things. The fact that everyone was scattered in unfamiliar locations and those locations were constantly morphing would require her complete attention. That would leave her exposed to the coyote. Her darkness was her strength and weakness. The coyote had the ability to exploit it.

Could she do it? Could she make herself vulnerable in order to save those for whom she cared? Would her body and mind allow it? Perhaps. If her will was strong enough. Perhaps.

She drew a deep breath and surrendered her focus to her darkness, to the thicket of thorns, to pushing them into prison cells and down corridors. Her darkness coiled around the moving roots of the prison, following their paths, searching their properties. Every barb was an eye, every stem an arm, every leaf an ear.

Search, she demanded of her darkness. *Find.*

The first things it found were the tiny cages of souls left behind by the Devourers after they'd consumed the inmates of the prison. They were bait for Coyote who survived by draining souls of life experiences. Neither the Devourers nor the trickster would get those prizes. No. Bix used gates to deliver the ripe souls to Phobos. It was the least she could do for the god who fed her.

Next, her darkness sought the pockets of excessive Mids' magic. Three points resisted her more than the rest. The creationist superpowers. The twins and Samael. Her darkness homed in on the greatest source of magic first. The dragons had found Tobek and his men. Devourers surrounded them, blending with the shadows she'd created. The men had formed a protective ring around Raspoine. The dragon queen ascendant glowed like a bonfire, casting precious light around the Berserkers and her brother. Why didn't the Devourers attack? Wards. Tobek had warded himself and his men to keep the Devourers at bay, probably a variant on the wards he'd used at the coal plant. But even the strongest wards could resist a sustained assault for only so long.

"Foolish dragon queen, drawing the Devourers to her," the coyote whispered, far too close to Bix. "She is pure native magic, a feast befitting an army. Even now, more of the old foes come to our humble home, hungry for her."

Raspoine was anything but a fool. The dragon was making herself bait. She either knew where Fymmi nee Tashka was or knew…

Ashtad and Drew. In pulling the magic of the World close for their inspection, the twins must have found Ashtad and Drew. Ashtad was Bix's known associate. Were they trusting Bix's team to locate their lost kit? Highly unlikely under normal circumstances, but the presence of Devourers changed the roles of hunters and prey. The twins were definitely prey now.

Ashtad and Drew weren't. Ashtad was a demigod. His body

wasn't made of native magic nor did he exude the divine essence of a full god; therefore, he was beneath the regard of the Devourers Drew's suit was a creation of native magic, but it didn't radiate enough to interest the Devourers. Why would Devourers settle for a crumb when there was a whole bakery down the hall? Ashtad and Drew were uniquely positioned to slip past the Devourers to reach Fymmi. All Bix had to do was track Ashtad, which would be infinitely easier and more expeditious if he lit himself up like a Tesla coil. Come to think of it, Tesla had been his code name way back when she'd been a rookie on his team. He'd know for sure she was the one calling to him, not the coyote.

She shifted her focus from the dragons' distraction to search for Ashtad.

Ashtad, she called through her darkness, along with a singular command. *Tesla.*

"Ashtad," the coyote mimicked, drawing closer still. "Tesla."

The prickles Bix felt along her darkness did not come from electricity. It was the coyote simulating it. She'd spent enough time with Ashtad to know the difference. She dug her nails into her palms and willed herself not to retaliate. Focus on the mission. Focus on her friends.

Ashtad, she repeated with more force. If the coyote could use the pool to deliver blank sheets of paper Worlds away, she sure as hell could use her own darkness to deliver a simple vocal message in the same building. *Tesla.*

A thin stream of light pierced her darkness from a far tangle of the prison, causing her darkness to judder. It repeated the pulse nine times. Three short. Three long. Three short. S.O.S.

Bix zeroed in on the spot and found…a pile of half-eaten corpses? More denizens of the prison. What remained of them. A bright spark within the heap repeated the distress call. Her darkness knocked aside the dead.

"Bixie?" Drew's head peeked from a lump of flayed flesh. "Oh, shit, if that's you, we've got her. Now get us out of this nightmare."

Bix readied gates as her darkness removed the corpses until all that remained was Drew curled over Ashtad, who huddled over a mess of rags and a wealth of hair. Darkness scooped them up and verified that no Devourer tainted their bundle. There were only hammering pulses. The World changed shape and, with a cursory glance, gates opened. Darkness delivered them to the safety of Drew's apartment, then slammed the passage shut as the World changed again.

You have the broken kit. Now I will take your broken mind.

A pike of solid shadow rammed up Bix's spine and pierced the base of her skull. Agony unbridled poured from her. It blasted through her darkness and reverberated through the walls of the prison, shaking the very structure and making the World wail her distress. The coyote hesitated for a beat, then redoubled its assault. Its claws ripped and tore through her mind, searching, grabbing. The incursion drove Bix to her knees.

Instinct surged. Her magic retaliated, but not against the coyote. It went after the Devourers. Her darkness impaled the ravenous troops amassing around the dragons and the Berserkers. It raised the anti-gods up like stacks of hematite rings upon splayed fingers of ephemeral night.

Yes. Destroy them, the coyote cheered in her mind. *Yes. Show me how. Show me.*

She grappled with the torture of the coyote's presence within her as her mind spun. *Finish the mission. Get everyone clear. Get everyone out.* Yet the pain was such that she couldn't guarantee the size of the gates for the exfil. One miscalculation would cause the destination World to implode. Plus, she still had no idea where Samael was. She tried to reach out with her senses to locate him but to no avail. He was either gone or—

Stop dawdling. The coyote jabbed a second spike of shadows into her spine. *Kill them. Show me how to kill them.*

She screamed in anguish, teetering on the brink of control, yet relief lay within her grasp. All she had to do was *choose* to take it. One choice. One easy decision and no one could stand in her way. It'd be a mercy to her, and to those who were relying on her to save them, right? A simple choice.

It wouldn't make her an addict. It was a practical decision, really. If she didn't do it, the coyote would husk her, leave her as an emptied casing with no memories at all. If she was husked, she couldn't stop the faction inside the Consortium from locating and taking Tashka before the cloaking tech was destroyed. If she was husked, she couldn't protect her friends from the blowback of the prison break. If she was husked she couldn't stop the Devourers from consuming the Mids. Those were certainties.

There was only a chance the monster within her would be unleashed. There was only a chance it wouldn't go back in its cage. There was only a chance that she'd never again be able to care for the people she cared about right now.

There was only a chance she would deeply regret this.

A tear dribbled down her cheek as she fed from the Devourers, hating the way her body embraced the numbness. Hate was short-lived as ego separated from id, allowing instinct to run riot.

There was no calculation of risk, no second thought as her gatekeeper magic dumped the Berserkers and the dragons outside the coal plant. There was no concern as her darkness scanned the prison for any lives beyond those of the Devourers and a mad god, confirming Samael had bailed on the mission. There really wasn't much of anything getting through the miasma suffocating her empathy and compassion.

She wrapped her arms around her injured body and laughed as the drug of Devourers coursed through her. Her laughter carried the atonal discordance of malevolence, of a monster. Gates opened, and she yanked the platoon of helpless Devourers to her.

What are you doing? Why are they are not dying? Did you bring them here to trap me? To use them against me? Dozens against one? I will never allow them to imprison me, to husk me. No. No more tricks, Chimera. I am the Trickster, there is no one better at deception than I. Show me how to kill them, or I will leave you a drooling husk of an entity.

215

"You want to know what it takes, Trickster?" she mewled aloud. Her skin blackened past pitch as she drained every bit of sustenance she could from the anti-gods. She expected to hit a point of fullness, but she apparently had stores no one had mentioned to her. She fed until there was nothing left to take.

Yes. Show me, damn you, the coyote insisted, gouging her mind, yet unable to remove anything. *I must destroy the old foes. At last, I will rise up a champion of multiple pantheons. I will have the respect long denied me.*

Satiated with zero fucks to give for anything, Bix looked over her shoulder at the very large coyote and sneered.

"You foolish god," she derided, standing. Her emboldened darkness overpowered the shadows invading her body. "You prideful, pitiful excuse for a deity. Stealing from *me?* The Chimera? I possess more wherewithal in my fractured state than you ever could in the whole of your existence."

"We had a deal," the coyote brayed aloud as it tried to withdraw its shadows from her. She held them fast until they quivered with the god's panic, then she released them. The coyote shuddered and shook its coat, growling as it backed away.

"Gods and their contracts. Fine. You want to know what it takes to kill a Devourer? Trash. An excess of trash." She chuckled with malice as she flipped the switch from withdrawals to deposits. All her effort to stay anchored in the prison, to bathe the surroundings in darkness, to search, to grow, to heal, to wield; it had all produced a remarkable surplus of rubbish.

Devourers shouted and screeched, their voices not of fear but of glorious achievement. One by one, they popped, spraying their toxic blood everywhere.

All over the coyote. Black goo burned through fur and blistered flesh. The god brayed again, but this time, there were no words, just pain. The coyote shrank, giving up its dominating size for a smaller spatter target. She tried to feel pity for it but couldn't. The emotion just wasn't there.

She loomed over the collapsed god and tutted. "Now then, I

believe you have something that belongs to me."

"No," the coyote gasped. "They're mine. You gave them to me. They are my motivation, my reason. Do not take them from me. Please."

"I *lent* them to you." She stroked the warm knot of green and silver glowing across her bosom. "You're a Shadow Caster. You know better than to fight this, so just relax. Let it all go."

Her darkness pierced the god and reached past its physical constructs, past the primordial essence of divinity, past all that made the god a god to cull the motes of her memories hidden within. They came to her like metal shavings to a magnet, eager to return home.

For a moment, a brief moment, she remembered that she and Tobek had never located an artifact that could manage her memory merge and prevent her from destroying Worlds. The ones that were supposed to keep her from becoming a monster.

Too late about the monster. It was already free.

"Well, shi—" The curse died midformation as her displaced memories assailed her mind, searching out the puzzle pieces to which they fit. Images flashed behind her eyes. Pips of music played. Tastes ghosted along her tongue. Myriad sensations teased. Her awareness flickered in and out of the now, sputtering its grasp on reality. Her eyes twitched and her nose bled. She crumpled and rolled to her back, desperately seeking physical contact with the familiar.

Somewhere beyond her echoed the mournful cry of a beast. The beast. The god. She had to husk the god before she fully succumbed to the assimilation of memories. She had to take everything from the coyote. Everything. Until the god was just a shell. For the safety of the Mids.

Instinct obliged, bending to the task of completely draining the trickster.

The onslaught of divinity came as a furious deluge, but unlike her previous attempts to husk a god, she didn't try to contain what she took. This time she let it travel the paths of the excess fuel she'd derived from the Devourers. She focused only on keeping it out of her head. She didn't want the coyote's memories. She didn't want its mind. She didn't want its madness. Let all that pass the way of the forgotten. She couldn't escape the maelstrom of the trickster's emotions, but the numbness afforded by feasting on Devourers kept the god's feelings from causing her irreversible damage.

At length, gasping and exhausted, she succeeded. With the help of the monster she most feared, she'd finally husked a god. In between flashes of way back and not now, she glimpsed the translucent shape of a motionless coyote just beyond her fingertips. If only she could open a gate to dump the husk into the ether, she'd be done.

The notion of focusing on just two images when hundreds of thousands demanded her attention? That was…that was just funny. She snorted. Snickered. And finally gave into outright hysterics.

Strong arms, solid and firm, lifted her. A singular constant sensation amid many fleeting ones. The aroma of sandalwood, black pepper, and musk lingered when others faded.

"You're not a monster, Chimera. You never were."

Chapter 24

Amber eyes stared unblinkingly at Bix. She stared back at the Greek god of fear and sniffed. Rogue scents tickled her nose, scents that didn't belong in Phobos's domain.

Small flames danced in a blackened fireplace, casting just enough of a glow to lend a sinister air to the darkened study. Whorls churned amid the weave of the blue-and-black area rug. Demonic carvings in the frame of Phobos's velvet balloon chair whispered and wriggled, eliciting responses from the carvings covering all surfaces of her chair.

For most people, her chair would've been a horrific torture. For her, it was retraining her mind to sort sensations born of memories demanding context from very real contact happening in the moment. The chair varied the textures, motions, and frequencies so she never grew too comfortable or inured. Because she relied heavily on feeling surrounding magics' interaction with her for basic survival, the intrusion of the ghosting touches posed a risk she could ill afford.

Plus, with her body still under the numbing effects of the Devourers on whom she'd feasted, she needed all the help she could get.

"You're sure I didn't open a plethora of gates for the

Devourers to invade the Mids?" Bix asked for what was probably the hundredth time today.

"Quite positive," Phobos drawled, justifiably annoyed by the repetition as he uncrossed his legs and stretched them, resting his heels on a leather ottoman tufted with tiny skulls. "An answer you would know and believe if you could recall the better part of the last month. That your blackouts are now infrequent is an improvement. However, these uncontrollable bouts of traveling at random times to unknown locations remain a concern."

That was the ginormous problem of pictures from her past overriding her present. Wherever her mind envisioned, her body went. Gatekeeper issues. She had them. In abundance. She'd suffered an increase in them after the Coyote memory merge. Phobos, bless him, had been tracking all her weird ever since he'd brought her to his home after rescuing her from supermax.

"Timing may be random. Locations may be random, but the number of locations I hit is consistently seven." Bix dabbed at her eyes and nose with a handkerchief, coming away with blood. Hers. She tended to spring a leak when her memories got the better of her. "How long was I gone this time?"

"Total? Seven minutes out of the last hour." Phobos flipped the drained hourglass that sat atop a pile of books resting on an ornate side table of ebony wood. "Your episodes consistently involve clusters of sevens. Unsurprising, since that has always been your sacred number."

"If I can weed this back to one trip every seven hours, then I could get away with being normalish." She tried for a half smile, but it probably came out like a sneer. "Except I have no idea how to make that happen. I can't ignore the images like I do the sounds. Sounds are easy. It's like being in a crowded bar and choosing to tune out the surrounding noise."

"Unless that memory is louder than, say, me calling your name from across the room in the present." He threw his voice to demonstrate his point, and it was valid. Fortunately, the assimilated memories that were finding connections lasted less than a minute.

They'd started as isolated dots, motes, and singular notes. Now, they were like annoying GIFs interrupting at the most arbitrary times, trying to locate the rest of their sequence. The chances were high that she'd miss someone calling her name. It was only one syllable. As for conversations, she ought to be able to hang in for the gist.

"Missing seven minutes out of every hour has to be good enough for now. I really must get back to the Mids. I left balls in the air that I need to locate and put away, assuming no one else has run off with them." She stared at the streaks in her predominantly dark skin. Even after many lengthy grueling sessions with Phobos, she still hadn't burned through a fraction of the Devourer essence she'd consumed in supermax.

"Oh, but you've been to the Mids rather often over the last month, among many other places." He tutted. "Even though you can't recall doing so."

She lifted her brows. "Care to share my itinerary?"

"Unless you provoke fear in those around you or summon me through our bond, I can't track your precise location," he dismissed with a flick of his wrist.

"Figures," she muttered. "The one time I actually needed to be trackable for my own good."

"We both know I cannot stop you from going if the Mids is where you wish to be." He propped his elbow on the armrest and his cheek on his fist. "Understand, however, you left quite a few things in a state of chaos. They have not resolved in your absence. Indeed, many have gotten worse."

"You're referring to the pool?" She picked at the embroidery in the beautiful dress he'd made for her. He usually put her in shades of gold, but today his mood had called for ivory. She didn't know him well enough to know the deeper meaning of his choice of color, but she suspected there was one. "I'm aware that what transpired between the coyote and me was observed by every Shadow Caster out there. Even in the pool, being an object of attention carries weight. However, I was more concerned about the mortals and the Mids than I was about the delicate sensibilities of whatever is lurking in the dark."

"Your allies within the pantheons are doing what they can to mitigate the worst of the consequences of your actions." He turned his empty hand palm up and manifested a balloon glass of something thick like maple syrup but which smelled a lot like bourbon. Since he was a god, it probably was the best of both. "Your mortal friends are attempting to do the same, though their efforts are pitiful at best."

"I had no choice but to let my friends fend for themselves for a bit," she argued. "If I tried to return too soon, I'd do irreparable damage to them and to the Mids we're all endeavoring to protect. My friends understood the threat my memories pose—*I pose*—and they're not helpless."

Fact was, she wasn't at all sure how many of her friends and allies were still standing or in what condition, and that worried the hell out of her. Yes, she'd gotten them all clear of the prison World before she'd succumbed to her memories. But it'd been a month. The Consortium and the faction within it had had plenty of time to learn about the breakout and retaliate. Ditto for the dragons, Coyote's pantheon, the Fates, and whoever else had a bone to pick. Any number of bad things could've happened in her absence. Then there was the part about her not remembering what she did or where she went while in the throes of a memory trip. The dragons had told her she'd visited present-day Feng in her sleep. She knew for a fact she visited Tobek multiple times while she slept, and had done so from the day she'd moved in with him. Who knew what she'd done while out of her mind? It was terrifying to consider. Hence the many reasons she really, really needed to get home.

"You said you wanted to leave, yet here you sit." Phobos swirled his drink and inhaled its fumes. "Agitated. Restless."

"I'm not sure I'm safe company to keep yet, and I'd rather not use mortals to test that out. So would you…" She searched for the words. She felt like such a feeb. Upshot was that she'd burned enough Devourer goo that she *could* feel like a feeb, yet there was not enough salt in any World to go with the crow she was fixin' to eat.

"Go on," Phobos encouraged, his lips twitching, exposing one sharp canine.

"You're enjoying this," she muttered.

"Immensely," he purred, "but you will have to say the words, because I want to hear them from your plump, painted lips, Chimera."

She sucked in a breath and ditched her pride. "Would you come with me, please? To make sure I don't hurt anybody when a memory gets the better of me? And to help me understand if there is something I did while under the influence of my past to merit concern or contrition?"

"That would be a full-time job for which I am disinclined to volunteer. However, I will grant you one hour in the time of the Mids of visible assistance to test how well your training holds." He held up one finger and pointed behind her. "After you apologize to them."

Bix leaned around the side of her chair and grimaced. There, in the adjoining chamber, lay many, many of Phobos's beleaguered minions who'd suffered the wrath of the broken Chimera. There'd been a lot of…issues with her mental stability after her adventures in supermax. Cannon fodder best described the role his creations had played in bringing her back to a semblance of normalcy. Poor minions. Serving the god of fear had its downsides.

"Will words suffice, or is there more to it?"

His malevolent chuckle confirmed an apology involved more than words.

Chapter 25

Bix straightened her bangs with the edge of her nail as she closed one set of gates redirecting an apology shipment of souls to Phobos's minions. Not that she'd killed random masses of mortals. No. No. Those plump souls had come from mortals who'd recently died of whatever passed for natural causes in the Mids. She'd simply stolen them from a psychopomp who'd been delivering the souls to another god. Since psychopomps extorted the families of the recently deceased, she had no qualms about robbing one of those unethical degenerates.

Next, she opened a set of gates to Drew and Cian's apartment in the Primary Mid World with Phobos at her side. Last she could recall, she'd deposited Drew, Ashtad, and Tashka here after supermax. Ashtad would've taken the lead on securing Tashka, probably moving her to a safe house protected by demigods. Drew should know where they were.

It was as good a starting place as any…except for the wealth of Mids' magic battering against her Other World presence before she cleared the destination gate. Cian's apartment shouldn't have registered that much magic. Humanity was the grounding race. There should have been a lull in all magic. The kitchen and living room were empty, so why did the anomaly register?

Bix looked at Phobos, unsure if what she felt was real.

"Figure it out," he murmured. "Training is useless if you can't apply it when it's needed."

She pushed out with her unreliable senses. Native magic pushed back. Superpower level. Definite and distinct shoving, but not on par with a ranking superpower.

"Rank and file. Six of them."

Phobos arched his brow. "Where?"

"Four to the left. Two to the right."

"You're not reaching far enough," he chided. "Three on the roof, two on the street, and an easy four dozen in the surrounding buildings. You should be able to discern and sort a city block without effort. This is a regression in your abilities, not a matter of mental confusion."

"Maybe I'm still affected by the painkillers known as Devourers," she contended. "So maybe I'm trying to concentrate on a smaller area. One that I can easily verify."

"The smaller the focus, the more effort required. Scan the city, give me the rough estimates. No?" He leaned toward her. "As I said, regression. One that should be investigated. I've warned you repeatedly that we don't understand the long-term effects of you feeding on the old foes. This could be one of them."

A door to the bedroom adjacent to the kitchen opened. A lean, toned, platinum-blonde woman emerged.

"Drew?" She took a step forward and froze.

Black eyes. Angel.

"Chimera," the angel hissed.

Doors to the second bedroom and the bathroom swung wide. More angels emerged. This was either Drew's cockamamie plan to use angels to hunt nutter gods gone predictably awry or Samael had some explaining to do.

"I was very clear with your archangel regarding your presence around my friends." Bix sniffed. Was that warm vanilla bodywash? Not a normal smell for angels or teenage boys. She counted to seven to see if the scent lingered. No. Yes? Gah. She couldn't tell.

And was that the sound of the shower running? Using hot water in this apartment caused the pipes to knock, and that she didn't hear. Was Cian taking a cold shower right now? Poor kid.

"Bix?" Ashtad emerged from Cian's bedroom limping and looking a bit grizzly but not abused, if one disregarded his collegiate gamer attire. He pointed at the blonde angel, then at Drew's door. "Let the draugr out. There will be no cooperation from the Chimera until she has proof of life."

Proof of life? Uh-oh.

The scamper of tiny nails clicked across the parquet floor, followed by scrabbling along a cabinet. A pea-green, pink-polka-dotted rat hustled across the counter with a squeal.

"Bixie," it squeaked.

"Drew?" Bix caught the rat mid leap and held it at eye level.

"I explained the whole decaying suit issue to our houseguests, and this is how they resolved it." Drew bared its little rat teeth. "Daily fresh rat suit. If you think this is horrid, you should've seen the Pollock dye job I had last week."

Phobos burst out laughing, a deep, rich, wholly evil guffaw.

The shower shut off. The sound of rings sliding along the rusty curtain rod rang in clarity. A snap of fabric. The telltale double thump of the loose towel bar.

"Deimos?" A very sodden woman raced out of the bathroom, securing a towel around her as she shouldered her way through the blockade of angels. "Deimos?"

Phobos sobered instantly as the woman threw herself at him.

Ever the almost gentleman, Phobos held his arms out from his sides as the woman hugged him tightly. She lifted adoring heterochromatic eyes to him. Her brilliant smile faltered.

"Your face? What happened to your beautiful face?" The woman released him and sized him up and down. "What's with the sourpuss suit?"

"That is my brother," grumbled a voice from the far side of the room as Other World magic surged, then settled. "My twin brother."

The woman spun around sharply, spraying water everywhere. This time the angels lunged out of her way. She planted one foot on the edge of the sofa and leapt the distance into the open arms of the god of terror. Other World magic spiked again, transforming her towel into casual attire as she wrapped herself around the glowering god. Deimos held her close. His scarred cheek pressed against her hair as he angled away from everyone. He curled a lip, daring anyone to advance.

"Ermahgerd," Drew gasped, scampering along Bix's arm to perch on her shoulder. "Is that…wuv? Twu wuv?"

"Bix, may I introduce Fymmi nee Tashka," Ashtad drawled, scratching his shaggy beard.

"Well, I think we've just learned which god found an orphaned dragon kit on an abandoned World." Bix bit her lip as delight, warm, gooey, actual delight, flowed through her. Not even her dorked-up senses could misconstrue what lay between Deimos and Tashka. She glanced at Phobos. "Did you know about this?"

Phobos lowered his arms and tugged his suit jacket into place. Nary a droplet remained upon his person from the soggy hug. "My family is averse to sharing certain aspects of our lives. Recall who our mother is and her penchant for irrational displays of jealousy."

Aphrodite. That goddess had self-worth issues.

"While we let those two reconnect, I'll accept a volunteer from the Angelic Host to explain to me what the hell is going on." Bix smiled with pure artifice at the angels struggling to tear their gazes from the god and the dragon. "Hello? Over here."

"It is our archangel," the blonde said. "He has not been seen since he left the Crimson Market with you."

"Samael?" Bix tilted her head. "He hasn't reached out to any of you? No mind melds, no directives, no…nothing?"

The angels shook their heads in unison.

Samael wasn't the silent type. He normally kept close contact with his choir, so something super-duper bad must have happened. True, he'd bailed on her in the middle of the op for reasons she didn't know, but she'd promised him trust all the way through the mission. She'd keep her word and give him the benefit of the doubt. After all, he *had* helped her stage a prison break from a prized Consortium storage facility that had ended with all the menagerie dead. The faction, the greater Consortium, or even the Angelic Host could've fitted him up for the blame when they couldn't locate her. Wherever he was, she owed him at least a welfare check-in.

"What about the Sage?" Bix prompted. "He was in your care. Where is he now?"

"We have moved him." Blondie lifted her chin. "When you return our archangel to us, we will return the Sage to you. A hostage exchange, I believe is what you call it."

Darkness wriggled under Bix's skin. "*Hostage* implies we are on opposing sides. Are we?"

Blondie blinked rapidly. "Your friends will remain here with us. The Sage with our brethren. All have had their basic needs met and have come to no harm. We will continue to care for them in this manner until our archangel directs us to do otherwise."

"House arrest, Bixie," Drew uttered in her ear. "We've been on house arrest while you've been absent."

"What about her?" Bix tipped her head toward Tashka.

"She has required extra care," Blondie answered, her brow furrowing. "We have muted her surroundings as they have proven to be overwhelming for her. We do not understand why it has been necessary. She has refused to explain."

"She's not staying here a minute longer," Deimos snarled.

"This is the one for whom our archangel has long searched," Blondie countered flatly. "Therefore, she remains with us until he says otherwise. Unless your pantheon wishes to challenge our choir?"

"It's okay, Deimos. I'm not worth a war." Tashka patted his shoulder. "The angels have been helpful. I need the rehab they're providing. Coming back to the Primary Mid World has been harder than I expected."

"Then I stay here with you." Deimos thrust his chin forward.

"Just to make sure they remain *helpful.*"

Everyone looked at Bix. Bix stared past them at the memories overtaking her surroundings and the images gaining dominance in her mind's eye.

She bounced, like a rubber ball through destinations, unable to linger in any one place as her gatekeeper magic responded to the images, searching for the connections in her mind. A whirlwind of sounds, scents, and sensations swept her up in their maelstrom. She steeled herself against the sensory onslaught, waiting out the break from reality.

A sharp pang in her neck pierced through all other perceptions and snapped her back into the moment, back to the apartment, back to a room full of puzzled and perplexed expressions. She winced and dabbed at the throbbing in her neck, feeling indentations.

"Yo, Bixie," Drew whispered, rubbing its teeth with its tiny paws. "What just happened? Better yet, why there, there, or *there?*"

Bix ignored the rat on her shoulder, who'd apparently come along for the ride, and looked to Phobos instead.

"Gone one minute precisely," he answered quietly without needing the question and manifested a clean handkerchief for her.

"Speeding through seven destinations," Drew complained. "And now I'd like some Dramamine with a whiskey chaser."

"Draugrs don't drink." Bix blotted her eyes and nose. "But you might want to get down before the next bout arrives."

"*This* is what a single dose does?" Drew sat up on its back legs. "This is what…this is why…? Naw, Bixie. Naw. I'm with you through all your crazy. You missed a spot on your cheek. There. No, the other side."

"I know you are, Drew, but I need you to stay here with the angels as a show of good faith." Bix caught Blondie's gaze. "I don't like that Samael's gone missing either. We've got too much at stake in the long game of protecting the Mids. We need him, and we need to show his choir that we respect them and their contributions to the greater cause."

"Are you fucking kidding me with this," Drew muttered against her collar. "*Angels*, Bixie. Do you remember what they did to us?"

"I remember." Bix set Drew on the counter and looked every angel in the eye. "I don't know how long this will take, but be assured that I am actively searching for your archangel."

The angels nodded once and in unison.

Bix shifted her focus to Ashtad quietly observing everything as he leaned against a wall. Before she could ask, he answered, "We're good. We'll wait right here for you. *All* of us."

"I too believe I will wait right here," Phobos drawled, his attention on his brother and Tashka.

"Tashka," Bix called across the room. Knowing Deimos's opinion of her, Bix opted to give him and his significant friend space. "When you have a moment, would you please sit with Ashtad and Phobos to understand the entities who wish to forcibly separate you from your enhancements?"

"Your friends and I have discussed my situation at length. The angels have offered their insight as well." Tashka slid down Deimos's chest and turned to face Bix. Deimos kept a possessive hand on Tashka's hip. "However, when *you* have time, Chimera, there are things you and I should discuss in private."

"Looking forward to it." Bix tried for a real smile, then turned to Phobos and murmured, "Make sure your xiphoi are within reach, okay?"

He inclined his head. "Mind the consequences. They await you."

Chapter 26

Bix opened a gate to the kitchen in the basement of the coal plant. A battery of hostile magic assailed her before she could exit, bringing her up short. Odd. Why had Tobek modified the wards in their home?

"Tobek?" she called from the threshold of the gate.

No answer.

She needed Tobek's help to locate Samael. Her Berserker wouldn't be pleased to do it, but he'd understand why Samael was necessary to the greater cause. She leaned half out of the gate and double-checked the state of magic encompassing the greater coal plant. No hints of Devourer toxicity registered, no pushes of Other World magic that a god or a Fate would emit, and no anomalous spikes in Mids' magic that would indicate a dragon or an angel. All the unwelcoming magic carried Tobek's signature blend, but it occupied a frequency on the spectrum of greater magic that she hadn't felt before.

Maybe the modifications were some sort of enhancement after his brush with Devourers in supermax? No way had he intended for them to repel *her*. He, more than most, knew nothing could stop her from going where she damn well pleased. Hell, even a prison built by the superpowers expressly to keep her out hadn't managed it.

The prison break.

Maybe his superiors in the Mid World Army had ordered him to beef up his security against her in the aftermath of that? Tobek would have had to inform the MWA of what had gone down with the Devourers inside the prison. Knowing him, he had framed it in such a way that her appearance had been to save him and his team. That was the sort of ally he was. The kind who had her back, regardless.

Pfft. Totally plausible. She and Tobek would probably have a good laugh at how pigheaded his bosses were, just as soon as she found him.

"Tobek? Gurp? You guys home?" she called again. Still no answer. The guys must've been upstairs in the shop.

Her gaze caught on the back wall of the kitchen where the eight-burner fancy-shmancy range sat. The range hood was missing. More importantly, the Bi Xie protector totem that existed as part of the range hood was missing. The last time the Bi Xie had come off the wall had been to fight in *her* defense. It was *her* protector, not Tobek's or Gurp's.

A shiver wriggled down her spine. Her darkness wriggled back.

She stepped fully into her home and shut the gate. Every nerve ending prickled despite the lingering effects of the Devourers' essence she'd consumed a month ago. The normally overstocked armory had been raided. Amber canisters of shelf-stable chemicals and inert bioagents lay shattered along the concrete floor. Fragments of detonated grenades and pale green ash lay in a film coating the kitchen island. Bookshelves, curio cabinets, and modular storage units that had once functioned as room walls throughout the basement had toppled like dominos radiating from a singular central blast zone.

Tobek's altar room.

What had once required a hike through the maze of passages to get from the kitchen to the altar room was now a straight shot across a sea of scattered artifacts and upended tomes from bygone eras. Solid white light surrounded the altar room. It didn't radiate outward like a normal glow. No, the light was concentrated in the circular footprint of the altar room.

Bix's throat constricted.

Tobek had built his altar room to contain the potent magic that he couldn't safely practice anywhere else on any other World. The stuff he did in that room was so powerful it had worn a thin spot in the protective barrier surrounding the Primary Mid World.

She held the image of his altar in her mind and tried to open a gate to it. Nothing. Not even a vibration. The only time she couldn't open a gate was if she didn't have an accurate mental image of where she needed to put the gate. That meant the inside of Tobek's altar room had been drastically...altered.

Not good. Not good at all.

"Tobek? Gurp?" she called again, glancing back at the missing Bi Xie. No part of her could come up with a positive spin on what had gone down in her absence. It wasn't like Gurp to let a mess linger any more than it was in Tobek's nature to leave his precious books with spines skewed and pages crumpled. She picked up three of the closest books, smoothed the pages, and gently closed them before setting them back on the floor. There was no clean, flat surface to put them.

Using gates to move through the blast area, she paused at random spots to look for any indicator of what had happened to her roommates. Directional droplets of dried blood led her to what remained of the bathroom. The curved stacked stone shower enclosure looked like a cannonball had shot through it. Her heart thundered painfully as she cleared the debris covering the shower drain.

"Gurp? Gurp are you down there?"

When no response came from the goblin's favorite hiding spot, she sent her darkness down the drain to look for him. It followed the forks and twists to the sewer at one outlet and the Potomac River at another.

Nothing. If Gurp had been here for whatever had happened and had escaped, he could've taken either route to any number of allies.

"Damn it, boys, what happened?" She chucked the rocks into the pile of rubble, dusted her hands on her skirt, and toed a pile of towels that had tumbled from the mangled vanity. No blood on the towels and no puddle anywhere around the bathroom. Whoever had been bleeding hadn't bled enough to exsanguinate. Small favors.

She resumed her circular approach to the tower of light. No other blood trails lent her a clue. Odd was the lack of scorch marks on the toppled furniture. Odder still was the lack of ash that she'd spotted back in the kitchen. The real kicker was the hint, just the faintest tickle of something calling to her gatekeeper magic. It wasn't the programmed gateway upstairs. No, it was more of a lure, a magnetized draw that started seventy feet from the altar room and grew stronger as she approached the light.

She stopped arm's length from the barrier constructed around the altar room and held her hand in front of her eyes in a futile attempt to lessen the brutal luminosity. Thankfully, the numbness of the Devourers' essence still coated her pain receptors, but it didn't dull the summons coming from within the light.

"Tobek, can you hear me? Can you feel me? I'm here." She closed her eyes and cast out with all her other senses, searching for the interplay of his magics with hers, searching for that playful tug and push of their colliding magics whenever they were in physical proximity to each other. She worried the Devourer stupor had mucked with her ability to detect him. She worried Tobek had used too much magic to create this containment field and fried himself to a crispy critter again. She worried he'd finally ripped a hole in the protective layer surrounding this World and was adrift in the ether that lay on the other side.

He couldn't die. The Fates wouldn't let him. She had to tell herself that six, better make that sixteen times, before she finally calmed the rioting of her pulse.

Whatever he'd trapped inside that tower of light had to be a Big Fucking Deal. The energy radiating from the light was one hundred percent Tobek's magical blend, but it was running shy of what he'd expelled in the subcity to break the wards. Of course, he'd had her help in the subcity.

Time to find out what had happened in her absence.

Bix opened a very small gate in the wall of light, as large as a fingertip, and slowly let the gate grow. Pitch-black was very much alive inside the confines of the tower. It swelled. A great tarry fist punched through the gate, fingers opening, grabbing for her.

Instinct overrode everything.

Bix's darkness formed a shield and rammed the fist, shoving it back inside the tower. Staggered gates engulfed the tower, adding layers of security for the coal plant as she ducked inside the tower and closed the opening.

Night buffeted her. Not common night. No. It was the pool, the thing she normally had to use her darkness to engage with. How was it surviving the light? Why had it come to Tobek? What kind of magic had he tried that had provoked this...presence? Yes. Definitely a presence within the pool. A singular dominant presence far more powerful than a god and possibly a titan. It was aggressive, desperate even. Fierce, decidedly, and very masculine. It clutched at her repeatedly only to be repelled by her darkness. Each collision of her darkness and the presence within the pool caused a frisson of recognition. Intrigued, she flipped her tactic. Instead of rebuffing the presence, her darkness laced with it. Flickers of memories pushed toward the surface. This was something she knew. Some*one* she knew. Yes. Someone she knew well.

But who? Whom had Tobek summoned through the pool? And what had this presence done with him? And if she pissed off this presence what would it do to him in response?

Tobek, she called through the pool. *Tobek, where are you? Are you okay?*

The presence within the pool surged around her, trying to wall her in, to corral her. It tried to block her access to anyone else within the pool. Its power and aggression made her skirmish with Coyote in supermax feel like a toddler's squabble.

Who are you? she demanded of the presence. *Where is Tobek?*

Tobek? The presence laughed, bold and harsh with a hint of manic indulgence. *To-bek. Designation To-be-k. To be killed. Naughty, naughty executioner. You defied a direct order. The rotting godling is To-be-k. To-be-killed.*

Bix's brain short-circuited. One piece of intel too unexpected. One answer too far out of left field. Her brain refused to process it.

Chapter 27

Bix endured the pool rippling with the laughter of an arcane masculine presence. The presence latched on to her and dragged her farther into the pool. Not just her tentacles of darkness; it yanked her body. Actual body snatching.

The movement kick-started her brain.

Oh hell no. Nope. Nope. Nope. She did not tolerate that shit. Devourer. God. Titan. Tobek. Didn't matter. No manhandling of her person, ever.

She turned her full focus on the masculine presence. She'd scared the denizens of the pool by throwing a tantrum after they'd dicked her around while she'd hunted Fymmi nee Tashka. That was long before she'd overfed on Devourers and discovered the lethal joy of letting her instinct take over. Fear of pantheonic retribution? Pfft. Not when the big oogy was picking a fight in the middle of her home. Had to nip that at the root before other entities tried their hands at it. She didn't even care about extracting its identity before evicting it. It—whatever it was—was determined to screw with her head.

Tobek. To be killed, indeed. Twisted fucker.

Whoever the presence was had known Chimera version 1.0, the monster currently champing at the bit for a repeat appearance.

This was one foe her conscious brain didn't know how to tackle, but one her subconscious had already rebuffed. That was good enough proof of ability for her.

She dug into the glut of Devourer essence and allowed her id to rule, dictating reckless and ruthless attacks. A small part of her brain took note of the maneuvers but remained detached from empathy and control. The masculine presence countered each strike with ease. Too much ease, as if she and it had sparred in this manner for ages. The presence fed a curious joy into their surroundings, a joy she was incapable of reciprocating.

Instinct couldn't win this battle. Damn it.

Her darkness broke off the attack. She tried to stuff her monster back under the layers of repressed abilities and incomplete memories. It was a struggle. Her monster didn't want to retreat from the current threat. Her monster wanted to fight. It refused to see the futility.

Whoever it was in the pool knew the original Chimera *too* well. If she wanted to win, if she wanted to force the thing out of her World, it had to be done by the new Chimera. One who didn't know better. The one who was unpredictable because of ignorance. The one who didn't default to violence first. The one who trained as a spy to use her wits before her weapons.

Heat suffused her chest. Her Eternal Knot shimmered, sharing comfort and tenderness. Her monster responded with a ripple of sadness strong enough to pierce the stupor holding her emotions at a distance. Her monster yielded control and clarity back to her conscious mind, back to the new Chimera. Bix laid a hand over her warm heart and sent a silent prayer of thanks to the Berserker at the other end of the connection.

Tobek. To be killed. A direct order of execution. From whom, exactly? Not the thing in the pool. She had no doubt it could have ended Tobek if it chose. It could have ended the entire Primary Mid World, for that matter; it had that much primordial power. All it wanted to do was take her, and every brain cell said not to let it.

Why do you want me? she asked the presence.

Broken, you are broken, it said woefully. *I can fix you.*

I can fix myself, she contested. *Why are you attacking my home?*

Never an attack, the presence responded indignantly. *Perhaps, I am too strong for your little house. For your little Worlds? All these toys you claim as yours. Never allowed to keep your toys. Never allowed to care.*

Unwise to threaten me, she seethed as her temper spiked.

Not a threat, never against you, the presence fiercely denied. *You railed to the omnipresent night. Many heard you. That was unwise.*

Bix straightened. *The pool? Are you referring to my tantrums in the pool?*

They know where you are now. They felt your compassion. They know you learned to care. They will take it all from you. The presence spoke each sentence with rising emphasis and anger. *Punishment for rebelling. Punishment for failing to execute the rotten godling.*

That was the second time the presence had referred to Tobek as a rotten godling. She'd suspected for a while Tobek was a demigod trapped in the Mids, unable to ascend due to the Fates, his pantheon, or both. Tobek wouldn't discuss it, of course. Neither would Phobos or any of the other gods who deigned to speak to her. It explained a lot about Tobek though; about the way he interacted with Mids' magic, the way he could exist beyond the Mids just like Ashtad. The marked difference between her friends was that a demigod was only meant to exist in the Mids for five hundred years; overstaying their welcome affected the primordial essence accumulated within their bodies. The best she understood it, the longer a demi lingered in the Mids, the more powerful they would become when they finally ascended. It was why the pantheons didn't let their kids linger. Gods were capricious, competitive, power-hungry immortals constantly jockeying for supremacy. Tobek had been in the Mids for eons. He'd be on par with a titan by now, able to overthrow the leadership of his pantheon and many others to boot. Probably was the cause of the execution order the original Chimera had ignored.

That all assumed she trusted anything the presence said, but it was an unsolicited answer. An answer more likely to contain truth.

Talk about a truth bomb. Holy hell.

I can help you. I can help you save your toys, the presence cajoled, *if you set me free.*

Every hair on her neck stood at attention. She'd dealt with conniving deities for far too long to not recognize a trap. This time, she wasn't going to spring it. Nope. She was still recovering from the last trap she'd intentionally sprung. Phobos had warned her that there were things in the pool that were more dangerous than the Devourers. This presence definitely qualified, but then again, she couldn't afford to eschew a potential ally just because it didn't arrive in the shape of a puppy.

No, she said flatly. *If you want me to consider your request, you'll help me from the confines of wherever you are. You'll do so without harming—directly or indirectly—any of my toys and you will do so with respect for the time of these Worlds.*

We are older than time, the presence scoffed.

Time exists in the context of events. Events are what feed our minds… unless you have completely lost yours? she taunted. *In which case, I have no reason to believe you can do what you claim, thus I have no use for you.*

Always demanding proof, the presence harrumphed. *Very well. Your first toy returned. The harm is his own doing. Mostly.*

A large body thudded at her feet. The feeble push and pull of familiar magic confirmed which toy had been returned, if the brilliant teal and navy glowing Eternal Knot had somehow failed her notice.

You have altered the rotten godling, the presence said with petulant surprise. *I wish to keep him to study these changes, instead I return him. Proof of…cooperation, yes?*

It's a start, she conceded, desperately wanting to draw Tobek into her arms and inspect him for damage, but doing so in the pool would be exposing herself and him to unknown factors. More unknown factors, that is.

I will go. I will help. And when your toys are well and truly safe, I will expect you to free me.

The presence departed the pool before she could correct his

erroneous assumption of freedom. One problem at a time.

The pool retreated from the light of Tobek's containment tower, no longer supported by the entity forcing it to invade the altar room. Bix closed her eyes and crawled to the nearest cardinal compass point where a steel canister filled with fuel gel provided the element of fire. Cursing under her breath as the canister singed her fingers, she moved the damn thing out of alignment, breaking the containment spell.

The burning light faded, allowing Bix to finally see. The remaining base elements rested at the other cardinal compass points, and the base metals sat at the ordinal compass points. All unharmed. At their point of intersection lay Tobek, gaunt and wan. His bones pressed too closely to his skin. His glorious bulk had shriveled. Long, discolored scabs crisscrossed his torso. He didn't wear his prosthetic, or shoes, or any clothes for that matter. There was new ink on his feet and new scarifications on his thighs and shoulders.

Yet healthy and flush amidst the blood that had dried on his torso, shone his Eternal Knot.

Bix knelt beside him and placed her hand over his knot. A gentle tug of magic answered, followed by feeble but playful batting. Calloused fingers, large and strong laced with hers. His eyes opened, dull and unfocused.

"I don't know how much longer I can hold him at bay, sweetheart," Tobek rasped. "Come back to me soon."

She did have somewhere she needed to be—wherever a certain archangel had opted to sequester himself—but Tobek was her bigger priority. Drew, Ashtad, and Tashka were in good enough hands with the angels. Phobos and Deimos would make sure of that. At least in the super short term.

"Silly man, where do you think I'm going?" She bit her lip and pushed his blood-crusted hair from his face. "Better yet, where have you been? And for how long?"

He garbled something in a language she didn't understand.

"English, you old fart," she teased even as her voice quavered.

She'd come so close to losing him and hadn't even known it. Sure, he couldn't die, but the presence in the pool had planned on keeping him. The altered him. Whatever that had meant.

"We only have seven seconds until you disappear again." Tobek struggled to sit up. "We have to…we have…."

"Tobek, I've been here for a lot longer than that." She steadied him when he teetered. She used gates to bring the pile of towels from the bathroom to his lap. He didn't care about modesty in so much as he cared about not crossing a line of unwelcomed intimacy with her. She had a lot of baggage when it came to that stuff, so he went out of his way to make her feel comfortable in his presence. The least she could do was respect his efforts. "The house is a wreck. Gurp is missing, and you summoned a big bad from the pool who is very certain there is a standing execution order with your name on it. Said Tobek isn't a name at all, but a designation."

She'd meant it as a joke, but a glow dawned in his Berserker's blue eyes as his attention focused on the moment. He blinked rapidly and glanced around the room. His grip tightened on her hand. He brought their laced fingers to his lips and held them there for long, long moments. She didn't rush him. He'd obviously been through some serious shit.

"It's the name you gave me on the day we met." He cried out and his back bowed as the curse of silence bubbled and bled through his knot.

"Shh, shh, shh, don't make things worse, you pain-fetish freak," she soothed as her brain whirled. The presence *had* been telling the truth. Rotten godling and all. She wasn't too sure what to do with that at the moment. She was more concerned about getting Tobek the help he needed. "Do you want a glass of water? A cheeseburger? I'd offer to put you in the shower, but it's broken."

"Gurp," he rasped through a groan. "Where did you take Gurp?"

"I didn't take Gurp. I know how he feels about me in this state." She gestured at her skin and frowned. The fuel gauge of

Devourer essence had faded. The streaks of black and grey had disappeared. Her veins were no longer mapped as some zombie horror effect. Her nails were only slightly discolored. Her scuffle with the presence had apparently taken quite a bit out of her.

"You travel in your sleep. You travel to me multiple times, regardless of where I am. Here, in the shop, on maneuvers, or even testifying before the MWA brass about a Devourer invasion of a supermax facility." Even breathless, Tobek managed to imbue that last part with a wealth of droll amusement. "That's been your norm since you moved in here. However, shortly after the incident in supermax, you were followed by that entity in the pool."

Her blood ran cold. "I brought it here?"

"No, I think I own the blame for that." He let go of her, albeit slowly, and clapped his lone hand over his festering curse. Feeble magic stopped the bleeding but did nothing for the blistering. He probably didn't have much more magic to give, not even to himself. "The entity would appear moments after you did. You two would fight, you would drag it into the pool of omnipresent night, then you two would vanish."

"That's why you changed the wards, to try to keep it out?" She tucked her hair behind her ears and wrinkled her nose. "I have to say those wards are not precisely pleasant to experience."

"The modifications are intended to target the new class of Devourers we encountered in the prison. An unanticipated side effect is a beacon that summons the greater entity whenever your presence triggers the wards." He gave her a chagrined smile. "Gurp and I were refining the spells after each of your visits until Gurp crossed the path of the entity. You rescued Gurp from it and vanished. While you've returned many times to battle the entity, you have not returned Gurp."

"Aw, shit," she groaned, as worst-case scenarios threatened to play through her mind. She blocked the images and their associated detours. "I don't know where I took him. I've bounced to so many locations in the throes of memory assimilations, I don't even know where to start."

Gurp was a mortal, long-lived, yes, but unable to leave the Mids. He'd die if she took him to an Other World. Phobos knew her affection for the goblin; he'd have said something if Gurp had died. She'd very much mourn her favorite goblin, like exploding-Worlds level of mourning. Phobos wouldn't risk her finding out like this. Not while he was hanging out upriver with his brother and his brother's special friend. No. Gurp was somewhere, still alive. Finding people was what she did, so she'd find him…right after she found Samael….and right after she got her rotting godling some help.

"The boys upstairs are actively looking for him," Tobek assured. "If you think of anything that could narrow their search…"

"Yeah, of course, I'll let them know." A stray horrifying thought flitted through the riot of consequences she was trying to process. "Wait. You said my presence triggered a beacon that summoned the entity. It obviously still does."

"I can change the wards." He waved off her comment. "I can put them back to the last version we had in place before the new strain of Devourer crossed our paths."

"Keep the wards as they are. Make them stronger, in fact," she urged. "The Devourers have successfully hacked the gateway tech, that's how they got into supermax. If they could break in there, they could break in here. You need to protect your men and the surrounding community. I've got other places I can stay."

Not that she really wanted to go. She loved living with Tobek and Gurp. She liked being surrounded by the wealth of testosterone and infectious camaraderie that came from hanging out with the battalion. However, the battalion had repeatedly had her back; they'd even lost men supporting her missions. So, yeah, she'd choose isolation if it meant protecting Tobek and his Berserkers.

"No," Tobek barked, his gaze snapping to hers. He cleared his throat and softly repeated, "No. There's a better solution out there. We can figure it out. We just need time, not distance."

"It's my presence that poses the immediate threat. Just because I convinced one über entity to retreat, doesn't mean there aren't others out there eager to exploit the vulnerability in your security." She layered the bath towels over his lap, suddenly obsessed with fussing over him.

"This is your home, here with me." He captured her hand in his, stopping her from covering him with a blanket of towels "Nothing is going to drive us apart, not again."

"You have to admit, my subconscious ability to hunt your ass down is pretty impressive." She tried for a smile as she tugged her hand free of his. "However, because of that, you need to boost your wards to the point that they'll hurt me if I try to cross. We both know you can't stop me from coming, but if you can inflict enough pain, it should awaken me. At least then I'll stay back."

"I can't hurt you, sweetheart." He shook his head. "Don't ask it of me."

"My temporary discomfort or the lives of your men," she pressed. "We've had a long history, by your own account. I'm pretty sure you know at least a handful of ways to wake me up."

His smile was wholly wicked.

She rolled her eyes. "Tobek."

"A compromise, since you're right about the risk to the men." He tempered his wicked mien down to playful. "I'll take up temporary residence in a less populated area while I work out the kinks in the wards."

"Thank you." She laid her hand over his knot. A tendril of her darkness coiled down her arm and pierced his skin, unbidden by her conscious mind.

Tobek inhaled sharply but didn't fight her; his presence greedily welcomed her invasion of his person. Her brain told her to withdraw, but her body wouldn't. It insisted on the connection to him.

He raised a hesitant hand toward the knot hiding beneath her skin…then stopped. A blush streaked his cheeks as he dropped his hand. "Sorry."

K. A. Krantz

She took his hand in hers and set it across the top swells of her breasts, needing the contact, to complete the circuit. His jaw clenched. He didn't speak; he didn't seem to trust himself to do so. Instead, green and silver shimmered from his hand. Tiny silver spears pierced the frame of his Eternal Knot on her skin. Pierced, like few other magics could. It didn't hurt. On the contrary, it was like coming home, like snuggling on a couch beneath a big fuzzy blanket on a cold, damp evening. It was warm but never hot.

The power of their bodies and magics connected rippled through the air, creating a song, a gentle melody with a whispered harmony. Both knots brightened to flood the basement without blinding the bearers. Masculine magic wended with the feminine, bending reality and time, senses and thoughts. Bix's darkness unfurled around them, shimmering with starlight. Tobek's amputated arm spawned bands of intricately engraved silver, bands that articulated on rivets of polished brass, bands that morphed and fitted into a full arm and complete hand. Tobek raised his silver hand and cupped her cheek.

Bix's heart threatened to burst from the joy infusing every piece of her being.

It dawned on her, finally, what the presence had meant when it had said she had altered the godling.

"You carry a piece of me inside you, a part of my essence," she whispered. "That's what these knots are. I have a piece of you, and you have a piece of me. Unlike my memories, the part of me you carry isn't eager to return. It is content where it lives."

For a moment, Tobek's smile was beatific...then it fell. His eyes rolled to white. The arm of silver vanished. The arm of flesh flopped limply at his side.

A breath later, he collapsed.

246

Chapter 28

Bix stared at the lump of a man passed out before her. A surfeit of emotions left her no other option but laughter. To share such a beautiful, tortured, bemusing, and cherished moment... then, you know, flump. She verified Tobek was still breathing, then used gates to deposit him upstairs in the clinic. A beat later, the silent alarm flashed annoying red lights across the basement, heralding Tobek's appearance on a steel slab.

His men would take great care of him. His lieutenants might even know what the hell had just happened. Sure, the poor guy had carved himself up to power some sort of blood spell to trap an über entity in a tower of light, had been snatched by said über entity to some place beyond the pool, unceremoniously dumped back home, and then tormented by his roommate with some kind of intimate magic exchange.

Wow, she couldn't wait to razz him about this.

First, however, she had to move out before other bogeymen showed up, then she had to hash out a Plan B for locating Samael, then she had to come up with a Plan A for locating Gurp—poor, frightened Gurp; what an asshole she was to abandon him—and then there was the whole finding someone to modify the spells on Tashka's spine without killing the woman, and then, and then...

No "and then."

She picked her way across the basement to her bedroom, what was left of it. All the shelves that had stored her clothes, shoes, and assorted other things had tipped over to form a little pyramid around her bed. Gates moved all that to her bolt-hole on Vuornis. She'd deal with the details of establishing a new home later. For now, her Plan B for Samael started with the floating headboard suspended from the ceiling on cables. Massive black feathered wings had been encased in crystal etched with potent spells to hide the wings from their rightful owner. Whether Samael had earned the return of his wings depended a lot on where he was and why he'd vanished in the middle of the Fymmi op. Meanwhile, she needed a few feathers to locate him. She'd intended to ask Tobek for help with the spell work, but clearly, his help was no longer an option.

Tiny gates bored teeny holes in the crystal until the satisfying crackle preceded the more satisfying crumble of a few chunks that gave her access to the feathers. She grabbed a handful, crossing her eyes at the thrust of potent Mids' magic imbuing them, then sent the wings to a separate building on Vuornis. She wasn't too sure how effective the spells hiding the wings would be what with a hole in the crystal now. Better safe than sorry.

Yep, she had a half-baked Plan B. One that involved calling in a humongous favor. She tried to open a gate to the last confirmed location of Samael, the supermax prison. The gate wouldn't open; her skirmish with Coyote must have changed it too much. So, she moved prison-adjacent.

Chapter 29

Bix stood on the World adjacent to the supermax prison; rather, what had been the prison. There was nothing there now. No World. No prison. No echoes of potent magic to stain the sepia filter of ether. She clutched Samael's feathers to her chest. So much for easy. She was fairly certain she hadn't destroyed the World. The Consortium must have seen to it upon hearing their precious menagerie had been compromised.

Asking the dragon twins for their help locating their archenemy was out of the question. She couldn't turn to Tobek for obvious reasons. Lesser angels couldn't locate a greater angel unless the greater angel wanted to be found, which was why Samael's choir was depending on her. Samael was the only archangel who put up with her, and his own kin had booted him out of the greater Angelic Host, so no help from that front.

That left her with one super long shot. She jabbed all but one feather in her hair in case the ask went sideways. She pressed one black feather into her palms and cupped the pendant of the creationists' parts that she wore.

"Okay, Feng, there's a war on the doorstep of the Mids. I need your help to stand up our defenses. The Consortium is tearing them down, you know this. You knew it before I did. We need to find Samael, so he can rally the angels to the greater cause." Bix clutched the pendant more tightly and willed her innate defenses to relax. Feng could only help her if she let him…and if he was inclined to do so. "Wakey, wakey, Phoenix. We have a job to do. Help me find Samael. He's somewhere in the Mids. You can go right back to sleep once you show me where he is."

The only warmth surrounding the pendant came from her own touch. Yes, there was a huge risk in rousing Feng. He could misconstrue her request for help as the summons future-Feng had mentioned, the summons that had aborted his recovery. However, she'd asked the dragon twins to make sure the Feng of the present stayed out of her way, and they'd yet to let her down. Hopefully, Feng helping her now and Feng staying in the dragon's rookery were not mutually exclusive. She really didn't want to muck up the Phoenix's recuperation. However, Samael was important, and Feng was her best hope.

Samael and Feng. She worried for both of them. Admitting that about her erstwhile adversaries felt…strange.

"Oh, come on, you big baby," she groused to the pendant as if Feng himself were trapped in there. "I know you can find him. You're the only creationist whose magic outranks an archangel. If he can track me across Worlds using your resonance dandruff, then you've got to be able to track his pure aura from your mud crypt. Don't be a dick. Help a girl out. I even made it easy, I'm holding a piece of him. Please? Pretty please?"

Nothing.

Figured. It was probably too much to expect. The collection of Mid Worlds was a lot of ground to cover. Not knowing the intricacies of how Mids' magic worked, she might well have been asking for more than the Phoenix could manage at this stage of his recovery. On the other hand, she also had a tainted future-Phoenix hiding in a library. Nah. There was that whole "existing out of time" thing that couldn't accommodate finding Samael in this moment. Maybe Yukiko knew of a warlock who could—

Fire scorched her palms. She yelped and released the pendant, hunching forward to keep it from burning her chest. Samael's feather didn't burn. The rachis of the feather separated from the vane. Thin black barbs separated into teensy threads that tumbled and twirled into a pattern, no, a picture, no larger than a dime. Bix held her sleeve behind the tiny image, the white providing a contrast to the black. The detail was minimal. Hopefully, it was due to the location being rather plain. It looked like a partially collapsed mine shaft or the ruins of a dungeon in an abandoned castle. Neither structure should've trapped Samael. Archangels could move through the Mids as they pleased unless some creative spell work was in play.

Bix pressed the image into her mind and tested a gate. It vibrated in readiness.

"Yes, thank you, Feng," she whispered. "Thank you so much. Now go back to bed. If anyone asks about this, it never happened, okay? We don't want anyone else getting trapped like Samael, right? Right. Thanks again."

Seriously, whatever was keeping Samael incommunicado couldn't be good. If spells were containing him, and he hadn't summoned his choir to free him, then he—and Bix by extension—had a new problem. A new Chwed high warlock must have come on the scene. Perhaps a co-conspirator of Isoba's? Isoba himself couldn't be the spell caster. The patchwork man had died along with all the other horrible creations in supermax. Then again, there was the faction, the other archangels, and the dragons who had other means of imprisoning an enemy like Samael.

Shit.

Going in blind sucked, but until she knew what brand of danger had captured an archangel, she wasn't going to call in reinforcements. She was, for all intents and purposes, the most resilient of Samael's allies.

He was so going to owe her for this.

More dungeon than mineshaft, Bix decided as she quietly slipped through gates into a dank and dim oubliette. The air was thick and metallic. A thin ray of moonlight struggled through a rusted grate in the ceiling, hinting at rough-hewn walls slick with moss and fungus.

The sputtering presence of another gate called to her gatekeeper magic. Mids' magic nudged her. Poisonous presences recoiled from her.

Devourers. Samael had been captured by Devourers.

Shit. Shit. Shit.

An archangel couldn't defend himself against the anti-gods. He couldn't kill them, wound them, or fight them. Devourers fed on Mids' magic, and he was pure potent magic, as pure as a dragon queen.

His only salvation was that he was too pure for the rank and file of the Devourers. If an anti-god tried to consume an entity whose magic was greater than their own, they'd get violently ill and physically weak.

Judging the sounds of vomiting filling the pit, it hadn't stopped them from trying to prove they were more powerful than an archangel.

Samael's bellow of outraged agony slid up the walls of the oubliette, drawing Bix to the edge of feeble moonlight. Audible lip smacking, gnawing, and grunting came from a ring of Devourers on their knees, shoving and elbowing each other as one after the other turned away to be violently ill. All wore Isoba's patchwork form, all except one. That one Devourer stood to the side, native body, bronze uniform pristine. It crossed its arms over its long waist. The Devourer's platinum eyes pinned their hatful regard on Bix.

Behind the anti-god wavered the liquid frame of an unstable gate that allowed tendrils of ether to drift into the oubliette. Black Devourer blood coated the walls around the gate, a testament to those who'd died trying to come through.

The guard at the gate spoke to her. Words she didn't

understand. The tone, however, was decidedly adversarial. Frankly, it could've been friendly as heck; Bix would've still had the same reaction.

Her darkness ripped from her spine, spearing the Isoba clones. They cried out in surprise, then rapture, then horror, and finally they burst. The gate guard didn't flinch as black gore bathed it. Instead, it held up a hand. That hand vibrated, and from it came a sound, a horrible sound of a single note that made Bix's teeth ache and brain throb. Louder and louder the sound built, shaking the walls of the oubliette and spreading the vomit, blood, and gore. The unstable gate collapsed on itself, melting into an oily puddle and stranding the guard.

The guard continued its assault. Mist and midnight poured from Bix's eyes, nose, and ears. She glanced at the ground and tried not to hurl. Samael lay in a pool of black gunk atop a bed of razor-edged algae. When angels bled, their blood turned into plants, part of their creationists' magic. Curiously, the plants created by Samael's blood didn't appear to be of interest to the Devourers. No, they'd wanted his body. They'd hungered for the native magic in his flesh and bones. Chunks of flesh were missing from his cheeks and torso. His limbs were missing entirely. Yet his black eyes remained unmarred and staring at Bix. They, more so than his chewed-up features, conveyed a victorious rage.

The sonic assault from the remaining Devourer adjusted its pressure, drawing Bix's attention back to the lingering anti-god. Had she still been able to hear, Bix might have noticed if the tone had changed along with the pressure. Still, she endured the attack. Yes, it would have been less painful to bear had she fed from the Devourers before she'd killed them, but she didn't want to become the addict of whom Tobek had cautioned her. She had enough bad habits; she didn't need to create new ones, especially ones involving anti-gods.

This Devourer, this guardian of an unstable gate must have been a higher-ranking Devourer. Someone of greater consequence than the scouts; someone of greater power than the hangry forward troops. Bix's instinct wanted to kill it forthwith. Training stayed her darkness. She'd trained to be a spy, and for a spy, information was everything. The first time she'd fought the scouts, they'd lobbed blobs of destructive black energy at her. The sonic attack was new. Painful, but the longer she stood in its cone of sound waves, the more certain she became that this new attack didn't present any greater threat to her than the lacerations from a Shadow Caster. The pain just pissed her off, and not being able to hear was a bit of a reprieve considering the mucking around her memories were doing. If this was the worst the Devourer could inflict upon her...

The Devourer raised a second hand, and the pressure evolved. Bix's darkness trembled and retreated, driven back by the sonic offensive. Not particularly pleasant, but not enough to end the experiment. She wanted to know the worst this thing could do to her. Curiosity held sway. A soft sheen developed along the temples and throat of the Devourer as its gaze narrowed and its body shook. It opened its mouth and bared its pointy teeth. A shout, perhaps. She let it continue its futile defense, curious as to which would end first—its efforts or her patience. For a race unfamiliar with self-doubt, surrender didn't seem likely.

As long as Samael didn't explode, they could wait out the storm. When the Devourer's knees buckled, Bix opted to give it a wee bit of mercy. Okay, not really mercy. She owed a particular god of war a replacement prisoner since the last one had responded to her panic attack. A pair of gates delivered the Devourer to the god's doorstep. One debt paid with interest.

Unobstructed by the sonic resistance, her darkness swarmed the oubliette, confirming she was truly alone with the archangel. Samael opened his mangled mouth. She held up her hand and pointed to her ear. They'd both need a few minutes to get back to minimum senses. She plucked the extra angel feathers from her hair and laid them across the worst of his injuries. His body absorbed them, building new muscle, sinew, and bone. There was nothing quite like witnessing an archangel reconstruct himself.

The feather-assisted parts healed first, the rest took time.

When he reached the point of looking less like a Halloween appetizer and more like an amputee, she opened gates.

A crisp wind carried smoky rosemary and cedar up into the wide boughs of ancient trees forming a large grove. A full moon played peek-a-boo with the clouds. Far below, simple-minded giants gathered around a bonfire. Leaders from the assorted tribes stood upon stumps, extolling trials and tribulations. Bix tugged on her earlobe as her hearing returned, allowing her to listen to the slurping and slushing symphony of the archangel's body restoring itself. They sat side by side on a burl, their legs stretched before them, erm, her legs, his nubs.

Samael scratched his back against the tree trunk and huffed. "The Airing of Grievances from the giants. I haven't attended one of these in ages."

"Well, we missed all the big ones on the Primary Mid World, and I figured you'd be hungry after being repeatedly eaten by Devourers."

Angels fed on negative emotions. Shame, guilt, and depression for an angel were akin to pizza, pad thai, and quarter pounders for a teenage human boy. After a month of being someone else's food, the archangel likely needed to partake of his own feast.

"Thanks for coming to get me," he mumbled.

"Trust all the way through the mission, right?" She grinned, knowing that the gratitude panged his precious pride.

"I did intend to come back to the prison." He flexed his arms and splayed his fingers, testing their form and function. "I took Isoba, put him in holding in that oubliette, and had planned to come right back to help you find Tashka. More fool me for realizing too late what I'd really freed was a Devourer."

"I would've come sooner, but that mission didn't go the way any of us had planned." She poked the holes in her skirt from where anti-god goo had burned through her god-created dress. She needed to work on shaping her darkness as a hazmat suit whenever she was in proximity to detriments to her attire.

"Glad you didn't, actually." He looked up at the moon. "Gave me time to study the enemy, once I got past the initial…um, yeah."

"You going to be okay after that?" She gave him the side-eye. "Riding the edge of death with those entities, I can't imagine what that does to you."

"Oh, it'll take me a while to get near the vicinity of 'okay.'" He inspected his face with his fingertips. "Upshot of being long-lived is that I've got the time to get there. Being their food helped me to focus on understanding what sort of entity we're up against. I've never met the likes of it before, and I say that having battled some really reprehensible gods."

"Downside is the Devourers have learned you regenerate despite their toxicity. You guys can't kill them, so you make the ideal prey. They'll start gathering up angels, penning them. Keeping them weak by feasting on them." Bix grimaced. It was what the Devourers did to gods who lacked the weapons to kill them. Devourers hid those captives in Devourer strongholds. However, the Devourers would have to keep the angels in the Mids because angels couldn't exist beyond the reach of Mids' magic. That meant Feng and the archangels could track any captive angel straight to a Devourer camp. It wasn't the sacrifice she would choose to make, but she wouldn't put it past the Angelic Host to deploy foot soldiers with the intent for them to be used as location beacons.

"I made no effort to hide my experience from the other archangels. In fact, I summoned every one of my brethren to share what the Devourers were doing to me." He waggled his brows as their black arches regrew. "They are very aware now, and they are very displeased that the Consortium has allowed this type of entity to enter the Mids. The rot should begin to feel the walls closing in as ambivalent allies turn to dedicated foes."

"Yet no one came for you. No one used their relationship with the pantheons to send in a rescue team." Bix shook her head.

"How do you endure that? That deliberate callous snub, even at your weakest and most vulnerable?"

He kneaded his thighs as they took shape and smirked. "Don't fret over what can't be changed. Don't look to others to decide your value. I could send a mountain of motivational posters to the coal plant. The goblin might eat them, but it's the thought that counts, right?"

Bix's smile was fleeting. She wasn't going to get into a discussion about how she'd misplaced her favorite goblin. The guilt for that rubbed her raw. "You should let your choir know you're alive and on the mend. There are eleven people in a two-bedroom apartment, and none of them is the tenant named on the lease."

Samael laughed in earnest this time. His attention drifted upward again, his mind and magic likely connecting with his minions. His fingers twitched as though typing dictates. He snorted a few times. Grunted. Tsked twice. Then turned his head to stare at her.

"You got Tashka." He held up a fist for a bump. She didn't leave him hanging. "The dragons are going to demand you turn her over to them. I strongly recommend against that."

She shrugged. "Before I make any decisions about Tashka, I need to talk to her. Get her take on everything, judge the where and how of her mind."

"Speaking of states of mind…" He wiggled his toes and rolled his ankles. "We should discuss your draugr and his challenge to my choir to hunt down crazy gods."

"Ah, right." She sighed. "You should call them off."

He licked his teeth and clenched his butt a few times, bouncing beside her as he manifested clean clothes for himself. "You know, I don't think I will."

She did a double take. "What?"

He stretched his arms out from his sides, stopping shy of knocking her across the chest. "Nope. I think we're going to do just as that annoying abomination asked."

"Samael, no." Bix shook her head rapidly. "No, don't. Imagine the optics of that. Angels hunting gods. No. Bad, bad idea. Especially with the faction, erm, *rot* looking for ways to distract the Consortium from the real problems."

"See, that's the thing, though. I'm disavowed. My choir fallen. The pantheons aren't going to bitch if we're looking to take problems off their hands." He thumped his chest like a gorilla. "Hunters, remember?"

"Samael, please, don't," Bix reiterated, knowing it was futile.

"The great thing about being an archangel is that every member of your choir is a spare body part. The things they witness, the snippets they overhear…They can't place those bits into the greater picture because they can't see the greater picture." He bumped his shoulder against hers. "Mad gods hold your memories. Your memories hold the keys to defeating the Devourers. I just spent a month being eaten by Devourers. Call it self-preservation, but I'm getting you your mad gods. Trust all the way through the mission, right? The mission is to save the Mids. We're far from done."

Bix squeezed her eyes shut. There was no way she'd dissuade him. Being snack food kind of cemented that. Truth be told, if she could negotiate a delivery schedule, it'd allow her to focus on thwarting the faction, fighting the Devourers, and dealing with whatever that presence had been in the pool instead of looking over her shoulder.

"Four," she groaned. "There are four Mid World guardians who hold my remaining memories."

He snorted. "There are far more than four gods who've lost their damn minds, but it'll be good for my choir to practice the hunt."

"Don't bring all the trophies in at once. You'll have a storage problem since I can't assimilate more than one set at a time. Recovery is fairly calamitous for an undefined amount of time."

"That explains the month you were gone. You need time to fix your shit." He grinned. "Got it. Can empathize at the moment."

"Oh, and one other thing…" She held up a finger and opened

gates.

Two wings of plush black feathers encased in broken crystal landed across their laps.

He stared at her with eyes wide. "Is this a pity gift?"

"You said you'd need them back when it came time to defend the Mids." She gestured to their surroundings. "It's time."

He crossed his arms over his chest. "Keep them."

"Why?" She cocked her head. "I'd thought you'd be happy."

"I'm happy that you *want* to give them back, which is why I trust you to keep them safe for me." He puckered his lips and shook his head, leaning away from his wings. "If I'd had these when the Devourers held me prisoner, one of them would've discovered the power they could have over me through my wings and the power they could have over a lot of others. No, you keep them. Hide them again. Not having them gives me leeway in the actions I might not otherwise be able to take. If circumstances change, I'll let you know. But until then, with these new enemies, my wings are a weakness."

"Alrighty," she drawled, and gates took the wings away. She wasn't sure how she was going to repair the broken crystal and redo the wards since Gurp and Tobek had done it the first time. Eh, problems for later.

"The Sage should be home by morning. I believe he's thoroughly hacked all the syndicates by now. You don't have to broker an official deal with the market for existing intel anymore." Samael folded his hands behind his head and closed his eyes. "If I need to get in touch with you, I'll use him or the draugr."

She dodged the elbow threating to thump her upside the head. "Enjoy your dinner, Samael, and thanks for all your help."

Chapter 30

Bix returned to the parquet entry of Cian and Drew's apartment. A superhero movie played on the big-screen TV. Deimos lounged at the far end of the sectional while Tashka rested her head in his lap. The two ardently debated the merits of magic versus technology. The god of terror gave Bix the two-finger wave but never took his attention from his very special friend.

The rank funk of teen boy had been replaced by the wonderfully warm scent of ginger and cinnamon. Ashtad pulled a tray of cookies from the oven and set them atop the range.

"Admit it, you miss the delicate palate of your demi years," Ashtad baited Phobos, who'd removed his suit jacket and hung it on...nothing. It floated in the corner where a hook could've gone.

"I'm a god. If I want to taste a damn cookie, I can taste a damn—oh, this isn't bad." Phobos grabbed three cookies off the hot sheet.

"It's the pinch of clove and cayenne that gives them a nice echoing heat." Ashtad peered under the top cabinets obscuring the entryway from the kitchen. "Welcome back, Bix."

"How delightfully domestic of you all." Bix grinned, completely yet pleasantly surprised by the normalcy of the most unlikely gathering. "I take it the angels went home?"

"Departed the minute their archangel made contact," Phobos answered, dusting sugar from his vest. "There have been no attempts by the Devourers to retrieve Tashka."

Bix leaned over the edge of the counter. "And Drew? Where's the draugr?"

"Out getting a new suit." Ashtad took the tray of cookies to Tashka and Deimos, hobbling. "I suspect that'll take a few days. You know how Drew gets when stuck inside a body, especially a living one."

Drew would spin through suits like a debutant through champagne. Drew had once likened being stuck in a suit to being stuck wearing grungy underwear. The chafe. The stink. The slime. He was not a fan of the bodily functions required to maintain a living suit.

"I see why the archangel was indisposed." Phobos raked Bix with a critical eye.

"There was…" Bix paused as her dress changed, the damage of the Devourers erased, the winter white replaced by vibrant blue, "…a higher-ranking Devourer there this time. It used a sonic attack on me."

Phobos stiffened. "Sonic? Just sound, or were there words?"

"It said something to me before it attacked. It blew out my eardrums, so I was focused more on the pressure of the attack." Bix's attention moved to Deimos and Tashka as they stood, concern plain in their expressions. Deimos joined his brother by the fridge. "Is that bad? Worse?"

"Did you kill it?" Deimos demanded.

"I sent it to Ogun." Bix held up a finger as both brothers scowled at her. "I did not feed from it. I didn't even touch it. I let it exhaust itself, then repaid my debt to that god of war for running off with one of his prisoners."

Phobos grabbed his jacket and draped it over his arm. "Sonic attacks are a specialty of a certain branch of the Devourer army. They are not from the same branch as the scouts we hosted at Dad's."

"They must have sent them after what she pulled in the pool," Deimos groused, his glower intensifying.

"It gets worse. They're field-testing prototype gates." Bix closed one eye as the brothers swore in unison. She opted not to mention the entity who'd used the pool to invade the coal plant. It was more powerful than a titan, and she didn't want the brothers trying to go after it. "There was an unstable gate in Samael's prison. It was porous enough to allow ether to seep through. However, based on the surrounding gore, the flaws are costing them a lot of lives to get just a few soldiers across."

"You guys should probably go and let your pantheon know about that, right?" Tashka slid her hands in her back pockets and gave Deimos a pointed look.

"But we've only just—" Deimos objected.

"The Chimera and I need to close the loop on our mission," Tashka interjected, leveling a breathtaking smile on the god of terror. "Only then can you and I hash out how we go forward, right?"

Deimos nodded once, saving all his hostility for the look he gave Bix. Bix held up her hands before he could unload on her.

"I promise not to hit on your girlfriend." Bix bared teeth and batted her lashes. "I'm not your mom. I respect boundaries."

Deimos grabbed his long coat from atop the fridge and stepped next to Bix, snarling, "Don't leave her unprotected."

"I'm partial to letting the lady make her own decisions. If you want a happy future with her, I suggest you do the same," Bix whispered, her heart about to burst with joy despite his overprotective Neanderthal behavior. For a god to experience love, real actual love, was beyond rare. They were masters of faking it, every last one of them. Manipulating affection was a game to the deities; they did it primarily to amass followers whose souls they could then own. Phobos and Deimos, as the sons of a goddess of love with brothers who were gods of specific kinds of love, totally got shafted. They were intimate with the ugly, horrific side of passion. They knew the thousand and one ways love went catastrophically wrong. Phobos carried the proof with him in his vest pocket. Yet, despite all that, Deimos had fallen anyway. That, that right there, was hope and beauty, and everything worth fighting for.

"Chimera," Phobos sighed, his usual stoicism sliding back into place. "We have not completed your training or evaluating the changes wrought by your latest diet. When you are ready, you know where to find me."

Clouds of navy and mulberry built around Phobos and his twin.

"If she needs me for any reason, any at all, you get word to my brother. I'm relying on you, Chimera," Deimos spoke through the mist swallowing him.

In a breath, they were gone.

Tashka gave Bix an apologetic smile.

"Well, ladies, I love being the third wheel, but I don't think you need me here." Ashtad pushed off the sill of the front windows, favoring one leg. "Bix, if I may impose?"

Bix pointed to the old battle wounds he'd clearly reinjured. "You okay?"

"I will be," he assured. "Nothing a little tea can't help."

"Home, Bruce?" Bix asked with a grin.

"Home, Alfred." Ashtad winked and dropped through gates.

At last, Bix was alone with the infamous Fymmi nee Tashka.

Tashka wiped her hand on her jeans and extended it in a formal shake. "Hi. I'm Tashka. It's…well, it's nice to finally meet you, Chimera."

Bix laughed and shook her hand. "It's ten years overdue, and for that I am sorrier than you'll ever know. But call me Bix. And mind the third cushion there."

Tasha hopped in front of said offending cushion and poked it. "I fixed it. Nasty little surprise that was."

"We should sit." Bix motioned for Tashka to join her. "We need to discuss the dragon in the room."

Tashka folded a leg under her as she sank gracefully into the huge couch. "Ashtad told me that you'd only recently rediscovered you were the Chimera. Drew said the CWIG knew who you were all along but never bothered to tell you."

"All true." Bix nodded. "I'm more surprised they admitted their ties to the CWIG."

"Oh, they didn't tell you? I guess they wouldn't, Ashtad especially. He was always very good at compartmentalizing." Tashka coiled her hair at her nape. "I was their training officer for a while. I was stuck overseeing the demigod probationary agents for a few decades. They made me hate being a manager. I realized I was more of an individual contributor thanks to those reprobates. Drew was a member of the final class I mentored."

"No shit?" Bix cried softly. "At no time during the planning of your pre-prison rescue did he mention he knew the package."

"The dirty secret of Dark Ops agents is that we don't expose the connection until it's absolutely necessary." Tashka smiled, but it faltered. "But I've now been filled in. I know about your trial before the Consortium. I know about the conviction, the exile, and the parole. I tell you that because I know you didn't have to come get me this time. You could've left me in supermax. The traitorous faction within the Consortium would never have found me."

"The Devourers would have," Bix said, raising her guard, wondering what scheme was going through Tashka's head. For an agent who'd *trained* Ashtad, well, that put a different scope on the timing of everything. Ashtad had been part of the spy guild for well over a century. The whole Isoba, Tashka, traitorous dragon royal…that shit was a deeply rooted secret that Bix had forced to light. Doubtful that the royal dragons would thank her for that.

"I see you doing the math in your head and you're wondering how long I'd known Isoba and whether I willingly blew up the Crimson Market subcity." Tashka rubbed her palms along her thighs. "You want to know if my integrity was compromised by my unusual past and if I can be trusted now."

"As an agent, you insisted on working solo," Bix said. "My

guess is that you used your tech to justify the isolation, but the truth was—and is—you didn't trust anyone to have your back. Not surprising, given what's attached to your spine. So, when you got in over your head on your final op, you didn't know whom to call. It wasn't Isoba who worried you, it was whichever dragon helped install the bomb garden."

"When I was a child, Isoba and his father took me to the Crimson Market to watch the whores, so that I would understand my role in their breeding plan. In the core of my being, I knew they were wrong. I wasn't born to be a womb, I was born to protect and defend. When I started to rebel, they took me to the dwarves and had me fitted." Tashka tapped her neck, a flawless neck that gave no hint whatsoever of the tech beneath it. "That was the first time I'd ever met a dragon. He was wholly intimidating. Regal and cruel all in a glance."

"He?" Bix interrupted.

Tashka nodded. "Centuries later, I'm tracking a weapons buyer who turns out to be Isoba. I'm set to report him to my handler at the CWIG, when lo, who should appear in the market?"

"The dragon."

"I knew him, despite his disguise. Our interaction was call and response, his magic to mine." Tashka wiped a tear from her cheek. "He had stories to tell me. About my origins. About my family. About how I ended up in the care of monsters. All I had to do to get a little bit more of the story was help him build the bomb garden."

"You became an addict to information, to information about yourself." Bix inclined her head. "I've been there."

Tashka rested her fists in her lap. Her knuckles turned white. "I built flaws into the grid. It should never have been able to blow. That parts of it did is solely on my shoulders. I accept full responsibility for those deaths."

"You deliberately provoked the syndicate security into arresting you and Isoba before you completed the bomb garden." Bix set her elbow on the back of the couch. "You didn't count on the other dragon finishing your work, then setting it off."

Tashka's gaze jerked to Bix. "Is—is that what happened?"

"You and Isoba were on the prison ship when the clusters blew. The only person who could've done it was the other dragon." Bix massaged her temple as memories threatened to intrude. "Tashka, you could've escaped the transfer on your own, but you chose to escort Isoba to the Undine prison ship. You made yourself a prisoner to keep him from being released again. When that ship sailed into supermax, you stayed because you believed you deserved the punishment. You let the people of the subcity die. You enabled it. You allowed it. If you'd told the CWIG—"

"They would've told the Dragon Horde, and I would've been executed. Isoba would've called on his old buddy in the Horde to let him slip through the cracks." Tashka bit her lip. "Any Dark Ops agent caught is disavowed by the CWIG. We know that going in. I had no protection, and I had no means of making sure Isoba stayed in that damn supermax cell unless I held him there."

"So you did. You fell on your sword to protect the Mids. I get that. I understand it. I appreciate it. I value it." Bix tugged on her ear as random sounds pitched around her. "Your actions and decisions aren't what worry me. It's what is fused to you. If the Devourers get their hands on you and your cloaking tech, they will replicate it and run amok through the Mids, destroying Worlds as they advance toward the heart of native magic. Unbeknownst to us."

"If they try to take the tech from me, they will kill me in the process. It is as much a part of me as the bomb garden was to the Crimson Market."

"Roots and shoots," Bix mused. "Yet as long as you live, you will be hunted. The faction inside the Consortium will ensure you are outed as a public enemy; I say this from firsthand experience. Your ability to hide is compromised when everyone is looking for you. Not even your tech can shield you."

"Then kill me and melt my spine," Tashka said with a zealot's fervor. "I don't want to be the reason the Mids fall to enemies like that."

"That's the tricky part, Tashka." Bix inhaled strange scents not associated with ginger cookies. "I *can* kill you, right here and now. However, the dragon queens know you live, so killing you is an affront to them. There's an entire choir of angels keen to keep you alive as well, if for no other reason than to spite the dragons. Then we have dear Deimos, who would love any excuse to unite his pantheon against me."

"But you and Phobos? Aren't you two… I mean… It looked like…" Tashka sputtered and stumbled through her words.

"No, we are nothing remotely akin to you and Deimos." Bix grinned, then sobered. "I think you would be a valuable asset in the war against the Devourers and against the faction within the Consortium who is aiding them, *if* that's a path you want to take. On the other hand, you might prefer to vacation for a few decades with Deimos and try for a fairy-tale life together."

"He's incapable of loafing and so am I," Tashka noted drolly. "I've been an agent for centuries. You don't stop protecting the Mids just because the CWIG stopped protecting you. That's small-minded. Success was never about individual glory, not for a Dark Ops agent. Nobody knew we existed. No, the whole point was to serve the greater good. Ten years in supermax may have rattled me, but it didn't change my core values."

"Good, good." Bix tugged on the corner of her eye, willing the trip down memory lane to wait just a little bit longer. "Then we need to figure out a way that your tech self-destructs if anyone attempts to remove it. That's probably going to require some very unpleasant experiences for you."

Tashka snorted. "You mean that someone is going to have to carve open my back, modify the spell work on my spine and neck, and then pray that it doesn't kill me in the process?"

Bix nodded. "Yep, that's the gist."

Tashka slapped her thighs. "Then we should get started on locating someone who can do that kind of work."

"Which leads me to the second issue." Bix dabbed at her nose as blood welled. "The dwarves made your hardware, but it was a dragon who produced the spell."

Tashka immediately sobered. "You want me to face the Horde. The very race who abandoned me multiple times during my life. The race who enabled some of the worst agonies I've ever experienced."

"Not the Horde as the whole," Bix dismissed with a wave. "However, you are being hunted by royal dragons as we speak. I'd rather we face them, get the big intro over with, and get a feel for where they stand with regard to you. If they want you dead, then we need to know so we can shape our strategies accordingly. If they want to bring you into the fold, you need to know so you can make your decisions appropriately. I suffer no delusion that this will be easy for you. Similarly, you should not allow one dragon to cement your opinions of the whole race, nor should you take one interpretation of your story as gospel."

"A fan of facing the fears, are you?" Tashka drawled.

"Considering whom you're dating, I hope you are too," Bix countered with a smirk.

"Then let's do it." Tashka stood and held out a hand. "Right now. Get it over with, as you say."

"Give me a few minutes to prepare, then we'll go scare the hell out of some dragons." Bix leaned back on the couch as another memory parade marched down Brain Street.

Chapter 31

Bix closed the gate to a hibernating World. When the weather was warm, the entire World was a jungle of lush canopies, exotic animals, clear rivers, and more plant species than one could count. During the cold season, everything went dormant. Rain and snow fell in soft tumbles, securing the winter wonderland. Leafless trees provided the support for ethereal ice sculptures. It was all very white, very fragile, and very quiet.

Tashka shivered beside her, pulling the fur-trimmed hood of her parka tighter around her face. "Not exactly what I imagined the dragon home World to look like."

"Pit stop." Bix grinned and tipped her nose up to catch a snowflake. "The Dragon Horde doesn't like me at all. Rather than ruin any chance you might have with your family, I've requested a meeting with one of the dragons who's discovered the advantages of putting up with me."

"This place is a good spot for a meet, then." Tashka grunted her approval. "We can see and hear if we have extra company. The dragon has to wear their human form lest they get a tree up the butt."

"In the warm seasons, this World provides thirty percent of the fruit and floral imports to communities favored by the dragons.

If those communities don't get their natural joy—"

"The dragons can't feed from that joy," Tashka finished for her. "They have every reason to want to preserve this place. I see you paid attention in the CWIG academy on how to set a meet."

"Blame falls fully on Ashtad and his relentless on-the-job training," Bix admitted ruefully. "He had to break me of the habit of holding meets atop gates to the ether."

Tashka laughed. "I would've paid handsomely to see his face when he realized it wasn't a stunt to impress him, but a habit."

"Siege face." Bix mimicked the thin-lipped, mulish jaw, and narrowed eyes Ashtad inevitably donned when confronted with a long-term challenge. "That's what our team called it."

"Yes," Tashka cried softly. "That's exactly it. You can see him mentally digging in for the battle."

Bix turned toward a surge of native magic and the flare of deep purple light accompanying a whisper of a song. "Here we go."

Tashka stood straighter, all mirth fading to be replaced by her game face. Bix couldn't imagine what was going through the other woman's mind. Hope? Fear? Hate? All of it?

Rummir emerged from the portal, dressed in finery. Lavender embroidery rose up the outer seams of his black leather pants. The sleeves of his lavender blouse billowed around the fur trim of his long-tailed black vest with his royal crest emblazoned down the front placket. His plum gaze narrowed as it swept Bix.

"Chimera," he greeted curtly. "I see this has been an eventful time for you as well."

It took Bix an extra beat to remember the grumpy dragon hadn't seen her post-Devourer-gluttony. "Some girls gain a few pounds when they eat too much, but, you know me, I had to be different."

"If that's what you wish to call it." Rummir sniffed and his attention shifted to Tashka.

"Prince Rummir, may I introduce Tashka." Bix gestured to the woman at her side. "I think you've been looking for her."

"P-Prince," Tashka stammered, dipping into a curtsey.

"The lost kit." Rummir twitched his fingers, motioning for Tashka to stand. "The formality is noted and perhaps could be taught to the Chimera."

Bix laughed. "Dude, you've seen me in my pajamas. We're way past formality."

Rummir's lips quirked for the briefest moment. He held out his hand, palm up, to Tashka. "Forgive me, but I must be certain."

Tashka placed her hand in his. Dark plum magic flowed from him to envelop Tashka in a translucent cloud. The jewel-toned scrollwork running from his nail bed to his scalp glowed.

"Remarkable," he murmured. "May I press further?"

"Um, sure." Tashka hitched a shoulder.

Bix had no idea what he was doing to Tashka other than it involved a notable amount of Mids' magic that was slapping Bix in the face like a pissed fish. She wasn't going to get in the middle unless Tashka asked her to, but she stayed close enough for moral support. At length, Rummir withdrew his magic from Tashka and ratcheted down the wielding.

"My sister would very much like to meet you, if you are amenable?"

"Does that mean I passed your test?" Tashka rubbed her hands together, more due to nerves than glee.

"I merely verified you are the lost kit and not a tragic creation of the men who took you from us. Your…" He paused, and his brow furrowed.

"Enhancements," Bix offered.

He nodded. "Yes, your *enhancements* are…"

When the silence grew uncomfortable, Bix piped up again. "Reminiscent of something you've recently undone? Honestly, Tashka, his sister is much better at speaking than he is."

Laughter like wind chimes filled the grove as Raspoine joined their little gathering, sweeping across the snow without leaving a print. Snowflakes played with the pearls forming her royal crest over the back and train of her lavender-and-white cloak.

"The fault for my brother's gaffs is mine. I was nattering on with a thousand questions, distracting him." Raspoine held out both hands to Tashka.

Tashka took them and curtseyed again. "Queen Ascendant Raspoine, I am honored."

Raspoine tugged Tashka to her feet and cupped Tashka's cheeks. "You are a wonder. Strong and determined. Dragon kits do not survive their adolescence away from the Horde. You did. You took a life that would've destroyed even a queen and became a warrior, despite—or perhaps because of—the misanthropes who were determined to break you."

"I think you overestimate me, Majesty," Tashka whispered, staring at her boots. "I am a corruption of nature, an abomination of dragon purity. I don't feed on positive emotions. I eat greasy pizza and fluffy beignets. I can fill a teakettle with water from a tap, but not a lake from my desires. I can't shapeshift. I've never assumed my native form. The only smoke I've ever produced was from the end of a lit cigarette. I am special by the standards of humans, average by the gauge of Chweds, but I am grossly inferior as a dragon."

Dayum. That was one harsh self-assessment.

"What you are is what native magic decided you ought to be." The brusque tone arrived before the woman who spoke it as six portals of assorted shades of purple opened around the grove. From those portals stepped the other queens and their enforcers. Thankfully, all wore their humanoid forms. Less awesome was the uptick in Mids' magic that poked and pushed Bix.

The reigning queen swept into the center of the large circle forming around Tashka and Bix.

"Majesty." Raspoine bowed and retreated to the perimeter of the circle along with Rummir.

The reigning queen raked Bix with flagrant contempt. "Chimera."

Bix snorted and inclined her head, but did not move away from Tashka. "Tashka, the reigning queen."

272

Sure, introducing the reigning queen by her full title and given name would have been appropriate, but Bix couldn't pronounce her name. Four of the seven queens had names that sounded like something caught between a banshee's wail and a dog's sneeze. Better to skip over that insult waiting to happen.

"The reigning queen," Tashka groaned and curtseyed again. "Oh gods."

"Don't bring them into this," the reigning queen sniped, gripping Tashka by the chin and raising her. "It's true, then. The mismatched eyes. The light skin. The feeble body. A nadir dragon."

"A what?" Bix asked.

"Go on, Jekora, educate the forgetful Chimera." The reigning queen kept her grip and attention on Tashka. "You know better than most about nadir dragons."

A barrel-built woman and her equally brawny enforcer stepped forward from the ring. Tashka inhaled sharply and clutched Bix's hand. Her heterochromatic gaze locked on Jekora's enforcer, and her skin paled. So, he must've been Tashka's tormentor.

Had the twins not brought charges against the dragon who'd laid the bomb garden? Darkness wriggled along Bix's spine as she looked over her shoulder to Raspoine. Raspoine met and held her gaze. Mids' magic prickled Bix's free hand, depositing something…

A pen.

What is proof without motive? It is a book with no words. When building a case, you must be mindful of who owns the pen. Those had been Raspoine's words back in the subcity.

Bix spun the pen between her fingers and switched her focus back to Jekora, who stared at Tashka. The barrel queen chewed her lips, her jaw quivering. Still no words. Jekora's enforcer, well, he was a closed book.

Dude was not going to like what Bix was a-fixin' to write.

"A nadir dragon is born at the end of the cyclical Great War during the reset of Mids' magic when native magic is at its lowest point," the reigning queen explained with a lash to her tone. "Dragon eggs laid during this window are usually destroyed before they hatch. A nadir dragon is inferior, weak, and unable to rise to the challenges set forth by the queens, demanded by the Dragon Horde, and necessitated by native magic. They are a drain on our society and an exploitable weakness in our constant vigilance."

"Wow." Tashka jerked her chin out of the queen's hold. "Good to know I was abandoned because you all preferred I'd been killed."

"Oh, we didn't *all* abandon you, dearie." The reigning queen cast a side-eye at Jekora's enforcer. "Did we, Offrem?"

"My queen?" Offrem asked, his tone ever so innocent.

"Jekora was the reigning queen at the time of your birth, Tashka." The current reigning queen paced the inner curves of the circle. "It fell to her enforcer to burn all the nadir eggs, which he did. All but one."

"Because it was my egg," Jekora whispered. "I kept it. Hid it. Hoped that against the odds, you'd be the exception that would allow us to overturn that dreadful, cruel tradition borne of our cowardice and our fear. I am so sorry."

Tashka's grip on Bix's hand tightened, but neither of them said anything.

"You're sorry because you're selfish and short-sighted," Offrem hissed causing the other dragons to gasp. "You had no plan, no strategy for raising an illegal child. Her existence was a threat to our place in this society and to the continued rule of the seven queens. You didn't care about the future of your people. You cared only about your immediate emotions for a cluster of cells that had yet to be born."

Jekora hung her head.

"I had to move quickly to keep the other queens from detecting your precious egg." Offrem sneered at his queen. "The anomaly of a nadir dragon would hit their radars, and they'd go looking for your kit. They would've killed her, and you and I would've been precisely where we are now."

"Not precisely where you are now, Offrem." An enforcer Bix didn't know stepped forward, his expression as grim as his tone.

"Back then, your actions were driven by loyalty to your queen and because you shared her hope. They were forgivable transgressions."

A second enforcer stepped forward. "However, once she was no longer the reigning queen and you were no longer afforded the deference to which you'd become accustomed, you focused your resentment on her *child*."

"When rumors of a rogue kit reached the Horde, you took the lead for the searches to ensure she was never found." A third of Offrem's peers joined the ring.

"The abominations of the grifter and Isoba were supported, funded, hidden, and sheltered by you." Another enforcer added to the circle of damnation.

If Bix had been human, Tashka would've crushed her hand with the force of her grip. Still, neither of them spoke or moved as the ink set in the book of motivations.

"You shackled the child, denying her heritage and her bond with native magic." Rummir joined the other enforcers in the inner ring. "You crippled her, abandoned her, then decided to sell her to foreign invaders as a weapon against the Mids."

The reigning queen's enforcer completed the circle of enforcers. "You've betrayed your queen, the noble line of Dreigiau, and the whole of the Dragon Horde. In the process, you've colluded with traitors among the Consortium to lay open our borders and weaken our defenses."

Offrem looked at the bright sky, shrugged, and flicked his wrist; his flash of magic shook ice from the boughs, sending watery spears crashing around the circle. Bix and Tashka flinched, but not one dragon so much as blinked.

"And what are you going to do about it, eh?" Offrem swept his contemptuous glittering gaze around the circle of his peers, then settled on the reigning queen. "Execute me? To damn me, you'll have to explain to the Horde that a venerated queen was corrupted and fallible, that she believed the laws didn't apply to her. It will give your detractors all the fuel they need to tear apart the rule of the seven queens. The Horde will descend into civil war, dragging the Consortium down with it. That will allow our foreign friends to arrive, break apart these unending cycles of tradition, and finally allow native magic to evolve in leaps and bounds unfettered by our close-mindedness."

"Have you ever met these foreign so-called 'friends'?" Rummir curled a lip. "I have. I have stared them in the eye and watched in horror as they consumed our creations. I have experienced firsthand the poison they introduce into native magic. It is not a poison that provokes evolutionary mutations. It is a fatal infusion from which native magic cannot recover. We are naught but food to them, and you would offer up our people as a banquet."

Offrem's confident smile faded. His brows drew to a fine point. "No. That's not our agreement with them. We have a contract."

"Contracts only matter to the Consortium," the reigning queen ridiculed. "They are only valuable when they can be enforced. How are we to punish these foreigners when they are in breach? Wag our fingers at them? Tell them they're naughty, then ask them pretty please not to eat us? You are a fool who has compromised far more than your place among this court."

"Majesty, if you make us prisoners for our crimes, the same outcome holds." Jekora wiped more tears from her cheeks. "The Horde will learn of my transgressions and his. Our enemies will use it to destroy us and the Horde. For the greater good, we *must* be executed. Both of us. Here. Now. Before word can spread."

"No," Tashka blurted as discomfited whispers rippled among the other queens, some agreeing, some not. It was a hell of a sticky wicket for the reigning queen. Damned either way.

Bix opened her mouth to offer to be the bogeyman of lore and do their dirty work, but the pendant on her chest burned, causing her to blurt a curse instead.

The reigning queen leveled a quelling look at her. "No, Chimera, your involvement will speed the dissolution of the Consortium during this critical time when all races must work together."

"Then it is settled." Offrem tugged on his lapels, his confidence solidified once again. "You can't touch m—"

Wings of fire blazed behind him. A hand of flames punched through his chest, ripping three hearts from his torso and turning them to ashes.

"The Phoenix rises," shouted an enforcer.

And from there, everything moved in slow motion. Jekora fell to Feng's wrath next, her final expression a mix of sad relief.

"No," Tashka screamed, lunging forward. Darkness caught her and threw her through gates to Samael's tower in the Crimson Market. If the dragons were going to fight, the angels were the safest place for her to be. They at least knew the gist of the sitch and her importance. Better still, Tashka knew them and might not try to run from them.

"Phoenix, is this the price you demand for your restoration?" The reigning queen raised her arms, and potent native magic swelled.

"Majesty, no." The reigning queen's enforcer raced to her side. "Only the Chimera can bring him to heel."

The remaining dragon royals formed a circle around their queen. Their wide serpentine eyes pleaded with Bix.

"Oh, now I'm not so evil, eh?" Bix closed a hand over the pendant smoldering against her chest and advanced on the living inferno, her darkness dancing around her. "Feng…"

He roared his rage and his fire grew. His wings lifted, and damn if there wasn't a fiery tail lashing out at her to boot.

"You were supposed to stay in bed, you big baby," she groused and opened gates.

Chapter 32

Bix stood on the World once adjacent to the supermax prison and waited while Feng calmed his fire and threw up.

"Thanks for the warning, I guess." She averted her gaze and poked at her pendant as it cooled. "But now where am I supposed to park you while you recover?"

Feng wiped his mouth with the back of his hand and gaped at her. "I don't remember being this sick when I traveled with you before."

"The first time we did it, you were totally healthy, and I hadn't leveled up yet." She wrinkled her nose and gave him the once-over. He looked like he was suffering from the flu, not five years of protracted torture. Yes, he was too skinny, his wings had bald patches, and a few barbs were missing from his tail, but all in? Not bad. "I expected you to look a lot worse."

"Mids' magic is still pure and building toward its apex, plus your stunt with your warlock in the market gave me a big infusion." He stretched one arm in front of him, then the other. "I am the living gauge of its welfare, so I can't help but look my best…ish."

"Vanity, methinks it is your weakness," she teased. "How are your marbles?"

"Out of the jar, rolling off the table, tripping people, also known as completely fucked." He straightened slowly and beat his wings. "Feels good to be outside. Let the wind clear the molt. Reconnect with native magic in a different way."

"Your timing was curiously impeccable, again." She pieced together the times of his assistance, seemingly random, yet possibly not. "Safe to assume you've been eavesdropping on everything I do from your mud crypt?"

"Better than a podcast." He nodded. "But only in the Mids. The reception sucks when you bounce out. Your voice occupies a frequency I find soothing, particularly when the nightmares get too real. Good job managing the memory merge, by the way. I really expected that to go far worse than future-me said it would."

"You've been yakking with future-Feng?" She blinked rapidly as her mouth opened and closed like a guppy. The wonders of Mids' magic. She really didn't understand it. It was forever doing sneaky shit as if it enjoyed subverting logic.

"Bix, you've got to execute him, for his sake and the Mids. He is completely tainted by Devourer toxin. That's why he refuses to show his true self to you." Feng crossed his arms and rocked up on his toes. "He and that library may exist in a pocket out of time, but Mids' magic is still aging without him. That's the gauge that matters. The length of this op has run him past his expiration date. Whatever the Devourer toxin does to Mids' magic, it's preventing him from burning. The inability to do what he was created to do is akin to being unable to breathe. The body demands it, the mind is singularly focused on achieving it. He blacks out, only to restart the cycle again once he regains consciousness. You are the only one who can end his torture."

"But the resources of that library," she groaned. "If you'd seen—"

"I have seen," he said gently. "Through his eyes, through his mind. He tried to impart to me everything he could about the missions and the key moments that can change the tides. It was a struggle for him and for me. Neither of us is mentally whole."

She wasn't surprised that future-Feng wasn't right in the head.

She'd suspected as much when they'd met. She just wished she'd had more time to understand the messages she'd sent herself.

"Future-me went through all this effort to send the library back in time, and it's good for only one mission?" She gnashed her teeth. "The timeline hasn't yet changed enough. He said you would rise after I got my third infusion of memories, and here you are. He said the Devourers were going after Fymmi nee Tashka, and they did. We haven't won enough skirmishes to stop the Mids from falling."

"He said I would rise to contain you, but that's not why I emerged. He said you'd be insane, and you're not. He said Tashka had to be killed to stop the enemy from getting the tech when modifying the spells will suffice. She never reconnected with the Horde in his timeline, but that she's done it in ours has started the dragons' response to the faction and Devourers years ahead of schedule. Little things are already changing. Don't lose sight of that."

"Seems more like Tashka is going to be the cause of a civil war," Bix groused. "Through no fault of her own. She can't catch a break in any timeline."

"I executed Offrem and Jekora because that was the only possible solution for the dragons that *wouldn't* end in civil war." He scratched his thick beard, shaving it with his mere touch, and reshaping it into the thin-lined Drake he customarily wore. "The reigning queen is a mistress of spinning yarns. I suspect Offrem and Jekora will be grieved as martyrs who sacrificed themselves to the will of native magic so that I may rise glorious and restored, ready to preside over the upcoming transfer of rule to Raspoine. The events will be retold in such a way as to remind the Horde that all magic is an exchange, and that their traditions are built to respect and nurture that exchange."

"Wow, that is some crafty repackaging." Bix pressed her fingers to her lips. "What of Offrem's associates?"

"The other queens and enforcers are actively backtracking his network, particularly his ties inside the Consortium. Remember, this is the highest echelon of dragons we're talking about, not vacuous dilettantes or poorly resourced inspectors. These are mistresses of political intrigue and masters of military strategy. Offrem's treason has united the other queens behind the reigning. Bickering is a luxury of peace, a luxury they now realize they cannot afford."

"What will they do about the rumors? Tashka is living confirmation of them." Bix didn't like the idea of those rumors painting a bigger target on Tashka. Sure, Tashka could cloak herself from sensors and magic, but she wasn't Bix. She couldn't vanish.

"This is hardly the first time a scandal has slithered through the royal court. They'll leave the rumors to run their course. An absence of disquiet would raise suspicion. However, the Horde is soon to have a new queen, and that is a joyous celebration of pageantry and racial pride. It will refocus the dragons. Offrem's and Jekora's great sacrifice will be footnotes of a departing era." He laughed, a sound full of sunshine and coconut beaches. "As for Tashka, there is every likelihood her role in the greater fight against the Devourers will lead to changing the policy on nadir dragons as her mother had wished. Ripples, Bix. Ripples. What we do matters."

Getting a pep talk from the guy who'd dragged her unhappy ass to stand trial before the Consortium? The same Consortium they were each trying to save? Very strange.

Bix forced a weary smile. "Good to know we didn't ruin Raspoine's turn on the throne."

"Raspoine's rule will be very different from her predecessor's. She is a queen who strongly believes the dragons should be active participants in the Mids, not passive observers. This is why she's allying with you now, to forge lasting bonds."

"Here I thought it was because she liked me," Bix drawled.

"She does. This iteration of you fascinates her because it is so different from who you were. I think you and Rummir used to have a thing, by the way. I couldn't quite hear that whole story.

Mud in the ear and whatnot."

"Rummir? And original me? Really?" Bix tried not to picture that happening. Failed. It'd probably been hella satisfying, pleasuremonger that the enforcer was, but no way would that happen these days. Dude had a personality that begged to be annoyed, and this version of her was hard-pressed to resist. "At least it wasn't you and me. Wait, it wasn't, was it? We haven't, have we? I mean, I know not *you*, you, but like past Phoenixes?"

Feng snorted. "The story of the Phoenix and the Chimera is integral to many traditions for many races for many reasons. Sadly, those stories long ago lost the nugget of truth that you and I cannot forget. The Great War is waged because I burn and raze entire Worlds. My fire is as inexhaustible as Mids' magic. At its apex, Mids' magic is so powerful that I cannot and will not stop burning on my own accord. Your place is to terminate me, to extinguish my fire that rages beyond my control. In so doing, you salvage life and prevent native magic from devolving due to being pruned back too far."

"Wait, wait. I'm *not* the bogeyman of the Mids? The ruthless terror that ravages Worlds? That's you? Yet everybody makes *me* out to be the villain?" Bix crossed her arms and pouted…then tossed him a wink.

"It's not my fault you're a foreigner and your PR is tragic." He chuckled. "Never fear, you're still the thing that goes bump in the night to the superpowers. I could never take your place in that role."

If she couldn't resist feeding from Devourers, then she would become the addict of which Tobek had warned her. That addict wouldn't want to feel; that addict would be incapable of caring for anyone or anything. Pursuing an addict's fix would open the Mids up to a slew of other problems. Plus, she was only three memory pieces into the full set of seven. Each section of memories she reclaimed brought the original Chimera closer to the surface. Yes, fine, Feng letting her in on the "old Chimera isn't wholly evil" nugget did assuage some of her concerns about reverting to what she'd been, but she still didn't want to lose who she was right now. Call it selfish, but she liked the woman who greeted her in the mirror each morning.

"You're glib," she said, "like you're totally okay with me executing you. That's weird. You know that, right?"

"My Zen acceptance of inevitability wavers. Part of my fallibility." He closed his eyes and tilted his head back, inhaling deeply. "The lone advantage of the war with the Devourers and dismantling the faction inside the Consortium is that it gives me something else to focus on. It makes it seem like I have a chance to do a lot of good before I do a lot of bad."

She respected that and him for admitting it. "Now that you've pissed off the dragons, do you need me to find a haven for you?"

He laughed. "I'm the Phoenix. The Mids are my playground. I'll be fine."

"Will you?" She wasn't so sure; he didn't have a great track record. "Or am I going to have to hunt you down and put you in a pretty prison ahead of schedule too?"

He finally looked at her head-on. His bright aquamarine eyes were haunted, but also happy and brimming with anticipation. "I have PTSD, Bix. I'm a mess. Talking to my future-self made me realize it's not enough to heal the body this time. I need to heal my mind, and for that I need professional help. There is a brotherhood of kobolds who excel at psychology. Their particular strength is in group therapy, and their magics…well, their magics should allow me my weaknesses without jeopardizing them or their patients."

"Kobolds you say?" Bix perked up, grinning. "I think you're going to be welcomed with open arms and scarified backs."

He cocked his head.

"You'll see." She waved aside her comment. "If you need me…"

"I'll reach out. You do the same, okay? I don't know that I'll be able to listen in as much as I used to, so make sure you ask. It might take me a minute to answer, but I will, even if you still call me a big baby." He smiled.

She snorted. "Heard that part, did you?"

"Before I check in with the kobolds, I'm going to visit Tashka at the Crimson Market and alter the spells Offrem embedded in her spine." He held up a quieting hand before she could unleash her concerns. "Don't worry, it's minimally invasive surgery. She'll have some new challenges as a result, yes, but the changes should repel the Devourers in as much as your warlock's spells repel them. Though, I will endeavor not to create a beacon to primordial entities in the process."

"Seriously, is there any part of my life you didn't spy on?" she cried.

"Any time you are exposed to puissant Mids' magic, I am drawn to investigate its cause and your reaction to it. It's how I know when and how to help."

"Oh, well, yes, that makes total sense," she mumbled drolly.

"Speaking of being helpful, I'll put together a list of action items and clues that the future-me imparted once I'm better able to sort the madness from the meaning." A touch of sadness dulled his smile. "When I get a few marbles to stay in my jar, I want to join the fight for the Mids as an active player, so save me a place among your motley misfits. Deal?"

"You got it. Remember, I'm also never more than a summons away." She waved goodbye as Feng beat his wings and caught a breeze to a portal he'd opened. An extra twitch of his tail and he was gone.

What a bizarre time to be alive.

She'd just agreed to ally with her mortal enemy after having a not unpleasant conversation with him. Then there was the future version of said mortal enemy she was supposed to end forthwith to free him from the panic-laden hell of dying without ever achieving death. She'd been there. Done it. Starvation had been her malady, not asphyxiation. But she'd been meant to survive it. She was immortal, even if she hadn't known it at the time; she'd deduced it eventually. Feng, on the other hand, was meant to die and knew it.

Alas, she didn't want to let go of the library. Realistically, she couldn't use it without future-Feng since he and the library were a package deal. Plus, she couldn't translate what was in there without him. She needed a third option, an option that allowed her to put future-Feng out of his misery while retaining her access to the library. But with Mids' magic so corrupted in the future, there were countless ways that could ripple back to dork up the present with the library as its focal point.

No, she had to stop viewing the library as a permanent resource and more like a damaged hard drive recovered from a building fire. Enough intel had been salvageable to put her on a path, but nothing more. Yeah. Damaged drive. That was the right perspective.

Time to fully destroy it.

Chapter 33

Bix's first six attempts to access the library failed. She couldn't open a gate, not to the atrium, the balconies, or any of the shelves. Either the library had been destroyed, or something inside had changed drastically. She tried a gate to the front door itself, and that finally worked.

The moment she crossed the gates, she understood why getting into the library had been hard.

Unlike her very first visit, there was no great fall from the frescoed ceiling. There was no plummeting down seven stories of overstuffed antiquities. No plush carpeting, no gentle lighting, no soothing scents of myrrh and cardamom.

There was nothing but future-Feng unconscious on a dirt floor with two stacks of books to his left and a cluster of potent artifacts to his right. The glorious gilded library had been a manifestation of his magic. More tangible than an illusion, but still unreal. Real was this small hovel, barely large enough for the two of them.

The glamour of the library wasn't the only thing gone; so too was the glamour Feng had used on himself. Her heart broke into a thousand pieces as she knelt beside his shriveled and malformed body. No wonder he'd been so determined to project an image of health and relative vitality. Every scar he'd ever earned was augmented in black weeping tar that spoke of the poison of the Devourers imbuing Mids' magic. His head was as bald as his wings. His long tail nothing more than a nub. There were deep scratches along his throat and in the floor around him. Dirt had caked under his broken nails, evidence of the panic and struggle of repetitive asphyxiation.

How cruel the Fates to make him die like this.

Yet now she understood why—part of why—she always showed up for his execution. If no other entity could kill him and he couldn't naturally expire because the fire with which he burned would never exhaust itself, her intervention was an act of mercy. It had nothing to do with violent opposition. It was compassion.

Even the original Chimera, High Executioner for All Worlds, had operated on a principle of clemency.

The Chimera version 1.0 hadn't been a complete monster. The cyclical battle between the Phoenix and the Chimera was a display of grace, grand and fierce to all those who witnessed it because the individuals involved were mighty, powerful, and numinous.

She wasn't horrible. She didn't have to be afraid of the original Chimera. That Chimera had been emotionally crippled. She'd had her compassion used against her, so she'd chosen to be impassive and apathetic. She'd become addicted to the stupor caused by consuming Devourer essence because it was easier than dealing with pain. She'd chosen to live detached from feelings.

Being numb was not a way to live.

Perhaps that was why the original Chimera had exchanged pieces of herself with Tobek, so that she could understand emotions and empathy through the filter of a man who'd learned how to manage them. Perhaps the original Chimera had wanted to feel again. Perhaps it still did. Perhaps she should stop assuming the worst of herself—past and present.

A huge chip tumbled off her shoulder with that resolution, allowing her to draw a deep, cleansing breath. She patted Feng's limp hand in gratitude, then shifted her attention to the artifacts and books that were keys to stopping the faction within the

Consortium and the Devourers. She inspected each artifact, committing its details to memory. Those, she might be able to find in present time, including the prism that future-Bix would eventually use to record her message. She made mental note of the magical resonance of the artifact and of the World source—be it Mids, Upper, Under, or Other. Once she'd learned all she could by manhandling the artifacts, she turned to the books. Not a single one was written in English, Greek, or Norse futhark, which put their contents out of her ken. The best she could do was memorize the covers, the weight, and the magical signature.

She was halfway through the first stack when Feng twitched.

His hoarse gasp was followed by a series of increasingly desperate attempts to breathe. His fingers clawed at the floor, weak and trembling. His eyes fluttered open, and his head bobbed as he tried to lift it.

Bix set aside the books and took his hand in hers.

"Enough, Feng, it's enough. You've fought well. You don't have to die alone." She let the tears fall as she opened gates and took the Phoenix out to the highly destructive ether of the present day.

Bix wrapped her arms around Feng, holding him as he convulsed, gasping. It didn't last long. Too far from the vital Mids' magic that had given him life, his body disintegrated.

One tiny spark—barely the size of a grape seed—was all that remained of the Phoenix's fire. Bix cupped it in her hands. In a heartbeat, it went out.

Chapter 34

Bix returned to the quiet of Vuornis, walking the arid paths to the rotunda as grief gave way to the grim satisfaction of a duty done. She entered the rotunda and fumbled for a glow stick. She must have knocked the box of them off their perch the last time she was here. Rubbing her hands over her face and stifling a yawn, she sent her darkness to locate one. Her tentacles located and cracked three of them. Pale green light cast itself over the absence of décor. The skeletons were gone. So was her rocking chair and the collage of Tobek's drawings. So too were the deposits from her bedroom.

"Damn it, Phobos," she sighed, too exhausted to be angry. She knew she should've relocated her stuff after he'd paid her a visit here. Her interpretation of habitable and his interpretation of squalor tended to coincide. She should open a gate and read him the riot act, but he'd insist on interrogating her about the Devourers' impact on her, and she'd lose track of time, which she couldn't afford to do right now.

Somewhere out there was a beloved goblin frightened out of his mind. She couldn't rest until she had him home with his battalion. No wonder little dude had kept a wide berth of her darkness. She had no idea how she could ever sufficiently apologize to him for what she'd done. Hell, he might not even let her. He certainly didn't have to.

Speaking of lost friends… She toed off her shoes and used her darkness to carve a message into the soles.

Tashka at Crimson Market. Needs a hug. Might be woozy after Phoenix's help.

The shoes, she flung through a gate. Phobos had made them for her, so they were better than personalized stationery. If he tripped over them, then he deserved it for mucking with her sanctuary. If Deimos tripped over them, then it'd be due to him wearing a rut in Phobos's study, assuming the worst had happened to Tashka. Bix, for one, was happy to give the two lovebirds an excuse to be together. As long as Tashka was with Deimos, she was safe from the faction, and Feng would ensure she was safe from the Devourers. Tashka would contact Ashtad or Drew when she was ready to get back to saving the Mids since she knew those two best. The primary mission had been successful: liberate Fymmi nee Tashka. Done. Finally. No agents lost this time around. Yay.

Just one goblin misplaced. Doh.

Recalling her darkness to the confines of her body, Bix plopped down on the edge of the empty crystalline basin, tipped to her side, then rolled to her back with arms wide.

"Okay, memories, where did we take our favorite goblin?"

She closed her eyes and braced for the barrage. Muted music played, and fragrant flowers drifted across her senses. She waited for her brain to unleash the images that should accompany the scents and sounds, but sleep threatened to show up first.

"Pretty lady okay?"

She bolted upright.

A glow stick illuminated bulging eyes and a large nose wart.

"Gurp," she cried in delight, wrapping her arms around the squat goblin. "Gurp, oh my… Gurp, I'm sorry. I'm so sorry. Oh, thank the powers that be you're okay."

He clucked and patted her head. "I okay. I okay."

She squeezed him tightly until he ripped the most pungent

of farts, then she let him go. "You've got to be starving. Let's get you home."

"Wait, wait." He backed up and waddled to the mosaic wall. Holding up the glow stick, he knocked on the crystals. Each rap was a musical note.

The bottom of the basin rotated ninety degrees, sections sank, allowing slivers of light to reveal a crystalline stairway wrapping around a clear pipe. The music she'd heard earlier came from below; so did the fragrance of flowers.

"What the...?" Bix stared at the goblin. "How did you know this was here?"

Gurp tapped his temple and headed for the stairs. "Come, come."

Dutifully, she followed him down the winding staircase into the ruins of a massive cistern shaped like an eight-pointed star from which tunnels sprouted. Towering crystal columns—chipped and cracked—braced the barreled ceiling and reflected the light coming from a tunnel to the southeast.

Gurp hummed along with the music as they made their way toward the light source. Bix's bare feet registered the cool ground worn smooth by waters long ago evaporated. Three of the tunnels they passed had collapsed at some point, spilling boulders into the plinths of nearby columns.

A few steps into the southeastern tunnel, she stopped and gasped. Nooks and niches lined the walls, each filled with some sort of artifact, doodad, or trinket. Familiar trinkets. She picked up the one nearest her, a bloodstone urn that pulsed with Other World magic. There was a memory tied to it. And to the pile of scrolls in the neighboring niche. A heap of gold and silver bangles caught her eye next. Oh, and there was her smartwatch, the one Cian had made and Ashtad had taken to make security enhancements.

"You bring me. You bring things. I put things here. Yes?" Gurp grunted proudly and motioned for her to follow him farther down the tunnel. A cluster of rose quartz, taller than the goblin, sat in the middle of the floor, providing the gentle light that filled the cistern. On the walls between the cubbies were Tobek's sketches along with paintings, sand casts, and thin aquariums where the colorful liquids changed shapes. Beside the quartz sat her rocking chair.

She took it all in, breathless and humbled.

"Come, come." Gurp tugged her hand and led her around the bend. A tunnel collapse had made it a proper chamber with vaulted ceilings and only the one entrance. Her bed and her hot-pink comforter occupied the center of the room. A side table made of bones hosted a music box that turned the mechanisms of a pin-dotted lamp shade that cast shadowy dancers over the walls. Her clothes had been neatly folded and stacked in the shelves from her bedroom in the coal plant. Her shoe collection had been artfully arranged on the boulders forming the back wall. Samael's wings—wings she had deposited in another building on this World—had been recessed into a side wall, the crystal hole patched, and new spells chiseled into the surface.

"Okay, yes?" Gurp asked.

At a loss for words, Bix knelt before the goblin and hugged him again. He grunted sounds of reassurance, patting her hair.

"You spoil me rotten," she whispered. "I am beyond blessed. It was wrong of me to force you to come here. I should have taken you to one of the Berserker outposts after the entity attacked you. Then I had the gall to abandon you for who knows how long. You have every right to be furious with me. Instead, you took care of me, going out of your way to transform my sanctuary into a home. You excel at selflessness and always make me feel wanted. I don't know why you put up with me, but I am ever so grateful you do."

He wriggled free of her hold, then took her hand and tapped her temple with it. "One day. Yes? One day."

"One day, I'll remember, eh?" She gave him a weary smile. "Regardless, know that I want to be worthy of your kindness in this moment and the future."

He blushed and rubbed one foot atop the other. "We go home now? See Chief?"

"Absolutely." She stood and smoothed her skirt. "I'll send you home."

His wide brow furrowed. "You come too, yes? Home?"

"It's best I keep away from the coal plant for a while. Between the entities in the pool and Devourers, I'm too much of a security risk." She pouted then smiled. "Our boys are too important and so is Tobek. All of whom, by the way, are in a panic looking for you. I've never seen a bunch of men so utterly helpless than that battalion when they're short their most valuable player."

He scowled and shook his head. "But Chief and you? Chief happy when Chief and you. You happy when Chief and you. You come home. Yes?"

The sound of metal scraping brought her up short. She pushed Gurp behind her and headed back to the main tunnel.

In the mouth of the tunnel stood a large silver-and-gold Bi Xie. The one missing from Tobek's kitchen. Its lion's head turned toward the sound of her approach. It dipped its long, gold, spiraling antelope's horns in formal greeting. Its steel feathered wings flared from the side of its gunmetal leonine body, blocking any attempt to access her new abode from the main cistern.

Bix bit her lip and curtseyed to the sentinel who protected wherever she considered home. After the fight against the entity, she hadn't had time to think about where the new place would be.

Apparently, her subconscious had.

The Bi Xie grumbled a sound of approval, turned around, then took up its post at the entrance to the tunnel.

Gurp hung his head. "No home?"

"This is where I'm going to live until we defeat the big bads. Thank you for making it a home." She kissed the top of the goblin's head, then dropped him through gates to the armory in the basement of the coal plant.

Gurp's safety, indeed the safety of all those at the coal plant, far outweighed her desire to be enmeshed in a friendly community. She had no doubts that once Tobek was back to rights, he and Gurp would work tirelessly on adapting the wards. Perhaps she could introduce Tashka to Tobek, and those two could discuss cloaking tech and deflector spells. She'd wait until Tashka had time to heal, of course. Deimos wouldn't let anyone near his special someone while she was injured, so there was no point in rushing that meeting.

A beam of green light shot through the gates from the coal plant as they closed, propelling a silvery origami swan into her sanctuary. The paper bird fluttered around the room, then came to rest on Bix's hand. Fold by fold, it unwrapped itself until it was a smooth sheet of paper. On one side, a message in flowing script:

> *It is said every man fails to perform at least once in his life.*
> *Immortals aren't spared that indignity.*
> *Forgive me.*

"Aw, my little rotten godling," she chuckled and pressed the note to the knot warming her chest.

Silver flake on her fingers caused her to flip the paper over. It was a sketch of her holding his hand against her knot as the tiny silver claws of his magic pierced her skin. That wasn't what snared her attention. It was the woman standing behind her. A giantess made of diaphanous night with eyes of the darkest nebulas, her expression one of satisfied amusement. The shapes of her features were the same Bix saw in the mirror every morning. The original Chimera. Tobek's vision of her, at least.

Guess her subconscious had really, really wanted to reconnect with Tobek in a more intimate way than her conscious mind would allow.

What was the deal with his silver arm, though? It hadn't been a hallucination. She clearly recalled his metal touch. Why did it manifest only when they were connected by body and magic? Why, if she'd been so infatuated with him as the original Chimera that she'd exchanged parts of her body with him, had she cursed him to suffer great agonies when speaking of her? Why, if they were so close, hadn't she helped him ascend to full godhood?

Things didn't add up.

She'd figure it out. She was a spy. Learning secrets was what she did.

She added the drawing to the wall with Tobek's others, then returned to the back chamber of the tunnel for her comforter. She dragged it to the gallery and flung the comforter over the top of the rose quartz, dousing the room in near pitch-dark. With a weary sigh, she collapsed into her chair and bid her darkness to slowly rock her. The liquid art gave off a soft bioluminescent glow. It was pretty, but why had she wanted that? Why now? From where and from whom had she taken it?

The same could be asked of everything in this tunnel. Why had her subconscious deemed these things necessary? What was her mind trying to tell her?

So many questions. She had no idea how she would handle the answers when they finally arrived, devoid of order, context, and completeness. One way or another, she wouldn't fall into the traps of her past. She wouldn't be an addict, a monster, or a bogeyman. No, she was actively surrounding herself with the most crucial elements for an immortal's sanity. Friends. The more relationships she could strengthen, the more promising her future.

Other Books

The Hanged Spy
Available Autumn 2018

Want to be notified when a new book is released?
Subscribe to K. A. Krantz's email newsletter at
kakrantz.com

**If you enjoyed this book, please spread the word and
leave a review with the retailer of your choice.**

Acknowledgments

To my family, for understanding when I make myself scarce and for keeping me in bonbons. To Jenn Stark, for bourbon deliveries and enduring the booger jokes. To Linda Ingmanson, my development editor, for pointing out where emotions matter most. To Toni Lee, my copy editor and fact checker, for resisting the temptation to turn this into a frisbee. To the team at Gene Mollica Studios, for not running away when I asked for tentacles.

About the Author

KAK splits her time between Cincinnati and the DC 'burbs with her faithful hairy beast. When not writing, she indulges in a shoe obsession, conducts a love/hate affair with paint, and makes epic messes in the kitchen.

Visit her website at kakrantz.com for free flash fiction, blog posts about her latest fancies, and more. If you're on Twitter, she'd love to hear from you. Tweet @KAKrantz.

www.ingramcontent.com/pod-product-compliance
Lightning Source LLC
Chambersburg PA
CBHW052023240626
47153CB00006B/1926